BATHING BEAUTY

It was not until Brandon cursed, stumbling over a misplaced stool, that Alana became aware of his presence. Her clothes and towel were on the counter behind her, just out of her reach. The fear of his peering around the screen just as she got out to grab them trapped her in the water.

Alana bunched the bubbles around her as she offered a silent prayer. But her prayer went unanswered; Brandon's stumbling search for the coffee pot led him around the screen.

Retaining what dignity she could, Alana said sharply, "Sir, if you don't mind, I'm taking a bath!"

An evil grin crossed his face. He gathered up her clothes and towel and held them just out of her reach. "Seems I have a slight advantage here," he boasted. "Yes, I guess I'm holding the winning hand, and I intend to use it."

We will send you a free catalog on request. Any titles not in your local bookstore can be purchased by mail. Send the price of the book plus 50¢ shipping charge to Tower Books, P.O. Box 511, Murray Hill Station, New York, N.Y. 10156.

Titles currently in print are available for industrial and sales promotion at reduced rates. Address inquiries to Tower Publications, Inc., Two Park Avenue, New York, N.Y. 10016, Attention: Premium Sales Department.

THE THORN BUSH BLOOMS

Rosalyn Alsobrook

TOWER BOOKS  NEW YORK CITY

A TOWER BOOK

Published by

Tower Publications, Inc.
Two Park Avenue
New York, N.Y. 10016

Copyright © 1981 by Tower Publications, Inc.

This book is lovingly dedicated to my beautiful parents: To my father for instilling the love of books into me and to my mother for teaching me my "this" from my "that."

There is nothing holier in this life of ours than the first consciousness of love—the first fluttering of its silken wings—the first rising sound and breath of that wind which so soon to sweep through the soul, to purify or to destroy.

Longfellow

The Thorn Bush Blooms

Chapter One

"Madam, you dropped your purse," Alana heard as her thoughts refocused on the present. She nodded a thank you to the gentleman holding her small drawstring bag out for her hand to reclaim.

The young man watched his fellow passenger as she returned her gaze to the scenery beyond the small window beside her. It was quite evident that this young lady was unaccustomed to having strangers speak to her. But with such a beautiful creature sitting right across from him in the small confines of this stagecoach, he felt it would be a great loss not to at least try to make her acquaintance.

"You really should be more careful," he spoke softly.

Alana realized that she was again being addressed. "Sir?" she asked as she took notice of this man who had boarded at the last stop, replacing the matronly woman who had occupied that seat so quietly before, only breaking the silence with an occasional command to sit up straight to the small child perched impatiently beside her. When the pair got off, Alana had hoped she would have the coach to herself.

"You really should be more careful with your purse. It is apt to be stolen if allowed such casual attention," he gazed down at the strikingly beautiful dark brown eyes that peered up uncomfortably at him.

"I shall try to remember that. Thank you," she replied timidly. She lowered her eyes and stared at the purse she held so preciously in her lap. She could feel that his expressive black eyes were still looking at her, as indeed they were. He was drinking in the smoothness of her velvety skin, the slenderness of her features, the slight upward curve of her nose, and the high cheeks that were blushing slightly as he continued to heed the beauty of this awkwardly shy female. Her dark hair, which he judged to be of some length, was piled on top of her regal head and held in place by a small dark blue hat that matched the dark blue sashes adorning her simple-cut, pale-blue traveling dress. Why should such a woman as this be so ill at ease?

"My name is Don Andrios Valis," he said with some pride in his deep warm voice. Not having the effect he had hoped, he continued, "Might I inquire as to your name, *señora?*"

"My name is Alana Stambridge," she managed to say with a smile.

"Ah, should I call you Mrs. Stambridge, or might I have the honor of calling you Alana?" he asked hopefully.

Looking up at him through partially lowered lashes, she answered politely, "Sir, I am a Miss not a Mrs. I guess you may call me Alana if you wish." She realized now that this Don Andrios Valis was harmless enough as she took in his appearance. He was tall, slender, and his dark complexion held a handsome face of about thirty years that sported an ample mustache drooping over a gentle smile. He wore a short, embroidered brown jacket and a casual open-necked tan shirt. His pants were also brown and slightly flared from the knee down. He sat erect, his well-developed shoulders arched out slightly. He seemed nice enough to Alana.

"Well, I am headed to my home in El Paso. My family owns a *ranchero* near there. Are you traveling that far?" Don Andrios continued, keeping the conversation alive.

"No, I am to get off in the town of Gilmer just the other side of Louisiana," she answered more at ease.

"It does not sound as if this Gilmer is your home," he proceeded. "Why do you go to this town, if you do not mind me asking?"

"I have a teaching job waiting for me there," she replied as she relaxed back against her seat. She was actually enjoying talking with this Don Andrios. "I recently earned my teaching certificate at the Boston Women's College in Massachusetts and was offered a job on a ranch near Gilmer." She pulled a folded piece of paper from her bag and offered it to Don Andrios. "There are few teaching jobs in the North right now and I was lucky to receive such an offer," she mentioned as he took the letter from her.

Don Andrios opened the letter, noticing the worn appearance around the edges from an obvious number of readings. It read:

> *Dear Madam,*
>
> *We appreciate the promptness of your reply to our inquiries of a live-in tutor for the children of Montaqua.*
>
> *This Alana Stambridge you referred to sounds quite capable of handling the job.*
>
> *As was previously mentioned, we guarantee and expect a year of employment which can be extended if she meets our requirements and if we meet hers. The wages you mentioned are quite satisfactory with us.*
>
> *The tickets are enclosed. She is to come as far as St. Louis, Missouri, by train. There she boards the stagecoach that will bring her to Gilmer. She is scheduled to arrive on the eighth of May. We will have a driver with carriage waiting for her there.*
>
> *Yours sincerely,*
> *Lilian Brams*

"Today is May eighth, is it not?" he inquired as he studied Alana's shining brown eyes. This was not his idea of a schoolmarm, no indeed.

Alana flashed a worried look at Don Andrios, "Yes, we are running a day behind schedule because of a bridge that was washed out due to heavy rains and flooding. They had to reroute us to a bridge downstream. Then, of all the worst luck, the front wheel broke and had to be replaced. I hope they gave this driver they mentioned instructions to wait. That stage driver assured me this morning that we should be arriving in Gilmer late afternoon tomorrow, if all goes well," she said anxiously as she looked upward toward the direction she knew the driver and the rider with him to be seated on top.

"Have you ever been to Texas before, *señorita?*" he inquired as he refolded the letter and handed it back to Alana, almost dropping it as the stage hit a bump and jerked sideways.

"No, but I have done quite a bit of reading on the area. I do know that it gets hot and dry during most of the months and that there are few trees to shade the flat, sandy earth. I have read that the trees they do have are squatty with only a few branches, rarely reaching the height of twelve feet and thorny plants called cactuses grow as tall," she stopped her description when she noticed a wide grin stretching across Don Andrios's face.

"You think that you have described Texas well, no? *Señorita*, you will not see the Texas you speak of. You have described the *Tejas* I live in near El Paso. You are headed for the eastern part of Texas. The land is not flat, but has many hills covered with many trees, mostly pine trees, that grow to the height of more than ten men. There is green the year round and rain is quite plentiful, except maybe in the month of August. There are rolling grassy pastures and wooded land as well. Oh, yes, it does get hot; but it is not dry and a cactus is rare. You may be in for quite a surprise," he mused.

"Indeed, I may," Alana said shortly, feeling quite the educated fool. She was searching for a way to turn the conversation elsewhere when the stagecoach came to an abrupt halt, throwing her forward. The door opened as the man that had been accompanying the driver on top eyed his only passengers. He could remember a time when a stagecoach hardly ever traveled with less than six and usually as many as ten or even twelve passengers. But that was all before those railroads started moving in. As they made progress, the stage lines suffered. Some lines that had run parallel to railroads were forced to quit business altogether. Luckily, the Civil War had damaged two-thirds of the track in the South and railroads were just now getting a strong foothold again. He felt sad for he knew the stagecoach's days were numbered. For now, he had these two passengers to tend to. He took a deep breath and said, "Fixin' to git on the ferry to git across this here river. If'n ya want to get out and stretch them legs a might, now'd be the time to do it. Won't be another stop until we bed down outsidda Shreveport this evenin'."

Don Andrios gestured with a wave of his hand for Alana to step out first. She put the letter back in her purse, which she hung high on her arm, remembering clearly Don Andrios's warning of the evils of carelessness. She gathered up her skirt a bit, using a hand on each side, so that she could step free of her hem. As she got up, the stagecoach shifted, and without a hand free to hold on to something, it caused her to stumble. Don Andrios caught her by the arm. His hand remained at her elbow until she had both feet firmly on the ground. Alana blushed as she turned to thank Don Andrios for his supportive hand. She felt uncomfortable about his touch, but did not know why she should. It was quite proper for a gentleman to help a lady.

Don Andrios followed Alana aboard the ferry and stood silently beside her as the men coaxed the horses to bring the stage aboard. Alana allowed her thoughts to drift as she tried to understand her present discomfort. Maybe it was because she had never had a gentleman, or any other man, gentle or not, extend proper courtesies to her. She was amazed at the difference her loss of weight had caused. Not only did people act differently toward her, she was different somehow. It was more than her new figure, her own outlook was beginning to improve as well as her attitude toward men, which had actually never been given a chance to form.

As her mother stated when the chubby daughter that had left home to study teaching returned as a slender young woman, "It is going to take a while to get used to it!" She caught her mother staring at her several times as if she were seeing her youngest daughter for the first time.

Alana had grown up shadowed by her beautiful older sister, Bethany. The attention Bethany always attracted caused a void in Alana's young life as she never received much notice. Alana had turned to food to fill this emotional vacuum that existed as early as she could remember. The physically satisfying feelings food brought never lasted long, but the effects the food had on her body did. Alana felt ridiculous pretending to be ladylike and playing the ladylike games many of the other little girls seemed to enjoy. She quickly gave up these proper little girlish traits to excel in marbles and in the playing of games such as pioneer. She could climb a tree like a monkey and run like a rabbit, in spite of her weight. Her mother insisted that Alana was a complete disgrace to her family.

As she grew older she noticed how popular Bethany was with the boys. A great many suitors came a calling. Alana was popular with the boys, too. But she realized that she was only popular as a teammate, and that realization hurt. She was just one of the boys. When her female peers started seeing their special fellows, going to dances and on Sunday picnics, she found she was not included. Having become too old to play War or Kickball, she turned her full attention to books and always seemed to have a nose in a book. She only brought it out to eat or, in the springtime, to keep her rose garden. The rose garden became an obsession with her when she discovered that she could receive compliments through the attractive blooms. She did not allow a weed near her precious roses and watered them faithfully. She learned through books about fertilizers and her rose bushes bore twice as many roses as most. She never received an unkind word about the extraordinary garden, except once she overheard her mother complain that she worked it like a man would. Well, it was just easier to plant her knees into the ground than to kneel down delicately as a proper lady would.

When she returned from Boston last month to her family home in New York, the rose garden was the first thing she noticed. After two years of her absence, the rose garden had been allowed to run down. Someone had obviously watered the plants, but the weeds were allowed to grow unchecked among the bushes. Alana pursed a frown as she knelt down and started pulling, even before going inside to announce her homecoming. Her mother looked out of the window to see an attractive young lady kneeling down ever so properly, pulling weeds with a gloved hand and wondered who this lady could be. She was absolutely speechless when she discovered that this lady was the transformation of Alana.

How had such a change come to be? There were several factors involved. First, Alana found that between her studies and the part-time job in the Dean's office taken to help meet expenses, there was little time to eat. Second, the need to eat lessened as she came out from the shadows of her older sister into the glow of the attention she received at the college. Her many years of constant reading had rendered her a quite knowledgeable young woman. Her teachers let her know how impressive she was with excellent grades. She was given a chance to stay with the college as an assistant to the Dean, but her heart truly lay with the children. Choosing the job offered to her in Texas not only involved children, it was far away from any reminders of her not so rewarding childhood. Somehow just the thought of Texas intrigued her.

The jarring movement of the ferry as it docked on the far side of the small river brought her attention back to the present once again. Don Andrios was gazing out at the river, which was narrow, slow moving, and muddy, with huge trees lining the banks that bent down graciously to shade a good part of the water. Alana had not noticed her surroundings until she looked to see just what had captured Don Andrios's keen eye. Now that she looked out over the golden river and listened to the tranquil rhythm of the water splashing lazily against the ferry's side, she stood in awe of its beauty. In the distance, a group of children were enjoying their play in the cool water. Echoes of laughter and splashing drifted past her. Slowly, Don Andrios turned to her and sighed, "Magnificent, is it not?"

Alana nodded an agreement, for only a fool would believe otherwise. "Well, madam, I guess we should get back in the coach so that they might proceed," Don Andrios said as he noticed the driver motioning to them to hurry up.

He held the door open for her and again lent her arm his support with his free hand as she climbed to her seat.

She smiled as she thought how pleasant it was to have a gentleman extending proper courtesies to her—Alana Stambridge.

The next couple of hours passed rather quickly as she and Don Andrios talked of many things. He told her of his *ranchero* near El Paso and of all of his brothers and sisters. She spoke of the college and of her home in New York. That evening he invited her to dine with him in Shreveport instead of eating another tasteless meal at the stationhouse.

Alana put on her finest dress, but still felt awkward and plain. She had never seen a need to buy a frilly evening gown. The dress she wore was amber gold with a high neck and a small white collar edged in brown lace that matched the sash around her small waist and the lace at her short white cuffs. She wore her hair pulled back high with long curls dangling down to her neck.

Don Andrios greeted her at her door and escorted her to a carriage that he had waiting just outside. He was dressed in a short black jacket embroidered with gold thread and matching flared trousers. He wore an open white shirt. Underneath was a gold chain around his neck. They took the carriage into town and dined elegantly at the renowned "French restaurant." Alana tried not to let on that this was the first time she had accompanied a man to dinner. After dinner, they took the open carriage through the many streets of Shreveport, making a point to drive by the Centenary College that one of Alana's teachers had spoken of on several occasions.

They traveled down to the banks of the Red River and stopped a moment to admire the view. Don Andrios casually slipped his arm around Alana as he openly compared her beauty to that of their surroundings. She was indeed quite beautiful, even in her simple dress. But it was evident that she did not believe in her own beauty. His words put her on edge, and she really did not know why. He decided against any further advances as she withdrew more with each well-deserved word of praise that he gave her. He chose to return instead to the stationhouse and retire early.

Having slept soundly, in spite of the hard bunk with insufficient cover supplied by the stationhouse, Alana awoke early and prepared to board the stagecoach. Today was the day. If nothing disastrous happened, she would be in Gilmer by late afternoon. She felt excitement along with growing anticipation. Realizing that she knew very little about the people at this Montaqua ranch, she began to wonder if they might not be of Spanish descent as was Don Andrios. The name Montaqua sounded Spanish enough. Knowing nothing more than what the letter had contained, she knew that she would teach more than one child and that this Lilian Brams who was hiring her had enough money to employ a special teacher for them. This woman had obviously had schooling herself as the letter was written in her own hand and worded quite well. Alana took a deep breath and went downstairs to eat breakfast.

As the day passed, Don Andrios found that Alana talked less. He could see her dark eyes clouding with concern.

"All will go well, you shall see," he tried to reassure her.

"I am not so sure. What if the driver with the carriage is not there? What if he has already left? What if he was never there? What if they have changed their minds and do not want me?" Alana cried as she let her fears run wild.

"If the driver is not to be found, you go to the sheriff and ask his help. This town is big enough to have a sheriff, no? Besides, you have your letter confirming your employment. Everything will be just fine."

"I do not know how big Gilmer is; I could find it only on one of the many maps that I looked at. But, apparently it is small. Maybe it does not have a sheriff," she worried out loud.

"Well, there should be someone there in charge who will help you. Do not expect the worst." He paused before continuing, "Here, you must eat. It will make you feel better." He pulled out the boxed lunch that had been provided for them, hoping it would help get her mind off of her worries.

"No, thank you," she replied quickly. She knew now that food did not solve anything. She would wait to eat. "I wonder how far Gilmer is from here. We should be arriving soon," she said nervously as she looked at the timepiece that hung from a chain around her neck.

"You are going to wear that thing out with all the attention you have been showing it. It should not be long now. The time would pass easier if you would not keep checking on it," Don Andrios assured her. And it was not much longer. Less than two hours later, the stagecoach came to a stop in front of a small wooden building with a rough-planked ramp leading to an open door. Overhead, hung a sign that read in large bold letters: POST OFFICE. Beside this post office was another wooden framed building with no evident identification. On the large covered porch of this building sat several older men watching the stagecoach with seemingly little interest as they discussed the more important events of the day.

Surrounding these two buildings, in the form of a huge square, many businesses lined the dirt-packed streets facing inward. A few shops as well as the livery stable lay on side streets stemming off of the square.

"I guess this is good-bye. *Señorita,* I will miss your beautiful smiling face. Please, if you ever find reason to come to El Paso, visit me. Ask anyone where to find the *Ranchero de Valis,* they will give you the directions," Don Andrios said with a remorseful expression.

"I will," Alana promised as she gathered up her skirts to step out. Don Andrios took her arm in his hand and accompanied her down. Before releasing her, he pulled her hand to his mouth and kissed a short, gentle farewell. He quickly turned and climbed back inside. Alana looked at her hand and then at Don Andrios waving from within the coach. She was stunned, as a very warm pleasing sensation stirred somewhere inside of her. She returned his good-bye wave knowing that she was going to miss him, too.

Standing beside her two trunks, she watched as the driver climbed back up to his seat and started the team of eight horses. The stagecoach pulled away and was soon out of sight. Suddenly, Alana felt strangely alone. She looked around at the new surroundings and wondered where the stage office was as she searched the storefronts for a clue. Directly across the street from the post office lay a local lodge, a newspaper office, and a couple of small shops, neither of which was the stage office.

She was developing grave doubts about her situation when she noticed that a young man with blond hair showing beneath a Western-styled straw hat was staring openly at her. He sat in a shaky wooden chair that was tilted back, resting awkwardly against the front of the lodge across the street. He got up with a grin spreading across his boyish face and walked directly toward her. She turned her head away, mistaking his actions as improper advances.

"You Miss Stambridge?" he asked as he stopped directly in front of her. Alana turned her head to look at him at the mention of her name. He was an attractive young man. She guessed his age to be near her own, maybe twenty-one or twenty-two. He wore a red plaid shirt with the top two buttons left undone, dark brown pants, and heavy leather boots with pointed toes. His smile easily involved his entire face.

"Yes, I am Alana Stambridge," she replied as she eyed the man suspiciously.

"Well, it's 'bout time ya got here!" he remarked with a good-natured Southern accent, "I was supposed to pick ya up here yesterday. Mister Brandon's gonna be madder than a wet hornet as it is, me havin' to stay the night and a good part of the day waitin' on ya. We were supposed to fix a busted fence this evenin'." He abruptly turned away as he finished talking and started walking.

"Where are you going?" Alana wanted to know. She did not know whether to follow or not.

"Gonna get the surrey. I don't wanna tote them trunks of yours that far," he shouted back over his shoulder. He walked a short distance to a small carriage made to seat approximately six, including the driver. Both seats faced forward and had an open-boxed area for large parcels behind them. Alana was accustomed to carriages that had two seats facing one another and a separate little bench for the driver on the front in which parcels were put in a compartment either below the driver or at the back. After untying the team of two horses from a short hitching post, the young man led them over to stand by Alana. "Here, hold them while I load her up," he said.

Alana was unaccustomed to "holding" horses, but obliged as he handed her the leather strap that came from the bit of one of the horses. The trunks were placed in the back with two ropes tied across them to hold them securely in place.

"By the way, my name's William, but most folks 'round here calls me Billy. You gotta name I can call ya 'sides Miss Stambridge, or is that what I am supposed to use?" he asked with a twinkle in his bright green eyes.

"My given name is Alana, please use that. Are you one of Lilian Bram's sons?" Alana inquired wondering if it would be proper to use first names if she might have to teach him.

"Heck, not me. I am just a hired hand. Mister Brandon took me on to help him work the ranch, since I am real good with cattle. I live with my folks on a farm near Pleasant Grove, only a couple of miles past Montaqua. Someday, I hope to make a ranch out of it. I am saving up most of the money I make to buy me a herd of Angus. Mister Brandon just got him some shipped down here special from over to Scotland. They sure are a pretty animal. Someday I will have a whole slew of them," he said with obvious pride as he climbed into the seat.

"And just who is Mister Brandon?" Alana wanted to know.

"Get up here and I'll tell ya," he said simply.

During the hour drive to the ranch, Alana questioned Billy about everything that she could think of. She found out that Mr. Brandon was Brandon Warren, the owner of Montaqua. He inherited the ranch when his father, Lowell Warren, died last spring. It was clear that Bill liked and admired his Mister Brandon.

She also discovered that Lilian Brams was Brandon Warren's sister. She had six children, of which four were boys. She moved back to Montaqua after her husband died a year ago from last Christmas. Brandon needed her to help nurse their ailing father. After he died, Brandon asked his sister to remain at Montaqua with the children. The main house at the ranch was evidently large enough to accommodate all of them.

It was Lilian's six children plus three more boys that Alana was to teach. The other three boys belonged to Brandon's older brother, Douglas, and his expecting wife, Anne. They lived on a nearby ranch, part of which was given to them by Anne's grandfather. They raised some cattle, but relied more on the sawmill that Douglas and Anne's grandfather were partners in.

Many local plantation owners and farmers had lost a lot of their land and possessions to "the cause" nearly two decades ago. But Lowell Warren did not support slavery and never had. He was not fond of the way Northerners made fun of Southerners, but his dislike was not strong enough to make him want to give to "the cause." When the war was over, his was one of the few places that was not crippled in some way. His plantation began to delve more into cattle as it transformed into the prosperous Montaqua, meaning mountain water. It was named for the Warren Mountain that it encompassed and for the several streams and ponds that interlaced it.

As she glanced ahead to see if she could spot Montaqua, she realized that Don Andrios was certainly right about this part of Texas. It was breathtaking. Huge trees loomed over her head, forming an arch that shaded most of the road. There were oak, elm, sweet gum, walnut, pecan, persimmon, and many other trees mingled with the most prominent pine trees. The pastures beyond were deep in green and thick with grass. Pretty little blue and gold wildflowers dotted the fields. Beyond the fields rose large hills covered with many shades of bright green. The earth was a deep, rich brownish-red; not dry and sandy as she had expected. An occasional fence appeared on the roadside, but they were not made of wood as most Alana had seen were. They seemed to be made of posts joined by several strands of wire spaced about a foot apart.

Heading toward the largest hill, Alana wondered if it might be the mountain of Montaqua. Her silent question was answered as Billy announced, "We're almost there.

It's just around that next bend."

Alana tried to see through the brushy wooded area that they were passing through, but saw nothing but more brush and trees. She was hoping the house was not in this thicket. Then the woods ended at a fenceline. There was clear pastureland beyond, broken only by small clusters of trees until the woods started again in the distance. Among several huge spreading pecan trees was quite an impressive house, very large and stately, that faced north. Alana remembered seeing hotels and boarding houses that were smaller. The outer walls of this house were made of dark roughwood boards with stucco sealing any crevices between the boards. There was a long covered walkway across the front with thick angular posts used as columns.

When Billy pulled the carriage around behind the house, she was surprised to see that it was built in the shape of a U around a fabulous terrace with several gardens encircling a beautiful ornamental pool. The inside wall of this U-shaped house was also lined by covered walkways with the support of the large angular posts. Planters rich in greenery hung from each of the posts. Two boys that had been seated on one of the benches along the covered walkway scurried into the largest area of the house near the front.

"Everyone will know you are here, now. With those two, news travels fast," Billy said as he gestured toward the door the boys had just disappeared into. He jumped down and started untying the trunks.

Alana came down, keeping a careful eye on that door. As she waited to be told what to do or where to go, a woman appeared in the doorway wiping her hands on a small towel. She laid the towel down just inside the door and walked toward Alana. She ordered Billy to put the trunks in Miss Stambridge's room as she held out her hand to Alana.

"Welcome to our home. Are we ever glad to see you! I was beginning to worry. We thought maybe that you had changed your mind or had run into an ill fate. Come in and meet everyone. Oh, I guess I should introduce myself.

I am Lilian Brams, the one who wrote the letters to the college asking for a teacher," Lilian said, still clasping Alana's hand in both of her own.

Lilian was not at all like Alana's vision of a dried-up little old widow dressed in black. The way Billy had talked, Lilian was a saintly old woman struggling to raise her six fatherless waifs. Instead Alana was impressed by a warm beauty that glowed from within this tall, stately woman. And Lilian Brams was quite tall for a woman. Alana guessed that she stood five feet plus another eight or nine inches, probably two inches taller than her own five feet, seven inches. Her dark brown hair was tied back into a ponytail that hung low on her back. Alana judged Lilian's age to be around thirty, but was given only one real clue to this age from the small wrinkles beginning to form at the corners of her huge, round eyes when she smiled. The deep blue of those exceptionally beautiful eyes was outlined with long dark lashes. She was dressed in a floor-length cotton floral-print dress of pinks and blues with a full, white pocketed apron over the front, tied by a sash in the back. Alana definitely liked Lilian.

Lilian released Alana's hand as she motioned for Alana to go ahead of her. They entered the same door that Lilian had just come from. Once inside, Alana found herself standing in a spacious living area with a huge rock fireplace and hearth making up the entire opposite wall. The other walls were made of a light brown stucco with heavy wooden beams. Two long cloth-covered couches with wooden arms and delicately carved wooden boards high across the backs were the the main pieces in the room. The long tables in front of the couches and the smaller tables at the ends matched the wood accenting the couches. Hurricane lamps of porcelain and brass sat on the smaller tables. The couches were back to back, one facing the fireplace while the other faced a huge window with a view of the terrace. Two matching stuffed chairs were angled toward the fireplace directly beside the end tables. Several fancy hand-carved, high-backed wooden chairs were lined perpendicular to and on either side of the couch facing the window. It was a well-planned room.

To her right, she noticed part of the wall seemed cut away revealing the dining area. A crew of fidgeting children sat with their eyes keenly focused on their new teacher. A large Negro woman walked in from a swinging door on the opposite side of the room and stood behind one of the older boys seated at the end of a long, wooden dining table as they entered. The children occupied six of the twelve high-backed, thickly carved, wooden chairs.

"Well, children, this is our new teacher all the way from New York—Miss Stambridge. I want you to introduce yourselves, starting with Jacob," Lilian spoke with a firm look, reminding them to use their manners.

"Glad to meet you, Miss Stambridge. I am Jacob Brams, most folks call me Jake. I am the oldest," Jake announced proudly as he stood erect beside his chair in military style.

"Very pleased to make your acquaintance," Alana said with a proper nod as she looked over the fourteen-year-old boy.

Jake was on the verge of becoming a very handsome man. There were not many boyish features remaining on his lean face. His thick black hair was parted to one side and combed away from his face. He had inherited his mother's deep blue eyes, which were surrounded by a heavy growth of dark lashes. His height already matched that of his mother. He was muscular through the back, yet slender at the hips.

"I'm Jim," an eager voice said from behind her. Alana turned to find that the voice came from a small boy who had gotten up from his seat and circled around to stand directly behind her. "I am twelve years old next month." His dark-brown curly hair hung over his very blue eyes that were not quite the same deep blue as Jake's, but were outlined by the same long dark lashes. A patch of freckles crossed the bridge of his nose, which wrinkled as he studied his new teacher. His slender frame stood about four and a half feet.

"I am pleased to meet you, Jim," Alana said graciously, devoting her full attention to the little boy.

"And I am John," came from another voice, again behind her. Alana turned and stared in amazement. This boy was an exact replica of Jim, right down to the last little freckle. "I am twelve next month, too."

"Twins!" Alana exclaimed, "Identical twins! How will I ever tell you two apart?"

"Even I have trouble sometimes," Lilian admitted. "Sometimes I have to lift up their hair in order to tell them apart. John, here, has a small scar on the right side of his forehead." She pulled back John's curls to reveal the telltale scar near his hairline.

"I shall have to remember that," Alana said as she made a mental note of the identifying mark. The twins returned to their seats giggling with total delight over the teacher's confusion.

A small girl seated beside the twins looked down at her hands folded neatly in her lap as she barely spoke, "I-I am Brenda Sue Brams."

"Such a pretty young lady," Alana complimented the nervous child. Brenda looked to be around ten. She had thick black hair pulled back into a single braid that hung down below her tiny waist. Her long dark lashes hung so low as she studied her thumbs, that Alana could only guess that her eyes were blue, too. "Glad to meet you, Brenda."

"She's scareda ya!" the smallest boy seated on the edge of his seat next to Brenda said. "She's afraid of everything. She even runs from harmless old lizards."

"Michael Brams, you apologize to your sister this instant. You have no right to talk about her that way!" a reddened Lilian reprimanded her youngest son.

"I'm sorry," he said quite insincerely as he turned his pugged nose up at his mother.

"This is Mickey. I am afraid that he has a problem with his manners," Lilian apologized to Alana, who remained silent.

Mickey appeared to be around seven. His shaggy dark brown hair was highlighted with streaks of blond and hung partless over his ears and forehead. The two upper front teeth were gone, giving his pudgy face an almost comical look. He sported his oldest brother's eyes and the twins' freckles.

After a moment of silence, the last and youngest of the Bram children stood up to introduce herself.

"My name is Angela. I usta be called Angie, but that was when I was just a little kid," the chubby figure said with a great show of dignity.

"Then I shall be certain to remember to call you Angela," Alana promised the pretty amber-haired girl. Angela, it turned out, was the painful image of her father. She had acquired not only his amber hair, but also his pale green eyes. With her hair braided at the ears, she displayed the same high forehead. She showed signs of a weight problem as she was very near to being plump. But, her weight did not seem to bother her as she posed to be the proper little lady of five years.

Alana turned to Lilian and complimented her on having six such fine children, remarking that she did not look as if she had even bore a single child.

"I have borne seven, actually," Lilian spoke softly. "My last child was stillborn shortly after Mark, my husband, died." Her eyes filled with tears as she continued, "I only carried him eight months. He was amber-headed just like his father." She paused a moment to regain her composure, "But you are right, I am lucky to have these six fine children. Come, I want you to meet our housekeeper, Lizzie."

The large Negro woman showed a hearty smile as she shook hands with the new school teacher. Alana was told that Lizzie was practically part of the family. Lizzie shook with laughter at the suggestion that she was tied to the Warren family. A sparkle in her shiny black eyes could warm the coldest heart. She was a tender, loving woman who, whether she admitted it or not, was as much a part of the family as Lilian herself.

"Lawdie, Miss Lilian, you given me more praise than a body should have. I best be gitten back to my chores in the kitchen before I be gitten the big head. Master Brandon be coming in hungry as a bear after skippin' lunch like he did," Lizzie said as she backed through the swinging door that led to the kitchen.

After Billy came rushing by with the announcement that Alana's trunks were in her room, Lilian escorted her outside. She led Alana down the walkway to their right and down what she referred to as the West Wing. She stopped in front of the last door and searched her pocket with her hand, "I have a key here somewhere. Ah, here it is. This is your room. It has a lock so that you might enjoy your privacy," Lilian said as she handed the key to Alana and guided her inside. "I hope it meets your standards. Anything you think it needs, just ask and I will see what I can do."

The room more than met any standards Alana may have had. The walls were made of smooth pink stucco with dark wooden baseboards and doors. To the left, was a double-sized, brass canopy bed with a dark rose-colored spread and a pink mesh cloth surrounding it, reaching to the floor, to prevent the pestering of insects on summer evenings when it was far more comfortable to sleep with the windows open. On one side of the bed was a small table supporting a glass oil lamp with a shiny brass base. A brass candelabra and a large ceramic pitcher with basin were set on the dresser on the opposite side of the bed. Across the room a beautiful rock fireplace took up half of the wall. Two upholstered chairs with a small table between them were just in front of and facing the fireplace. Short logs were stacked high on the hearth beside the fireplace. There were two ceramic owls over the mantel and beside the fireplace was a door that was slightly ajar. Alana supposed it was a closet. There was another door in the wall on the right that was partially covered by a huge wardrobe cabinet that stretched half the length of that wall. Beside the door through which they had entered was a small brass table with a matching mirror on the wall behind it. A dainty brass stool with a pink cushion was set before it. The two small windows on either side of the door were open as well as the two on either side of the bed. A slight breeze swept through the room causing the open doors to sway.

Lilian walked over to the door by the fireplace and

pulled it completely open. "Your room adjoins the room that is to be your classroom," she mentioned as she waited for Alana to peek in.

The room was similar to the one they were now in. It also had pink stucco walls with the dark wooden trim. Another rock fireplace was directly behind the one in Alana's room. A large wooden desk was set out from the wall on the left with two open windows behind it. The desk faced two long tables with benches on the sides opposite the desk. Directly across was a door that led to the outside as did the windows on either side. Alana felt a slight twinge of excitement as she viewed her very first classroom. She could hardly wait to arrange her books in the bookcase behind her desk.

"Brandon had long tables and benches made for the children and one of Papa's old desks moved in here for you. He was even willing to let me order a slateboard for you once he finally gave in," Lilian told her.

"Once he gave in?" Alana repeated questioningly.

"Well, to tell the truth, Brandon was not all for hiring a special teacher from up North. He was satisfied with sending the children into Gilmer every day. I did not like it because by the time they stopped and picked up our brother's boys and rode into town with the wagon, well over an hour had passed. I did not complain so much for the near to three hours' total traveling time as I did the overcrowding. More and more people have been moving to Upshur County as of late, and there are more children in the schools than the teachers can really handle. The townfolk have talked of hiring more teachers, but some claim that it would cost them too much, so it is still just talk. There are a few little community schools around, too; but they are not run by qualified teachers and are just about as far away as Gilmer is anyway. The only one that was worth considering was at the Glenwood Crossing about four miles from here. It was run by Reverend W. H. McClelland who seemed to know what he was doing, but it burned down just before Christmas. And, since he lost a son in the fire, Reverend McClelland shows no desire to rebuild it or even to return to teaching at all. As for now, I am not satisfied with just any school and I am determined to see to it that my children receive a proper education. Brandon just needed a little convincing. Actually, it took quite a lot of convincing. Lizzie cooked up all of his favorites and the children sweet-talked him; they promised to do more chores as they would have more spare time. Brandon finally gave in. But, I do want to warn you, he is still dead set against the idea of spending good money on what he considers a needless luxury—never did like school himself," Lilian cautioned. She added as if a second thought, "Please do not take it personally if he seems irritated by your presence at first. It is just that he hates not getting his way."

But Alana was already taking it personally. She could not help but let her wild imagination take over. Education was very important to her, and it was beyond any understanding of hers that a man could have such little concern for properly educating these children. What kind of man would try to blockade the path of knowledge? She was beginning to imagine all manner of things about this Brandon. She was forming a picture of an uneducated old tyrant. She could just see an overweight, overbearing, slothful man that talked too loud and pounded the table as he spoke. She compared him with King Henry VIII as she decided that he was probably against church as well. Her temper flared as she wondered if he might even try to run her off. Well, she just was not going to allow this brute to bully her. Alana Stambridge might have to teach him a thing or two as well!

Chapter Two

"Where is that Billy?" Brandon thought angrily as his deep blue eyes squinted against the late afternoon sun, trying to judge the time. He looked toward the house with hopes of seeing his tardy helper riding up. "He ought to be back with that fool teacher by now. That stage is never this late," he grumbled aloud.

Brandon had replaced the rotten posts of the damaged section of fence by himself, but needed help stringing the wire. This new barbed wire was tricky, and it took at least two men to put it up. Until they did get this stretch of fence fixed, the cattle would keep wandering off into the woods directly behind it. He might have to have Abe stop rounding up the cows that were still strayed on the mountain and help him stretch the wire, if Billy did not show up soon. It was too dangerous a task to attempt after dark, no matter how much help there was.

With his patience wearing thin after waiting only another few minutes, Brandon stalked over to the nearby wagon and untied his horse from the back. He mounted his golden horse to search for Abe. He was tucking his gloves into his vest pocket when he heard a horse approaching. It was Billy.

"About time, I'd say. What did you do, lead the old lady in on a leash?" Brandon asked curtly.

"Sorry, but the stage was late and then your sister had me tote the trunks in for her. Lord, she musta had rocks in one of them. I could hardly lift it," Billy tried to explain, knowing by the flare of Brandon's nostrils that his temper was riled.

"Probably the trousseau that the old maid never got to

34

use," Brandon snorted as he climbed back down from his horse and tied it back to the wagon. "Hurry up and get your gloves on. There's a lot of work here that won't get done jawing."

"She ain't exactly old, Mister Brandon. No siree, I bet she ain't as old as me. And if that was her trousseau, there's still plenty of time for her to be using it," Billy said with a grin and a raised eyebrow. "She won't be havin' no trouble at all findin' her a fella when she takes the notion—she's awful pretty."

"Say she's pretty?" Brandon asked, letting his anger slide.

"Prettier than most girls I ever saw. In fact, she's beautiful, and seems quite the sophisticated lady. I never woulda guessed her for a schoolteacher," Billy remarked as he shook his head displaying a look of incredible doubt.

"Well, let's get to work. We need to get this fence fixed this evening," Brandon reminded him again as he pretended not to be even slightly interested. But, he did wonder why a young woman would be willing to uproot herself and come to Texas to teach such a small bunch of children, especially if she was as pretty as Billy seemed to think. He decided that she must have been fresh out of that teaching school his sister insisted writing to. "Well, she just better be a good teacher," he thought bitterly as he carefully undid the first roll of barbed wire.

Wanting to impress Brandon Warren as an authoritative woman and as a quite competent teacher, Alana used careful planning in getting dressed for dinner. Hoping to look a few years older as well as a few years wiser, she twisted her hair back into a tight little bun. She chose her most matronly gray skirt with a high-necked white blouse that tied with a narrow black bow at the throat and fastened down the front with small black buttons. A black square-shouldered jacket gave the outfit a certain masculine quality. The entire ensemble was very large as she bought it the summer before college when she herself was greatly oversized.

Most of her wardrobe was still too big. She had

purchased a few new dresses during her weight loss, but could not afford to fill her entire wardrobe needs with new clothes. Since alterations and sewing were two of her weaker talents, she had to make do with the oversized clothes she had. But, in this case, Alana was glad that her clothes were too big. It seemed to help her create the effect that she was after.

Alana decided not to touch perfume to her neck since she still smelled of lavender from the soap Lilian had provided for her greatly appreciated but most disturbing bath. All baths in this house were taken in a large brass tub behind a tall woven screen in the far corner of the kitchen. Lizzie filled the tub with water warmed on the stove and stood a vigilant watch over the bath area to make certain it was not disturbed. If anyone entered by mistake, she quickly chased them out with a broom, a ladle, or whatever was handy.

Occasionally, Lizzie would peek around the screen asking Alana if she needed anything. This discomfited the modest Alana immensely and forced her to hurry through her bath. Once out of the tub, she kept her towel wrapped securely around her as she quickly dressed, hoping Lizzie would not peek in on her again before she was decently covered. Yet, in spite of the way she rushed her bath, she found that she felt quite relaxed afterward. Some of the anticipation she was building had temporarily been eased. Now it was rapidly building again.

She paced the floor of her room as she waited for dinnertime. Lilian had told her that the family generally dined at 7:30, but Alana had gotten ready too early. She spent the extra time practicing different speeches, hoping to find one that would so impress Mr. Warren that he would completely change his mind and welcome her employment.

Just before time to go, Alana rechecked herself in the mirror. Then, taking a deep breath, she locked her door and walked to the dining room. Lilian was waiting for her at the dining-room entrance.

"Lizzie was just about to ring the outside dinnerbell that calls everyone to supper. Please, go ahead and be seated," she said as she escorted Alana to the table, which was already set with dishes, silverware, and filled water glasses.

Alana was seated next to one end. Angela was the next one to sit down as she slid into the seat next to Alana. Jake stopped a moment to say hello to Alana before sitting at the opposite end. Mickey, Brenda, John, and Jim lined the other side of the table leaving the place opposite Alana for Lilian. That left one setting empty. Nervously tapping her fingertips together, Alana waited for Mr. Warren to come in and fill the empty seat. Lilian watched her a moment, wondering what had happened to the pretty young woman she had greeted earlier as she noted Alana's plain, unattractive clothes and her simple, almost ugly, hairstyle.

Finally, she spoke, "Brandon has not come in yet; but, we will not bother waiting for him. You just never know when he will come in."

She then nodded to Jake who said the blessing, after which all eyes turned to the swinging door to the kitchen.

Shortly Lizzie backed through the door carrying a huge tray covered with bowls of food. She set the tray on the buffet table behind Lilian and began serving the food. She placed a large platter of sliced ham in front of Lilian and bowls full of black-eyed peas, fried okra, boiled cabbage, and mashed potatoes in various locations along the table, before gathering up her tray and returning to the kitchen. Jake slapped Mickey's hand as he picked at the okra with his fingers instead of waiting for Lizzie to return with the big spoons and the basket of rolls.

As Lizzie placed a spoon in each of the bowls, they heard a door shut in the kitchen.

"Master Brandon's home. I better be gettin' him a towel. He'll be wantin' to wash up and eat right away," Lizzie reported as she hurried off.

"Would you care for some peas, Alana?" Lilian asked and then handed the steaming bowl to her. Alana accepted it and spooned a few of them onto her plate before automatically passing it on. Her thoughts were not on the food; they were on the muffled sounds coming from the kitchen. She could feel her pulse racing as she waited for the appearance of Brandon Warren through the closed door.

The children began eating as Brandon washed and changed into the clean shirt that Lizzie had waiting for him. They were nearly finished eating when Brandon started through the door. As he entered the room he was looking down and buttoning the cuffs to his sleeves. When he looked up, Alana was stunned. Instead of the old tyrant that she was expecting, she found Brandon Warren to be surprisingly young, about twenty-eight she guessed, and extremely handsome. Alana could not remember ever having seen a man so handsome. He was tall and broad across the shoulders yet narrow at the waist and hips. His thick black hair was parted on one side and swept back away from his gentle blue eyes, which were outlined with very long black lashes. He wore a pale-blue shirt, unbuttoned at the neck, and dark-blue denim pants, which seemed to bring extra attention to his fabulously blue eyes.

Lilian introduced Alana to Brandon and a gorgeous smile spread across his face, forming two long, slender crevices in his lean cheeks. His deep voice carried softly as he spoke, "Pleased to meet you, Miss Stambridge."

He stared curiously at her as he waited for her to reply, unable to believe that Billy was so taken by this woman. She was pretty enough, in a strange sort of way, but not nearly the beauty that Billy described. He wondered if Billy might not have been out in the sun too long. He felt that she was just too plain to be warranted as beautiful and not at all like the charming lady Billy claimed her to be. This woman looked more like a schoolteacher than anyone Brandon had ever met.

Alana found that she could not speak and nodded politely instead. She looked down at her clothes and wished that she could just slide under the table and disappear.

Sitting down at the end of the table beside Alana and Lilian, he turned his full attention to his meal. He continued to eat as he listened to Lilian's account of the day. The children each excused themselves as they finished eating and went outside to play.

Before Brandon was able to finish, Lilian also excused herself, "I need to get Angela ready for bed; I will be right back." Alana was just about to make her excuses to retire early when Lilian added, "You two keep each other company while I am gone."

Right after Lilian walked out of the room, Alana noticed a short frown purse on Brandon's lips that reminded her of the tyrant she had originally pictured. "So you are Lilian's new schoolteacher. How long have you been teaching?" he asked wondering just how old Alana was.

"Actually, this is my first real teaching job, but I have assisted several college teachers," Alana replied, hoping that her apprehension was not evident.

"You have never taught before?" Brandon asked incredulously with one eyebrow raised as if in judgment.

Feeling her temper rise, Alana forgot any fear and tried desperately to restrain herself. "I assure you, sir, that I am quite qualified as a teacher and am confident that I can give your nieces and nephews a proper education," she managed to say calmly, overcoming the desire to stamp her foot.

"Think so?" Brandon asked with his eyebrow still cocked high as he pierced her with his ice blue eyes.

"I am certain of it," Alana said with a stubborn 'I shall show you' quality in her voice.

Brandon stared openly at Alana. He frowned as he noticed her rigid jaw clenching in anger. He was not accustomed to a woman with such a display of temper. Deciding to forego that line of conversation for the moment, he asked instead how her trip went. His voice displayed a certain lack of interest.

The conversation had lagged when Lilian walked in and found the two of them just staring hatefully at each other.

"Well, Angela's tucked in," she said as she took her seat. Neither Brandon nor Alana attempted to carry a conversation as they continued to stare oddly at each other. "I see that we are all finished. Why don't we move out to the patio and enjoy the cool evening breeze?" Lilian suggested hopefully.

"I think not, thank you. I am rather tired from the wear of such a long trip and really do need my rest," Alana coolly excused herself before she pushed her chair away from the table.

Lilian was curious as to what had been said between her hot-tempered brother and this obviously offended woman, but did not pursue the matter as she walked with Alana to Alana's door. Lilian answered several questions that Alana had about the classes. Alana would teach early mornings during the summer and through to mid-afternoon in the winter months. Whenever Alana had her classroom in order, she could get started. Before leaving, Lilian reminded Alana that breakfast was served at 7:00.

Once inside her room, Alana pulled the combs from her hair and let the thick brown tresses fall across her shoulders. As she sat in front of the mirror to smooth its thickness with a brush, she caught a fair glimpse of herself. She pouted at what she saw and wondered how she could have worn such atrocious clothing. Turning her head at an angle, she closely studied herself. Hoping to improve her face, she pinched her cheeks, bringing a pinkish glow to them. Then, she tried out a few different smiles, none of which satisfied her.

"I might as well come to terms with it, Brandon Warren could never become interested in someone like me." She sighed remorsefully.

After she brushed her hair, Alana went to bed. She had trouble falling asleep as her mind kept recalling the blunderous evening. She wished that she could control her temper better, hoping that somehow she and Brandon might be able to get along and that, just maybe, he might even grow to like her.

Early that following morning, Alana started getting ready for breakfast. This time she was going to plan her attire quite differently. She searched through her trunk until she found some of her newer dresses that fit. She chose a yellow and gold print cotton dress with pale yellow lace across the high-neck and down the front in five even rows. The short puffed sleeves were edged with the yellow lace and two rows of lace circled around the hem, nearly brushing the floor.

Still not ready to wear her hair down in front of people as Lilian did, Alana decided to pull it up high off of her face and neck, shaping curls around the crest of her head. After digging into the trunk once again, she came out with a small yellow ribbon that she wove in and out of the curls. As a finishing touch, she pinched her cheeks and bit her lips for the added color.

She felt that she was almost ready to meet Brandon again. Determined to hold her temper as well as her tongue, she was going to show Brandon a different Alana from the one he met last night. For the final touch, she put a bit of perfume on her neck. Then as she remembered seeing Bethany do, she added an extra touch behind each of her ears.

With a different kind of anticipation this time, she locked her door and proceeded down the walkway to the main part of the house. Catching her reflection in a window, she stopped in disbelief. Could that slender girl in the reflection be her, it was still such a pleasant surprise to find that it was. She took a few more steps and noticed that she did not walk quite the way she knew a woman could. She practiced a few more steps, swaying slightly at the hip, but it was not exactly right. It would never impress Brandon. She decided that she would just have to practice later, as she passed on by the window.

With her head held high, she entered the dining room to find Lilian alone, sipping a cup of coffee at the table. Places were set for breakfast, but she noticed that Brandon's was not. Her heart sank as she listened to Lilian explaining that Brandon, having already eaten, had run over to his brother's sawmill to get enough lumber to repair the holding pen and build a new stall in the barn.

After a breakfast of hot oatmeal and honey, Alana returned to her room to begin unpacking her things. She spent most of the morning hanging up her dresses, skirts, and blouses. Refolding her undergarments and gowns, she carefully organized them into separate drawers. She put her shoes and boots away in the wardrobe chest as well as several hats and her umbrella. She placed all of her grooming aids on the vanity and hung her hair ribbons on the mirror behind it. Choosing the mantel as a perfect spot, she carefully displayed the small framed portrait of her family. She shook her head in disgust as she looked at the plump figure sitting awkwardly beside the poised and beautiful Bethany. She knew that it was none other than herself. Her mother and even part of her father were partially hidden behind the large frame of their youngest daughter. The picture was not a very complimentary one of Alana, but it was the only picture she had of her family and it did serve as a reminder of what she had let food and her emotional insecurities do to her in the past.

After finally reaching the bottom of the first trunk, it was too close to lunchtime to begin unpacking the other trunk. She decided to walk out to the patio and rest a minute. She corrected the few loose strands of hair that had fallen and tidied up her dress before the mirror in case she happened to run into Brandon.

It was a beautiful morning. A cool breeze swept past her as she made her way to a bench under a small tree near the end of the patio. She sat facing away from the house, which enabled her to view the barn to the left of her. It was a huge structure made of materials similar to the house, and was shaded by huge pecan and walnut trees. She could also see a large orchard of pear, apple, and peach trees to the right of her. In the center of the orchard was a small well with a housing shaped from the same rough wood boards as the house and barn. On the far side of the orchard was a neatly planted garden with many rows of vegetables in various stages of growth. Beyond the garden was a huge rolling grassy pasture spotted with pink and yellow wildflowers. Large, black muscular cattle grazed lazily on the green grass. A long stream wound lazily through the pasture's thickness which, at one place, had been dug out and partially dammed to form a pond. The languid pool of crystal blue water was accented by the deep greens of the grass and the tall pink and red wildflowers that dotted its shoreline. Several oak and sweet gum trees surrounded the pond, blocking part of it from sight and forming a private little haven of peaceful beauty.

Beyond this large pasture was a hill covered with timber. Off to each side were smaller pastures stocked with the same black cattle as the main pasture. It was a beautiful ranch, one Brandon had a right to be proud of.

While Alana continued to view the grounds, Angela came running by.

"Where are you going in such a hurry?" Alana shouted to her as she passed.

Angela stopped with a look of surprise at the sound of her name. She had not noticed her new teacher sitting in the shadows. "I am headed for the orchard to get me a peach. You want one?"

"Oh, no, it is just not done. Besides, if a lady eats too much, she might lose her girlish figure. That would never do," Alana said in a sincere tone, hoping that her message was getting through. She would hate to see such a pretty girl as Angela suffer the horrible fate of fat as she had done.

Angela looked down at her chubby little stomach and then at Alana's trim waistline and pursed a frown. A peach certainly would taste good, but she did so want to be a proper lady.

"I guess that I did not realize how close it is to lunchtime. How silly of me," she said with her nose held up almost snobbishly. She climbed up onto the bench next to Alana and folded her hands in her lap as she knew a lady would. Smiling up at Alana, she sat silently, blinking her large pale green eyes. After a bit more silence, Angela remarked, "I am going to be a beautiful proper lady like you someday."

Alana was startled at such a sudden and totally open compliment. Could she actually seem beautiful in the eyes of this young child?

"Why, thank you, Angela. I am absolutely certain that you will be very beautiful. You are quite pretty, now."

Angela sighed, "I am going to be very beautiful and marry a man just like Uncle Brandon."

"You must be very fond of your Uncle Brandon," Alana

probed.

"Oh, yes, he is the best. He gave me a store-bought hat for Easter and then walked with me arm and arm to church. He also got me my very own horse after I proved that I could ride good enough. We named him Sawdust cause that is what color he is. You want to meet him?" Angela said as she hopped down.

She led Alana around to the far side of the barn to the tall rough-board fence of a small corral. Three horses were standing lazily under the shade of a tree. Two were the color of golden honey and the third was coal black. The smallest of the blond-colored horses turned at the sound of Angela's voice and slowly walked over to get his nose rubbed.

"Want to pet him, Miss Stambridge? He don't care; he likes it. Ain't he great?"

Alana flinched at Angela's poor use of grammar, but decided she would start correcting that soon enough as she reached out to rub Sawdust on his handsome white forehead.

"He is beautiful. Is he all yours?" Alana asked, truly impressed.

"Sure he is all hers," a masculine voice remarked. Alana gasped as she turned to find Brandon leaning on the fence right next to her.

"You frightened me. I did not know that you were there," Alana stammered.

"Didn't mean to," Brandon said simply as he stared in wide-eyed amazement at Alana. He was not certain that this was the same woman that he had met just last night, until he heard Angela call her Miss Stambridge. Maybe it was he who had been in the sun too long. Billy was right when he called her beautiful. As she looked shyly away from him, he took in her appearance. He liked the beautiful crown of curls formed by her thick brown hair, the slender upward curve of her nose, and her haughty little chin. But he was mostly impressed with those deep brown eyes that now revealed the embarrassment of being caught off guard as she was.

Alana could not think of anything clever to say to

Brandon, as she found that she could not take her eyes from his steel-blue gaze. Instead, she directed her words to Angela who was still busily rubbing Sawdust, "Angela, you must be very proud of such a fine horse."

Before Angela could answer, Brandon replied as he continued to stare at Alana, "Oh, she is. In fact, she helps Billy curry him every evening." A moment of silence followed, which was shortly broken by the sharp ringing of a bell and Lizzie's shrill voice announcing that lunch was ready.

"Shall we go?" Brandon asked as he stepped aside to allow Alana and Angela to walk ahead of him. With Brandon following her, Alana wished that she had taken the time to practice a more stylish walk. Walking in front of Brandon to the house seemed endless as she felt that he might be watching her too closely. Angela babbled constantly about her horse, but all Alana could hear was the pounding of her own heart.

A basin of hot soapy water was waiting for them to wash their hands before sitting down to a table of broiled sirloin steaks, mashed potatoes, field peas, sliced tomatoes, and Spanish cornbread.

Lilian noticed the trio as they entered together, hoping that Alana and Brandon had settled whatever differences they seemed to have had last night. She raised an eyebrow as she watched Brandon display his best table manners; he even remembered to place his napkin on his knee. It usually remained at the side of his plate until needed. After an awkward exchange of glances between the two, she saw that someone was going to have to start a conversation, the silence was deafening.

"Well, did you see Douglas at the sawmill?" she asked Brandon.

"Yes, he said to give you his best and to have you send for the boys when the new schoolteacher was ready for them. When do you think that will be, Miss Stambridge?" he asked as he glanced over at Alana.

"I hope to be ready to begin next Monday morning, if that is all right with you," Alana replied.

"So soon?" Mickey's small voice whimpered. He was

hoping for a long vacation.

"Hush, Mickey," Lilian scolded and gave him a sharp look that conveyed a special meaning Mickey knew only too well. A smile then returned to her face as she asked Alana, "Are you certain that you can be ready that soon? You must be a fast worker."

"I'll be glad to help her get ready," Angela piped in.

"With a fine helper at my side, I know for sure that I will be ready on Monday morning," Alana remarked. Besides, she would enjoy having someone to talk to while she sorted her books and supplies.

"Seems you have made a new friend, Miss Stambridge," Brandon remarked as he nodded to Angela.

Angela sat up straight and proudly announced, "I am going to grow up to be just like her. I'm going to go to college and become a schoolteacher and everything."

"Now, you just settle down a might. Girls don't need to be going off to college. It doesn't do them any good anyway. Just pick out a husband with some land and you'll do all right." Brandon made the mistake of saying that in Alana's presence.

Alana's jaw flinched as her temper climbed to its boiling point. "What do you mean it does not do a girl any good to get a college education? I suppose that I wasted two years of my life attending classes instead of searching for a prosperous man to marry! Let me tell you, there is a wealth of good usable knowledge in books that a woman can utilize as well as a man. One way a person learns is by reading of the accomplishments and mistakes that others have made in the past. That is the key to knowledge. And a woman can put that knowledge to as practical a use as any man can! Even those who marry can still learn through books how to be more efficient and how to manage a tight budget. To quote Disraeli: 'The more extensive a man's knowledge of what has been done, the greater will be his power of knowing what to do,'" Alana spoke as her voice wavered with anger.

"Ah-ha, he said man's knowledge, not woman's knowledge. All a woman needs to know is how to cook a decent meal, sew a stitch, and raise her children. She don't learn that in books," Brandon said, letting his voice rise.

"She doesn't learn . . ." Alana haughtily corrected his improper grammar with a look of arrogance. A scowl came across Brandon's face as Alana continued, "Whether it is a man or a woman that he spoke of, the principle is the same. There are a lot of things that a woman can learn in books about cooking, sewing, and life in general. She can come to understand fully what actually happens to her body during childbearing and what she should and should not do at that time. Or she can learn to help manage a budget or even a business. There are many things a woman needs to know, and one of them is when to excuse herself before she says something she might regret later," Alana said as she pushed her chair away from her half-eaten meal, gave her apologies to Lilian, and gracefully walked out.

A completely stunned Brandon Warren watched Alana exit with total amazement. That was the first time a woman had ever gotten the best of him in any type of disagreement. He shook his head as he decided that if college continued to teach women like that, more men would have to go to college just to learn to deal with them. "Just a waste of time," he thought to himself as he resumed eating. When he looked up, he saw all of the children and even Lilian giving him icy stares. He took a few more bites as they continued to frown at him. Finally, he threw his fork down and marched out fuming, "That new teacher lady can cause a lot of trouble." He continued to mumble under his breath on his way to the barn.

Chapter Three

Angela tapped the door lightly with her foot and waited patiently as the tray she carried grew heavy in her little arms.

"What are you doing carrying such a large tray? Where is Lizzie? She should be bringing that," Alana remarked when she opened the door to find Angela almost hidden beneath the huge supper tray. She bent over and accepted the heavy load from Angela's trembling arms. "Do you have time to sit with me while I eat?"

For the past few days, since she and Brandon had exchanged their varied points of view, Alana requested to have her meals in her room. Afraid there might be repercussions, she chose to avoid him as long as she possibly could. She spent most of her time getting the classroom and her teaching program set. Angela had spent a great deal of each afternoon helping Alana dust books, put up curtains, tack pictures on the wall, and do whatever else Alana would let her do. They talked constantly of many things, but Angela's favorite subjects were of parties, travel, and of the many fine qualities that made a proper lady. Alana was growing quite fond of her new little amber-haired friend. And, although she hated to think of having a teacher's pet, she did have to admit she felt Angela was indeed special. The little girl was smart, very outgoing, and quite eager to learn.

"I can stay until the dinnerbell rings. We have not eaten yet. Well, Uncle Brandon already ate before he went into town," Angela said as she followed Alana into the classroom.

"Your Uncle Brandon is not here?" Alana asked, feeling

a limited freedom. She could safely venture out of her room this evening if Brandon was gone.

"Uncle Brandon likes to go into town on Saturday night. If he and his friends are not in town, they are at a party somewhere. He don't usually stay home on Saturday night," Angela replied.

"He doesn't . . ." Alana inserted. She had already begun correcting Angela's grammatical errors.

Angela accepted the correction and repeated correctly, "He doesn't usually stay home on Saturday nights."

A delighted smile crossed Alana's face as she asked, "Do you think that you might have time for a stroll with me after you eat? I am eager to put my work aside and get some fresh air."

"I'll ask Mama. She will probably let me go, if I promise to be in bed by dark. We have to get up early and go to church tomorrow. Are you going with us?" Angela asked hopefully.

"Tell me, does your Uncle Brandon go with you to church?" Alana questioned, hoping and rather expecting the answer to be no. It was.

"He goes on Easter and Christmas Sundays, but usually he stays home and sleeps, because he sometimes don't— doesn't get home until early morning."

"Well, I would love to go to church with you, if your mother does not mind," Alana said, wondering which church the Warrens were affiliated with. It really did not matter, though, she would be happy to be able to get out and meet new people.

"She doesn't care. Anyway, she told me to ask you," Angela explained as Alana set the tray on her desk and began to taste the beef stew, cornbread, and spiced tea that had weighted it so.

The dinnerbell rang and Lizzie's shrill voice rang out, "Supper, come eat!" Angela hurried off to eat, promising to meet Alana on the patio when she was through so that they could take that evening stroll.

Alana found that she had an unusually vigorous appetite as she quickly finished the large bowl of stew and the generous square of cornbread. Rather than wait for Lizzie to come by for the tray as was her custom, Alana chose to carry it to the kitchen herself and wait for Angela on the patio.

Shortly, she was joined by both Lilian and Angela. It was a cool evening compared to the hot muggy afternoon that plagued them earlier. They walked along a worn path that led them through the thick green grass to the pond, which looked almost spooky as it succumbed to the dark evening shadows created by the many huge shade trees that so closely surrounded it. Then, they crossed over to the barn, where they paused long enough to let Angela run in and see that Sawdust was bedded down properly. Abe had bedded her down before bunking down himself. Abe was the part-time help. He lived with his older sister in town, but usually slept in the bunkroom of the barn while he was working on a job for Brandon. For the past two weeks, he had helped Brandon round up the strays and mend fences. Both spring and summer almost always found reason to keep Abe around. Lilian explained that he cut and sold firewood to the folks in town during the cold winter months. She was still telling Alana all about Abe as they approached the house. They found Lizzie sitting on a bench outside the kitchen door snapping green beans.

"Miss Lilian, I got Angela's bath ready. It be getting dark and she ain't ready for bed yet," Lizzie said, giving Angela a direct look that warned of the consequences that surely would fall on her if she did not hurry into that bath.

"And I suppose you will be slipping in late for your bath as usual, Miss Stambridge," Lizzie said with a curious look. She could not understand why a person would want to bathe so late.

"Yes, I imagine I will. You just go on to bed. I can heat up my own water," Alana replied.

She had begun taking her baths after everyone else was in bed, mainly to secure herself a bit of privacy. Lizzie was noticeably uneasy about not being around to assist Alana with her bath, but allowed herself to be dismissed from the task.

Lilian and Alana had joined Lizzie on the bench, when Angela finished her bath and came running out to kiss her mother goodnight. Then she trotted over to Alana, paused a second, and kissed her too. Alana was deeply touched by the honest show of affection. A smile curved across her lips as she watched Lilian walk hand in hand with Angela down the walkway, under the warm and gentle glow of lanterns hanging along the walls, to tuck the child in bed. Angela's short legs were moving twice as fast as her mother's in order to keep up. After they disappeared through the open door of the room Angela and Brenda shared, Alana leaned back and watched as the fireflies danced gaily to the distant sounds of the night. The occasional ribbing of frogs blended into a rhythmic background produced by the many talented crickets and katydids. There was a strange silence to the many noises of the night that softly encompassed her, but she could not decide just what it was.

Lizzie broke in on her thoughts as she stated, "Sure is quiet around here with the boys gone."

The boys were gone, of course, that was what was missing. There were no little voices laughing with their final playtime of the day. No raspy arguments penetrated the air.

"Where are the boys?" Alana wanted to know.

"They sleepin' over to their cousin's house this evenin'. They seem to get a thrill out of it. Lilian will pick them up at church tomorrow, I reckon," Lizzie said matter-of-factly, finishing the last of the beans.

"Did Brenda go, too?" Alana asked, wondering why Angela did not go if everyone else did.

"No, Missy Brenda had another spell with her coughing and fever. Lilian put her to bed this afternoon. That poor child has been plagued with the cough and fever since she was born. Sometimes it gets so bad she can hardly breath. It has kept her out of school a good bit. But, now that you is here, she might get caught up on her schoolin'. I feel so sorry for her sometimes, she don't hardly have no friends, they are afraid to let her do anything. There ain't nothin' to do but hope she outgrows it, or so the doctor says," Lizzie said regrettably, watching Lilian tiptoeing out of the girls' room.

Alana talked with Lizzie and Lilian until Lizzie reminded them of the time it was getting to be and carried the washpan of beans into the kitchen to soak in cool water until time to prepare Sunday lunch. Then she went into her bedroom next to the kitchen and closed the door.

Lilian agreed that the hour was getting late and also retired, leaving Alana alone on the patio. She enjoyed a moment of solitude. The nights here were so calm and peaceful in comparison to the noisy nights of New York to which she was accustomed. Soon she decided that she was ready to enjoy a long, hot luxurious bath. She went to her room and got her gown, robe, and the bottle of foaming bath oil she had brought with her. She poured some of the oil into the tub and then filled it with water so hot that it was almost unbearable to the touch. The steaming bubbles caressed her tired body as she slowly eased into the sensuous water. She laid her head back against the curved edge of the tub, letting the water gently rise to her neck. She was so immersed in the warm sensations encircling her that she did not hear the door open. It was not until Brandon cursed, stumbling over a misplaced stool, that Alana became aware of his presence. Her clothes and towel were on the counter behind her, just out of her reach. The fear of his peering around the screen just as she got out to grab for them trapped her. A chill came over her, in spite of the tepid water. She listened quietly as Brandon cursed again, trying unsuccessfully to kick his boots off. Then he tried to push one boot off with the other. Finally, he sat down on the stool that had just accosted him and pulled his boots off with a loud groan. "Damn things must have shrunk," he mumbled to himself, kicking them aside.

Alana bunched the bubbles around her as she offered a silent prayer. She turned the lamp out that was on the stool next to her, hoping that Brandon would not notice. "Where is that blamed boiling pot?" Brandon growled as he shuffled noisily through the many pots in the cabinets. His search led him around the screen where he stopped abruptly and stared in amazement. "I'll be damned!"

Retaining what dignity she could under the circumstances, Alana spoke sharply, "Sir, if you do not mind, I am taking a bath!"

"Heck, no, I don't mind," he said, continuing to stare down at her. An evil grin crossed his face as he realized that he finally had this woman at a disadvantage. He walked closer in spite of her sharp protests. Finding a box of matches near the lamp, he carefully relit the wick.

"What have we here?" he asked nonchalantly, noticing her clothes and towel. He then gathered them up and held them just out of her reach. Anger cut through her lowered lashes as her tightened jaw flinched rhythmically, a sign of her temper Brandon was becoming well acquainted with.

"Seems I have a slight advantage here," Brandon boasted, dangling her gown in front of her. "Yes, I guess I am holding the winning hand, and these are my aces." He continued waving her things around before ending his little dance by tossing them on the floor across the room from her.

"Give me my clothes!" Alana demanded. Brandon shook his head defiantly. "Sir, I order you to return my clothes to me," she said, shaking her head so as she made her demand that a lock of her long brown hair came loose and fell into the soapy water, floating delicately in the fading bubbles. Brandon stared in amazement at the beauty that the gentle glow of the lamp seemed to magnify.

"Ma'am, I do not believe that you are in any position to be giving me orders. Get your clothes yourself, if you want them. As your bubbles there disappear, I believe that you will find the need great enough for them, won't you?" Brandon replied as the idea played on his mind.

"Sir, you are intoxicated," she pronounced simply.

"So what?" he asked with a slight slur in his speech.

Alana took a deep breath before speaking slowly and quite distinctly, "If you do not give me back my clothing, I am going to scream and wake the entire household." Her eyes narrowed and her nostrils flared as she prepared to fulfill her threatening promise.

A scowl covered Brandon's face. He had not considered that.

"Damn!" he cursed aloud as he reached over and picked up her clothes. He then threw them at her, getting the towel wet as it sank into the water. Then, in a cold silence, he grabbed up his boots and walked out in his stocking feet. "That damned schoolmarm is just a little too big for her britches." He growled under his voice. But, then a devilish grin replaced his frown as the thought crossed his mind. "What britches?"

Throughout the morning services of the small church in a community she heard referred to only as West Mountain, Alana could not keep her concentration on the sermon. Instead she found herself reviewing the previous night's disturbing events. The thought of Lizzie's presence during her bath was not as distressing as it once had seemed. In fact, she might prefer to have Lizzie back at her side during her baths. She was worrying about what might have been revealed to Brandon through the thin covering of bubbles as she rose to sing the closing hymn with the congregation. Angela's sharp voice singing slightly off key brought her attention back to the small room housing a throng of people singing of their amazing grace. The melody seemed odd without an accompanying piano as Alana was accustomed to hearing in the huge elaborate churches and cathedrals of New York. But, she realized as she looked around, there really was no place for a piano in this small room. The heavy wooden benches left little space for much more than the small raised platform near the front, which held the simple-fashioned pulpit high enough for everyone's view. There were no fancy statues or colorful windows, only a tiny cross hung on the wall behind the pulpit. These un-adorned surroundings did not seem to hamper the congregation's high spirits as they sang the final refrain in perfect harmony.

After a short final prayer asking for safe passage home, the members filed outside where they gathered in small groups under the shade of the several oak trees. Alana followed Lilian from group to group. Names were tossed at her from every direction as she greeted the people who welcomed her to East Texas. When the time came to leave, she found that she could not place in her mind any names with the faces. All she could remember was that there were several people named Morgan, many were Mackeys, and she thought she remembered the name Todd being presented at one time.

Her head was still spinning from the confusion when Lilian greeted a small, pretty woman, radiant with child.

She quickly turned to Alana, "This is my dear sister-in-law, Anne Warren." Lilian paused for Alana's "pleased to meet you" before continuing proudly, "And this is Alana Stambridge, our new teacher."

"I have been wanting to meet you so badly; but, as my time nears, I am not allowed to travel. Douglas does not really like for me, or should I say us, to make the ride to church," she confided as she patted her protruding stomach.

Alana looked around to see if she could pick Brandon's older brother out of the men still remaining. Not one of them seemed a likely prospect.

"Is your family with you? I would like to meet the boys I will be teaching," she said as she searched the mingled faces for boys that might belong to this fair-skinned blonde. She looked for a child with a similar long, slender nose separating light blue eyes.

"Certainly, but they are already in the wagon, ready to go home and eat their Sunday lunch. You would think that I never feed them except on Sunday. Come with me," she said as she took Alana gently by the hand, leading her across the church grounds to a wagon overloaded with boys. Four of the children Alana immediately recognized as Jake, John, Jim, and Mickey Brams. But three of them were little strangers.

"Here we have Andy, Phillip, and Robbie," Anne announced as she pointed to the boys accordingly.

Andy, at nine, was the oldest. His sandy blond hair hung straight over his forehead, cut straight across at the eyebrows and tapered downward to cover his ears. His dark complexion contrasted with his translucent blue eyes, making them seem almost clear. A long nose and jutted chin gave his face an expression of obstinate pride. The dress clothing he wore was beginning to show signs of strain at the seams as the material found it difficult to contain his tall, muscular body.

Phillip's hair was a shade darker than Andy's, but his complexion was the same and his blue eyes were nearly as crystal in color. He was not as muscular as his older brother, but was still pretty thick across his arms and legs for a child of seven.

All that could be seen of little Robbie was his dark curly head because the siding on the wagon was nearly as high as he was tall. Two blue-green eyes sparkled delightfully from under his jet black lashes. At the age of two, he still had a babylike pudginess about him. His rosy cheeks were so chubby that there was hardly room on his face for his darling little open-mouthed grin displaying a tiny set of pearl-like teeth. His small upturned nose wrinkled across the bridge everytime he laughed, which he seemed to do a great deal. The fellow was quite a little charmer as he batted his big round eyes at Alana flirtatiously.

After Anne finished her introduction, Andy quickly asked, "Are you going to be the new teacher?"

"I certainly am. Are you going to be my most studious pupil?"

One eye closed as Andy contemplated the thought, "Well, I suppose there is always that possibility," he said with a sheepish grin.

"And what about you?" Alana said as she turned to Phillip, "Are you a fine student?"

He gave her more of an answer than he realized with his "I dunno." Then he looked up at the towering pine tree overhead trying to dismiss anymore attention that might be coming his way. Alana was easily diverted and turned her attention to the youngest Warren. When she spoke his name, he sank down in the wagon so that all she could see were his two dark, round blue-green eyes between the wooden planks making up the sides of the wagon. He watched her closely through the tiny space as she asked if he was ready to start school. When his mother tried to dismiss the idea by telling Alana that he was too little, his eyes narrowed and a notch formed in his forehead in between his dark eyebrows. Then, in a determined voice, he jumped up and shouted a sharp shrill, "Big boy!" His pouting face relaxed when he heard everyone laughing at his antics. He began to laugh, too.

"I think you are a big boy, too," Alana chuckled, "I just might find room in my class for such as you. Would it be permissible for him to come one or two days a week? Children are never too young to learn," Alana asked Anne.

"He might get in your way. Robbie's quite a handful."

"It is worth a try. Why not start by allowing him to accompany his brothers one day in the middle of next week?" Alana asked convincingly.

"We shall see. I must first discuss this with Douglas, of course," Anne replied.

"What do you have to discuss with me?" a tall bearded man in his early thirties asked in a low, husky voice as he walked up to the group.

"Miss Stambridge wants Robbie to attend her classes once or twice a week. Since we have not discussed that, I was telling her I could not answer until we had, and had come to a decision together," Anne said as she shifted from one foot to the other in an effort to make her little passenger more comfortable.

"He is already too smart for his own good," Douglas said jokingly as he reached over and tousled Robbie's curly hair. "Do you think you could do him any good? He is a pretty tough customer."

"I can certainly try," Alana answered as she looked over Brandon's older brother curiously. Douglas was shorter than Brandon, not much taller than herself. Most of his face was covered by a heavy black beard, neatly trimmed, no thicker than two inches. His long straight black hair was combed down and away from his face. The only resemblance between the two brothers were the deep blue eyes surrounded with those same long dark lashes that most of the Warrens seemed to claim. Douglas was indeed as handsome as Brandon; but in a different, more rugged sort of way. The suit he wore looked to be tailor made to fit his broad shoulders and muscular legs. There was one other noticeable difference between the two Warren brothers: This one seemed to like her.

"I think we might be able to spare him once a week, that is until you come to your senses and refuse to have him around. In fact, you might be refusing to teach any of these boys. You don't know how wild they can get," Douglas chuckled, presenting a wink to the boys.

"I plan to get to know everything that can be known about them, starting early tomorrow morning. Can they be in class by nine o'clock?"

"Why don't you start getting to know them this afternoon. We are having a cookout for the children this evening. Lilian and Brandon are bringing her children over early enough for those wanting to get in a swim. We surely would love for you to come. There will be plenty of barbecue. Please, say you will come," Anne asked as she looked pleadingly into Alana's eyes.

At the mention of Brandon's name, she knew she would have to decline. She made up a plausible excuse of having several last-minute details to take care of before tomorrow morning; but added that she would certainly accept if invited again.

Alana also declined lunch when they returned home and found Lizzie had it waiting on the table for them. She claimed that she had too much of the cheese, eggs, and bacon that was served at breakfast. Instead, she went to her room and removed all of her clothing, except for her white cotton camisole and her brief lacy step-ins. The small confines of her room were beginning to depress her. She wished that she had been able to become friends with Brandon. He was such a handsome man. She wondered how she could allow herself to get on his bad side. Her temper was the cause of it all. Why could she not keep her tongue to herself? She hoped that time would help ease these conflicts as she shook out the dress that she had just taken off. After putting away the Sunday dress of yellow and white gingham, she stretched across her still unmade bed to rest a minute or two, but soon fell asleep.

Over an hour passed befor Alana awoke. A quick glance through the window told her that everyone was gone. She put on the coolest thing she could find. She chose a sleeveless cotton dress with a rather low, almost daring, neckline. It was the only dress she owned that did not have a suitably high neck. Not exactly certain as to why she wanted such a dress at the time of purchase, she was glad she had it, now. The day was turning out to be a hot one.

Feeling a little hungry, she decided to see if there was any food to be found. She was surprised to find Lizzie sitting at the counter on a tall stool, eating her lunch. For some reason, she had assumed Lizzie would be at the Warrens' eating barbeque with the family. "Come on in and join me, Miss Stambridge. I got plenty enough here," Lizzie invited when she noticed Alana at the door. Lizzie got up and brought in a second stool from the next room. "You don't mind sittin' with the likes of me, do you?"

Alana did not mind. Actually she was delighted to have someone to talk to while she ate.

"I would love to join you, Lizzie. But, tell me, why did you not go with the family on their outing?"

"That's a family doin'. I don't like to butt in on a family dealin'. But, if the truth was to be known, I don't like to do the work I end up doin'. Sunday afternoons is my time for myself. Master Lowell, he gave it to me, and Master Brandon, he said I could keep it."

Alana sat down and started filling the plate Lizzie handed her. "Why do you refer to him as "Master Brandon"? He does not own you nor can he. You have no masters; you are no man's property. Certainly you know that he is in no way your master."

"That's exactly what Master Lowell told me when he bought me and then handed me my own papers. But, I didn't call him or do I call Master Brandon 'master' because he owned me. Naw, it's just 'cause he owns this place and is the man in charge. He is 'lord and master' of this property and home. Since I consider this place my home, too, that makes him the master. So, I calls him so."

Alana was not certain that she understood the logic, but

knew she did not want it explained again. Instead, the mention of papers had caught her attention, "Did you say that Lowell Warren bought you and gave you your papers?"

Lizzie took a long drink of water before answering, "Actually, it was Miss Chrissy, his wife, that got me bought. They was down in New Orleans celebrating their tenth wedding anniversary late in June, back in 1852 as I recollect. Anyway, Master Lowell had brought her to New Orleans to pick her out something special for the occasion. He was always buying her things. She had things he bought her that she never even used. She liked gettin them things though. Anyhow, it was while they were signing into their hotel that they saw me. The man who owned me back then was having to sell some of us slaves off to pay up some bad debts his card playing got him into. He made me stand on a long table in the big room right near the front door of that big fancy hotel while white folks came up and looked me over like I was some sort of animal." Lizzie's black eyes showed the hatred and anger she felt just talking about it, "They put their sweaty hands all over me. They forced my mouth open and looked at my teeth. They even undone my clothes and looked over my personals, feeling of whatever they took a notion to."

Alana sat in wide-eyed horror as Lizzie continued, "Oh, I had seen worse happen, but Miss Chrissy had not. She, being from Ireland and all, had never seen the likes of a slave sale at all. When they handled my private places so roughly, I could not help but cry out. I was only nineteen at the time. Well, Miss Chrissy turned to Master Lowell and said to buy me. She told him I was what she wanted for her anniversary. After convincing him that she really needed more help with the chores and the children as well, Master Lowell up and bid on me until he got me. I brought a pretty price, too," she said proudly.

"Then what?" Alana prompted her to continue.

"Miss Chrissy, she got so mad that she commenced telling those white folks off. She looked them right in the eyes and shook her finger up under their snobby noses. She called them everything from 'trash' to 'gutter animals.' I knew right then I liked her. Master Lowell, he just stood back and nodded in agreement until she got through. He always said there wasn't no use trying to stop what he called her 'wild, Irish temper.' Since Master Lowell did not believe in man trying to own other men, he never felt it was God's way; he up and gave me my papers. He was not a regular churchgoer, but he knew a lot about the Lord and liked readin' on the Bible. He was dead set on lettin' me free. But when he found out I had nowhere to go, he up and offered me a job as housekeeper with pay."

"Did you not have someone you cared for? Someone you wanted to return to?" Alana wondered how anyone could have absolutely nowhere to go.

"I found my man when I was seventeen. We paired off and had a son that same year. He was shot in the back while trying to escape from the plantation. They called him a 'bad nigger,' but he was a good man. They told us that any the rest of us trying to leave would get the same. Bad get hurt and killed. But, Rufus was a good man, really he was. If only he would a stayed put a while longer. He probably would have got sold off the place with most the rest of us. At least he would be alive. But he just could not tolerate one more strappin' on his back." Lizzie paused as she bit her lip. The pain was still there.

"Well, what about your son. Did you not wish to return for him?"

Lizzie's eyes filled with tears as she shook her head, "He was sold that same summer as Rufus was killed, back in 1851. I never could find out what happened to him. Even those working the main house could not find out. Mr. Lowell went to see about it for me later, but that fool master we had did not keep proper records and could not remember who bought him. He did not even remember me havin' a baby."

Alana's eyes were fighting back tears as she tried to comfort Lizzie, "How horrible. I am so sorry. I wish there was something I could do for you."

She placed her hand over Lizzie's in a show of her sincere concern. She was shocked. What little she had read about slavery never mentioned such horrors. She had always assumed that slaves were treated as any laborer was expected to be treated. She had always thought slaves rather lucky to have food and shelter provided for them. She actually had pictured them as a carefree lot, singing a cheerful song as they worked the fields. Where had she gotten such a misconception of slavery?

"There ain't nothin' nobody can do. At least there ain't no slaves no more. Besides, I got to be freed early and I found a family. I got to take over Master Lowell's children. Miss Chrissy, she died two years later when she was only seven months along with child. The doctor said there was something wrong with her blood. Master Lowell took it hard. He never remarried. He never even courted another woman. I was given a free hand in raising all three children. It is like they are my own." Pride sparkled through Lizzie's still tear swollen eyes as she spoke of them. Then, noticing Alana's empty plate, she offered her some peach cobbler for dessert. After accepting Alana's refusal, she continued, "Yes'm, I watched them grow up. I was there for both Douglas' and Lilian's weddings. And someday, I hope to see Brandon wed."

Alana's curiosity got the better of her as she asked, "Why has Brandon never married?"

"It's a long story. Before I start, let's go out on the patio and sit a spell. It's much cooler out there," Lizzie said, tugging at her blouse to let a bit of fresh air flow through.

They left the dishes sitting on the counter and walked outside.

"I think we would be more comfortable in Brandon's chairs," Lizzie said as she pointed to a couple of large chairs at the end of the covered walkway. They were made with large wooden frames and small flat boards. The corners were bound together by rope. "That's Brandon's study behind us," Lizzie remarked as they settled down in the chairs. Alana noticed they were seated directly across the patio from her room.

After scooting her chair away from the wall and tilting it back against it, Lizzie began again, "To answer your question about Brandon's not ever being married, I'll have to go back to when he was about eighteen years old. Or maybe he was seventeen. No, I think he was eighteen. Understand first that Brandon was an ambitious boy. He was a good worker and didn't spend a whole lot of time loafin' off as most boys do. He was always full of dreams and was bound and determined to see that they all came true. One of those dreams was to marry Miss Stephanie DeLane. He and Miss Stephanie had been courtin' for over a year and he had made his intentions of marrying her known to everyone. She was very beautiful and I felt sure she was as deeply in love with Brandon as he was with her. But, she had ambitions, too. She up and married a stranger one day, a stranger that had stopped in her daddy's store to buy supplies. The way I heard it, he asked her to dine with him that night and before the sun came up the next morning, they was gone. Seems he was the son of a rich gold miner in California. That's where they went off to live, in a place called San Francisco. She chose wealth over Brandon's love. All she left him was a letter and a ring that he had bought her earlier that summer."

Lizzie shifted her weight as she tried to make herself more comfortable. The chair moaned at the strain of such a large woman's weight.

"It hurt him deeply. He loved her so much, still does love her as far as I know. He even swore to me that there would never be room in his heart for another woman. Oh, quite frankly, he has carried a few to bed since then, but has never carried them in his heart. It's likely he is afraid of gettin' hurt again. So he never has married and doesn't ever plan on it. It's a shame, too. There is so much love trapped up inside of him that it has just got to be bustin' to get loose. He needs a woman and a passle of kids," Lizzie sighed. She paused to wave her hand at a fly that had begun to pester her. "Problem is, he tries awfully hard not to get along with most women, especially the young attractive unmarried ones Lilian keeps inviting to dinner. If they pose a threat to his solitude, he manages either to avoid them or offend them somehow. He does not trust any females either, thinks we are a conniving bunch," she flashed a wide grin across her dark face as she added, "I reckon sometimes we are."

"Surely he does not think of his own sister, Lilian, as a conniving woman," Alana insisted.

"Oh, he knows just how conniving Lilian can be. You are here, aren't you? Then there is the time she decided she wanted to attend a fancy boarding school in New Orleans, Master Lowell was against it. But, one evening, he and Lilian went on a walk and she turned her charms on him and next thing we know'd, she was packing. Then, when Mark followed her home that next summer to ask for her hand in marriage, Master Lowell was completely against it. He spat fire at the thought of it. Not really cause he didn't like Mark, mostly cause they wanted to return to New Orleans to live. Lilian didn't seem too bothered by his reaction. One evenin', she took him a whiskey into his study, stayed an hour or so talking, and came out to announce her comin' marriage. I've always 'spected maybe she threatened to come up with child just to get her way.

"Douglas and Brandon were kind of jealous of the way Lilian always got anything she wanted from their father. Douglas was especially jealous because he never seemed to get his way. When he was growing up, he was usually at odds with his father. He always was a little naughty as a child, but after his mother died, he became wild and uncontrollable. He stole whiskey from his own father and got drunk a lot. One time he forced his attentions on a young girl and was nearly jailed for it. He never liked to work, and played a lot of hooky from school. Eventually, he refused to even go. He was always getting into fights, even with Master Lowell. He would call his father ungodly names right to his face. There were just too many things he did wrong to even try to cover them all."

"But, I met Douglas this morning after church. He seemed quite nice," Alana remarked as she found Lizzie's words hard to believe.

"That's Miss Anne's doin's. After he met up with her, he began to change. Master Lowell could not see it, but I could. They still fought, even after Douglas married Miss Anne and moved out. It wasn't until Andrew was born, more than four years later, that Master Lowell's contempt for his eldest son began to mellow. By then, Douglas had become a respectable businessman. He and Miss Anne's grandfather had opened up that sawmill on Clear Creek. Mister Pilgrim, Anne's grandpa, put up the money and Douglas did most of the work building and runnin' it. As it grew, he tried to get Brandon to work for him as a foreman, but Brandon's heart is here at Montaqua. Douglas even tried to get Mark, Lilian's husband, to move to Gilmer and come to work for him. That was just before Mark died." Lizzie reflected a moment and then asked, "Am I boring you rattlin' on like this?"

"Not at all," Alana answered sincerely. "Tell me, how did Lilian's husband die?"

"Well, the first we knew of anything being wrong was when we received a letter saying he was really sick and they needed money to help pay the mountin' doctor bills. Master Lowell himself was too sick to go, so he asked Brandon to do what he could. He was gone over a month and we got no word. Then one day, he shows up here with the children and all their belongin's, telling us Mark had died of pneumonia. It was a week before Lilian arrived. She was with child and had to come by taking short stagecoach trips and restin' in between rather than come in that wagon. It was still pretty rough going. When she finally got here, everyone wanted her to rest; but she refused to. Instead, she immediately started to unpack and help take care of Master Lowell, who was ailin' real bad. She never showed her grief once. Then one night she collapsed at Master Lowell's bedside. She broke out in a cold sweat and started with her pains. She was only eight months along. The baby boy was born dead. Everyone around here cried, everyone except Lilian. All she would say was how much it looked like Mark. Sometimes I'd think she was gonna cut loose with some tears, but they never came. In fact, that next spring, when Master Lowell died, I never saw her shed a single tear. Yet, I know she was grievin' deeply. It isn't good for a body to keep them things inside. It will take its toll." Lizzie shook her finger ominously as if she was warning Alana of something specific.

"How did Brandon and Douglas take their father's death?"

"They both took it hard, but Douglas was the one who broke down and cried like a child. He felt guilty for ruinin' so many years of his father's life. With him gone, there was no way he could pay off the debts he felt he owed the man. I truly felt sorry for him. Brandon did not cry as openly, though the tears flowed down his cheeks in a steady stream. It was fittin' to cry. Master Lowell was the best man I ever knowed." Indeed, tears once again filled Lizzie's eyes as she spoke. Alana realized that she was blinking back tears herself as she listened. After a moment, she said in a lighter tone, "Here I am runnin' my mouth and you still got plenty of chores to do before mornin'. You should have hushed me hours ago."

"But, I have enjoyed talking with you," Alana insisted. "Yet, you are right, there are a few things I should tend to this evening. I hope we can talk some more over supper."

"Sure can, you just mentioned my two most favorite things—talkin' and eatin'," Lizzie laughed goodheartedly. "I will just clang the bell when it is suppertime. We can even eat at the big table, Miss Stambridge."

"Please, call me Alana."

"Alrighty, see you this evening, Miss Alana."

Chapter Four

Her first few weeks in Texas went by rather smoothly, with the exception of the first couple of days. Alana began to eat many of her meals at the dinner table with the family, but Brandon seemed to miss a majority of them as the days grew longer. Longer days provided him more working time and he usually came in after dark, too late to join the family for dinner. Occasionally, Billy joined him for a late meal in the kitchen. But, usually Brandon ate alone. As Alana saw less of Brandon, her fears of sudden reprisal subsided. She was now able to concentrate more on her duties as she established the children in their individual studies. As she had expected, Angela was her prize pupil. It impressed her to find that a child of five had learned her sums and knew the sounds and order of each letter of the alphabet. Alana placed her in the same group as Mickey and Phillip. Although Angela was two years younger, she surpassed them in every subject.

Alana grouped Andy and Brenda with the twins, and gave Jake special attention. She introduced him to several high school level subjects. She started him in the history of the world, simple biology, and science as well as the staple subjects of English and arithmetic.

Her teaching schedule had become a set pattern now. Classes were from nine until noon. On Mondays through Thursdays she had the children work on their various assignments and tested them on Fridays. Little Robbie came on Thursdays and she presented him with busy work. She had him stack small wooden blocks or flip through cloth books and point to things he recognized.

Although Mickey caused more trouble in class, Phillip

was the problem child. He could not seem to hold his attention on his work; instead, he would busy himself with pushing his dark blond hair out of his face or watching the bright yellow butterflies dancing from wildflower to wildflower outside the opened door. Alana often had to remind him of his place and purpose. He was not at all argumentative; he just seemed to forget what he was supposed to be doing. On the other hand, Mickey would get his work finished quickly and find little tasks to do in order to fill his spare time. He especially enjoyed drawing on his desk with his chalk or throwing spit wads at the ceiling. Alana was constantly calling him down for one of his naughty deeds. Between the two seven-year-olds, Alana found little time to devote to the older children.

One morning Alana decided that she needed a helper. The older group was wasting time waiting on her to get back to them after each assignment. She asked Brenda to be the younger group's leader. A bit reluctant at first, Brenda finally agreed to help. At first the project seemed doomed. After assigning a few extra projects for misconduct, Alana convinced the boys that Brenda was going to be boss.

As time went by, Brenda began to ease out of her shell and assert herself. Oddly enough, her health improved. She was not plagued by her coughing and breathless spells as often. She soon gained the confidence necessary to pursue her new duties. A list of assignments was handed to her every morning and she saw to it that they were completed by the end of the class period. If arguments broke out, she had the authority to issue extra work.

Generally, the classes went well. The mornings seemed to fly by. All too soon, the dinnerbell clanged, dismissing class and announcing lunch. Douglas's boys usually stayed for lunch before heading for home. They rode double on a tall, brown horse they called "Auntie." On Thursdays, Robbie was set in a little harness that hooked on to the saddlehorn and rode in the saddle with Andy while Phillip rode on the horse's rump. It was beyond Alana's reasoning that anyone would willingly allow a two-year-old to ride a horse without an adult, but no one else seemed concerned. She was told that most of these boys were riding a horse unassisted by age four. She was also assured that "Auntie" was a very gentle mare and absolutely trustworthy.

After Douglas's boys left, the other children set about doing their chores. The growing summer heat did not seem to slow them down. Once finished with their work, they were free to do whatever they wished. Usually they ran down to the pond and went swimming. Occasionally Alana would go with them and from the shade of a nearby tree watch them play. If the boys were not around, Alana sometimes joined Angela and Brenda in the cool water.

Evenings were devoted to washing up, eating supper, and then retiring to the patio. The children continued to play but quieter games. Lilian usually worked on the cover that she was crocheting for Brenda's bed. Alana liked to use the time reading or grading papers. If Lizzie joined them, she brought a pan of beans to be shelled or a pot of corn to be shucked. Many times, if it was too hot to concentrate on busy work, they just fanned themselves while they talked, usually about how hot it was or about how they should be doing something. Then, just before dark and before Brandon was due in, Alana would retreat to her room for the night, wishing that she did not feel such a need to.

On one such evening, as Alana prepared to leave, Lilian invited her to attend an afternoon tea with her at Anne's house. A special cousin of Anne's was visiting from New Orleans and Anne was having the tea in her honor. Many of Anne's friends were invited. It would be a perfect opportunity to meet new people.

"I would love it," was Alana's reply. "When is it?"

"It will be day after tomorrow at three o'clock. She always chooses Fridays for her gatherings. Robbie will come Friday instead of tomorrow. The boys will stay here for the afternoon. I have already warned Lizzie. We should be back in plenty of time for supper," Lilian explained.

"Are you certain that Anne wishes to include me as one of her invited guests?" Alana asked wondering why Anne had not mentioned it Sunday after church.

"I am quite certain. Andy handed the invitation to me during lunch. It was addressed to us both. Apparently, this is one of her famous last-minute decisions. As is her custom, she assumed that Lizzie would be glad to keep the boys. Oh, I guess she usually is. Anyway, we should leave around one-thirty so we can offer our help in the preparations. Is that agreeable with you?"

"To tell you honestly, I can hardly wait. I am anxious to meet more of your friends," Alana replied. "In fact, I think I will select my dress tonight and air it out. I might have to ask Lizzie to press it for me." A sense of urgency was in her voice as she noticed Brandon, Billy, and Abe approaching the barn on horseback.

"Then it is settled," Lilian remarked in dismay as she realized the reason for Alana's sudden nervousness was the approach of her brother. She wondered why the two could not seem to get along and avoided each other like the plague. Yet, they often questioned her about each other's welfare. Something needed to be done to bring peace beween them, and she was the one who had conjured up the perfect scheme to do just that.

Time did not allow Alana the chance to eat lunch that Friday. Immediately after class, she put away the books and began getting ready. She decided to wear the yellow-and-gold print dress she had worn that fateful day she had wanted to impress Brandon. Maybe it would impress the ladies at the tea. As a last-minute addition, she pulled out a bright yellow cotton shawl to drape across her shoulders to shade the sun from her arms. Her hair was pulled back high off of her forehead with several fat curls encircling a full bun. It was the best she could do with so little time.

It was a little past 1:30 when Alana joined Lilian on the patio. "Sorry that I am late. I assure you I did not mean to be."

"That is just fine. I only now walked out myself. Billy is supposed to be fetching the carriage, but he certainly is taking his time about it," Lilian remarked as she kept her eyes on the barn door.

"My, but you look beautiful," Alana offered an honest compliment.

"Why, thank you," Lilian replied politely as she checked the high pile of dark curls with a light touch. The pale-blue dress she wore accented the deeper blue in her eyes. She wore a silver cross on a delicate chain, which brought special attention to the white lacy edge of her scooped neckline. A touch of color had been added high on each cheek, giving her cheekbones more prominence. "You look quite stunning, yourself. That gold color becomes you," Lilian said.

The barn door swung open and the creaking of the carriage could be heard as it rolled out.

"Well, it is about time Billy brought that thing," Lilian said as she waited for the carriage to circle around to the patio. As it came closer, Alana realized it was not Billy seated behind the reins. She managed to resist the overwhelming urge to run and hide when she saw that it was Brandon. Instead, she acted as if she was not at all concerned with the fact that Brandon was so near and causing her heart to pound ferociously.

"What happened to Billy?" Lilian wondered aloud.

"He is in the barn putting salve on Honeysuckle's foreleg. We just noticed a deep cut. It was not bleeding, but still needed attention."

"Well, climb down. We are running late," Lilian spoke impatiently.

"Are you certain you would not like for me to manage the reins? After all you have never driven a carriage with Starfire hitched to it," Brandon offered, as he referred to the high-spirited brown stallion that seemed to have trouble standing still.

"Brandon, you know I can manage that horse. Besides, this tea is for ladies only. Now, get down and let us go!"

"I certainly would not mind escorting two such beautiful ladies, but I see that my presence is not preferred here," Brandon replied with a crimp in his voice, making his speech sound all the more pathetic. A broad smile endeared his face as he turned to Alana and reported, "You, my dear, are really quite lovely. I do believe you will truly impress everyone at the tea."

Alana eyed him suspiciously as she thanked him and allowed him to support her arm as she climbed into the carriage. Lilian looked somewhat bewildered when he also gallantly helped her into the carriage.

"Why is he in such high spirits?" Alana asked after they were a fair distance away.

"I think it is his way of making amends for the irritable way he has been behaving lately. He is not the type to ever say that he is sorry or admit that there is even the slightest chance he did something wrong. Instead, he proceeds to act as if nothing ever happened. But, it usually takes him longer to come to his senses than this."

Alana hoped Lilian was right, yet something inside of her still distrusted Brandon. Maybe it was just a front to gain her confidence until he could find a way to get even with her. She felt he surely still held a grudge against her. He probably always would. He just wanted to catch her off guard.

She was remembering the wonderful feeling of his gentle touch on her arm when Lilian mentioned a few of the women who would probably be at the tea. Alana listened as Lilian filled in a few details about Anne's visiting cousin, Cynthia Helton. She explained that Cynthia usually lived with her parents in New Orleans. She and Anne were best friends as well as inseparable cousins when Anne also lived in New Orleans with her parents. When Anne was only nine her parents were killed in a fire. Her grandfather became her legal guardian and had her sent to Gilmer to live with him. Anne and Cynthia visited back and forth afterward. Although she had never had children herself, Cynthia came to help Anne through the final days of her pregnancy and planned to stay for a month or so after the baby came. It has been five years since they have seen each other.

"After several relationships with the different men in her life failed, she decided to travel abroad. While she was in Europe, she actually was courted by a duke and a count, but never offered marriage by either."

As they came to a stop in front of Anne's stately white

frame house, Lilian whispered as though what she had to say was strictly confidential and was not to be overheard, "That last time she was here, she pursued Brandon quite shamelessly. And, although she did receive more of his attention than any girl had managed in a long while, she found that she could not get him to vow his heart. There never was a proposal. I hear she plans a second attempt for him while she is here, at least that is what Douglas seems to think."

"Does Brandon know she is here?"

"Anne mentioned her proposed visit to him a couple of weeks ago. She did not have a definite date to give him at that time. Then he saw the invitation to this tea confirming that she was actually here. He did not say much more than to offer her a fond hello for him," Lilian remarked as she climbed down and straightened her skirt.

Alana wondered what this Cynthia looked like, hoping that she was no real beauty and had aged to Brandon's distaste over the past five years. Even before meeting her, Alana was certain she would not like her and hoped her stay would be a short one—very short.

A young boy led the carriage away to strap the horse to a post under a large cluster of tall pines nearby. Alana followed Lilian up a pathway made of huge red flatrock carefully placed into the ground. Several fat green bushes, cut to identical height and width, edged the walkway leading to the front steps. Large wooden columns supported a small balcony that served as an awning for the long, narrow front porch below. Flowers were arranged according to their various heights and encompassed the entire two-storied structure. Dark-green shutters accented the many windows. The doors added more dark-green accents, as did the woven wicker furniture carefully arranged on the porch.

After tapping lightly at the door, Lilian let herself in. "Where is everyone?"

"In here," Anne's voice came from a doorway to the right. Alana followed Lilian through the large entranceway into a huge, elaborately decorated room. Two long tables were draped with fine tablecloths made of delicate ivory lace. They were both laden with large silver platters of small cakes and tiny iced pastries. Silver tea sets surrounded by matching silver cups centered each table. Small floral decorations of pink and red blossoms were pinned to the corners. Anne was busy straightening the extra chairs brought in for the occasion.

"Can we help in any way?" Lilian asked, noticing that everything seemed to be in order.

"I really do not think there is anything left to do," Anne answered. She then added, "But, I am certain we forgot something. It never fails. Does it look okay to you?"

"Well, I think it is as fancy as any tea I have ever attended," Alana offered as she glanced over the well-arranged tables.

"Yes, Anne, you have outdone yourself again," Lilian added as Anne took her drawstring bag along with Alana's shawl and carried them into the next room.

When she returned, Lilian asked, "Where is Cynthia?"

"She is upstairs putting the finishing touches to her hair. Wait until you see it! Over in Europe they have gone to cutting it short on the top and front. She pulls the longer hair in the back up and shapes it into wide curls and then sweeps the shorter hair back, leaving some of it to cover her forehead. You will just have to see it. I cannot do justice to it with words," Anne reported with the animation of an adoring child. "I wish I had some of her uncanny beauty."

"Why, Anne, you look simply radiant, or should I say you 'both' do," Lilian assured her as she lightly patted Anne's protruding stomach.

Alana agreed with Lilian. Anne was attractive in her own gentle way. The lavender of the dress she wore brought out a special glow of pink from her broad cheeks. Her fine blond hair had been braided and encircled into a small bun on top of her head with a sprig of deep purple violets carefully woven in the front.

The sound of a carriage approaching caught Anne's attention and she politely excused herself. She called to someone in the kitchen, and then went to the front door to greet her guests. Lilian followed closely behind her, leaving Alana alone, thus giving her a moment to gather her thoughts.

As Alana reflected now, Brandon's sudden change in mood was not any form of an apology. His presently jovial mood was undoubtedly due to Cynthia's return. The longer Alana thought about this conclusion, the more positive she became. Brandon must be absolutely delighted over Cynthia's reappearance in his life. A pout deepened across her face at the thought of Brandon with Cynthia. The bothersome chatter of women's voices from the hallway cut Alana's thoughts short. Two older women followed Lilian into the room.

They were discussing something about Anne's dress when Lilian spoke, "Ladies, I would like to introduce you to Alana Stambridge. She is the teacher we sent for, and I am pleased to say that she is really quite divine. Even Mickey likes her."

The women stopped talking in order to give Alana their full attention. The shorter of the two leaned forward and said stuffily, "How do you do? I am Mrs. Lula Hart, my husband is the owner of the largest hotel around these parts, the Commercial Hotel. I am sure you know which one I am speaking of. It is well known throughout the South. This is Mrs. Lynn Walton. Her husband is postmaster of the Gilmer Post Office and her son, Dean, plans to run for a seat in the State senate. He is certain to win."

"I am pleased to meet you," Alana replied rather uncomfortably. She felt as if this woman was being a little too condescending, to the point of showing a bit of contempt.

"Where do you reside, Miss Stambridge? I assume it is 'miss.' Certainly a young woman such as yourself is not living at the same residence as an unmarried man such as Brandon Warren," the little woman pried with a tilt of her head.

Alana did not know just how to reply to such an accusation, as she knew stemmed from this sharply pointed question.

Luckily, Lilian was not at a loss for words, "I assure you,

with all of the chaperones we have around Montaqua, the arrangement is quite innocent and can certainly do no more than remain so."

"But, Lilian, dearest, people are going to talk about the fact that such a beautiful young girl is living in your brother's house," Mrs. Hart said with more of a rise of her nose than her eyebrows.

Lilian knew that people would indeed talk because Mrs. Hart would be certain of it. She took it upon herself to see to everyone's affairs and make public anything that did not suit her.

Lilian tried to handle her as best she could, "Well, anyone with a mature sense of values will know that we are doing nothing out of the proper. We will just have to try to overlook such idle and malicious gossip as might suggest differently."

Mrs. Hart and Mrs. Walton gave Alana one last disdainful look before turning away to view the elaborately decorated tables and make their requests to the women standing behind each of the tables waiting to serve them.

"Do not pay those two witches any mind; no one else does," Lilian whispered to the disheartened Alana before returning to the doorway to greet three new guests that had just entered.

After several more guests arrived, Alana was beginning to feel a little more at ease. Most of the women greeted her warmly. She became the center of attention with the younger women. Many wanted to know what was happening in New York, which plays were being performed and what fashions were popular. Some of the guests Alana had met previously in church, but had never really had the chance to talk with them. She and one such young lady, Katy Ford, were busy talking about a mutual friend they discovered they had when Anne's sharp voice cut all conversations short, "May I have your attention, please. Ladies, your attention, please. I would like to take this opportunity to thank you for coming, especially on such short notice, and to introduce my closest cousin and dearest friend to those of you who do not already know her. This is Cynthia Helton."

Everyone's attention then fell on a young blond woman standing slightly behind Anne. A smooth smile curved across her full lips as she nodded politely to Anne's guests. Alana was disappointed to see that she was absolutely gorgeous. The regal way she held her head let Alana know that Cynthia knew just exactly how beautiful she was. The European hairstyle Anne spoke so fondly of made the twenty-six year old woman look like a young girl. As Anne led her around the room, making personal introductions, Alana eyed Cynthia's natural gracefulness. She walked with the same easy, refined style that Alana had so dearly wished she had. Her laugh was charming and her smile so fair that Alana found herself hating her. Even little old Mrs. Hart seemed enchanted by Cynthia's *prig grandeur* as she clasped her hand receptively.

Alana watched the two of them as they continued to make their way around the room. After a short introduction between Cynthia and Katy, it was inevitably her turn. "And this is Alana Stambridge. She is the teacher Lilian sent for. You remember, the one I was telling you about. The boys absolutely adore her. She has Andy believing he is a scholar," Anne boasted.

"I am pleased to meet you," Alana replied, relieved that she did not choke on the words.

"I am sure," Cynthia muttered as some of the charm eased in her voice. "So, you are the new schoolmistress the boys spoke so highly of last night throughout the evening meal." Her voice stiffened as she remarked, "I must say you are not as I had envisioned. We must get better acquainted later. By being under the employment of dear Brandon's sister, we shall certainly be seeing a great amount of each other." She then coolly turned her back to Alana and initiated a conversation with another woman, causing Alana to feel quite a jolt from the condensation of Cynthia's voice and the chill from her shoulder.

The afternoon seemed to drag endlessly for Alana as Cynthia basked in the glowing adoration and open admiration bestowed on her by Anne's many friends. Alana found herself constantly at the tables nibbling on one sweet concoction after another as she pretended not to notice Anne's beautiful but arrogant cousin. She avoided most of the guests for fear of hearing one more word expressing in detail just how lovely Cynthia Helton is. Instead, she remained at the tables with her back to the room.

When she finally did turn away from the tables, she saw Cynthia leaning toward Lilian as they discussed some confidential matter. Alana had no doubts the conversation was about Brandon. She could not understand why it should upset her so, but she knew it did. She wanted to look the other way and just act as if she had not noticed the two of them standing so closely in the corner exchanging confidences. Yet, she could not keep her eyes off of them. Just as Alana had decided to return for another cake, she saw Lilian waving for her to join them. The thought crossed her mind to just pretend she was not aware of Lilian's motions; but, for some reason she was not certain of, she walked casually over to them.

"Oh, Alana, I have persuaded Cynthia to join our shopping excursion tomorrow. She mentioned she needed to get to town and buy Anne's baby a nice birthing gift. Silly girl ran off and left the quilted comforter she originally planned as her present at her father's house. Since we were going into town tomorrow afternoon anyway, I suggested she join us. She has also graciously agreed to dine with us tomorrow evening, is that not marvelous?" Lilian revealed as she watched Alana's reaction carefully.

"Yes, it is simply marvelous," Alana replied with a sober face that failed to reveal the sullen reaction occurring somewhere deep inside of her.

"Then it is settled. We should pick you up shortly after lunch on our way into Gilmer. I can have Brandon bring you home sometime after supper tomorrow evening," Lilian said as she kept a careful watch on Alana's response.

Alana propped a slight smile across her face as she pretended to be satisfied with Lilian's decision, giving Cynthia the opportunity to be alone with Brandon.

"I had better let Anne know you are going with us tomorrow. I will return shortly," Lilian said as she went off in search of her sister-in-law.

"Do not mention my plans to purchase the baby a gift. I do so want it to be a surprise. Besides, she would just proceed to talk me out of it," Cynthia told her as she left.

After a brief pause, Alana decided to attempt a civil conversation, "It is nice that you have decided to join us for dinner tomorrow." The words did not come easily.

"Oh, then you dine with the family?" Cynthia asked incredulously. Her eyes narrowed as she continued, "Well, I must admit I am looking forward to supper tomorrow evening. Brandon and I have a great deal in common. I expect I shall be dining over there often while I am here. I just cannot seem to get enough of Lizzie's delicious cooking nor can I deny myself such delightful companionship as Brandon offers."

"We are looking forward to it," Alana emphasized the word 'we.' "We enjoy having dinner guests so." She used the same condescending tone as Cynthia seemed so fond of as she spoke through a frozen smile.

"Until tomorrow then," Cynthia admonished as she turned ever so gracefully and moved smoothly across the room and disappeared through the door, leaving Alana suffocating in the fumes of her own anger. "Until tomorrow indeed," she thought hopelessly.

The ride home seemed burdened with a heavy silence as Lilian guided the carriage down the well-trodden dirt path leading to the larger clay-topped road to Montaqua. It was not until they were nearly home that Lilian spoke, "Did you enjoy the tea, Alana?"

"Yes," Alana lied, "I most certainly did." Her anger had subsided and left her rather weak and overly tired. "I must say, it was decidedly a day I feel I shall not soon forget," she added more honestly.

It was well after six when they arrived home. Billy came out of the barn to take the carriage. When Lilian asked what he was doing in so early, he explained that he and Brandon had spent most of the day tending to a couple of sickly calves and repairing the door of the bunkroom that had come loose at the hinges. Both of them had stayed close to the house all day.

"Then Brandon will be eating with the family to-night?" Lilian wanted to know.

"I expect so, ma'am. He and Angie are inside currying and combing Sawdust. If you want me to, I'll go ask him," Billy offered.

"That's not necessary. I imagine Lizzie will know. Come on, Alana, let's go. I need to get Anne's boys on the road. She wants them home before dark."

Once the three boys were off, Alana excused herself with the explanation of wanting to rest before dinner. In reality, she wanted time to freshen up and look her best since Brandon was joining them for supper. This might be her last opportunity to impress him favorably before Cynthia got her chance to turn him totally against her, as she was certain Cynthia would.

She busied herself with all the necessary preparations a lady had to make in order to look her best. The dress she chose was a deep pink floral that billowed from the three flounces of delicately designed material that crossed her shoulders. Pale pink lace edged all three layers and matched that of the inset lace across the bodice and around the hem of the full skirt. It fit loosely when it was purchased, but did not fit so loosely as it had. No doubt the now tight fit was due to the ravenous way she attacked the many pastries and cakes at Anne's earlier.

Deciding to completely rework her hair, she pulled it further back on her head and dropped long ringlets to the nape of her neck. She finished in time to touch her favorite scent to her ears and neck and evaluate her appearance. The mirror reflected a job well done, but Alana only saw a simple girl who could not possibly measure up to the fascinating beauty Cynthia possessed. Rather disheartened, Alana felt that even at her very, very best she could never be considered as attractive as Cynthia. The sound of the dinnerbell, followed shortly by Lizzie's warning to come to supper, caused Alana's heart to jump.

"Well, here goes," she thought as she carefully locked

her door behind her. Although she was the only one who seemed to take the trouble to lock her door, it was a habit she learned as a child growing up in New York, where most people had two locks to each door. Habits were very hard for her to break.

Checking her reflection in the window of the room next to hers, she noticed that heavy drapes were drawn tightly behind the dusty pane. She felt this was unusual, since most of the windows were opened this time of year to allow a breeze to flow through. Remembering the half-hidden door in her room, she wondered if it led to this room instead of a closet door as she originally assumed. When she turned to continue her way down the covered walkway, she saw Brenda sitting on a bench watching her. Before Alana could offer a friendly 'hello,' Brenda jumped up and ran to her with a pitifully desperate look on her little face.

"Miss Stambridge, you have just got to help me. Please, please, say you will help me. I have just got to go, I just have to, please!" she pleaded randomly, twisting the end of her long single braid nervously with her fingertips as she reached behind her back.

"Slow down. What is it you have 'just got to' do and how is it that I am the one to help?" Alana asked as she knelt down and looked up at the worried face Brenda displayed.

"It is Linda Arnold. You know the girl with the red hair who sits with me in church sometimes. She's gonna have a sleepover tomorrow night. She stopped here this afternoon to see if I could go. I want to go. I won't get sick, I know it," the words poured rapidly as she tried to explain her problem.

"Now, slow down. Linda plans to have some of her friends to stay with her tomorrow night and you are invited?" Alana checked to be certain she was getting the gist of what Brenda was trying so hard to say. Brenda nodded. "And you think I can help convince your mother you should be allowed to go?"

"Not mother, it is Uncle Brandon I have to ask. I already asked mother. She said that she did not know if I should go or not because I sometimes get sick when I do too much or I get excited and have one of my spells. But I have not had a spell in weeks now. I am better, I know it. Mother said that if I could get Uncle Brandon to say yes she would let me go. She would drop me off on the way to town tomorrow afternoon. I have never got to go to a sleepover before, and I do so want to go. I just have to go. Please help me get Uncle Brandon to say yes," she pleaded. "You do think I should get to go, don't you? It really is important."

Alana nodded reassuringly. Indeed, she did think it was important for a girl of ten to enjoy the company of other little girls of the same age, remembering how she longed to be included in such get-togethers when she was young. Bethany had often been invited to such parties, but Alana was always overlooked by the neighborhood girls when they planned anything like that. She ached to be included in sleepovers where deepest secrets were revealed in the dead of the night to trusted friends who swore to cut out their tongues if they should repeat any of their confidences. She could not reason why Brandon might refuse to let Brenda attend her friend's innocent little sleepover.

"What makes you think Uncle Brandon will need convincing?"

"Uncle Brandon is really strict, especially when it concerns me or Angela. He will find some reason to make me stay home. If he does, I will die; I will curl up somewhere and die!" Brenda exclaimed, showing a bit of the dramatics with her wild arm gestures.

Alana agreed to help Brenda's cause if she saw that Brandon might need a little convincing. A trembling hand grasped Alana's arm as Brenda thanked her and allowed a smile to ease across her trouble strewn face. Before entering the dinner room, they agreed to wait until after dinner to bother Brandon with a decision.

Several times during the meal, Alana and Brenda exchanged knowing glances of what was to come. Lilian noticed it, but said nothing of it. Instead, she continued to relay the many events of the day to Brandon. While describing in fair detail the decorations set about and the incidents that took place during the tea, Lilian mentioned

Cynthia would be joining them for dinner tomorrow evening and she expected Brandon to put off his Saturday night out until he had escorted her home.

Still showing a great change in his attitude, Brandon agreed with a flash of a smile that it would not be right if the whole family was not home to entertain Miss Helton and assured Lilian he would not only see her safely home, but would be the perfect host. Alana feigned an agreement to Brandon's words by showing a pleasant little smile pressed lightly into an otherwise expressionless face. She wondered just what Brandon considered the perfect host's duties.

As the children finished eating, they excused themselves. They all filed outside except Brenda, who still picked at the plateful of food sitting in front of her. She looked so nervous that Alana felt sorry for her. She wanted to go ahead and ask Brandon for her now and get the agony over with, but she waited patiently for Brenda to choose the proper time to approach her uncle.

When Brandon placed his fork across his empty plate and sat back in his chair with his usual satisfied sigh, Brenda looked up. "Uncle Brandon?"

"Hm?"

"Uncle Brandon, I . . . I have a question," she spoke so softly she could hardly be heard.

"Well, who knows, maybe I will have an answer," he spoke lightheartedly and winked at Alana who was watching closely. She felt certain that his good-natured reply was a good sign.

Brenda stood up and courageously walked around to stand face to face with her uncle, "Well, sir, Linda Arnold and her mother came by today and invited me to a sleepover at her house tomorrow night. I can go to church with them and then come home with mother. May I please go?"

After a short pause, Brandon replied simply, "No."

Her eyes were stricken with tears gleaming heavily in her eyes and her face tightened as she tried not to cry. Lilian looked away from the child so as not to reveal any expressions that might be present on her face. Hopelessly devastated, Brenda ran from the room. She was followed closely by her mother. Open-mouthed, Alana sat in total disbelief of the cold-hearted way he had snuffed the idea of Brenda's attending a friendly little sleepover. A study of his seemingly unconcerned reaction made her angry.

"You, sir, are an imperturbable tyrant!"

Not quite certain of what she had just called him, he asked, "What is that supposed to mean?"

"That you are a most formidable, cold-blooded, unfeeling, iron-hearted dictator that ever oppressed a small child," she replied slowly, revealing how strongly she felt about her own words with the flinch of her jaw.

"Ma'am, I do not see that this is any of your affair," Brandon replied shortly.

"Brenda is one of my students. I happen to be very fond of her. She is also a friend, and I am quite concerned about her. And when she solicited my support, it becomes my affair," she replied with a determined glint prevalent in her dark eyes.

"And I suppose you think I should have allowed her to go?"

"I cannot see why you refused so quickly. What harm could a little sleepover do? You could have at least softened the blow with a gentle explanation. Children are real people with real problems and very real emotions. Just because you have turned off your emotions and cut off your own feelings does not mean others are not sensitive to pain and sorrow. You just crushed a little girl's heart. I guess you do not realize how important it is to a young girl to have special friends of the same age. I would have given my eyeteeth to have been invited to such a party when I was young. Special times with good friends mean the world to a ten-year-old. But do you care? No! You do not even bother to tell her why she will not be allowed to go."

Forcing a word in, he replied, "I did not feel she needed an explanation—"

"That, sir, is exactly your problem," she interrupted him, "You do not feel at all. I propose that if you were to unlock those chains binding your cold, desolate heart, you just might find a compassionate human being locked inside. One who would not only be considerate of others, but actually care about even the feelings of a small child."

"Miss Stambridge, you seem to forget that you are talking to your employer," Brandon reminded her.

"Oh, well, excuse me, Master Brandon. I will try to remember my humble place in the future, Master Brandon. I should never have burdened you with the truth, Master Brandon," she spat the sarcastic words through gritted teeth, putting an extra emphasis on each use of the word 'master.'

"That is enough of that!"

"Oh, then I am being excused. Oh, thank you, Master Brandon, thank you!" With that, she sarcastically attempted a royal bow and flounced out of the room.

"Damn that schoolteacher!" he shouted and slung his plate against the wall, breaking it into several pieces. As he raked his fingers through his black curls, he asked himself aloud, "Why does she hate me so?"

Chapter Five

The bright July sun threatened another scorching afternoon as it effortlessly climbed to its peak position in a cloudless blue sky. While the carriage was in motion, a slight breeze kept Lilian and Alana comfortable under the protective shading of the cloth top that was sufficiently covering the surrey-styled carriage. When they stopped at Anne's house, Lilian climbed down to see if Cynthia was ready to go, leaving Alana sitting in the summer heat with no breeze to cool her. Since Cynthia was not yet ready, Lilian stepped inside to hurry her. Moments later, they appeared through the door with Anne following closely behind. As they reached the carriage, they noticed Alana's face was flushed and beads of perspiration dotted her neck and forehead causing the tiny ringlets at her temples to cling to her face. Cynthia, looking fresh as a morning flower, offered a snub little apology for being late as she placed a small case in the back. After remarking how wan Alana looked, she suggested Alana sit in the rear seat in case she felt any need of lying across it. Alana agreed, not because she felt any need of lying down, but rather because she would feel fearfully uncomfortable with Cynthia at her back. Also, by switching to the rear seat and letting Cynthia take her place beside Lilian, Alana felt she could keep a better eye on this crafty little ingenue.

"Hope you do not mind that I brought a few things to change into before dinner this evening. But, as you can see for yourself, this dress would never do," she commanded as she straightened her light-blue skirt. Alana did not know why this perfectly beautiful dress would not do for dinner. It was very fancy with its full skirt, puffy white

90

blouse, and trim blue vest laced across the front with a dark-blue cord. A pert blue satin hat adorned a flawless hairstyle. Alana wished she could afford something as nice.

Just as Lilian was about to snap the reins, Anne teased, "Now, you be sure to stop in at the Blue Swan Restaurant and let that nice Mr. Sobey serve you some of his fresh cool lemonade."

"Now, you just hush!" Lilian demanded as she blushed a shade of pink.

"Well, you do know how sweet Archibald Sobey is on you. Last time we stopped in, he would not even allow you to pay for your refreshments. Never hurts to remind a nice man like him that you are still around," Anne explained with a mischievous grin and a wink directed at Alana. "Alana, you see that any refreshments y'all have are at the Blue Swan. It is right on the square by the shoe repair shop. You cannot miss it."

With a slight smile, Alana replied, "I shall see what I can do."

Keeping quiet during the ride into town, Alana listened as Cynthia brought Lilian up-to-date on her many suitors. She placed special emphasis on the dukes and counts who persisted to court her during her stay abroad. Incessantly, she talked of the many fabulously intriguing places these suitors insisted on carrying her. Even Alana had to admit she was a bit awed by the many eventful tales of adventure and romance that Cynthia claimed as part of her past. But she could not help but wonder if all of what Cynthia was accounting for in these wondrous tales was factual or maybe a little of it was contrived. She also wondered just how unimpressed they would be over her single evening out with Don Andrios, and let her mind trail away to that evening at the riverside when Don Andrios had such beautiful things to say. Her vivid imagination then slipped Brandon's handsome face in the place of Don Andrios's. There was a melancholy type of pleasantness in dreaming of such impossible folly that allowed the time to whisk by. Soon Lilian was slowly guiding the carriage to a stop under several shade trees near the courthouse and just behind the post office.

"Goodness, but Gilmer has grown since I was here last," Cynthia remarked. Sardonically, Alana thought that this was the first sincere comment she could remember slip past Cynthia's sweet little lips.

"Oh, yes, Gilmer is growing very rapidly. And, I hear the Cotton Belt wants to come through Gilmer within the next few years as it crosses East Texas. They say the huge freight trains will not only boost the cattle and timber business around here, but will aid in local travel as a passenger train will run as well. I expect Gilmer will really boom then. Railroad towns always do, you know." Lilian boasted, "Brandon can hardly wait until then. He will only have to drive his cattle as far as Gilmer, instead of to the Red River when he needs to sell. Not too many of the locals want to fool with purebreds, but he has quite a market for the Brangus cattle in the North. With the railroads making it easier to sell, Brandon will no doubt have more money than any of us will know what to do with."

"Yes, Brandon should be able to save a small fortune then," Cynthia replied thoughtfully. Alana could have sworn she saw little gold dollar signs reflecting in those bright blue eyes.

The post office was their first stop since Lilian had several letters to mail for Brandon. While Alana and Cynthia waited outside the open doors, several men walked by and tipped their hats politely. Cynthia pretended not to notice as several walked out of their way in order to pass by and nod or tip a hat. Instead, she seemed faintly interested in the square itself, not the people in it.

Alana watched Cynthia closely and wondered why she chose not to recognize these friendly gestures. When she happened to notice a hat being tipped her way, she felt obliged to either smile or nod as did Lilian when she returned.

"Why don't we start with the dry goods store? Alana can get the hand mirror she mentioned needing and I have several items I need to purchase. They have a fair selection of baby items, too. So, is that agreeable with y'all?" Lilian asked as she fanned her face with a letter she had just picked up for Brandon.

Trailing slightly behind Lilian and Cynthia, Alana observed the smooth way the two walked, even over the roughly packed dirt street. Taking mental notes, she decided she was going to learn to walk as casually from the hip as they did.

Inside the large dry goods store, the three separated to do their individual shopping. Cynthia involved herself with looking through the many scarves and hats near the front window. Picking up an arm basket, Lilian systematically went down each of the narrow aisles, quickly selecting those items she needed from the tall wooden shelves stacked abundantly to the ceiling with all manner of merchandise. In search of hand mirrors and stockings, Alana ventured down the first aisle. When she wandered up the next aisle looking high and low, an elderly gentleman in white shirtsleeves walked up to her and asked in a gentle voice, "May I help you, miss?"

"I truly hope so. I am looking for a nice-size hand mirror and cannot locate a single one."

"Follow me, please," he spoke softly as he pushed his thick, wire-rimmed spectacles up high on his nose, just to have them slip back down again because his lean slanted nose lacked a bridge and fell straight with only a slight upward curve near the end, which prevented his spectacles from slipping right off of his face.

On a high shelf behind the front counter sat several boxes of mirrors. The old man was so short he had to use a foot stool to reach them. Carefully, he pulled the box out and opened it on the countertop.

"Here we are," he said as he raised his thick bushy gray eyebrows, the only noticeable feature on an otherwise bland face. He showed her several mirrors with long handles, short handles, two handles, and no handles. A couple of decorative long-handled mirrors with matching brushes sold in sets caught Alana's eye. Picking up one of these mirrors, she looked into it at her reflection to check it for flaws. She noticed something else reflecting in the mirror. She saw several crumpled rose bushes laying across a tall wooden crate. Turning around to get a better look, she exclaimed, "Rose bushes!"

"Oh, those things. They were specially ordered for Mrs. Lula Hart for the garden outside the hotel, but she refused to purchase them because they were not absolutely perfect. I guess she expected them to come in looking just like that pretty picture in the catalog," he said with a slight scowl. "I tried to convince her that, with proper care, these would turn out nicely. But, she said these would never do for her gardens," he wagged his head haughtily as he imitated the woman.

"Well, of course these bushes should revive nicely. What did she expect of plants packed together so closely and kept from light so long?" Alana asked as she bent one of the branches, "Oh, yes, there is plenty of life left in these bushes. I cannot imagine her refusing them." Actually, she could imagine it very well having met the formidable pillar of society.

"Would you be interested in buyin' them? I will gladly sell them to you at my cost, all six bushes. Would you care to purchase them?" he asked hopefully.

"I would love to have them, but I do not have any place to plant them, unless—wait here. I shall be right back," she spoke eagerly as she went off in search of Lilian to ask if it would be permissible for her to plant a rose garden somewhere near the house.

Moments later she returned smiling, "Yes, I do want to buy those bushes."

While he wrapped the bushes loosely with brown paper, Alana chose a pretty yellow handled mirror and brush set and two pairs of white stockings. He wrapped them into a second neat package, tied it securely with white string, and laid it beside the bulky rose bushes.

"If you can wait until my boy gets back from deliverin' an order over to Mr. Langford's just down Buffalo Street here, I can have these carried out for you," he offered.

"That's fine. I have to wait for my friends to finish their shopping anyway."

"I would carry them out myself if my salesgirl had not

sent word that she is sick and cannot work today," he continued to explain the delay. "I do not believe we have met. My name's Franklin DeLane. I am sure you figured out that I own this store."

"I am Alana Stambridge. I imagine you know Lilian Brams." He nodded that he did. "I have been hired to tutor her children as well as Douglas and Anne Warren's boys," she replied, wondering why the name DeLane seemed so familiar.

Once he had these facts, Mr. DeLane proceeded to tell Alana how he had known Lilian since she was a small schoolgirl, stopping in occasionally to buy a stick of candy. He also mentioned he had known her mischievous brother Douglas just as long. Then, he told her how he knew Brandon especially well, "In fact, he almost became part of the family," he boasted. "My daughter and he nearly got hitched." Alana's odd notion as to the name DeLane seeming to mean something was valid. This was Stephanie DeLane's father. Not able to resist hearing the other side of the story, Alana just had to ask, "Oh, really? What happened?"

"One day a fancy pants and his duded-up brother stopped in here and bought a considerable amount of supplies. While Stephie waited on 'em, they asked where the best restaurant in town was. She told 'em about the Sun Room at the hotel. That young one asked her to join him, and although I was against it, she let him take her to dinner. Next day, she left me a note tellin' me she was goin' off and weddin' that rich boy and would write when she got set up in California. The note also asked me to tell Brandon not to think she did not love him, 'cause she did, but somethin' inside her decided to go with the Californian. I knew just what that somethin' was— money. Oh, and maybe the adventure attracted her. But, his pa has a gold mine near San Francisco somewheres. I did not tell Brandon that when he came callin' later on that evenin'. I just gave him her message as it was and I reckon he filled the rest in himself. I never saw a boy look so pained as he did that night. But, I reckon he got over it; young hearts mend in time. Stephie seems happy.

I got a letter last week tellin' me what a fine Christmas they had. Takes several months for a letter to get back this way," he explained as he pushed his glasses up again only to have them slide right back down to where they were.

Just as Alana was about to ask if Stephanie ever visits Gilmer, Lilian walked up with her overloaded basket in one arm and a bolt of deep gold material in the other. "Mr. DeLane, I need about six yards of this material and cannot find Shirley anywhere to have her measure and cut it for me."

After explaining that Shirley was feeling poorly, and, as a result, had stayed home today, he asked Lilian if she would mind watching the door while he carried the material over to the cutting table and measured six yards. A few minutes later, he returned with the material folded into a neat square. He and Lilian discussed his sister's failing health, as he added up her bill, "That'll be twelve dollars and ninety cents, Mrs. Brams. Shall I add it to your account?"

"Please," Lilian replied simply. "Is Tony around?"

"He ought to be back any minute. Just tell me where your buggy is and I will have him load all these things in it when he gets back," he offered politely.

"It is just across the street, behind the post office. But, we have to wait on Cynthia anyway. Maybe he will be here by the time she finds what she wants," she remarked as she looked around the store to catch sight of her.

"Maybe I should see if she needs any assistance," Mr. DeLane said as he wandered off searching the aisles for her.

"Does he know Cynthia?" Alana asked as she leaned toward Lilian in order not to be overheard.

"I guess he remembers her. The last time she was here was for well over three months and she did spend a pretty amount in Mr. DeLane's store. Even if he does not quite remember her, she is probably the only other woman in the store," Lilian explained as she resumed fanning herself with Brandon's letter. A young boy, about fourteen, meandered in the front door and came to rest on a stool behind the counter.

Lilian offered him a friendly hello to which he smiled and replied, "Hi."

"You look tired, Tony," Lilian observed the droop of his hazel eyes.

"Feel tired," is all he would say and slumped down against the wall.

Mr. DeLane escorted Cynthia to the front counter. He was loaded down with a large pink and blue patch quilt, a light-blue knitted shawl, an assortment of colorful silk scarves, and a wide-brimmed white straw sunhat decorated with a slender dark blue sash. Cynthia carried a small box that held a tiny bottle of imported perfume.

"Will this be all for you?" he asked as he carefully unloaded the selections on the countertop.

"I guess so," she answered hesitantly. "No, wait, I would like several of those large English cigars. Yes, those in the glass jar there."

Carefully pulling the top from the jar, he slipped his small hands in and selected six of the cigars.

"Excellent selection," he remarked, knowing they were his most expensive brand. "Now, will there be anything else?"

"I guess not," she replied as she looked around her at the many displays.

After he wrapped Cynthia's purchases, he called Tony, "You need to carry all of these packages here to Mrs. Bram's buggy for her. It will take several trips. Don't go overloading yourself so that you drop everything," Mr. DeLane warned.

Tony scooped up several of the parcels and followed Lilian out of the door. Alana reached over and carefully picked up the rather bulky package containing her new rose bushes and proceeded to the door. With a look of total indignation, Cynthia crossed in front of her and sternly suggested Alana wait and let the boy carry everything, as that was his job.

"After all, you, even as a mere employee, represent the highly respectable Warren family. It would never do for their friends to see you doing such a menial task as this."

Trying to keep her temper under control, Alana replied

in as even a tone as possible, "Actually, I would rather carry this particular bundle myself. It contains several delicate rose bushes."

"Surely the boy can handle the load as well as you. Please, remember your position," Cynthia said a little too sweetly as she pointed to the counter where she felt Alana should set the package.

Reluctantly, Alana returned the roses to the counter rather than argue publicly with one of Lilian's and especially one of Brandon's friends.

"Come, let us find Lilian," Cynthia turned and walked triumphantly out of the store. Enraged, Alana followed, at a distance. The muscles in her jaw tightened at the bitter thought of the presumptuous way Cynthia actually felt she could offer such direct suggestions.

Lilian had shown Tony where the carriage was and met Cynthia and Alana near the front of the store. "Where have y'all two been?"

"Just getting acquainted," is all Cynthia replied. Alana feigned a slight smile as she thought with growing animosity that she already knew Cynthia a little too well.

"Well, where do y'all want to go next?" Lilian asked politely.

"I would love to stop in and look about that exclusive little dress shop on the corner, there," Cynthia pointed to Nell's, a store that not only sold ready-made clothes for older children and ladies, but tailor-made clothing as well. "Is that agreeable with you, Alana?"

"Fine," Alana answered coolly.

Although the two tried to conceal the immediate dislike rapidly growing between them, Lilian noticed the way one avoided looking at the other, but showed little concern as she led them into Nell's dress shop.

Racks of ready-made clothing lined the bright floral-printed walls of the small shop. Several large yellow tables holding handbags, hats, or miscellaneous folded items stood in the center of the room. Near the rear of the shop were yellow shelves holding a variety of bolted materials, laces, trims, threads and other accessories for specialty orders. A huge catalog supplying the specifications and designs of all the latest styles sat on a tall slanted yellow table in the corner with two tall padded stools sitting in front of it. Between the front window and the door were a couple of high-backed armchairs, richly upholstered in a deep golden yellow. The room seemed quite cheery to Alana until she caught a glimpse of the terribly high prices tagged to each of the fine articles. Realizing this shop was greatly beyond her price range, Alana decided she might as well sit and rest while Lilian and Cynthia browsed. At first, she watched Lilian flip through the gowns on one of the racks. When she turned her back and began to look through the catalog, Alana let her attention drift through the room. Her eyes came to rest on Cynthia. Rather than watch her delight as she pulled several dresses, most of them blue, from the racks and place them on one of the special selection hooks, Alana chose to step outside for a minute. As she got up, her arm brushed against something.

"Excuse me," she said politely before realizing that the lady she had just apologized to was made of wood. "That is perfectly all right," she answered for the wooden damsel with a silly bright red smile painted on her delicately carved face. Alana's arm had caught one of the many flounces of white lacy material edged in pale blue. With great adoration, Alana stepped back to gaze at the beautiful gown that was being displayed so prominently near the front window to catch the eye of anyone who might be passing by. The bodice of this dress was the same shade of blue as the lace encircling the skirt. It had a daringly open neckline edged in soft white lace. Three full flounces of broad lace made the short billowing sleeves. It was one of the fanciest gowns Alana had ever seen.

Out of curiosity, she peeked at the price tagged to the waist trim and gasped aloud at the cost. It was as much as a month's wages, more than she had paid for all three of the dresses she had bought just before making this trip to Texas, and four times as much as the dress she was wearing. She was still thinking with some awe about the outrageous price when she walked outside. A soft afternoon breeze was beginning to stir as she stood just outside of the front door. Casually she began to watch two elderly men playing an intriging game of checkers on a large heavy wooden board. It lay across the upturned end of a tall wooden cheese barrel in front of the nearby barber shop.

Each move was being carefully thought through, as time seemed of little concern to the two old gentlemen. Jumps were moments of total ecstasy. Their guffaws and kneeslaps after each jump caused Alana to step closer in order to enjoy the game. The two seemed equally matched; both had about the same number of checkers still on the board and each complained equally as loud. They were even matched in size; both were short and lean. Although their frail bodies seemed a bit wasted, they were full of vigor and life. About halfway through the game one old man, lost in deep concentration, noticed an opportunity to jump and took it. The other became infuriated.

"It ain't your turn, you silly old coot!" he shouted as he threw his hat on the wooden planked walkway, almost knocking over the spittoon sitting between them.

"Yes, it is, you musty old goat!" he defended himself, pounding one hand with the other.

"No, it ain't, you stupid senile snake!"

"Heck fire, you moved last, you old crosseyed gutter-snipe!"

"You better shut your mouth 'fore I put a lump on your head so big that you'll have to stand on your tiptoes to rub it!"

A grin started its way across Alana's face as she watched the two shake their bony fists at each other, shouting at the tops of their raspy voices. She decided, as a witness to the crime, she should speak up before the two came to blows, "Excuse me, may I say something?" The two looked up at her in surprise. "Sir, you really did move twice in a row. You had just moved your corner checker in to be crowned and then before your friend could move out of the way, you jumped his checker."

The old man looked at the checkerboard and then at Alana. He took his hat off and scratched his balding head as he thought back over his moves, "You sure about that?" he asked ready to take her word.

"Yes sir, I am. You should return that last checker and give him a chance to move."

"How come a lady like you knows so much about checkers? Most girls don't care beans about the game," he wanted to know.

"Most girls would not know a good game if it jumped up and bit them on their pretty little noses," Alana replied with a wink making the two of them cackle with laughter, which relieved the tension that had built up during the argument.

"Alana Stambridge!" Cynthia's sharp voice cut through her.

"Pardon me," Alana said to the two renewed friends and walked over to where Cynthia and a boy laden down with large boxes stood. "Did I not explain to you once already that as long as you are employed by the Warrens you are a representative of that family? How dare you tarnish their good name by delving into a conversation with the local riff-raff. Try to realize the importance of your position."

Again, rather than argue publicly with this overzealous friend of Lilian's, she kept quiet, allowing Cynthia to dominate this conversation.

"Now, Miss Stambridge, try to stay within proper bounds before I feel it necessary to speak with Lilian about your odd behavior," she warned as she signaled the open-mouthed boy toting her parcels to follow her. Before she led him away, she added, "Lilian is inside." Her words seemed to suggest Alana join Lilian inside.

By the time Alana took the several deep breaths needed to calm herself, Lilian came out of Nell's with a small paper bag under her arm. While waiting for Cynthia to return, Lilian showed Alana the fancy black silk choker with a golden teardrop shaped pendant sewn on it she just purchased. Alana wondered how much such a thing must cost and if she might be able to work such a purchase into her tight budget. She told Lilian how pretty she thought it was.

"Where to next, Lilian, dear?" Cynthia asked sweetly as she approached the two of them still admiring the choker. When Lilian showed it to Cynthia, her only comment was "How nice."

"To tell you honestly, I would enjoy a touch of cool lemonade about now," Alana suggested, "I see that the Blue Swan is only a few doors down and I did promise Anne if we had any refreshments that we would have them at the Blue Swan."

Cynthia waited to see Lilian's reaction before committing herself as for or against the idea. Although Lilian seemed a little flustered at Alana's suggestion, she did nothing to alter it.

"I guess a lemonade would be nice," she finally replied as she bit her lower lip. Cynthia was then willing to agree.

This time Alana led the group as Lilian seemed suddenly submissive and obviously needed someone to take charge. The closer they came to the front door the larger Lilian's eyes became. Alana smiled inwardly at the shaken Lilian because she knew exactly how her friend felt and realized just how important this man must be to her. Alana led them to a vacant table by the front window.

"Is this table suitable?" she asked.

"Fine," Lilian replied bluntly and quickly took the seat that would allow her back to be to the room. Alana sat across from her, with her back to the fancy smoked-glass window. Cynthia sat to the side allowing her back to be against the wall, able to see all about the room as well as anyone passing in front of the window.

"Do they wait on you here?" Alana asked as she looked around the room for a waitress.

The restaurant was nicer than Alana expected in such a small town. Along one side of the room were a half dozen little booths with dark-blue padded bench seats set back to back; divided by large wooden tables covered with blue-and-white checked cloths. A long smoked mirror reached from the tabletops to the ceiling and stretched the length of the wall, making the room seem larger than it actually was. Across the room was a tall dark wooden counter with several pies and cakes displayed under large glass domes.

A huge cash register sat at one end. Two wooden ceiling fans slowly circulated the air, being only as effective as the wind blowing outside because they were operated by wind forcing similar counterparts outside on the roof. This was a rare accommodation for such a small town. Near the back of the room was a long table meant to seat as many as sixteen. The other tables, arranged in the center of the room, could seat four as could the one they were sitting at. On each of the blue-and-white checked tablecloths, sat a large candle inside of an open blue glass globe. Highly polished silver-capped salt and pepper shakers sat on either side. At each place was a blue cloth napkin with a full setting of silverware. Tall wooden chairs with blue upholstered seats were set around the tables and a few extra chairs were lined against the wall near the front door. Except for two women occupying one of the booths, they seemed to be alone.

"Oh, yes, someone will wait on us," Lilian assured her uneasily as she peeked around the room. "At this time of the afternoon, they would only have one waitress."

Shortly, a young girl about fourteen or fifteen wearing a light-blue dress and a dark-blue apron came through a door at the back of the room carrying a loaded tray. She quickly set steaming plates of food and a basket of hot rolls in front of the two women sitting in the booth. After a few words were exchanged, the girl politely nodded to the women, tucked her tray under her arm, and came over to wait on them, "Would you ladies care to see a menu?"

"No, I do not think we should need a menu. Just bring us three cold lemonades, please," Alana replied.

"Would any of you care for water?" she asked as she looked at the three women, suddenly recognizing Lilian, "Oh, Mrs. Brams, what are you doing here?"

"Hello, Katherine Lynn, my friends and I were in town shopping when we decided a lemonade would be nice," Lilian answered awkwardly.

"Daddy will want to know you are here," she said brightly as she left.

Feeling an explanation was in order, Lilian said rather sheepishly, "That was Archie's, uh, rather Mr. Sobey's daughter. She sometimes fills in as a waitress on Saturdays."

"He's married?" Cynthia demanded with a look of shock forcing its way across her face.

"He is a widower. His wife and a son were killed nine years ago when their house in Virginia burned to the ground. Katherine Lynn was all he had left when he moved here last summer and bought this place from his uncle."

While Lilian was filling Cynthia and Alana in on Mr. Sobey's past, a tall brawny man came through the back door with his broad face easily carrying a wide grin. His eyes were concentrating on the back of Lilian's head as he came closer. "I think we are about to meet Mr. Sobey in the flesh," Alana warned as she tried to hide her amusement.

Lilian's eyes focused on the shiny cap on the salt shaker as she listened to the footsteps behind her coming closer. Inadvertently, she wet her lips with the tip of her tongue, leaving them parted slightly as if preparing to scream.

Cynthia's interest grew as the gently attractive man, seemingly in his midthirties, came closer. His hair was thick and black with touches of gray showing in his sideburns. Dressed in an extremely handsome outfit, complete with a black lightweight coat and a pretty red rose pinned to his lapel, he appeared to be a man of some means. He wore the coat open to reveal a delicate gold chain that crossed the small gray vest that met his black trousers at the waist.

"Hello, ladies, may I sit down?" he asked graciously.

With a wave of her hand, Alana directed his attention to the vacant chair, "Please, do."

Once seated, he directed his attention to Lilian, who was still focusing intently on the salt shaker, "Are you going to introduce me to your friends, Lilian?"

Avoiding his gaze, she spoke ever so cordially, "This is Alana Stambridge. She is the teacher I hired from New York," she nodded to Alana. "And this is Archibald Sobey, the proprietor."

"Pleased to meet you, Mr. Sobey. I have heard so much

about you," Alana said as she offered her hand.

"From Lilian?" he asked hopefully. He continued to watch Lilian, even as he clasped Alana's hand and shook it lightly.

"Well, actually, Mr. Sobey, most of what I have heard has been from Anne Warren."

He seemed disappointed in Alana's answer, "Well, Lilian has told me very little about you and, please, call me Archie as I have asked Lilian to do time and time again."

Alana was about to tell him that he should use her first name, too, when Cynthia, in an attempt to capture everyone's attention, casually cleared her throat. Fearing she might be excluded from meeting this man, she simply introduced herself, "And I am Cynthia Helton, Anne's cousin, visiting from New Orleans."

"Pleased to meet you. Why is Anne not with you?" he asked with a quick glance around.

"Doctor's orders are for her to stay near home these last few months. That baby may come just any time, now," Cynthia continued.

"Maybe she will finally get that baby girl she wants so badly," he commented, letting his gaze fall back on Lilian, who had returned her attention to the salt shaker.

"You, sir, are too kind to care about my sweet cousin so," Cynthia replied giving him an overdose of her southern feminine charms. When he did take his eyes from Lilian to look at Cynthia, she was certain to be looking up at him ever so demurely through heavily lowered lashes.

Unaffected by Cynthia's show of attention, he refocused on Lilian, "Is that why you and Anne quit coming to town so often? Doctor's orders? You have not been in here for a couple of months, now."

"I guess so. I do hate to shop alone," Lilian replied, glancing up at him quickly before looking away.

"I am glad you came in here today. It saves me a trip out to your ranch."

"How is that?" she asked curiously while holding her eyes on his, this time without looking away.

"I was bound and determined to ask you to join me for

the town's annual Fourth of July picnic. I plan to close up and spend the entire day. I would be proud if you would allow me to escort you to the festivities. You won't have to worry about packing a basket, I plan to have the cook fix something for us. Please, say you will do me the honor."

"I do not know if I should. I really need time to consider this."

"Fine, you think about it. I shall call for you at your door around ten. If you decide to go, I promise to do my best to show you a great time. But, if you decide against it, I shall try my best to understand. Oh, if it will make you feel better to bring the children, by all means, bring them. I think they would enjoy themselves."

"Will Katherine Lynn be going?"

"Most certainly, but not with me I am afraid. Young Paul Peterson has asked her to join his family," he replied with the raised eyebrow of a concerned father. "He seems to be awfully sweet on her. So, she will not be going with us, that is if you agree to join me."

Katherine Lynn had returned with the three tall slender glasses of fresh cold lemonade and set one in front of each of the ladies, "Well, Daddy, did she say yes?"

"Not yet, nosey. But she has promised to think about it."

"I sure hope you say, yes, Mrs. Brams. Daddy needs someone to look after him and keep him out of trouble. I will not be able to, for I have a fellow escorting me to the affair," Katherine Lynn stated quite proudly as she tucked her tray back under her arm and walked determinedly away, holding her head overly erect.

"I do not know what I am going to do with that girl," he laughed. "She does not seem to realize that she is still just a baby."

"Do not look now, sir, but your 'baby' is turning into quite a regal young lady," Alana observed. Indeed, she was. Curves had formed in all of the right places and she filled out her dress quite nicely. Her manner was genteel and she walked as no child would.

"Don't tell me that. I have a difficult enough time sleeping as it is," he complained as he watched his daughter charm the two ladies seated in the booth into leaving a substantial tip.

Not to be withdrawn from his conversation, Cynthia added, "A man as handsome as you are should expect his daughter to develop into a thing of beauty. It is just a matter of nature and proper breeding." She touched her glass to her lips as she delicately sipped the sweet lemonade, not letting her gaze drop from his blue eyes.

"I hate to admit it, but she is growing up so rapidly that it scares me. And it makes me feel old. My dear Lilian, please consider cheering an old man in his declining years by accompanying him to the picnic. Please, before it is too late. So, do not forget, I shall be there at ten," he spoke definitely, pushing his seat back, "Just in case you are a forgetful one, here is a sweet reminder of me." Unpinning the small rose on his lapel, he laid it in Lilian's hand. He then touched the end of her nose lightly with his fingertip, causing her to wrinkle it slightly. "Until Monday."

Once he was out of the room, Lilian found she could no longer hold back the childish grin that was bursting to run freely across her face. "Imagine that!" is all she could say as she touched the same spot on her nose.

A pout pursed itself on Cynthia's face as she consigned herself to her drink. But, Alana was tickled over the idea, "What will you wear?"

"You do not think I should go do you? After all, what would people think?" Lilian's face grew sullen.

"They would probably think how lucky you are to have such a handsome man showing an interest in you and that he is fortunate to be escorting such a beautiful woman. Most would remark that you make a charming couple. They would be happy for you. Why would they think or say otherwise?" Alana questioned, giving Cynthia a terse frown for not helping convince Lilian that her reputation would not be in any danger.

"They may think I have not allowed enough of a mourning period; after all, Mark's death was less than two years ago. I might be doing his memory harm," Lilian spoke softly as she wrung her hands together.

"Would Mark want you to become a recluse to prove

that you indeed loved him? Would he believe feelings might develop for another man that could possibly lessen those you had for him? Is that how you think everyone else remembers him?" Alana demanded, even though she herself had no concept of the man other than what Lizzie had told her.

"Well, no, but—"

"But, nothing! If it makes you feel better about it, take the children. Let everyone believe you are going for their sake. Besides, they will love it. You would not want to hurt Archie's feeings in any way would you?" She watched Lilian slowly shake her head. "Well, then, if he comes back out here before we leave, you should go ahead and tell him that you will be proud to go. You do want to go, do you not?"

Biting the edge of her lower lip, she answered demurely, "Yes, I would love to go, but—"

"But, nothing! Go! Have a good time!" Alana sternly ordered her friend, looking her straight in her fearful blue eyes.

"Will you go, too?" Lilian asked hopefully.

"No, I shall not. I cannot. I promised myself I would use that day to write my mother a long letter. I have not written her since I arrived." Alana made up the excuse as she spoke. "But, you do not need me with you. After all, you will have six children lending you support. Besides, Archie does not look as if he bites. Therefore, you should not need me as a guard dog."

"I guess so," Lilian replied worriedly, but a gleam of excitement was shining in her eyes as her heart was winning the battle with her conscience.

"It is decided. You should go and enjoy yourself. That, my dear, is that."

Cynthia seemed disinterested in the whole conversation as she set her empty glass down. "Are you two ready to go?" Pausing a moment for a reply, she found that there was none. "Lilian, you have not touched your drink, did you not like it?"

"Hm? Oh, I guess I was not as thirsty as I thought," she answered, trying fruitlessly to concentrate on whatever

Cynthia was chattering about.

"I shall get the check," Alana offered as she signaled Katherine Lynn, who came promptly to see if there was anything else that she could do.

"May I have the check, please? We are ready to go," Alana asked softly.

"Oh, but ma'am, there is no charge. Daddy said the bill has been taken care of," she said simply.

"Then, thank your father for us. It was delicious lemonade."

"You can thank him yourself. Here he comes," Katherine Lynn nodded towards her approaching father.

Lilian seemed to stop breathing altogether as Alana turned to thank him for the refreshments. "Please, come again. It is a great asset for my business to have such beautiful ladies as yourselves frequent my tables," he spoke rather eloquently. Turning to face Lilian, he spoke softly, "I can barely wait to find out if you are going to join me at the picnic."

Alana signaled Cynthia to follow her on out of the door, but finally had to grab her arm and pull her towards the door. She did not pay heed to Cynthia's protests as she listened for Lilian's reply, "Well, if nothing drastic happens, I shall be proud to attend that picnic with you." They were looking into each other's eyes and setting their plans as Alana and Cynthia reached the door.

"Who do you think you are, pulling at me like this?" Cynthia demanded for the third time as she finally pulled herself free of Alana.

"Will you hush?" Alana ordered under her breath as she reached for the door. A little man standing just outside noticed the approaching ladies and stepped over to open the door for them. "Why thank you, sir," Alana spoke courteously as she and Cynthia passed through.

Waiting for Lilian, Alana walked over to a nearby vendor and pretended to look at the many fruits and vegetables. Cynthia walked up behind her and spoke sharply through her clenched teeth, "How dare you lower yourself like that!"

Without looking at her, Alana replied, "I do not have

even the slightest idea as to what you are referring."

"First, you rudely yanked on my arm and pulled me outside. Then you actually spoke to that lowlife. Just allowing ourselves to walk through while he held the door would have been reward enough for the wretch. But, no, you had to actually speak to a common stranger and thank him aloud no less." Alana remained silent, still refusing this woman an argument. "Another thing, what makes you feel you are eligible to give your own employer advice as you did in there? I have tried to warn you to stay within your imposed bounds, but you have continuously refused to heed my advice. I feel I must speak to Lilian and Brandon about your behavior."

"If you feel you must, then you must," Alana replied perfunctorily, trying to keep her temper in check. "Aren't these peaches lovely?" she changed the subject as if totally unconcerned. "How much for a single peach?" she turned her back on Cynthia as she made her purchase from the young boy tending the small stand set just outside of the Blue Swan.

Little was said on the way home as Lilian was deeply engrossed in her own thoughts and Cynthia had nothing else to say to Alana, for which Alana was glad. It was after 5:00 when Billy spotted the carriage from the barn. He hustled over to get the carriage and help carry in some of the packages. When he got closer he noticed a third person unfamiliar to him. He walked around the back in order to get a better look at Cynthia sitting so pretty on the other side.

"Howdy, I am Billy," he said as he offered his hand to help her down.

His feelings were crushed when she totally ignored his words while allowing him to help her down from her seat. Turning her back to him, she asked Lilian if the largest of her boxes as well as her small case might be placed in the room designated for her to freshen up in. Lilian furthered the request to Billy, who was openly irritated by now, "Put that large box and the case that is under all those things in the back into the spare room two doors down from Alana's."

After Lilian escorted Cynthia to the room, Billy mumbled something under his breath as he slung boxes around. Gently, Alana placed her hand on his arm as if to calm him, "Do not pay her any attention, Billy. She thinks she is a royal princess."

Allowing a grin to replace his scowl, he retorted, "A royal pain is what she is!"

"Frankly, I agree wholeheartedly. But, she is a friend of both Lilian's and Brandon's. We should try to tolerate her presence for their sake." The advice did not come easy as she herself was near the breaking point. "Want me to help carry some of these things in?"

"Naw—say she's Brandon's friend, too? You better go get ready for dinner. You may need to go an extra step tonight. We don't want her working her hooks into Brandon, do we?"

"The boy has insight. You have to credit him that," Alana thought to herself as she started for her room. As an afterthought, "Oh, Billy, there are some rose bushes in one of those packages. Would you mind putting them in water for me until I can plant them?"

"Would mind it a bit if it weren't you askin' me," he replied good-naturedly. "Consider it done. Now, you go get ready."

"It is nice to have at least one good friend Cynthia will not be able to influence against me," she thought as she unlocked the door and went inside with every intention of following his orders.

Time seemed to evaporate like water spilled on a hot stove as Alana hurried to do her best with what she had. When she opened the package containing her new handled mirror, she found that Billy had delivered the little sack containing Lilian's choker. After a battle with her conscience of whether or not she dared to wear it, she put it back in the sack. She did feel she would need something drastic to divert Brandon's attention from Cynthia. She chose the sundress she once believed a little too daring, but now she was glad she had it. With a lacy shawl wrapped around her shoulders and the little gold heart on a dainty gold chain her father had given her just before she left, the sundress could do rather nicely. After hanging the sundress from the bed canopy and arranging her underclothing and shoes on the bed, she went to the pitcher and poured fresh water into the large basin to wash the road dust from her face. As she awkwardly reached behind her to undo the many hooks and stays of her dress, there came a light knock on her door. Alana walked over to the window and caught sight of Lizzie outside knocking for a second time. Opening the door and letting Lizzie in, she asked, "Can I do something for you?"

"Oh, no, ma'am, Miss Alana. It is just that Miss Cynthia sent for me 'cause she wants me to press out her dress. I just thought you might want me to press out yours while I am at it. The iron will be hot anyhow. Can't hurt nothin'."

"That would be nice, but are you certain you have time? With dinner to prepare and serve, you surely do not need extra work," Alana pointed out.

"Aw, supper's on the stove and cookin'. All it needs is time to get done. So, give me that pretty dress. We don't want Miss Cindy impressin' Master Brandon with a neater dress than yours, do we?" Lizzie said with a wink.

"No, we do not," Alana replied cautiously, with a frown questioning Lizzie's motives.

"Didn't think so. You need to be lookin' your finest tonight. Is this the dress? It is, isn't it? Fine choice," Lizzie said as she tossed the dress over her arm. "I'll give it the best pressin' out it ever had. It'll look just right."

"Why are you doing this for me?" Alana wanted to know.

"Because I know how much you likes Master Brandon, even though you two fights like two mama cats over a single scrap of meat. And, personally, I don't like that Miss Cindy," Lizzie replied openly.

"What makes you think I like Brandon?" Alana wanted to know, wondering just how transparent her feelings were.

"Oh, I see'd you lookin' at him outta the corner of your eye. I also see'd you standin' at your window once or twice watchin' him as he came in from the barn in the evenin's late."

"I have not!" Alana denied sharply.

"Yes, you have. I see'd you. But, don't you go frettin' about it, I ain't about to mention it to nobody," she promised as she patted Alana on her shoulder. "I knows you likes Brandon, but I don't reckon nobody else has to know."

"Oh, I do like Brandon, awfully so," Alana could not believe she blurted that out. Until now, she had not even admitted it to herself. "I only wish he could learn to like me. He hates me so!"

"He don't hate you, Miss Alana. It's just that you're so different from most of the silly witless girls around here. You are as smart as he is. He ain't useta that. Plus, I think the fact that he could really like you scares the hell out of him, excuse my language. He don't want to really like no woman, as I once told you. He still remembers how Miss Stephanie was able to hurt him deep and he refuses to give any woman that kind of power again."

"I do not know. We just cannot seem to get along. We are just too different, I guess."

"If you ask me, you are too much alike. Both of y'all are ambitious and very full of determination. Y'all both useta doin' for yourself. Most of all, both of y'all are always protectin' that dern fool pride that's pinned up inside of you for whatever reason; afraid to leave it be for even a moment. Just give him time, I know Master Brandon as well as anyone. He don't hate you. He just don't understand you. Maybe that is what makes him watch you outta the corner of his eye," she said with a wide grin. "The best advice I got for you is to just look pretty tonight and try not to argue with him about anythin'. Not tonight," she warned as she slipped out of the door as well as a large woman could.

Alana's heart soared at Lizzie's mention that Brandon might have been looking her way. But, then she let her spirits drop as she wondered if it might all be in Lizzie's mind. He may have been looking at something else. But, then, again, she had pegged her right.

Hurriedly, she finished her bath with a dampened cloth and began working on her hair. She pulled it far back and dropped long ringlets down to the nape of her neck. She shaped smaller finger ringlets with the shorter hair edging the neckline. Carefully, she fastened the delicate chain of her necklace behind her neck. She was sitting in front of the mirror in her undergarments searching her hair for flaws when Lizzie returned with her dress. Once inside, Lizzie complimented her hair and offered to help her with the hooks on the back of the dress, so she would not muss her hair. When Alana was in her dress, Lizzie went about straightening her skirt and touching up a strand of hair that had strayed. "You look beautiful, simply beautiful. Miss Cindy ain't got a chance with you in the same room!" she stated proudly.

"I do not know about that. She is not only very beautiful, she is so truly graceful and proper. I am not."

"Don't you feel like a proper lady dressed like that?" Lizzie demanded.

"Yes, I admit I do, but—"

"Well, you just act the way you feel and you will be as graceful as anyone could be."

"But she plans to undermine me. She told me so," Alana protested.

"That was probably just to scare you off and keep you from comin' to dinner. Keep your head up and show her you can match her anyday!" Lizzie offered as she pulled Alana's head up by the chin with her chubby finger.

"Thank you!" Alana cried as she gave Lizzie a big hug. "Thank you so much!"

"For what? I haven't done nothin'. You stop that before you wrinkle that dress up, Miss Alana," Lizzie told her. Before she disappeared through the door, she stopped to wave goodbye and offer a reassuring nod. With new hope, Alana did not wait for the dinner bell to sound. She gathered up her shawl and stepped out into the warm night air with her head held high.

Cynthia was already in the dinner room talking with Lilian. The smell of food filled the room as the time to eat neared. All of the places had been set and the water glasses had been filled. As she walked over to join the two, Alana wondered if Cynthia had spoken to Lilian about her, yet.

Evidently not, as Lilian greeted her cheerfully, "Alana, you look beautiful."

"Yes, you do," Cynthia admitted with less enthusiasm.

Looking down at Cynthia's attire in order to return a symbolization of a compliment, Alana was stunned. Cynthia was wearing that same beautiful white gown with the blue trim that she had been so impressed with earlier on the dress shop mannequin. It was all the more attractive on Cynthia. Her full breasts and small waist were accentuated by the fine curves of the bodice. Dejectedly, her gaze fell on her own dress that was not so voluptuously filled. Until now, she had not cared that she had failed to be as amply blessed or well proportioned as many of the others had been.

"You look quite beautiful yourself," she had to admit the truth.

"Thank you, I bought this little outfit this afternoon on a whim. I must confess, I rather like it," Cynthia boasted off-handedly.

The room's temperature seemed to rise as Alana listened to the casual way Cynthia referred to her dress. Knowing just how fine and expensive the dress was, she realized it was actually a special dress bought for a special reason. The same reason she herself put the extra touch of perfume at each ear.

While Cynthia continued the discussion of her casual purchase of the gown, Brandon walked in from the kitchen wearing a trim-fitting black dinner jacket over a white ruffled shirt and matching black trousers. He looked magnificent. The first to break the silence that followed was Cynthia as she sashayed over to his side, "Oh, Brandon, darling, I am ever so happy to see you again."

Taking the limp hand held out to him, he replied, "Why Cindy Louise, you look just as pretty as ever."

The familiarity suggested with his use of 'Cindy Louise' made Alana cringe. It took several heavy breaths to catch her breathing up with her jealous heartbeat as she continued to watch the reunion.

"Brandon, you are going to make me blush. You should

not go on so," she prompted him while batting her long lashes his way.

"But, you do look lovely. That gown is exquisite," he replied, letting go of her hand in order to kiss his fingertips in the style of a genteel European.

"This old thing? Do you really like it?" Alana felt that Cynthia's voice sounded almost sticky with sweetness, "You are just as gallant as ever, Brandon Warren. You always seem to know what to say to a lady."

"When a lady looks beautiful, she deserves to be told so," he stated simply. He then turned to Lilian and Alana, "I must say this room is filled with very beautiful and charming women."

Accepting the compliment as if directed only to herself, Cynthia remarked, "You always manage to make me blush." Carefully she slipped her arm around his and had him escort her to the table. "Did Lizzie get my little present to you?" she asked with a bat of her eye.

"Yes, I was planning to thank you for them later," he replied.

"Well, I know how a man loves a good cigar after dinner."

Just then, the swinging door opened and Lizzie came through frowning at the way Cynthia clung to Brandon. Giving Alana a look that showed her disapproval, she walked over to speak to Lilian, "I am ready to ring the bell. Y'all can go ahead and sit if you want. I'll be right out with supper." She turned around and spoke shortly to Cynthia, "How are you, Miss Cindy?"

"Lizzie, dear, I could not be better. I can assure you. I have missed all of you so very much. I just cannot tell you just how much. I could never possibly find all the right words to tell you."

"I am sure," Lizzie said bluntly, turning on her heel and marching out to ring the dinner bell.

"Do you still sit here on the end, Brandon, darling?" Cynthia asked as they approached the table. When he affirmed he did, she walked over and put her hands on Alana's chair, "Then, I shall sit right here so we can catch up on what has happened over the past few years."

"I do not know. Normally, Alana sits there," Brandon explained as he looked over at Alana, who managed to keep the rage inside of her from showing on her face.

"Oh, your little schoolteacher understands that we have a lot to talk about. I am certain she does not mind if I sit here beside you," she said innocently as she turned and gave Alana a cold warning through narrowed eyes and sat down.

"Of course, I do not mind. After all, you two are old friends; I think you should sit next to each other rather than have to talk across the table," Alana lied. "I shall just sit down here beside Angela." She managed to smile as she spoke.

"See there, I knew your little schoolteacher would understand," Cynthia repeated to Brandon.

Lilian said nothing as she watched the three with a careful eye. Silently, she walked over to stand behind her chair. Alana wondered if she had offended her by not warming up to her friend. She hoped not, for she had too much respect and admiration for Lilian to want to offend her.

Shortly after the bell had been rung, the children started entering and finding their seats. Curiously, they stared at the pretty blonde sitting beside their uncle. Jake remembered his manners and stopped to politely say hello. After listening to what a handsome young man he had become, he went on to his seat. All of the seats filled quickly except Brenda's. Alana and Lilian exchanged worried glances as they both feared the trouble the child was getting herself into with Brandon by refusing to come to dinner.

After a moment, Lilian interrupted Cynthia's constant chattering to excuse herself, "I think that I should check on Brenda. She must be feeling ill again. I shall be right back." She started to get up when Brandon stopped her.

"There is really no need. She is not here," he said simply.

"What? Why?" Lilian wanted to know more.

"Seems a friend of hers was having an all night party of sorts and she really wanted to go. Well, after talking it over with her, I just could not make her stay home. It seemed to mean so much to her. You know how little girls are when it comes to special parties with special friends," he looked directly at Alana as he spoke. "I carried her over there earlier. I realize her place should be here to greet our guest, but, I knew Cindy Louise would understand how it is," he glanced at Cynthia. "She did tell me to make her excuses and tell you 'hello' for her," he said as if the subject were a fresh one.

Tears glistened in both Lilian's and Alana's eyes as they exchanged smiles.

"Thank you, Brandon," Lilian said sincerely, the dampness in her eyes expressing how deeply touched she was.

"Well, I certainly do understand. I was always going off to parties when I was a young girl, still love a good party for that matter," Cynthia remarked dominating the conversation once again.

The heavy smell of delicious food wafted through the room just before Lizzie entered with her large tray loaded down with many of her specialties. As she set the bowls on the table, she caught some of Cynthia's conversation about the horrid evening her daddy refused to allow her to attend what turned out to be one of the biggest and finest parties of the year. It was an unfair punishment for some little innocent thing she had done. She was telling how broken-hearted she was when dear Anne returned with wonderful tales of the marvelous event it had turned out to be, when Lizzie looked heavenward and shook her head hopelessly for Alana's benefit. It seemed so comical that Alana laughed out loud without realizing it. Innocently, Lizzie returned to the kitchen, leaving Alana to receive the many frowns that followed.

"It was not funny for me to hear Anne's account of the party, I assure you, Miss Stambridge," Cynthia's eyes narrowed as she spoke. The children turned their attention from the food set before them to Cynthia when they heard the sharp tone of her voice as she spoke to their teacher. When she turned back to face Brandon in order to finish her tale, Mickey stuck his tongue out at her. The other children grinned and silently elbowed each other as

Mickey had just displayed how they all were feeling. Angela reached under the table and patted Alana on the hand reassuringly. All this show of support helped Alana keep from telling Cynthia just exactly what she thought of her.

Lizzie returned with a large platter of broiled steaks, a serving spoon for each bowl and a large basket of hot rolls. After setting the steaks and rolls in front of Brandon, she started placing the spoons into the bowls. But, when she got to the crowder peas set in front of Cynthia, she dropped the spoon into the bowl causing a bit of the soup to splash onto Cynthia's dress.

"Be more careful, you clumsy fool!" she snapped in a tone of voice more familiar to Alana as she tried to clean her dress with the corner of her napkin.

"Allow me," Brandon spoke as he dipped his napkin into his water glass and proceeded to dab at some of the spots on her sleeve and shoulder.

"Thank you, you are such a dear. But, some of the people you hire around here leave a lot to be desired," she pouted, although she deeply enjoyed the attention it was bringing her.

Alana seethed at that last remark that she realized was aimed directly at her. And the fact that no one took up for poor Lizzie after such an accident, well it could have been an accident, made her furious. The more she thought about it, the madder she became. She knew if Cynthia referred to her as 'your little schoolteacher' one more time, she surely would burst. Lizzie quietly returned to the kitchen to allow everyone to enjoy the meal without her presence. Before the meal could be eaten, Cynthia managed to downgrade women's colleges, emphasizing that only women of lesser breeding ever attended them. The muscles in Alana's jaw visibly tightened, but she said nothing. Even when Cynthia made a remark about how chubby Angela was after Alana had the child convinced the weight she had managed to lose over the last two months made quite a difference, Alana kept her tongue still. But, she did reach over and pat Angela's hand, returning the support shown her earlier.

The children were quick to finish eating and asked to be excused. They ran outside to play on the patio, since the darkness had crept in and prevented them from playing elsewhere. The conversation at the table continued to center around Cynthia's favorite subject, which was Cynthia. She repeated some of the tales she had previously related to Lilian earlier. Every now and then, she would pause to tell Brandon how remarkable he looked and how little he had changed, to which he always returned the compliment. Lilian and Alana generally were unwillingly silent listeners.

Cynthia fingered several flowers set into a pretty bouquet centering the table in front of her. As she began to run out of things to talk about, she mentioned the flowers, "Lilian, these flowers are so lovely. Didn't Lizzie arrange them nicely?"

"Alana arranged those. She has such a knack with flowers. She made that beautiful centerpiece on the buffet, too," Lilian replied, turning to point to a fabulous array of flowers and greenery set in a huge brass bowl. "Those flowers all came from the patio gardens."

"You did that? I did not realize your job extended to the garden," Cynthia spoke curtly.

"It is not my job. It is just something I enjoy doing," Alana explained. "I like it very much."

"Yes, I have noticed you generally seem to do whatever pleases you, no matter the consequences," Cynthia nodded snidely. Then she turned back to Brandon, "You really do need to have a long talk with her. She does not seem to realize the position she rose to when she became an employee of the Warren family. Do you know that she actually nods to strange men and talks with the local riff-raff, just like a common trollop? Once, when a particularly seedy-looking man had the gall to open the door for us, she actually thanked him aloud. She does not realize she is supposed to represent a family of much higher quality. She talked to this man as if she were on his level. That little schoolteacher of yours needs to be told the responsibilities that go with her position and how one representing our class does not lower herself by talking to just anyone." Cynthia's nostrils flared with a great show of disdain.

Any restraints she was holding on her temper vanished as Alana unleashed the rage boiling within her.

"I have had just about enough of you telling me what you consider right and wrong for me. Not everyone has the same high-and-mighty set of values as you do. I certainly cannot see putting one person above another. I do not consider myself any better than anyone else, and I most certainly do not believe you are any better than I am. I shall not and never could want to put myself on some sort of pedestal because I work for your precious Brandon Warren! No one is going to change me or the way I think. If anyone's values are warped, they are yours. And I do wish you would keep them to yourself. I am not about to be dictated to by the likes of you or anyone else. I cannot help it, it is the way I feel." She took a deep breath and continued. "Another thing, I do not speak from a certain class level or so labeled 'position,' my dear. I speak directly from something called a heart. I guess you could never understand. After all, you do not seem to have such a thing. I believe it has bloody well been bred right out of you!" When she paused to take a second breath, she realized what she had just said and done. Rather than offer a phony apology, Alana added more calmly, "It is getting awfully stuffy in here. I believe I could use a walk in the fresh night air. Excuse me."

She quickly pushed her chair back in hopes of making her exit before anyone could think of a retaliation.

"Just a damn minute there!" Brandon's voice boomed. "You wait right there," he demanded to a now paralyzed Alana. He then turned to Cynthia and, with a serious tone in his voice, he spoke, "She is right you realize. There just is no class system anymore. It died with the Old South in the Civil War. You act a fool when you pretend it still exists. She is also absolutely right about it being stuffy in here." He walked away from the flabbergasted, open-mouthed Cynthia to stand behind Alana. "If you would allow me, my dear, I would love to join you on your walk." He held his arm out for hers and escorted her out of the room.

Once they were outside, the reality of what had just happened struck Alana. The desire to laugh overwhelmed her, and she did little to hold it back.

"Shh," he warned her, "Wait until we are out of earshot!" Quickly, he pulled her down the walkway and into his study. After he shut the door, a deep laugh filled the darkened room joined by the higher toned laughter of Alana's. She laughed so hard she grew weak and without actually realizing it, she fell into his arms. Folding both arms around her, he held her close, laughing until tears formed in his eyes. When he could speak, it was chopped with helpless chuckles, "Serves her right." Looking down through the shadows at the face of the woman he suddenly held so close he said, "You really let her have it. Never even gave her a chance to open that snooty mouth of hers."

Alana had stopped laughing by now, but the tears of delight still clung to her eyes. When she realized Brandon was not letting go of her, even after their outburst had subsided, she looked up to see why. The torch that hung just outside the window cast only a dim light across his face. Unable to take her eyes from his, she spoke rather shakily, "Oh, but Lilian is going to be absolutely furious with me."

"She will get over it," he spoke softly now. "She is the type that never holds a grudge." He brought his face down to hers. Anticipating that she might turn away, he lifted one hand to cup her chin as he met her soft lips with his. Pulling her closer, he lingered at her mouth. He pulled back only enough to read her reaction, but found he could see nothing for the shadows darkened over her face. Again he kissed her long and hard. He eased her back a step, placing her face in the light. Then, pulling gently away, he found her face revealed nothing of the turmoil tumbling within her.

The small bumps prickling the skin along Alana's back and arms directly contradicted the deeply warming sensations that surged inside of her and spread to every part of her. It was like no other feeling she had ever experienced. Eagerly, she wanted more, yet, somehow she was afraid.

She could feel his warm breath softly on her cheek as she found it hard to speak, "I should go apologize to Cynthia. After all, she is a guest in your home." She spoke slowly, hoping to find time to collect the many thoughts that spun wildly through her mind.

"She deserves no apology from you," he spoke firmly as he lifted his head to get a better look at Alana's face. "You only spoke the truth. You were being honest."

"But, as usual, my honesty has gotten me into deep trouble," she protested. "I wish I would learn to keep my big mouth shut! Poor Lilian, we left her to take the brunt of this."

"She will handle it properly," Brandon assured her.

"Well, you better get back in there. Lilian expects you to carry Cynthia home," Alana pulled away.

"By now, she has sent for Billy to carry her home. I really should thank you for that. The thought of listening to her constant babbling a minute longer horrifies me." He walked over to the window at the sound of approaching footsteps. "Poor Billy did not know what he was getting himself into when he decided to move into the bunkroom permanently. Here comes Lizzie now. I bet a dime to a dollar she is fetching Billy."

Joining Brandon at the window, she watched a chuckling Lizzie hurry by on her way to the barn. On her return, she was able to restrain that impish smile somewhat; but her black eyes sparkled with amusement.

Lilian and Cynthia were standing just outside the window when Lizzie paused to speak, "He's gotta get his britches back on. It'll take a minute. He said he's gonna pull up by the patio when he gets ready."

"Thank you, Lizzie. Would you please see to it that the children get on to bed," Lilian spoke as solemnly as one did after a death in one's family. With deep sincerity evident in her eyes, she turned to Cynthia, whose back was now in the window's view. "I want to tell you how sorry I am that the evening turned out as it did. Although I realize my words cannot possibly undo what was said or heal the hurt you must be feeling right now, I must try to apologize. Please, do not dwell on this night. Do not feel any of it was your fault." The grim expression on Lilian's face showed how she must indeed have been deeply embarrassed.

Neither Brandon nor Alana could make out Cynthia's reply, but watched as Lilian placed a supportive arm around her.

"See, Brandon, she is upset. Lilian blames me. Why can I not keep my thoughts to myself?" Alana asked distressfully.

Taking her hand in his, he tried to comfort her, "Why should you? She was not keeping hers to herself." Their attention was drawn again to the window when they heard the carriage pull up.

Patting Cynthia on the back, Lilian turned to help her, "There is Billy now. You just go home and get some rest. We can sort this out later." Lilian continued to console her as they walked away. Cynthia's face was visible now as tears reflected the wavering light of the torches. She held her head up boldly, only attempting minor sobs and sniffs.

"I would say she is over-reacting. But, then, she always does," Brandon spoke with a slight tone of disgust edging his voice.

Billy waited silently in the carriage, not about to give this woman a second chance to insult him. He sat quietly, wondering why he had to carry her home anyway. Lizzie had not given him any details and by the looks on their faces he felt this was not the time to ask.

After helping Cynthia into the rear seat of the carriage, Lilian spoke briefly with Billy. She waved farewell until they were out of her sight. When she turned around the solemn look was quickly replaced with a look of relief. She turned her eyes heavenward with a slight raise of her eyebrows as if asking His understanding, then tried to squelch the smile teetering at her mouth as she gaily pranced off to her room.

"Why that little faker," Brandon exclaimed, wondering why his sister looked so satisfied. He knew by the look on her face she was up to something and he never did trust her on such occasions.

"I do not understand," Alana replied as she looked up into Brandon's deep blue eyes.

"Neither do I. But, you can be sure she is pleased about something. That was not the look of a mortified hostess at all." He rubbed his chin suspiciously with his left hand. Alana's hand was still clasped tightly in his other hand.

"Brandon, I am so sorry." Alana looked down at the floor rather than face him with her apology.

"Whatever for? Lillan does not seem upset by all of this; why should you be?" Brandon asked, lifting her chin gently with his thumb.

Even with her face lifted to face his, she failed to look directly at him. Instead, she diverted her eyes to the window.

"For everything. I simply want to apologize for everything. I have done nothing but cause you trouble and irritation since the day I arrived. I have openly and childishly interfered, when I had no true right to. I just cannot seem to keep my opinions to myself, even though I know it will make you angry with me."

"I think the reason I get so angry is because I have never had a woman giving me such strong opinions before. I really do not know how to handle it, especially when what she says seems to make sense," Brandon confessed.

"Well, I have absolutely no right to force my opinions on you whenever I do not happen to agree with you. We hardly ever seem to agree on anything, do we?" She smiled slightly as she now managed to look at him.

"We agreed with each other tonight, did we not?" he offered as he traced her narrow jawline with his fingers.

"Do you think we could try to be friends?" Alana asked hopefully.

Brandon touched her cheek lightly with his fingertips, "To be sure, I believe we can become the best of friends."

"I am glad of that. I never wanted to be your enemy," she replied with a sigh. She stared at him curiously for a moment, then quickly added, "I better go, now. But I do want to thank you, Brandon. Thank you so much for becoming my friend." She quickly pulled away. At the door she paused and repeated the word as if enjoying the mere sound of it. "Friends," then she slipped outside quietly.

Watching her walk swiftly across the patio to her door, Brandon questioned the darkness, "Just friends?"

Chapter Six

It was after nine o'clock when Alana finally got out of bed. With the children planning to join their mother for the July Fourth picnic, Alana had the entire day to do whatever pleased her. After checking the weather with a quick glance through her window, Alana discovered the rain that started late Sunday morning had finally let up. At last she could get started on her rose garden. But that was not the only reason she was glad the rain had stopped. Had it continued, the picnic would have been cancelled and Lilian would have missed this chance to be with Archie. The way Lilian was talking about the picnic Sunday afternoon when she came to Alana's room, it might very well break her heart to hear that the picnic had been cancelled. The reason she came to Alana's room was to set things straight about Saturday night's mishap. After Alana had failed to come to breakfast the following morning and then had sent word she felt too ill to attend church or lunch with them, Lilian decided that they needed to talk about it.

It took a great amount of convincing before Alana believed Lilian actually had no hard feelings and that there was nothing to be ashamed of. Lilian then explained how Cynthia seemed to be taking it quite well, too.

"In fact, right after church, she managed to get Dr. Marcus Morgan to ask her to the picnic. She seems to be handling Brandon's rejection rather well, I would say. She spoke to me as if nothing had happened," Lilian told her.

Alana was a little shocked that the new veterinarian, who was about her age, had asked Cynthia to the picnic.

Lilian laughed at that and remarked, "He probably does

128

not know how old Cynthia is, or maybe he just does not care, but he sure enough asked her. I know that for a fact, because I invited them to join us. That way I will not have to worry about keeping a conversation going. Cynthia never gives anyone else a chance to talk," Lilian confessed with a chuckle. Alana was glad to see Lilian really did not seem the least bit upset over her rampage of Saturday night.

Lilian also wanted to know if Alana and Brandon had settled anything between them during their Saturday night stroll. Alana assured her they had. "After I apologized for all of the terrible interference that I have caused him on several occasions, I told him I wanted to be friends. He said we could be the best of friends," Alana related happily. "I guess you could say we called a truce."

"Well, that is a start," Lilian thought to herself as she listened to Alana. She had hoped for better results than that, but at least it was a step in the right direction. By the time she and Alana were through talking, everything had been settled between them. They found that they were still the best of friends. Before Lilian left the room, Alana made her promise to tell her everything that happened during the picnic and mentioned that she hoped to see them off after breakfast. But, having overslept, Alana knew breakfast had long since been over. Hoping to talk Lizzie out of a piece of toast and a cup of coffee, Alana dressed hurriedly in a simple skirt and a blouse that buttoned easily up the front. She also hoped she might get ready in time to be able to say farewell to the picnickers. She quickly put her hair up into a simple bun. While she was buttoning her shoes, she heard a knock at her door.

"Come in, the door is not locked," she shouted.

"It is me," Angela said softly. A pout drooped across her little face as she eased inside, barely opening the door.

"What is wrong with you?" Alana asked, walking over and kneeling beside the forlorn child.

"I don't want to go. Please, may I stay here with you? I promise to be good," she pleaded in a hopeless voice.

"Why do you not want to go?"

"Because, he is not my Pa-pa! I do not like him. He is not

my Pa-pa!" she said bluntly, tears beginning to roll down her cheeks.

"Uh-oh," Alana thought. "Lilian does not need this."

"Please, Miss Stambridge, let me stay here with you," Angela begged.

"Maybe you really should stay here," Alana admitted. "Where is your mother? I shall have to offer her some sort of excuse. You just stay in here. I shall be right back."

Alana found Lilian sitting in the den waiting nervously for Archie. Not wanting to put a damper on Lilian's day, Alana told her Angela had a queasy stomach and should not go. Lilian agreed, having little suspicions since Angela had picked at her food during breakfast. Alana promised to take proper care of her and reminded Lilian to have a good time.

"I shall try," Lilian said cautiously, almost unbelievingly.

"If you leave with a negative attitude, you will have defeated your purpose in going, which is to have the best time possible and see that Archie enjoys himself, too. Now, smile and say you will have a positively marvelous time."

"Okay, I am going to have a positively marvelous time. How is that?" Lilian chuckled, feeling her tension ease somewhat.

"Better, much better," Alana said as she looked down at Lilian. "My are we not dressed nicely for a picnic?" she teased. Lilian was wearing a pretty white and pink gingham dress with as many as six petticoats underneath. Her hair was pulled back with a long pink ribbon and allowed to fall down her back. Alana wondered if her friend had risen at the first signs of dawn to begin getting herself ready. She was radiant.

Suddenly there came a short knock at the front door. Lilian scurried to answer, but paused in the entry hall long enough to check her hair in the large framed mirror that hung there. "Here goes," she whispered to Alana, who was following closely behind her. Alana wondered what the people around here considered a picnic when she saw Archie was as nicely dressed as Lilian. While Lilian escorted him into the den, Alana offered to round up the

children. When she returned with the small group, she
hustled them outside and into Archie's carriage. The
four boys were sitting on the rear seat and Brenda was
sitting on the far side of the front seat when Archie
escorted Lilian to join them.

Alana stood just outside of the front door waving
frantically to the group as they drove away. She chuckled
aloud when she noticed that Mickey had turned around
in the seat to peek under the blue and white checked linen
covering a very large basket sitting directly behind him.

When she returned to her room, she found Angela lying
on her stomach across the unmade bed with her head
propped up with two clenched fists.

"Thought you were coming right back," she complained sulkily.

"I meant to, but I ended up helping get everybody off,"
Alana explained, sitting on the bed beside her.

"They are gone? I get to stay here?" she asked
hopefully.

"Yes, you get to stay here. In fact, you can stay right here
and sulk all day or you can join me in the kitchen. I am
starved!" Alana said simply as she headed for the door.

"Wait for me!" Angela cried out in a shrill little voice,
running to catch up with her.

Much to Alana's surprise, Lizzie had a breakfast of ham
and eggs waiting for her when she walked in. Angela
sipped on a small glass of juice while Alana ate heartily.
After finishing, she told Angela about the rose garden she
was planning to create. She offered to let Angela help. But,
determined to be miserable, Angela said she was going to
spend the day in her room.

Alana walked with her to her door before going out to
the barn to borrow the large shovel and a small trowel she
needed to produce her very special rose garden. She
found Billy inside sharpening an axe with a huge gray
stone and asked him for the tools. With a curious glance,
he supplied her with three various shaped larger shovels
and two small hand trowels.

"You gonna do this yourself?" he asked with a cautious
look across his face.

"Any reason I should not?" she answered his question with a question of her own before walking out with the tools secured under her arms to the location she had in mind. She chose the yard area at the end of the house right beside her room. This area was her first choice not only because she could see it easily from her room, but because there was deep brown soil with plenty of morning sun and afternoon shade. This East Texas land baffled Alana, for one place might consist solely of a pale white sand and on either side of it might be rich brown soil or slick red clay. She knew that of her choices that the roses would do better in this brown soil. Selecting the shovel with a tall pointed and rather flat scoop, Alana placed it in position. Putting her foot on one side of the top of the scoop, she pushed down. The shovel did not sink into the ground as she had anticipated. It had failed to even cut through the grassroots covering the ground. Determination driving her, she hopped up on the scoop with both feet and jumped up and down. Still the shovel had not dented the ground. With a flinched jaw and all the strength she had, she again jumped on the scoop wavering it back and forth as she did. Gradually it began to cut into the ground. By the time she had sunken the scoop far enough into the ground, her forehead was covered with perspiration and long strands of her hair had fallen from their place, now dangling down her back. When she grabbed the handle to push down on it and break up the earth, she found that it would not budge. Realizing her weight loss had lessened the leverage power she remembered having, she decided extra effort was in order. Unbuttoning the top two buttons and wiping the sweat off of her hands on to her dress, she took a deep breath and pulled down with all of her might. Suddenly, the earth gave way and she tumbled to the ground with the shovel still in her hand.

Heavy laughter filled the air as she sat dumbfoundedly in a heap. When she turned to see who was considering her dilemma so funny, she found Billy nearly bent over with his loud guffawing.

Seeing how insulted Alana looked, he tried to apologize,

but it did not sound very sincere as he choked on laughter as he spoke, "I am sorry, but you looked so silly tumbling to the ground like you did. You did not hurt yourself, did you?" He offered her his hand to help her up. Finding his laughter contagious she began to giggle, "I imagine it must have been quite a sight at that. There is nothing quite like grace and sophistication."

After allowing him to pull her to her feet, she dusted the dirt and grass from her skirt. Looking around to see if anyone else might have seen her clumsy little stunt, she saw Angela running up the walkway with her usual curiosity.

"What is so funny?" she wanted to know. After Billy told her what he had just witnessed, she laughed, too. She temporarily forgot her determination to be miserable. Again picking up the shovel, Alana positioned it next to the hole she had just made, in order to shape the outside border of the rose bed.

"When at first you do not succeed—" Alana started to say.

"Give up!" Billy finished her sentence for her. Angela giggled with delight as Billy took the shovel away from Alana. "Mind if I help? You do not seem to be doin' much good with this weather-beaten ground." With amazingly little effort, he turned over a deep shovelful. "How big you want this thing?" he asked as he quickly turned over another shovelful.

Glad to have the help, she walked around the area, forming the boundaries of her rose bed, leaving markers of twigs or stones at the corners. With growing interest, Angela sat under a nearby walnut tree to watch and leaned against its trunk for support. It seemed as if only minutes had passed when Billy turned over the last shovelful of dirt. "Thank you, Billy. I must admit I was greatly in need of help. But I think I can take it from here. At least I hope I am able to pull the weeds and grass out and dig six little holes just deep enough to set the rose bushes in."

"I will fetch them over here for you," he offered as he headed back to the barn where he had them soaking in the water trough of one of the stalls. Silently watching

Alana as she knelt down on her knees and began pulling long runners of grass out of the dirt, Angela's curiosity reached its peak.

"What are you doing all of that work for?" she asked.

Continuing her work, Alana explained how she was preparing a garden bed to plant several rose bushes she had bought last Saturday. She was now pulling out all of the weeds and grass that would not only distract from the roses, but would drain the soil of its many benefits. She went on to tell her about the rose garden she had when she was much younger and how much satisfaction she had obtained from the beautiful blooms. By the time Billy returned with the bushes, Angela was sitting at the edge of the bed crosslegged, fingering the ends of one of her long amber braids.

"Here you go. Six rose bushes intact. You want me to undo these gunny sacks down here at the bottom?" he offered helpfully.

"There is really no need in that. The roots will grow right through them," she explained. "Just set them against the tree. I shall plant them when I am certain I have pulled every one of these weeds and all of this grass."

Angela looked suspiciously at the armload of prickly plants that Billy laid near her. "Are you doing all of this work just to plant them scrawny thorn bushes?" she asked, wrinkling her nose up in bewilderment.

"It is 'those' scrawny thorn bushes," Alana corrected her poor grammar, "and the answer is yes. It may be hard to believe by looking at them right now, but someday those 'thorn bushes,' as you call them, will bear gorgeous velvety blooms. Do you not know what a rose is?"

"I know it is some kind of flower. But I still cannot see those old thorn bushes ever being something worth looking at," she shook her head with hollow hopes for the limp, scraggly limbs covered with ugly spiked thorns.

"They may not bloom this year, but, with proper care and a lot of faith, those bushes will bear beautiful red roses so fair you will beg me for one to wear in your pretty auburn hair," Alana said proudly.

"May I help you?" Angela finally asked. With a warm

smile, Alana tossed her a trowel and showed her how to loosen the stubborn weeds at the roots so that they could be pulled out easily. Not keeping track of the time, they were surprised to hear the dinnerbell when it clanged loudly, calling everyone to the table.

"Go wash up and eat lunch. I shall get something when I am finished. I am almost ready to plant the bushes anyway," she told Angela.

"I shall hurry. I want to help put them into the ground," Angela said eagerly as she ran off to eat. Alana stopped a moment to catch her breath and push her hair back out of her face. Most of it had come loose by now and hung in her way. Being alone, she dared unbutton another button and shake her blouse loosely, allowing the air to circulate through the damp material. Tiring somewhat, she returned to the last few weeds with less enthusiasm.

Bending over a particularly stubborn weed, she pulled at it with all of the strength she could muster in her tiring arms. A twig snapped nearby, alerting Alana to Brandon's presence. Realizing that her blouse was partially open, she grasped it tightly; but, not before Brandon had caught a glimpse of her breasts showing over her low-cut white camisole underneath.

"What are you doing here?" she asked sharply, to which he answered simply, "I live here."

"I thought you were out checking fences. What are you doing sneaking up on me like that?" she snapped, more embarrassed than angry.

"I—I wanted to see if you are coming to eat," he replied, almost forgetting why he had come. "Lizzie has your place set."

"I cannot go to the table as dirty as I am. Look at me, my hair has fallen and my dress is completely soiled," Alana protested.

"Your dress looks fine to me," he replied, looking at the part of her blouse that she held so closely. "Wash up, brush your hair, and come on. If you do not eat, you will lose all of your strength; then how will you finish?"

She had to admit that she was beginning to feel weak and her stomach had begun sending distress signals at least an hour ago.

Still, she did not want Brandon seeing her looking so horrible. "Give me a minute," she finally replied. "I want to clean up a little. I shall hurry."

"I can wait for you."

Quickly she returned to her room and undressed. While washing her arms and neck with a damp sponge, she pulled a fresh dress of yellow and orange from her closet. She fumbled with the many hooks as she hurried to get into her dress. Lacking enough time to put her hair up, she brushed it out and tied it back with a bright yellow ribbon. She allowed it to hang loosely down her back as she had seen Lilian's hair many times. She was slightly uncomfortable about wearing her hair down, for her mother's voice echoed through her memory warning her that women who wore their hair down in public were bad women. Yet, Lilian was not a bad woman, nor was Anne. Occasionally, both of them wore their hair down. Even with this rationalization, she was still uneasy about going against one of her mother's strict taboos. But she was much too eager to join Brandon for lunch. She chose to ignore her mother's voice and not waste precious time putting her hair up properly. Out of the door she went.

By the time they sat down to eat, Angela was nearly through. Although Brandon suggested she take a short nap after such a heavy meal, Angela sat beside them and listened to everything that was said. When Brandon asked Alana why she was clearing that small patch of ground, Angela piped in the answer. She repeated everything Alana had told her, almost word for word. When he asked Alana if she knew much about gardening, Angela related the story about the rose garden Alana had as a child. Then Brandon asked Alana if there was anything that Angela did not know and they all laughed.

Noticing Brandon looking curiously at her, she asked him if something was wrong. Realizing that he must have been staring at her, he explained, "I was just noticing how beautiful your hair is. I do not think I have ever seen you wear it down before." Alana thanked him uncomfortably. She was pleased that he approved, but found responding to such a direct compliment awkward. Angela listened with obvious distress as they talked more and ate less. She kept insisting they hurry. She wanted to finish the rose garden so the flowers could hurry and bloom. Rather than listen to her whine, they finished their meal. Afterward Brandon walked with his two companions on either arm. They went back to the garden site, where they found Billy busy pulling out the last of the grass and weeds. He grinned sheepishly when the trio approached, "I thought maybe that it was too much for you and maybe you had to give up," he said. "Just thought I would lend a helping hand, is all."

"Thank you, Billy, you are so sweet," Alana replied. "Looks like we are about ready to plant the bushes, doesn't it?" She walked over to the tree to get one of the bushes. Angela also picked one out, imitating everything Alana did as she helped plant the first of the bushes.

Brandon watched feeling somehow distant from the group as they eagerly devoted their full attention to selecting the perfect spots and firmly planting the rose bushes. Standing back to admire their work, they complimented one another lavishly. Brandon was certain his words went unnoticed when he told Alana that he was going to his study to work on his records. The three of them were piling the loose weeds and grass into a huge bundle as he walked away, still unnoticed and feeling quite chagrined.

After everything was tidied up, Alana exclaimed proudly, "That looks just fine. What do you think, Brandon? Brandon?" Alana looked around. "Where did Brandon go?"

"I saw him go into his study a while ago," Angela replied offhandedly.

"Oh, well, I guess he had something important to do," Billy remarked. "But, I must agree, the garden looks real nice. Soon it will be just chock full of pretty roses."

"It will not be, if we do not water it," Alana noted. Angela eagerly volunteered to get the watering can and fill it from the pool surrounding the patio fountain. Each plant received an ample amount of water as Angela made several trips. While Billy was carrying the grass off, Angela and Alana decided a victory celebration was in order. They begged Lizzie to make something special for supper and have it on the table because they wanted her to join them in their celebration. Angela then dragged Lizzie by her hand out of the kitchen to see their fabulous rose garden.

"See those thorn bushes?" Angela asked proudly. "Those are rose bushes that someday are going to be covered with beautiful red roses. I helped."

As Billy returned, Lizzie expressed how deeply impressed she was and agreed a major celebration was in order. "You comin' to it, Billy?"

"I wouldn't miss it," he replied. "But, I better go get the horses fed and curried now. That way, I will have time to clean up before supper." He hurried away to the barn.

After a quick bath, Alana returned to her room in hopes of a short nap, but found that although extremely tired, she was too keyed up to sleep. She decided to go ahead and choose her dress for the evening. As she flipped through her dresses, her umbrella kept falling in her way. Finally, she pulled it out and laid it on top of the tall wardrobe cabinet.

After selecting the amber-gold dress with brown-lace trimmings that she had worn the night she dined with Don Andrios in Shreveport, she pulled it out and hung it on the canopy at the foot of her bed. When she reached up to get the umbrella, she accidentally knocked if off behind the cabinet. Searching the floor below it, she could not see where it had fallen. While looking in the dark space behind it, she found it had gotten caught on the knob of the door partially hidden by the heavy furniture. The umbrella was not easily retrieved as her arm could barely reach the knob from which it was suspended. When she rescued her umbrella, she discovered that her curiosity was mounting. She reached for the knob and turned it. It was not locked as she had supposed; but, it was effectively blocked. The door baffled her. Was it to a closet as she first assumed or was it to the mysterious room concealed behind those thick dusty drapes and a forever closed door? Appreciating that it was none of her concern, she pushed the door shut and put the umbrella back inside the wardrobe door. Then she returned to the task of getting ready for dinner.

Alana chose to wear her hair with the front pulled back, but allowing the rest of it to flow smoothly down her back. To the devil with her mother's silly notions, Brandon liked it.

In hopes of seeing Brandon by a calculated chance, Alana decided to wait out on the patio for dinner to be called. She sat on a bench near the edge of the patio, where she could easily view the rose garden. Her thoughts drifted as she imagined the little bushes bearing the richly scented blooms. A tapping of a finger on her head made her heart jump. She looked up wanting to see Brandon's deep blue eyes gazing down at her, but was disappointed somewhat. It was Billy.

"Mind if I sit beside you?" He sat uncomfortably beside her a moment before adding, "I see you are admiring our handiwork."

She smiled as she admitted she was, and described the beautiful garden she envisioned. While she was talking to him, she realized that this was the first time she had ever seen Billy dressed up. Usually, he wore heavy denim pants and a plain cotton shirt. He now had on brown dress trousers and a fancy yellow shirt with shiny pearl buttons down the front and at the cuffs. He had shined his boots and tried to tame his long blonde hair back with a wet comb. Alana hoped that all of this was not for her sake because the only affections she felt for Billy were the same as a sister would feel for a brother.

Just then, Brandon stepped out of his doorway and headed their way. He also had made a special effort to look his best. His attire included black dress trousers and a casually opened dinner jacket worn over a black vest with silver thread woven into the fabric. He wore a dark-blue scarf tucked into an azure-blue silk shirt. Alana's heart leaped as he came closer, looking so magnificent. Although she hoped Billy's special attire was not for her benefit, she did hope that Brandon's noteworthy appearance was just for her.

With little room left on the bench, he stood before them joining in on a conversation that was now commending the cool evening breeze. After such a hot day, it was nice that it had turned into a lovely evening with a delicate breeze softly stirring the trees and crickets beginning to warm up for their nightly concerto. An occasional bellow of a mother cow warning her young not to stray could be heard drifting in the distance joined in by the sharp barking of the many tree frogs. The sudden clanging of the dinnerbell broke nature's melody into sudden silence. Presenting his hand, Brandon offered his assistance in walking Alana to the table. Quickly, Billy volunteered to take her other arm.

As Alana was so graciously accompanied by a man on either arm, she remarked, "It certainly is nice to have my two gentlemanly friends usher me to dinner." She placed an emphasis on the word friends for Billy's benefit, worried he might have misunderstood their relationship as something more. But, it was Brandon's ears that were pricked by the hidden stress behind the word.

Just inside the door, Lizzie was waiting for everyone to be seated. It was not often she ate at the main table with any of the family members and had dressed in her prettiest Sunday-go-to-meeting dress for the occasion. She actually blushed when Brandon offered her a compliment telling him to 'hush up his sweet talkin'.' Angela was already seated and the food sat on the table still steaming. Brandon and Billy both reached for Alana's chair at the same instant; but, believing Alana would prefer for Billy to do the honors, Brandon politely stepped back. Waiting until Alana had been seated, he proceeded to sit down beside her. Billy hurried around to sit in Lilian's chair directly across from her. Lizzie walked around and stood behind the chair next to Billy. After a moment, she chuckled from somewhere deep within her, "Well, ain't nobody gonna pull out my chair for me?" Billy and Brandon both got up to assist Lizzie; but again Brandon allowed Billy to do the honors, wondering why he felt so perturbed about it.

The supper was nothing fancy and the conversation

consisted only of small talk. But, after everyone had set their forks down, Lizzie announced she had a surprise and ordered everyone to remain seated as she scurried off to the kitchen. When she returned, she was carrying a large triple layer deep-chocolate cake with mounds of creamy chocolate icing piled on top. She explained that it was for the celebration that Alana and Angela had asked for honoring their fine new rose garden. Angela was allowed to cut the cake, and generous pieces were passed around. Then, in toast-like fashion, they waved their first bite in the air in unison before proceeding to eat it, "To the rose garden."

To Brandon's dismay, the conversation returned to that rose garden. Angela wondered if a small rock-lined pond might not look nice among the bushes. Billy submitted the idea of building a sturdy fence around it to keep the armadilloes and 'other critters' out. Alana agreed they might consider a fence since the garden was somewhat away from the protection of the house.

"I will try to find enough lumber in those scraps up in the loft tomorrow and see what I can do about a fence," Billy promised.

"I really would appreciate it. I certainly hate the thought of the garden getting trampled," Alana replied.

Brandon listened patiently, waiting to find a chance to suggest that they remove themselves to the patio. Just as he was about to speak, Mickey burst in through the front door shouting, "We are back!" Everyone got up to greet the returning picnickers, including a disappointed Brandon. They met Mickey in the hallway. Excitedly he displayed a small shoe box as he gasped, "Wait until you see the great loggerhead I got here. Mr. Sobey helped me catch him down by the creek. His shell is about that long!" He held his hands about eight inches apart.

Alana looked at him questioningly, "What, might I ask, is a loggerhead?"

His little pugged nose, showing signs of being a bright shade of pink between his many freckles, wrinkled as he replied with disbelief, "A loggerhead is only just about the fastest, meanest snappin' turtle there is. Want to see?"

"Get that thing out of the house," Lilian ordered as she came up behind him. "If you insist on keeping that creature, it will be outside!" She pointed to the door as she gave him a little push for momentum. "That boy!"

The corners of Angela's mouth turned down as she listened to how the twins stumped everyone playing hide-'n'-seek. They laughed as they explained how they buried themselves in a huge stack of hay that was in the field where they were playing.

"Sounds like everyone had a good time," Lizzie chuckled, plucking hay straw from Jim's tousled hair.

"I should say so, or at least I think so. Jake spent all of his time with Karen Simms. I just assume he had a good time. I hardly saw him," Lilian said as she winked at the boy.

"Aw, Mama, we were just talking," Jake said unconvincingly. "It was Brenda here who you should be talking about. Craig Thomason sure did seem to hang around her a little more than was necessary." He grinned as he successfully turned everyone's attention to Brenda, who was looking down at her shoes while blushing.

"I think we all managed to have fun," Lilian beamed, as if enjoying a private thought. "But, now, it is getting to be bedtime and I know of some children that need to wash up and get on to bed—now! You, too, Angela, come with me," Lilian hurried them down the hall and into the kitchen for a quick scrubbing.

"Why don't we go outside to enjoy the cool evening air?" Brandon suggested, quickly taking Alana by the arm. Billy followed behind them, as the hallway was not wide enough to accommodate the three of them arm-in-arm. But, once they were outside, he latched on to the free arm. At Alana's suggestion, the three of them sat down on a bench near the fountain. It was the only one long enough to allow all of them to be seated. Before anyone was able to speak, Lilian shouted through a window for Brandon to come inside for a moment. Reluctantly, he promised his prompt return and left to see what Lilian wanted.

Billy noticed how Alana's eyes followed Brandon wistfully as he walked away. It was not until Brandon had disappeared through the door that she allowed her gaze to return to him. "He is the one you care for, isn't he?"

"Why do you ask?"

"I was hoping that maybe you could care about me," he replied with concern evident in his soft voice.

"But, Billy, I do care for you. I care a great deal. But, I feel I must be honest with you, I care for you only as a sister cares for a brother. If I have led you to believe otherwise, I have done you a great disservice and I am sorry. I would never intentionally hurt you because I really do care," Alana said as she gently took his hand in hers. "I treasure your friendship. I hope I have not lost it."

"I will always be your friend, Alana. But, I notice you have avoided my question. Is Brandon the one you care for? If you feel it is none of my business, just say so. Whatever you do tell me will be a secret between friends," Billy promised, continuing to hold her hand. "I would like to know, though."

"Please, understand that it is not because I do not trust you that I cannot answer you. I just am not positive what my feelings are for Brandon yet. I do know my heart races whenever he is near, but I am not certain why. I think it is partially admiration and adoration, but I also feel a sense of fear whenever he is around. I do not understand that either." Alana tried to explain her complicated emotions while Billy listened silently.

Brandon paused in the doorway as he watched Billy and Alana intimately holding hands and discussing clearly confidential matter. Their heads were very close. A strong petulant emotion overtook him as he felt he realized the depth of their affections for each other. It was obvious from the tender way their hands touched and the sensitive looks that were shared between them. He tried to ignore the curiously throbbing ache that resulted in his heart. Determined not to allow his deeper emotions to be reborn so easily, he tried convincing himself that Alana's interest in Billy was actually for the best.

"Seems Mickey had a little too much apple pie for supper. Lilian needed someone to carry him to bed," Brandon explained as he rejoined them.

"Is he going to be all right?" Alana asked, worried it might be serious.

"He will be fine. All he needs is a full night of sleep and to take it easy a while. After he named what all he put into his stomach today, I am surprised he can even move. Yes, I believe his best cure is a good night's rest," Brandon replied assuringly.

"Speaking of rest, it is getting late and I have to get up early. I have a lot I want to get done tomorrow. You will have to excuse me," Billy said politely and stood up to leave. Before he walked away, he added, "I will see you tomorrow, Alana." He turned and walked away.

"Nice fellow that Billy," Brandon probed as he watched both Billy and Alana.

"Yes, he is quite nice," Alana agreed.

After a lengthy silence, Brandon mentioned he should be getting off to bed, too. He had a full day ahead of him as well. He lingered a moment uncomfortably before taking a step toward his room.

"See you tomorrow," Alana replied hopefully, rather disheartened Brandon considered his rest so important. She watched him as he crossed the patio and went through his study door. She wondered why he seemed to avoid being alone with her. "Maybe he feels just as uncomfortable as I do," she thought to herself, remembering the turmoil that ran through her when he kissed her. Suddenly, it occurred to her that she probably kissed badly, not having any idea as to how it was done. Having never been kissed before, other than the peck on her cheek by her father, she might have done something wrong. And Brandon, having kissed many girls, probably noticed a horrid difference. Sadly, she resolved that he simply found out that he did not enjoy kissing her and really did not care about being alone with her as well. Tears tried to find their way into her eyes, but she managed to blink them back. She got up gloomily and went into her room not knowing that Brandon stood at his window watching her with questions of his own in his mind.

Pulling her curtains together and locking the door,

Alana prepared herself for bed. After putting on a light cotton gown, she washed her face and climbed into bed. She left the curtains closed, although her windows were open as she prepared to read a few poems to relax her before blowing out the light and going to sleep. The book had barely been opened when there came a quick knock at her door. Pulling her cover up around her, she asked aloud, "Who is it?"

"It is me, Lilian. May I come in? I want to talk to you," a whispered voice filtered in through the window.

"Just a minute," Alana whispered back. She paused a moment, wondering why suddenly she was whispering, before tiptoeing to the door and unlocking it. "Come on in," she said as she hurried back to her covers.

Quickly, Lilian slipped in, "I was going to wait until tomorrow, but I saw your light through the window. I hope you do not mind this intrusion," she explained in a rush of words.

"I was just reading a little poetry. Please, come on in and sit down," she replied as she patted the bed with her hand inviting her to sit.

Lilian sat on the edge of the bed, bursting to tell Alana the events of the day. "He wants me to help him celebrate the anniversary of his restaurant's first year by dining with him at the restaurant next Saturday evening. He is planning to send special invitations to his better patrons and have a large cake to offer them that evening. And he has asked me to dine at his table with him. He wants to pick me up early, around five or so, to be sure we are there in time to greet the early diners. He said he would bring me home right after he closed, which is usually around ten. What do you think? Should I go? The children are not invited. I cannot explain our togetherness as being for them as I did today. Everyone will know it is purely for my own pleasure," Lilian said worriedly.

"Is it? What I mean to ask is do you want to go?" Lilian nodded assuringly to Alana's question. "Well, as I see it, you want to go but feel the need of someone's permission. If you enjoyed being with him today and if you feel you will enjoy being with him in the future, I think you should go and enjoy the evening. Let me ask you this: Why would you not go?"

"I am not sure. I guess I have considered not going because of Mark. Somehow, I still feel guilty. Today, for example, I had a fabulous time with Archie and when he kissed my forehead in a fond farewell, my heart soared. I think I am becoming quite fond of him. Yet, somewhere deep inside of me is this feeling of guilt which condemns me for enjoying myself," Lilian replied, looking deeply into Alana's eyes for some phenomenal foresight.

"In time, I believe your feelings will sort themselves out. As for now, give Archie a chance. I believe he is a good man and deserves an opportunity. You might explain to him how you feel. Let him know your past emotions are struggling with those of the present. Be open and honest with him. He will understand and probably be proud you entrusted him with your confidences." Alana wondered from where she withdrew such wisdom. She certainly was no authority on love and emotions. In fact, she was totally confused about her own experiences with similarly fragile feelings.

"I think you are right. I should go. I shall go!" Lilian spoke determinedly as she pounded her fist into the bedcovers. "Thank you for helping me decide. You certainly have become a good friend in the short time you have been here. I really like you."

Alana smiled as she replied, "I feel the same for you. Actually, I have grown quite fond of the whole family and that even includes Lizzie."

"Oh, that reminds me. Brandon received a letter Saturday inviting the entire family for the Thanksgiving holidays to New Orleans. Uncle Lloyd is planning a huge feast for all of the relatives he can possibly round up. Brandon has already made plans to go hunting with some of his buddies in South Texas during much of November, but I really want to see Uncle Lloyd and Aunt Mary. I have told Brandon I plan to go. The children are going, too. So is Lizzie. Since that will leave you without a class to teach and no one will be around to keep you company, except Billy and possibly Abe, I thought you might want to go with us. We will be gone only a few weeks."

Alana thought a moment before answering, "I think not. I am not a qualified member of the family. I would be a stranger, not knowing anyone there. I do appreciate your invitation, I really do, but I feel I must decline."

"You are part of the family as far as I am concerned," Lilian insisted.

"Thank you, but I would not be comfortable intruding on a family gathering. No, I would be happier staying here. Besides, I could use the time to catch up on my reading. I also have letters I should write to my family and friends. And I shall want to start my Christmas gifts for the children. I do not mind being alone. Actually, I am rather comfortable with solitude."

Lilian could not understand how anyone could get used to being alone to the point of being comfortable with solitude. She tried several more fruitless arguments attempting to make Alana change her mind. Finally, she said, "If you change your mind, let me know because the invitation stands."

"If I do have a change of heart, I shall not hesitate to tell you," Alana promised.

"Since I cannot change your decision tonight, I guess I may just as well go to bed," Lilian remarked, getting off the bed. When Lilian moved away, Alana happened to notice the door that had her puzzled and asked Lilian where it led.

"That door just goes to a small storage room," Lilian replied uneasily.

"A storage room? Would it be possible for my trunks to be stored in there? They are quite bothersome. I put them in the back corner of the classroom, but they still seem to get in the way," Alana asked, wondering why Lilian seemed so uncomfortable discussing a storage room.

"Are they empty?"

"They are except for a few medications that I have had no need for since I arrived in Texas. I have not had any of my horrid headaches in months. There are also a few packing boxes and sacks that I have no need for in one of the trunks. I really would like to get them out of the way."

After a thoughtful pause, Lilian said, "If Brandon will let me have the key, I shall have Billy fetch the trunks tomorrow morning. Oh, by the way, I told the children they could sleep an extra hour in the morning. They are pretty tired. I hope you do not mind. I know I should have checked with you first."

"That is fine with me. After all you are the boss. I shan't mind an extra hour of sleep myself." Alana smiled, letting Lilian know she really did not mind.

"See you tomorrow then," Lilian said as she closed the door behind her.

Alana sat in bed staring at the part of the door that was visible. She wondered why they kept this room locked. She felt it was unusual as they locked no other doors. "They must certainly set a great value on whatever is inside or maybe they have something to hide," she thought, allowing her imagination to get the best of her. Whatever the reason, it certainly had her curiosity aroused. She contrived all sorts of wild ideas, even as she fell asleep.

In spite of the extra hour she could have slept, Alana was up early the next morning. She was in the classroom straightening her desk when Billy knocked at her door. To let him in, she had to return to her room. When she opened the door, Billy explained he had come for the trunks and followed her back into the classroom to get them.

One at a time, he carried them outside, setting them near the door to the storage room. Alana followed him as far as her own door watching curiously as Billy fumbled with the lock. Putting the key between his teeth, he quickly dragged the two trunks inside and promptly returned to relock the door. He checked the door's security twice before walking away. "I have to get this key back to Brandon immediately." He shouted as he waved to her, "See ya later."

"Certainly," Alana shouted back with her thoughts focused on the mysterious door. Suppressing her curiosity, she reminded herself that it was none of her affair what was behind this locked door or that shrouded window and returned to her classroom.

Alana rang her little bell at the door, signaling class time. Mickey came to class with the other children, but Alana had to send him to his room to rest shortly before class started. He complained of stomach cramps. She had the rest of the children practicing their sums when she heard loud banging just outside her window. While listening to Brenda recite her 'plus 10's,' she looked out the window to see what was making such a racket, but could not see anything unusual. She asked if any of the children knew what all of the noise was; no one did. Moments before she dismissed class, the noises stopped.

After the children left, Alana put the books away and locked the door. She stopped in her room to check her hair in the mirror. While she was running a comb through her hair, which she was wearing down again, Billy stuck his head inside of her opened door.

"I got something I want you to see," he said eagerly.

She followed him to the end of the walkway in front of her room and looked in the direction he silently pointed. There she saw a beautiful wooden planked fence around the rose garden. Four thin running boards were spaced evenly from just inches off of the ground to about waist height. Heavy posts anchored the fence at each corner and at intervals in between. A broad smile crossed her partially opened mouth.

"Billy, you built the fence, and such a handsome fence!" she exclaimed as gleefully as she threw her arms around him, "Thank you."

"You like it then?" he asked innocently.

"Like it? I adore it," she assured him, letting go of him to get a closer look at the fence now protecting her rose garden.

Brandon went again unnoticed as he stood in the doorway to the kitchen, watching Alana embrace Billy.

"No wonder she just wants to keep it as strictly friends between us. Well, I shall not interfere," he decided firmly as he turned his back to them and went inside.

Chapter Seven

For the third time, Alana tried to put her hair up into a spool of simple curls and for the third time part of it fell down over her face. It suited her fine to wear her hair down on cooler days, but this late August morning was particularly hot and she desperately wanted her thick heavy hair off of her neck. The summer heat seemed to cling mercilessly to her hair on such days.

Almost ready to scream in exasperation, Alana slowly and carefully attempted one last time to put her hair up. Finally, she had it up and bent over her dressing table to rest her throbbing head in her hands. She knew one of her frontal headaches was on the way when she started seeing dull white spots earlier that morning, but had hoped it would be a mild one. The bed beckoned her with silent invitations to its comfort as she finished getting ready and she planned to return to it as soon as class was over. But for now she had to get ready. There was nothing she could do to stop the pain. With Brandon already out in the pasture somewhere, there was no way for her to get the key to the storage room where her medications were. "I shall just have to brave it," she thought to herself, and walked into the classroom to ring the bell that summoned the children.

Rather than greet the children at the door as she usually did, she sat at her desk and explained that she felt a little under the weather. Brenda thoughtfully volunteered to pass out the spellers for which Alana was grateful. Recently Brenda had become her most outgoing pupil as Angela digressed into a shell of her own.

Even though Angela refused to discuss it, Alana knew

152

that Lilian's regular visitations from Archie Sobey had a great deal to do with Angela's growing depression. The closer her mother seemed to Archie, the further Angela sank into her despondent self. Seeing the need to spend more time with Angela these days, Alana hoped for a chance to help Angela understand her mother's growing relationship with Archie. They spent many afternoon hours tending to the rose garden, which was rewarding them early with many bright red blooms. Angela took complete charge of the watering and gave each bush an ample share everyday. Some days Angela would talk Alana into a horseback ride after she finished her watering. Angela preferred to ride bareback, but Alana had enough trouble with a nice padded saddle. Many times after a lengthy ride, Alana found she had to temporarily adjust her walking to suit her aching backside. Whenever she could, Alana talked Angela into a walk through the pasture or a swim in the pond instead. And, although she managed to lift Angela's spirits on several of these occasions, she could never get her to open up and release the emotions building up inside. By now even Lilian suspected Angela's disapproval and tried many times to convince her that there was nothing wrong with Archie's visits. Both she and especially Archie tried to win her affections for him by doing special things.

One Sunday afternoon, he managed to get her to smile by presenting her with a fluffy little gray kitten. Her depression was lost to her delight as she cuddled her new pet and announced gleefully that she was going to call the kitten Smoky. This happy reaction lasted only a few minutes. When she realized she had let her guard down, she again became sullen. She thanked him stiffly and quietly turned away and carried the kitten to her room without another word. Although she and the kitten became inseparable, she was no fonder of Archie. And, in order to get Angela's cooperation in class, Alana allowed the kitten in the classroom.

Today the kitten sat on the floor at Angela's feet resting peacefully and Angela participated willingly in the spelling bee Alana was directing from her desk. The throbbing in her temples made it hard for Alana to concentrate on each child's reply to the words she called out from this week's lists. Occasionally she got the younger children's list confused with the more complicated words for the older ones and chaos resulted. She was finding it hard to cope and was rubbing her forehead rhythmically with her fingertips when she realized John was talking to her, "I am sorry, what did you say?"

"When do you spell happy with only one p?" he asked somewhat impudently.

"You do not spell it with one p; there are two," she told him, wondering what this outburst was about.

"Well, Mickey just spelled it h-a-p-y, and you did not put him out. He should be out," John insisted.

"I am sorry. I guess I was not listening closely enough. What would you children say if I dismissed the class early?" Alana asked, knowing the reaction before she finished the question. "Then consider it done. You can explain to your mother that I do not feel well at all."

Once the children had left, she laid her head down on her desk, feeling its coolness against her hot cheek. She prayed for some relief, but it did not come. The throbbing worsened and by now had engulfed the entire front of her head. Her breath began to feel labored as she forced it through clenched teeth. It was almost unbearable. Her thoughts were submerged in the agony she was experiencing when Brandon came to the opened door of her classroom. When he had noticed the children outside playing so early, he was worried and came to see what had happened. She did not hear his footsteps as he walked across the bare wooden floor. He reached out and gently touched the back of her neck, "Alana, what is wrong?"

Hot tears flowed down her cheeks as she answered, "Oh, Brandon, my head feels as though it will burst any minute. I cannot stand the pain; I just cannot stand it!" She was reduced to sobs as Brandon took her into his arms. He lifted her from her chair and carried her to her still unmade bed. As he gently laid her down, he asked if there was anything he could do for her.

"My medication. I need my pain powders. They are in

my trunk. In there. In the storage room," she spoke
through short raspy breaths. "Please, get them for me.
Please. My medication." Alana was slipping in and out of a
delirium caused by the severe pain.

Frightened by Alana's heavy breathing along with the
perspiration forming on her forehead and down her
neck, Brandon did not bother to go for his key in his safe.
Instead, he grasped the huge wardrobe cabinet and
shoved it far enough to the side to be able to open the door
leading into the storage room. Stepping over a chest just
inside the doorway, he rushed in to find Alana's trunks.
The room was so dark he could barely make out the shape
of her trunks sitting near the outside door. He rushed to
them, nearly falling as he stumbled on a misplaced box.
Quickly, he yanked the first trunk open and felt inside. It
was empty. The second trunk had to be forced open.
Tossing the many empty boxes and sacks aside, he finally
found a cloth pouch with several bottles and a small tin
box.

He hurried back into Alana's room with the medicine
pouch in his hand. He found Alana now completely
unconscious. After readjusting to the light, he began
reading the labels on the bottles. None of them were for
pain. He opened the tin box and found several little
packets of white powder with no explanation as to what
they were for. Lifting Alana's head, he spoke loudly,
causing her to become conscious long enough to confirm
that the packets were what she needed. He mixed the
powder in a cup with a little water and helped Alana hold
her head up to drink it.

Brandon sat on the edge of her bed, massaging her
temples with his fingertips. Slowly, her breathing eased
and she seemed to drift into a restful sleep. He sat
watching her motionless form.

"You are so beautiful," he said aloud as he took in every
detail of her face without fear of being discovered doing
so. She reminded him of a sleeping angel. A smile crossed
his face as he remembered how that fragile jaw clenched
in warning of her fiery temper.

Although she seemed to be in better control of that

sharp tongue these days, she still had a tendency to explode when someone crossed her. Sadly, he attributed her calmer temperament to Billy. His own temper flared as he remembered the afternoon Billy and Alana spent painting that blamed fence white. Why their laughter and mutual delight should result in his own anger, he was not certain. He suspected he had feelings developing for Alana, but tried to squelch them. Now as he watched her sleep so peacefully, he knew that he did care for her. How deeply his affections went, he was not sure, but he had to admit that the feelings were there.

"I hope Billy realizes how lucky he is to have somehow gained the attention of one so dear and beautiful," he spoke aloud. He remorsefully touched her tender lips with his finger as he recalled the night his own lips caressed them. A heavy pounding possessed his heart even now as he relived those brief moments from what seemed a lifetime ago.

Alana slept most of the afternoon. When she opened her eyes she realized the headache that had forced her to tears earlier had subsided, but there was still a tenderness at the touch of her forehead or a quick turn of her head. Slowly she eased herself up to sit at the edge of her bed. At the sight of the open tin box on her dressing table, she remembered that Brandon had been there. She wondered where he was now and exactly what time it was. As she reached across the bed to turn the clock to face her, she noticed a single rose lying on the pillow beside her. Gently, she lifted the rose from its resting place and touched it to her nose to enjoy its beautiful fragrance. Then carefully looking over her treasure, she noticed each and every thorn had been removed so she would not prick herself. "How sweet," she thought as she lightly kissed its velvety petals. This was certainly a pleasant surprise to Alana, who had resigned herself to believing Brandon cared absolutely nothing for her. Over the past few weeks, Brandon seemed to avoid her, never allowing himself to be alone with her. When they happened to meet, he was cordial—too cordial as far as Alana was concerned. Then, just when she was ready to believe he could never care for her, he left her a rose to cheer her up, showing he did indeed care to some degree.

She lay back on her bed and dreamed of Brandon slipping in so as not to disturb her, being ever so careful in placing the rose on her pillow. With that thought in mind, she got up and waltzed around the room with her precious rose in her hands. Then, after checking her hair and smoothing out her dress, Alana left her room to see if Lizzie or Lilian had a small vase to put her special rose in. She found Lizzie in the kitchen preparing supper and asked her about a vase.

"My, what a beautiful rose," Lizzie exclaimed as she searched the pantry for a vase.

"Thank you, Brandon picked it for me," she said proudly. She no longer tried to hide her feelings from Lizzie for it was useless. Lizzie had some sort of sixth sense about her.

"Oh, Master Brandon did, did he?" Lizzie asked with a raise of her eyebrows. "Then, I must find a most suitable vase." She sorted through several before coming on a small footed cut-glass which she handed to Alana.

"He certainly has an eye for beauty. That is a fine rose," she remarked with a wink.

Alana placed her rose into the vase with some water and left Lizzie to her cooking. On the way to her room, she passed Angela sitting on the walkway slowly stroking Smoky. Angela looked up at Alana, when she heard her coming.

"Did that rose come from our rose garden?" she asked.

"I think so, your Uncle Brandon picked this rose," Alana told her.

"It is so pretty. It has to be one of ours," she decided. "May I see it?"

Alana knelt down beside Angela to let her get a closer look at the rose. "Yes, that must be one of ours. Do you not think so, Smoky?"

"You really love that kitten Mr. Sobey gave you, don't you?" Alana asked as she sat down beside Angela and Smoky on the cool walkway.

"I love Smoky a lot," she said softly. Her tone changed as

she sharply added, "But I hate Mr. Sobey!"

"Angela, how can you hate Mr. Sobey? You hardly know him," Alana asked, hoping to get to the bottom of this once and for all.

"I hate him, is all," she retorted with a scowl clouding her small face.

"But you have no reason to hate him. He likes you. He has as much as told me so. Why can you not like him?"

"He is not my father and I do not want him to be. I hate him," she replied, narrowing her eyes as she spoke.

"Do you think he is trying to replace your father? Is that why you hate him?" Alana asked as she began to analyze Angela's fears.

"Yes, if my mother likes him, she might marry him and then everyone will forget all about my father. I still love him," she answered with desolate tears trailing down her cheeks.

"Darling, no one is going to forget your father," Alana assured her as she gently pulled Angela to her breast, "You must not believe such a thing. Let me try to explain something to you. Since you got Smoky you have grown very fond of him, am I right?"

Angela nodded, while sniffing back her tears.

"I guess that means you no longer care for Sawdust and have forgotten all about your fine horse."

"No, I have not! I still love Sawdust," she answered and pulled away, angry that Alana could say such a thing.

"But you must not love Sawdust anymore because you just told me you love Smoky. You cannot possibly care for the horse now."

"I can too!"

"What makes you think your mother is any different than you are? Just because she has grown fond of Mr. Sobey does not mean she loves your father or his wonderful memory any less. Her new feelings for Mr. Sobey will not change any of her feelings for your father anymore than your new feelings for Smoky has changed any of your feelings for Sawdust." Alana hoped Angela understood the message she was trying to convey.

"It is not the same," Angela insisted.

"Isn't it?" Alana asked as she got up. "Think about it. Mr. Sobey is not a threat to your father's memory. No one can be. If you think about it, you both really have something in common. You both like kittens and you both care for your mother a great deal."

When Alana left, Angela was asking Smoky what he thought about it all. Alana hoped the cat was open-minded enough to agree with her and help Angela to soon become her bright, cheerful self again. There was one good aspect to the weeks Angela spent sulking. She had suffered a great loss of appetite and most of her chubbiness. With help, she should be able to keep her weight down.

When Alana got to her room, she set the rose on her dresser and allowed her thoughts to drift from Angela to Brandon. The rose had filled her heart with fresh hope. She could hardly wait until after supper. She was going to catch Brandon alone and thank him for the rose as well as for getting her medication. Vaguely she remembered that he pushed the wardrobe chest aside and entered the storage room through the door behind it. She turned to see if the doorway was still clear. It was not. Brandon had pushed the chest back. It only covered a few inches of the doorway now, but enough to prevent any use of the door. Her curiosity mounted as she wondered why he should bother to push the large cabinet back, blocking the door's edge. Again, she tried to suppress her curiosity by reminding herself that it was none of her business.

By suppertime, she had forgotten about the door and the room as well. During the meal, her thoughts returned to Angela who was pleasantly surprising everyone with her complete change of attitude. Laughter once again filled her tiny voice as she teased Mickey about one thing or another. Lilian stared at her in amazement. The entire family noticed it and exchanged curious glances. Alana was pleased except that Angela's appetite had returned as well and Alana had to remind her a lady never asks for seconds. When she finished, Angela once again joined the other children outside on the patio.

After the children had vacated the table, Lilian questioned both Brandon and Alana as to the reason for

Angela's sudden change in moods. Neither admitted knowing why; but agreed it was a pleasant change. They pushed their plates back as they discussed the possibilities. The heat in the room caused Lilian to suggest a move to the patio. Outside, they found the evening air had cooled somewhat, but was still pretty warm. Alana followed Lilian and Brandon on to the patio to rest on a shaded bench. While they sat silently enjoying a soft breeze, a horse could be heard approaching at a high gallop. They watched with growing interest as Billy leaped from his saddle, not bothering to tie his horse to a post. "It is a girl! Anne had a fine baby girl," he shouted happily as soon as he felt he was close enough to be heard.

"A girl?" Lilian asked as if doubting her own ears.

"Yep, a baby girl. Douglas delivered this one himself. The doctor did not get there in time."

"I thought Cynthia was supposed to help if the doctor did not make it," Lilian replied questioningly.

"Oh, she fainted dead away at the onset. She did not come to until after the baby had been born. You shoulda been there. It was hilarious. I was up a ladder paintin' the shutters like I was supposed to and Douglas was stirring up a new batch of paint when Cynthia came out on the porch screamin' at the top of her lungs, 'Her pains have come, her pains have come!' and waving her arms around like a chicken with her head cut off. Douglas, he ran to the porch, then back to me, then back to the porch, then back to me, only this time he asked me to go for the doctor. I took off and went as fast as I could. I had to track the doctor down at Mrs. Patton's. Her back is givin' her fits again. She claims to have these sharp little pains that shoot clean up her backbone . . ."

"Get on with it! What happened after you got the doctor?" Lilian demanded, not the least bit concerned with Mrs. Patton's pain right now.

"Well, me and the doctor rode back as quick as we could, but when we ran up the stairs to get to Anne's room, we heard the baby crying. Douglas came out holdin' his brand new baby girl in his arms. The doctor went ahead and checked over Anne and the baby while I followed Douglas down to the parlor for a stiff whiskey. When the doctor came down to the parlor, he said Anne and the baby could not be doin' better, but that Cynthia would probably need a weeks stay in bed. He said she was as pale as a ghost and barely able to speak," Billy chuckled at the thought.

"We must tell Lizzie!" Lilian said. "She told me all along it was going to be a girl. She certainly was right." Billy followed Lilian indoors to find Lizzie.

"I bet Douglas is ecstatic about now," Brandon said thoughtfully.

"I know he is. I imagine the whole family is," Alana agreed. "It is their dream come true. Anne especially wanted it to be a girl."

"I am glad," Brandon said rather wistfully.

A long silence fell over them as each tried to think of something clever that warranted saying. Alana was just about to revert back to the fine weather when Brandon spoke, "How is your head?"

"It is much better. Thank you," Alana replied.

"You had me scared there for a while. Do you have such headaches often?"

"I used to, but I have not had one since I came to Texas. I must say the one I had today was the worst I ever experienced. I really wanted to die there for a while," Alana admitted.

"At one point, I thought you might. You could barely breathe. I was terrified," Brandon told her with a look of honest concern in his blue eyes.

"Well, the pain is completely gone, now. I feel fine," she told him. She was about to thank him for his help and the rose when another horse was heard approaching the house. A single rider on a large white steed rode up to the hitching post at the end of the walkway by Brandon's study. He smiled and waved to Brandon as he secured his horse.

"Roth, over here!" Brandon shouted and waved the visitor an invitation to join the two of them.

Alana watched the handsome young man as he walked over and shook Brandon's hand. "I would like for you to meet Alana Stambridge. She is trying to teach Lilian's children a thing or two."

"If we had teachers who looked as beautiful when I was a boy, I never would have quit!" Roth remarked as he took his hat off for the introduction. When the hat came off, Alana got a better look at his curly dark blond hair and at the silver-blue eyes that were gazing over the length of her.

"You are too kind," she replied uncomfortably, as she did not care for the way his eyes traveled over her.

"Alana, this is Roth Felton, an old childhood buddy of mine. I may have been the oldest, but he was always the brains. I remember how he could con anyone into doing anything. He had the Widow Scales giving him anything he wanted at one time. When she first moved here, he actually had her believing he was a motherless waif. She was only too happy to fix pies, cakes, cookies, and plum jelly to take home to his suffering father. It was years before she ever met his mother, but Roth here told her she was his new mother. Roth could sweet talk honey from a bear if he ever had the notion to," Brandon chuckled.

"Is that so?" Alana replied coolly, not seeing the humor in tricking a kindhearted lonely woman. She found she had to look away from Roth as his stare seemed to chill her to the bone.

"He has been gone for nearly seven years. He returned only last month. You spent most of that time in California, did you not?" Brandon turned to ask Roth.

"Most of it was spent in San Francisco. But, I think I am home for good now. I never should have sold off the folks' place and left to seek my fortune. Fact is, the reason I came tonight is to see what kind of deal I can get from you on some cattle. I am thinking about buying the old Arnold place and running a few head on it. Think I can sweet talk say twenty from you on a promissory note? I will need all of my present cash for a down payment on the land," Roth explained with a look of desperation deep in his eyes.

With his glance finally off of her, Alana felt easier about looking at this strange friend of Brandon's. Why she felt distrustful of this exceedingly handsome man she was meeting for the first time, she did not know. There was nothing in his appearance to warrant her dislike. His large round eyes, slender nose, and jaunty chin with a dimple deeply etched in it should not cause her ill feelings, yet the feelings were there.

"Let's go into my study to discuss this. Alana, will you excuse us?" Brandon and Roth went into the study, stopping once in the doorway to laugh at something Roth had just said.

Narrowing her eyes as if trying to get a sharper view of this man, Alana wondered what had just been said. She wished she could get Brandon to laugh like that. "Maybe that is why I do not like him. I am jealous of him," she thought to herself trying to discover the reason she felt so.

"Whose horse?" Billy's words startled her. She had not noticed him behind her. He always seemed to come from nowhere.

"Some fellow called Roth Felton. Do you know him?" Alana asked, watching him carefully for his reaction.

"Roth? Goodness, yes, I know Roth. I heard he was back in town. Where is he?" Billy asked eagerly. It was obvious that Billy liked him.

"He and Brandon went into Brandon's study to discuss business," Alana told him, pointing to the open door they had just entered.

"Imagine, Roth's back. I gotta go say howdy to him. Roth Felton's back in town," he repeated as he quickly walked away to join them in the office. Meanwhile, Alana watched the doorway curiously, waiting rather impatiently for the men to return. When Lilian rejoined her, she also wanted to know whose horse was tied to the post. Alana simply stated Roth's name, expecting the same excitedly eager reaction from her as both Brandon and Billy had displayed.

"Roth is here," Lilian replied with a tone of caution edging her voice. "There has to be a reason for his return to Texas. Did he say what he came to see Brandon for?" she asked suspiciously.

"He wants Brandon to sell him some cattle. He says he

wants about twenty, but cannot pay for them right away," Alana told her, glad that Lilian's reaction seemed to agree with hers.

"That figures, he is probably flat broke. He never has any money; he gambles it away or spends it on his lady friends. Brandon will have a hard time getting the money and will not have the heart to take the cows back," Lilian said skeptically. "I know Brandon, always trustful. He will give him the cows. But, in all fairness, it has been seven years. Roth has had time to grow up. Maybe he has changed," she said hopefully.

Roth was the first to come through the door. Billy and Brandon were right on his heels. They stopped just outside of the door to discuss something Billy had just said. Roth turned so he could watch Alana. Avoiding his gaze, Alana gave her full attention to Lilian. While she was inventing a little small talk, the three men walked over to join them.

"Hello, Lilian, remember me?" Roth's voice came from closely behind Alana.

"Of course, I remember you, Roth. How can I forget the boy that tied the sleeves to all of my dresses together into one big heap?"

"Ah, well, I am not that mean anymore. I certainly hope you have not carried a grudge all of these years. I would hate to have anyone as pretty as you are mad at me," he said with a silvered tongue.

"I got over it," she said in a sweetened voice. He was winning her over rather skillfully, or so Alana decided.

"One reason I left California was the lack of beautiful women. By looking at the two of you, I know the decision to return to Texas was a sound one," he continued to win Lilian's favor.

"I do not know about that. I am certain there are beautiful women in California. Did you ever run into Stephanie DeLane while you were in San Francisco? She and her husband live near there, don't they?" Lilian asked.

"Yes, I saw her several times. In fact, she invited me to many of her parties. She was always having a party in that huge home or having catered picnics on their acres of lawn, that is, until her husband died," Roth told them as he kept his eyes on Alana.

"Until her husband died?" Brandon asked unbelievingly.

"Yes, he was robbed and killed in a side alley while visiting a friend in San Francisco. Did you not know? If you ask me, it was his good friend who did him in. She was cold-blooded enough."

"She?" Brandon questioned again.

"She was his mistress, Ruby Sweets. He paid for her apartment in exchange for—ah—well, in exchange for a few favors." Roth phrased it as politely as he knew how in the presence of ladies. "Walk with me to my horse, Brandon, my man, and I shall fill you in on a few details too delicate for the fragile ears of these lovely ladies."

Fear settled in the pit of Alana's stomach. Even though Stephanie was thousands of miles away, Alana hated hearing Brandon's true love was again available. She was terrified he might go to California to declare his love. The longer Brandon and Roth talked, the closer Alana came to crying. If Billy had not reached out and caressed her shoulder with a sturdy hand, she might have burst into tears in the presence of everyone.

"I am still feeling a little weak from my headache. I think I should retire early," she said, wanting desperately to escape to the seclusion of her room.

"Maybe you should rest tomorrow instead of holding class. I could run them through their spelling words and reading, if you want me to," Lilian offered, concerned for her friend.

"That will not be necessary. All I need is a night's rest. I shall be ready for class, I assure you," she told Lilian before leaving.

Once inside, she allowed her thoughts to run wild. Deciding Brandon was bound for California to reclaim his love as soon as possible, Alana started to cry. Just when she felt there was a chance for her in Brandon's heart, her hopes felt shattered. Through her tears, she noticed the rose on her dressing table, the proof that he might have been beginning to care for her. A tiny dash of hope still trickled inside of her as she picked the rose from its vase and brushed it gently against her cheek. There was still a chance Brandon's pride might prevent him from running into Stephanie's arms. Perhaps Brandon would be cautious before abandoning his Montaqua long enough to travel to California, find Stephanie, and return. Alana had not quite convinced herself, but was too tired to think about it any longer. Moments later she was asleep.

The next morning she woke early, still in the dress she had worn the evening before. Eager to see how Brandon was reacting to the news his friend had given him, Alana hurried to change clothes. She did take time enough to completely restyle her hair. She decided to wear it down since Brandon seemed to prefer it that way. With a tiny ribbon, she tied back only the hair at her temples and allowed it to blend in with the rest.

As she stepped from her room, she noticed Brandon tying a large satchel to the back of his saddle. Hurrying to catch him before he left, Alana's heart felt as though it might collapse. Although she was deeply afraid of his answer, she shouted to him while still several feet away, "Brandon, where are you going?"

"I have some business I must take care of," he said simply as he returned to strapping the heavy satchel down. "Why, do you need me for something?"

"No, not really. I just wanted to say . . ." Alana paused, not wanting to end the sentence with how much she cared for him as she had started to say.

"What did you want to say?" he asked as he stood close enough to smell her lovely perfume, intrigued by the searching gaze of her eyes.

"I just wanted to say, um, thank you for getting my medication for me yesterday and especially for the beautiful rose. I never got a chance to thank you. I was about to thank you last night when your friend, Roth, rode up and interrupted me," she said softly, equally aware of their closeness. She looked sadly into his deep blue eyes, wishing desperately he would not go.

"I had a feeling that a rose might help you feel better. I know how much you adore those roses," he said as he returned her gaze. Something kept him from adding the words that lay at the very tip of his tongue. He wanted to tell her that he hoped the rose might remind her of him whenever she looked at it and how deeply he felt about her. While he was trying to decide whether to say any of this to her, he saw Billy coming from the barn and was suddenly reminded of where he believed her heart to be aimed. He took a step back and turned to untie the horse's reins, "I am glad that the rose cheered you up," he added coolly. "After all, is that not what friends are for?"

"Indeed," Alana replied simply as she tried to keep the disappointment from her face, "That is exactly what friends are for."

"I'd better be off. Tell Lizzie I will not be home for supper. Roth and I have a great amount of business to tend to," he said offhandedly as he mounted his horse and rode away.

"Business with Roth?" Alana thought with relief. He was not headed for California after all. But her relief was short-lived when she realized that the rose was not a symbol of Brandon's love, only his friendship. She wondered how she could have been so stupid as to believe it was anything more, and firmly resolved never to allow herself to make such a dreadful mistake again.

Chapter Eight

"It's not fair!" Angela complained sharply as she entered the classroom.

"What is not fair?" Alana asked, surprised to see Angela there so early. The bell for class had not yet been rung.

"Mother will not allow me to take Smoky to New Orleans. It is not fair. After all, Smoky's part of the family," she said with her lips puckered into a pout.

"Yes, I can see your point. But, I also know why it would be better for Smoky to stay here," Alana told her, putting aside the papers she was grading.

"You, too?" Angela's voice wavered at the thought of Alana, her very best friend, betraying her.

"If you were to take Smoky, he would have to ride in a cage on top of the stagecoach. It is a rule, no animals inside. How do you think Smoky would like being caged and all alone, outside in the cold, for as many days as it takes to get to New Orleans?" Alana asked her.

"He has to ride in a cage?" Angela asked horrendously, "All alone?"

"Do you not think Smoky would be happier here with me? I would take special care of him, making certain he has been fed and is warm. I shall even let him stay in my room if he wants to. He would not be alone," Alana assured her as she pushed Angela's lower lip back into place with the tip of her finger.

"He likes milk best," Angela said, suggesting she was beginning to understand.

"I shall see to it he gets fresh milk every day. You can trust me," Alana pledged with her hand held over her heart.

170

"I do trust you," she told her as she threw her little arms around Alana's neck and gave her a big squeeze.

"Can I trust you to ring the morning bell?" Alana asked as she handed the bell to Angela, who eagerly ran to the door to call everyone to class.

Alana cut today's class short since everyone needed to be finished packing by tomorrow morning. After the weather had cooled somewhat during September, Alana began holding classes until four with one break for lunch and a short recess in the middle of the afternoon. But, today, she gave them a few reading assignments for the trip and held a quick review before dismissing the children at noon.

When lunch was finished, she helped Lizzie organize the clothes each one had chosen for the trip before putting them into a very large trunk. They were careful to put the traveling clothes on top. Alana was not looking forward to her chance for a month's solitude and that surprised her. Solitude had always been her friend before.

Tomorrow afternoon, Lilian, Lizzie, and the children would join Anne and Douglas with their children at the stage office and then they would all be on their way. The following afternoon, Brandon would also be gone. That would leave her all alone in this huge house. Billy and Abe would be around late in the evenings, but otherwise Alana was facing total solitude. She could not help but wish she had decided to go with the rest when everyone talked so excitedly about the trip during dinner. Brandon gave Lilian last-minute instructions. He warned her once again against seeing Mark's parents, "You will just be reopening old and painful wounds."

"But, they so want to see their grandchildren. They do have that right. Besides, I really do want to see them. I know that certain memories will be stirred up, but I can handle it," Lilian assured him.

"Do you need any extra money? You never know what kind of emergency will come up."

"I am taking more money than I should possibly need, thank you. Brandon, you are a worry wart," Lilian laughed. "We will be fine. Besides, Uncle Drake and Uncle

Lloyd will be there to help us if we have any trouble."

Supper went by quickly, after which everyone went to bed early except Alana who planned to sit on the patio a while. The chilly November night air soon forced her inside. She considered building a nice cozy fire, but decided it was not yet cold enough to warrant a fire. It seemed odd to her that although it was November there still had not been a frost. By this time of year, New York had experienced several frosts and everyone had donned their sweaters and coats. Here, the days were still pleasant and the nights, although growing much colder, were far from unbearable. Even though this evening was the coldest one yet, she still did not believe a fire was called for; there was only a slight chill in the room. She quickly got ready for bed and climbed under the covers to keep warm, but found she could not fall asleep. It was well into the night before she finally drifted off. She slept soundly past the usual time she awoke. The breakfast bell almost failed to awaken her. By the time she was dressed and to the table, most of the children had finished eating and were discussing the trip once again. Brandon was not there. He wanted to help Billy move the cows from the back pasture where the pond, which was the sole water source, had dried up from an unusual lack of rain over the past two months. He wanted to get them moved before the time the family left to catch the afternoon stage. Lilian planned to leave the house at 1:00 sharp.

The morning was used for last-minute packing and dressing. When 1:00 rolled around, everyone was ready except Angela, who was finding it hard to tell Smoky goodbye. Brandon finally had to take her by the hand and lead her away from Alana who held the cat closely in her arms. Alana waved goodbye from the patio with the cat snuggled at her shoulder, watching them climb into the carriage. She wondered why she felt suddenly homesick as she watched the carriage disappear around the corner. After all, she was not the one leaving. She would still be here. She most certainly was not missing New York. Yet she somehow felt quite homesick.

To help pass the empty time now facing her, Alana

decided to make dinner for the men. Lizzie had left an abundance of food in the cooler and showed her how to put water into it to keep the food from spoiling. She also had reminded her of the many jars of garden vegetables in the pantry. After a bit of exploring, Alana decided to bake a small ham, boil a pot of black-eyed peas, and bake a few potatoes. Since she did not know how to make cornbread, which Brandon preferred, she fixed sour-dough biscuits. It took her longer than she had planned, but luckily Brandon was late in returning and Billy and Abe did not come in with him as they usually did.

Having just taken the biscuits out of the oven, she was searching the cooler for butter when Brandon walked in. "What smells so good?" he wanted to know.

"I guess it is the biscuits. But they will not be very good without butter and there is none," she said with a pout.

"Do not get upset. There is probably some in the well box. I shall get it."

He returned shortly with a small jar of butter and, as he placed it near his chair, found the table set for four.

Alana was putting the vegetables down as she told him, "Thank you for getting the butter for me. If you would kindly light the candles, I shall get the ham and we can go ahead and eat while it is still hot."

She left to get the ham. Her heart fluttered at the thought of dining alone with Brandon. Now she wished she had dressed in a prettier outfit.

She returned with the ham to find that Brandon had lit only the candles on the table. He had not bothered to light the large candelabrum overhead nor the large lanterns hanging from the walls. He had already seated himself when she walked in, but quickly got up to help her with the ham. After allowing Brandon to take the ham, she noticed that her chair was positioned closer to his than usual. With the most gracious of manners, he pulled her seat out for her and helped her pull it to a comfortable distance from the table. He managed to close the distance between their chairs even more as he did.

Over the last months, she and Brandon had managed to remain the best of friends, yet their relationship was still a cautious one as each carefully guarded his or her own emotions effectively. Tonight something seemed changed. Maybe it was the soft candlelight or the fact they were soon to be apart for several weeks. But the thin icy wall between them slowly melted along with the candlewax.

They were leisurely enjoying each other's company more so than the meal, when Billy walked into the kitchen. When he saw them through the open door, he eased back outside unnoticed. He stopped Abe about halfway down the walkway and quietly motioned him back to the barn. Once a safe distance away, he explained to Abe why they would wait a while before eating.

Even after Brandon and Alana were finished, they continued to sit at the table talking.

"I hate the thought of you being left here all alone for so long," he said softly as he leaned forward, finding the soft golden glow of the candlelight against her hair and the delicate scent of her perfume intoxicating.

"It is only for three weeks and I do have letters that need to be written and a book of poetry I have been wanting to read," she murmured, feeling his closeness. "Besides, I shall have Billy and Abe to talk to in the evenings."

Jealousy tore at him with the thought of that lucky Billy having such a wonderful opportunity. He was certain Billy would find a way to get around Abe's unwanted presence and spend many an hour winning her affections. With no one around to keep a watchful eye on them, there is no telling where their relationship could lead. Brandon wanted desperately to cancel his hunting trip and spend the next few weeks trying to develop their own friendship into something more, but decided he would only be in the way, and Alana and Billy would still find a way to be together as they seemed to be able to do even now. Presently that relationship was growing at a strangely slow rate, and Brandon took an odd satisfaction in the fact. But, he knew the next few weeks would change that.

"Well, for now you still have me to talk to," he told her, touching a strand of hair that hung over her shoulder. She caught herself leaning forward, leading him in his casual advances. He ignored any feelings of betrayal to his friend as he took her hand in his and told her how much he was going to miss her. She then admitted she would miss him as well. Although they managed to avoid discussing their deeper feelings for each other throughout the evening, they parted a little more than just friends as Brandon placed a gentle kiss on her forehead, wishing her the sweetest of dreams.

Her dreams indeed were very sweet, but the warm peaceful feeling that they instilled in her vanished with the coming of morning. It was the last morning she would see Brandon for several long, lonely weeks. He would be leaving that very afternoon with Roth and a couple more of his good friends to go hundreds of miles away to hunt wild game.

Hurrying to dress, she hoped to be able to make coffee for the men before they left for Brandon's final check of the place. When she got to the kitchen she found she was too late. Three empty cups sat on the counter next to the sink and a nearly empty pot of coffee was on the stove, still warm to the touch. She reheated what coffee was left and sipped it down, hoping to force the morning chill out of herself. With little appetite to motivate her, she decided to forego breakfast.

The morning dragged along endlessly. After straightening her room and washing the dirty cups in the kitchen, she heated a stew in case the men returned in time for lunch. They did not. Wanting to be certain not to miss them when they did come in, she walked out to sit on the patio. There were signs of a storm coming in from the north and a cold wind was beginning to whip about the patio. Bright crimson and gold leaves of autumn had become magically animated as they waltzed about with the passing wind in a bustle of fading glory. As the northern wind picked up force, Alana moved inside to the den. Wood had been stacked by the many fireplaces in early anticipation of the inevitable winter. The room did seem quite chilly so Alana built a small cozy fire and curled up in a nearby chair to enjoy its warmth. Smoky sauntered up to her and mewed pathetically.

"Oh, come on," she told him as she patted her leg. Soon Smoky was snoozing comfortably in her lap as Alana stroked his thick winter coat. Laying her head against the back of the chair, she allowed herself to doze off.

Billy's shouting outside woke her from the peaceful nap. Laying Smoky aside, she walked over to the window to see what all the commotion was about. Billy had brought his horse right on the patio. There was something bulky draped over the saddle. As the horse balked sideways, Alana could see that Brandon was limp across Billy's saddle. Frozen by fear, she watched as Roth, Abe, and two other men—strangers to Alana—rode up. They did not bother to secure their horses as they rushed to help Billy pull Brandon from the saddle and carry him into his room.

"Oh, my dear God, no!" Alana cried when words could finally be spoken. Oblivious to the icy winds that nipped at her heels, she ran across the patio gardens and, totally ignoring the taboo of entering a man's private bedroom, rushed inside to find out what had happened.

"Snake bite," is all Billy took time to tell her as he helped one of the men, whose name Alana did not know, get a fire started. Abe and the other stranger were busy lighting all of the lanterns and candles in the room. Meanwhile, Roth pulled Brandon's boots off and laid them at the end of the bed. Then, he produced a large knife from a sheath hooked on his belt, and cut through the water-soaked hem of Brandon's pant leg. Quickly, he tore the front of the material its entire length in one easy motion. As it tore, she noticed that there was another rip at the thigh with blood staining the edges of it. To her horror, there was a wide gash on his thigh just above his knee and blood was oozing from the open wound. Roth used the knife to cut the material free and dropped it on the floor.

"I think he must have gotten most of the poison out himself before he passed out," Billy told Roth, who was examining the wound closely. The bloody gash cut deeply through the two puncture marks.

"How long from the time he was bitten until you found him do you think?" Roth wanted to know.

"Couldn't have been more than a few minutes. I was with him less than half an hour earlier when we first discovered the fence was down and that several cows had wandered down the creekbed. We split up to have a better chance of finding the strays. I was doubling back when I found him lying beside the creek. He had already tended to the bite himself, but had grown too weak to stand much less walk," Billy replied. "I summoned Abe with a gunshot and the two of us managed to get him on my horse. That was only minutes before we ran into you."

After holding his knife over an open flame, Roth opened the wound a little wider and milked more blood from his leg.

"Seems to be clear. If there was any poison left, it is well into his system by now. Only time will tell," he said sadly as he laid the knife aside.

Alana felt faint as the room began to spin around her at the sight of Brandon's blood flowing freely down his leg and onto his bed, forming a large red stain on the white sheet. The stain grew wider with each moment passing. She realized she needed to be strong and tried to shake this queasy feeling as best as possible.

"Alana, could you bring us some warm water and find us some clean cloth?" Billy asked as he frantically searched Brandon's drawers. Before Alana could walk out, she heard Billy shout, "I found it!" as he produced a small bottle of whiskey to cleanse the wound.

When she returned with the water and cloth, she found that they had removed his shirt, revealing the beads of perspiration covering his chest. There was also a great amount of perspiration forming on his pale face and along his neck. The bleeding had not stopped. Billy took one of the clean cloths and doused it in the warm water. He used the damp cloth to scrub the wound carefully. He then doused the clean wound with the whiskey. Although the leg jumped as the whiskey poured into the open wound, Brandon still did not come to. Getting another clean cloth, Billy folded it into a small square and pressed it firmly against the wound. He then tied it securely in place with a strip of cloth torn from a large towel. The cloth quickly stained with Brandon's blood, but was left just as it was. Taking another cloth and dousing it into the water, Billy washed the sweat from Brandon's face.

"Well, about all we can do now is wait. We will know in time," he said remorsefully.

"Aren't you going to get him a doctor?" Alana asked incredulously, ready to ride to town for him herself if necessary.

"There is nothing anyone can do about a snake bite but try to clean out the poison and pray. It is in God's hands now," Billy said as he knelt beside Brandon, continuing to bathe his forehead.

"Are you saying he might die?" Alana cried out; tears had begun to flow down her cheeks.

"But then he might not," Billy said simply, trying to get her to see from a more positive view. He stood up and walked over to her. "There's a good chance for him if he got most of the poison out."

"What if he did not get enough of the poison out?" Alana asked fearfully, trying to still one trembling hand with the other.

"We have to believe he did," Billy said firmly. "Come on, let him rest for now."

"That is right. He needs rest. Why don't you come with us to the kitchen and make up a large pot of coffee for us?" Roth asked as he placed a supportive arm around Alana before Billy could.

"No, please, I want to stay here with him. I shall be careful not to disturb him. I promise. Besides, Billy can make better coffee than I can," Alana pleaded to stay, not allowing her eyes to move from Brandon's inanimate face.

"It would be better for you if you did not stay. You really should come with us to the kithen," Roth told her, while gently trying to maneuver her to the door.

Alana looked pleadingly into Billy's eyes, making him realize just how important it was for her to be able to stay. "Actually, Roth, it might not be a bad idea to have someone here in case he does wake up and tries to get out of bed. If that were to happen, he would be too weak and could fall and hurt himself even worse."

"Have Abe stay, then. This pretty little thing would not be able to stop Brandon from getting up anyway," Roth replied sharply.

Billy ignored Roth's silver glare through his narrowed eyes and continued, "You must not know very much about Alana. When she has her mind set on something, even Brandon is helpless against her."

"Very well, I shall stay, too. Between the two of us, we should be able to keep Brandon in bed," Roth told Billy, turning his back to the door.

Alana was getting angry over all of this talk. Pushing Roth backward through the door, she told him in a steady low voice, "I do not need anyone in here to help me. Billy will make you a cup of coffee, which you can and will enjoy in the dining room. If I feel I need help, I shall scream loud enough that even the people in town should hear me."

While she was grabbing Billy and Abe by the elbows to escort them promptly outside, the two men she had never met scurried outside like a couple of frightened chickens. One of them did not bother to grab his hat, which lay on Brandon's chest of drawers near the door. Alana then closed the door on their shocked faces. Feeling surprisingly satisfied over what she had just done, Alana had to smile. But the sight of Brandon lying motionless on his bed with his leg still in a pool of blood reminded her of the seriousness of the moment and her smile faded. Dipping the last clean cloth in the now cool water and wringing it out, she knelt down beside Brandon and wiped his brow. Tears began to fill her eyes as she silently prayed for him again and again. She watched his eyelids for any signs of movement to give her a hope to hang on to, but the only movement he made was that of his labored breathing and at times Alana was certain that even his breathing had stopped.

After she bathed his face, she put the cloth aside and took his hand in hers. She found the hand was unusually cool, but that his forehead was very warm to the touch. She was not sure if these signs meant anything was terribly wrong, but she did not like it. As she massaged his hands, hoping to warm them somewhat, she gazed through her tear-swollen eyes at his face. His long dark hair had been pushed away from his face with the wet cloth, better revealing the handsome features marking him.

"Brandon, please, do not die. I could not bare to lose the only man I have ever dared love," Alana spoke while caressing his pale cheek lightly with her trembling hand. Feeling a warm flow of tears coming again, she buried her face into his chest and cried openly.

Many hours passed as Alana knelt by Brandon's side, leaning forward with her cheek against his bare chest, listening to his heartbeat. Her tears had finally subsided, but her fears were as strong as ever. Brandon meant everything to her, and she now fully realized that fact. A short knock at the door, brought her to her feet. She found she could hardly stand alone after kneeling for so long. From her knees down, she was numb. When she managed to answer the door, she found Billy with a tray. Its contents were covered by a white linen cloth.

"I thought you might be hungry," he told her.

"I do not think I could eat even a bite," she replied, opening the door fully to let him come in.

Billy carried the tray inside and placed it on a small table beside Brandon's bed. He stood over Brandon a moment before asking, "How is he? Has there been any change?"

"No, none at all." Alana's voice faltered as she tried unsuccessfully not to let her emotions show.

"Really, it is too soon," he assured her, then added, "I had everyone go home, since there is nothing for them to do here. They decided not to go on the hunt with Brandon in such danger. Oh, I took Brandon's rifle and canteen from his saddle, but I did not want to disturb him so I just left them outside of the door. I will get them. Now, I want you to get some rest. I will watch him awhile."

"I am not tired," Alana refused to admit. "You are the one that needs rest. You still have a ranch to run. I would appreciate it if you would help me change his sheets and maybe take his belt off of him. He cannot be comfortable like that."

It only took a few minutes for them to put fresh sheets on the bed. Alana worked at pulling the damp, stained sheets off at the head of the bed and began to put the clean ones on while Billy sat Brandon up by supporting his back. He laid Brandon's head on the clean sheet and pulled his legs up, being extra careful with the bandaged leg, while Alana finished stripping the bed and pulling the clean sheet down under him. Once the bottom sheet was in place, she laid the top sheet across him, bringing it up as far as his chest.

Billy tried once more to persuade Alana she needed a few hours of rest. Finally extracting a promise from her to at least catch a nap in a chair, he went to bed himself.

The next morning he tapped at the door, carrying another tray. He was aware from Alana's appearance that she had not slept at all during the night. Her dark brown eyes were hidden behind swollen lids and dark semi-circles were forming underneath. When he placed the breakfast tray on the table, he noticed that last night's soup and toast had not been touched. He doubted she even looked under the cloth to see what was there. "You did not eat anything," he scolded her.

"I was not hungry," she replied bluntly.

"Well, you are going to eat that omelet and ham I cooked up for you. I am not leaving this room until you do," he said sternly as he put his hand on the back of her neck, forcing her to move forward and stand in front of a chair. Then, with a push, he caused her to sit down.

"Eat!" he ordered her, placing the tray in her lap and pulling the linen napkin away to reveal the food.

Too tired to argue, Alana took the fork and placed a small bite of the omelet into her mouth and then another. She discovered she was hungry after all and the omelet was good. While Billy stood over her watching, she ate every bite and finished with the tall glass of milk.

"Feel better?" he asked as he took the tray and set it on top of the other one.

"Much better," she admitted.

"I have got to go feed the stock and make certain everything's fine out there. But, I will be back before lunchtime and help change the bandage. Meanwhile, you try to get that nap you promised me last night," he ordered. When he opened the door to leave, a cold gust of wind blew in. "When winter decided to move in, she wasted no time," he forced a cheerful tone into his voice.

"Be careful," she warned him before he closed the door. Now that she had eaten, she did feel like a nap. After checking Brandon for any signs of consciousness, she put on another small log to boost the lazy fire. Moving a large upholstered chair near the fire so she could watch Brandon, she curled up in it and eventually slept.

It was Billy's knock at the door that woke her. She got up to answer it, but before she could, Billy poked his shaggy blond head inside, "Can I come in?"

Not waiting for an answer, he stepped on inside with a clean cloth in hand. A chilly draft passed her as the door was closed behind him. He walked over to Brandon's bed, where Alana joined him, "No change, huh?"

"No, nothing," Alana answered sadly. "I am worried, very worried."

"I know you are, but realize that it has not been even a day yet. Sometimes it takes two or three before anyone starts getting better after a bad snake bite." He pulled the sheet back to reveal the blood stained bandage. "If I hold the leg up, can you put on a fresh bandage?" he wanted to know.

"I shall try," she said, taking the cloth from him.

Gently, Billy eased Brandon's leg up, giving Alana enough room to reach around and untie the strip of towel holding the bandage in place. When she removed the strip, she found that the bandage did not come off easily. Carefully, she worked the patch loose and examined the wound. There was a considerable amount of swelling and the area closest to the wound had turned a bluish-black. It was starting to bleed again in one spot, but otherwise the wound was doing fine. Folding the clean cloth into a similar square, she placed it against the wound and tied it back with a fresh strip of towel.

Billy eased the leg back down and pulled the sheet up to Brandon's waist. Remorse shot through him, causing him to bite his lip as he watched his friend. He knew Brandon should be thrashing about by now. The fact that he just lay there scared him more than he would dare admit to Alana.

A tiny meow broke the silence, startling both of them. When they turned around, they saw Smoky huddled on the window ledge peeking through the small parting in the curtains. "I forgot all about Smoky," she said, remembering her promise to take special care of Angela's pet.

"I would say that cat is hungry," Billy remarked. "You better go get him something. Maybe you could rustle us up something while you are at it. I will stay with Brandon."

Alana agreed reluctantly. Just before she opened the door to leave, Billy handed her his coat, reminding her that the north wind had brought winter with it. She was glad she had accepted the coat when she stepped outside. It was an extremely cold and cloudy winter day. A blustery wind cut through her clothes as she picked up the cat and, leaning forward against the icy wind, she made her way to the kitchen. Billy had a fire going in the stove, making the room just warm enough to be comfortable with or without the coat.

She poured Smoky a small bowl of milk, before searching the cooler and pantry for lunch items. She started to broil Billy a steak, but before she unwrapped the meat, she decided she did not really want to. Instead, she grabbed a couple of bowls and spoons along with the pot containing the last of the stew and carried it to Brandon's room. Smoky followed and entered the room right behind her. He made himself comfortable in front of the fire, while Alana hung the pot of stew over the flames to heat it.

Billy stayed with her most of the afternoon. Occasionally, they attempted a bit of small talk, but usually they sat silently watching Brandon or allowed the flickering flames of the fire to take their thoughts far away. As it grew dark, he had to leave. The stock had to be checked again and the horses curried and fed.

It had started to rain when he returned. Thunder and lightning had announced the nasty winter storm's arrival. When Billy entered the room, he found that Alana had not bothered to light a lantern or candle. The fireplace produced the only light in the room as Alana sat in a chair staring hopelessly at Brandon. Smoky lay silently at her feet, lifting his head from his paws enough to see who had intruded on them; then, after seeing it was Billy, he returned his head to its resting place.

"He has not moved," Alana answered Billy's silent question in a low monotoned voice. Billy knelt beside Brandon and placed his hand on his friend's forehead. It was quite warm, yet, there was a clammy sweat on his brow. Pulling the sheet back, he examined the bandage. It was still clean. No blood had soaked through to the outside, and he replaced the sheet over Brandon. He wanted to know how Alana was feeling.

"Who me? I am fine," she said tonelessly. In the firelight, he could see that her face was pale and her eyes still puffy from recent tears. She was not fine, not fine at all. Billy again tried to persuade her to go to her room and get some sleep. He knew before he made the request that she was going to refuse to leave Brandon, but felt it was worth a try. He sat with her in the dark for another hour before going off to bed himself. He left her with orders to call out if there was any kind of change at all. She promised she would, wondering if that call would be a joyous or tragic one.

She returned to Brandon's side and sat on the very edge of the bed washing the perspiration from his face and chest once again. She leaned over him and gently ran her finger through the damp hair on his chest pleading softly, "Brandon, please, open your eyes. Tell me that you are going to be all right. Please, I beg of you." Once again tears of anguish found her eyes as she dared lean over and kiss him on his rough, unshaven cheek, "I love you so much, I could not bare the pain if you should die."

She sat beside him for several hours, watching the firelight flicker across his damp face. While she was watching the dark shadows dance about his handsome features, she felt certain she saw his eyelids flicker. Hopefully, she leaned forward and watched closely for another movement. But his face was still. She felt that it must have been the sudden movement of a shadow over his eye that made it appear to have moved. Yet, she reached out and lightly touched his eyelid with her fingertip with hopes to feel a movement. As she did, he flinched and jerked his head away.

Breathlessly, Alana whispered, "Brandon, do you hear me?" fearing that she was so tired she was having unfounded delusions. She spoke louder, but there was no reaction. For the rest of the night she sat beside him washing his face with the damp cloth and closely watching his face and eyes for another movement.

The next morning when Billy came with breakfast, she told him about how Brandon had moved his head.

"Might be a good sign, all right," he remarked as he stood over his friend searching his face for any such movement, but found none.

"You better eat something. You will need your strength if you plan to see this all the way through," he told her as he uncovered another omelet, this time with sausage. He felt he'd better stay with something he knew she liked.

After she finished eating, she accepted Billy's offer to stay with Brandon while she freshened up and changed clothes. She put on Billy's coat and ran across to her room.

Although the day was sunny and bright the air was still very cold. She found her room was extremely cold, too. Rather than build a fire and wait for it to warm the room, she decided to gather up a change of clothes and go to the kitchen to dress.

While she searched the back of her wardrobe for a warmer dress, she thought of her medications that she had Brandon put back into her trunks so the children could not get a hand on them. Her pain powders might help Brandon if she could find a way to get him to take one.

The cabinet was still blocking the door by a few inches when she tried to enter. She pushed against the cabinet, hoping to move it out of the way. It would not budge; it was too heavy. Determined to get to those powders, she emptied most of her things out and laid them on the bed. Her bare hands were beginning to hurt with the cold as she again pushed the cabinet with all of her might. It moved an inch before she lost her footing and nearly fell. A second push moved it far enough to enable her to open the door. When she swung the door open, she saw why the door was never locked, only blockaded. The lock had been broken somehow.

Her conscience put up a weak front, causing her to pause a moment. After all, this was Brandon's secret room that held something so special or so horrible that it was always locked. But she wanted those powders for him badly, so she stuck her head inside. It was too dark to see with the only light seeming to come in from behind her. She lit a nearby lantern and stepped over several boxes blocking the doorway.

Inside, she found the musty-smelling room was completely furnished. Dingy white sheets were draped over many of the chairs and tables. A huge double bed with large heavy oak posts holding up a sagging blue canopy remained uncovered. On the dusty blue bedspread sat several boxes and crates. A large black spider had crafted a silvery web between two of the bedposts. Alana carefully stepped over a box that she guessed had fallen from the bed and lay in the middle of the floor. She saw her trunks sat opened near the front door and carefully made her way around the ghostly draped chairs to get to them. The medication pouch lay on top and she easily picked it out without disturbing too much of the dust filling the inside. Before leaving, she shut her trunks to prevent any further dust from collecting inside. When she did, some of the dust flew up in her face causing her to cough and stumble sideways. Once she got her breath back, she looked up to search the way out. She noticed a small wooden chest sitting alone on an uncovered wooden table. Strangely, this chest had very little dust covering it. It had either been newly set there or it was kept dustfree by use. Allowing curiosity to overtake her, she opened the chest to see if there was anything inside. There were dozens of aging letters filling the chest. Alana picked up the one that lay on top and, unable to fight this mounting curiosity, opened it. On the yellowing pages were faded words of love meant only for Brandon's eyes:

> *Dearest Brandon,*
> *It has been days since I have seen your handsome face and felt your strong, loving arms around me. I miss you so very much. I can barely wait until Saturday night when you will once again fill my soul with your love. Lizzie is in the store and has offered to carry a letter to you again. I just could not allow such an opportunity as this to tell you how deeply I'd love you to pass by. Brandon, my only true love, I shall need and love you until my dying breath.*
>
> > *Yours forever,*
> > *Stephanie*

Alana's heart sank as she refolded the letter and placed it back on top of the pile. This proved that Brandon did indeed still love Stephanie. Resisting the other letters, she opened a drawer at the bottom of the chest and found a small faded portrait in a tarnished silver frame and a small box not more than an inch in width or length wrapped in faded yellow paper with a tattered yellow ribbon around it. Alana carefully picked up the picture. It was of a beautiful young girl with flowing blond tresses falling over her shoulders. A rather demure smile was riding on her pretty face.

"So, you are Stephanie?" Alana remarked aloud, disappointed in the girl's remarkable beauty.

Replacing the portrait, she noted that the tiny gift could only be one thing, a ring. He had indeed been ready to ask her to marry him. It saddened her that Brandon had kept the ring, not only because of the jealousy it caused her, but because of the hopeless feeling Brandon must be carrying inside of him. As she closed the drawer and walked out of the room, she realized just how deeply Stephanie had affected him. It weighted her heart heavily to realize that it was true; Brandon would never have room in his heart for another.

Gathering up her coat, a dress, and her brush, along with the medication pouch, she left her room. The brisk air brushed against her face like a cold slap of a hand as she walked to the kitchen. As soon as she was dressed in a fresh outfit and had brushed her hair, she returned to Brandon's room. She found Billy sitting on the floor playing with Smoky when she entered. Returning his coat to him, Alana admitted she felt a little better.

"You look a little better," Billy remarked. "But, you would look a lot better if you would try to get some sleep. After I feed the stock, I am going to fetch some quilts and fix you a pallet. Then you can lie down and rest without leaving Brandon. I must say, you certainly are dedicated to seeing him through this."

"I love him," Alana admitted simply.

"Why don't you tell Brandon that?" Billy wanted to know.

"Because he could never love me," Alana answered him sadly.

"You are wrong. I think you should tell him how you feel. It could change everything," Billy told her.

"That is what I am afraid of," she replied, remembering the letter she found in that room. This way, she could at least have his friendship. Declaring her love to him would only put a strain on that friendship.

Billy just shook his head as he put his coat and hat back on, "I still think he should know." He looked her in the eye as he spoke. "Somebody should tell him," he stated firmly before walking out.

Somberly she sat down on Brandon's bed and looked at his unmoving form, "Oh, Brandon, if I had been Stephanie and had your love, I would never have done anything to chance losing it. Stephanie was a fool to desert you," she told him, knowing well that he could not hear her. She also confessed that she had been in his special room and apologized for learning his secret.

Feeling better at having said the words aloud, she picked up the damp cloth and wiped his face again. She rinsed the cloth out in the bowl of cool water and folded it into a small pad. After a moment, she placed the damp pad across his forehead, remembering that her mother had done the same for her whenever she was sick. It seemed to be the only time her mother had really seemed to bother with her at all.

After the cloth grew warm, she dipped it back into the water and wrung it out. Refolding it, she again placed it on his forehead. Several drops of water dripped out of the pad and down his face. When the cool drops hit his eyes, he rolled his head. Before Alana could say anything, he roughly spoke her name.

Tears once again filled her eyes only they were now tears of joy. "I am here, Brandon. I am here," she cried softly as she leaned over his face.

He opened his eyes and smiled up at her, "Alana," he repeated as he reached out for her hand. He closed his eyes, but kept the smile as he drifted off to sleep. His grip was weak, but his breathing eased. Brandon was going to make it. Alana's heart soared as she held his hand to her cheek. Brandon was going to live!

Chapter Nine

"You had better eat quickly," Alana warned Brandon as she sat a tall stack of pancakes in front of him. "That stage is due to arrive at ten and it is nearly nine now."

Brandon assured her they would be on time. "I thought about not telling Lilian about the snake bite. She would be angry with herself for not being here at such a time. But she is going to know something happened when she sees me. I am expected to still be in South Texas," he told her. "Just do not make it sound too bad when you explain it to her. She will fuss over me like a mother hen, not allowing me to run my own ranch."

"And you should not have returned to work so soon!" Alana scolded him, watching disdainfully as he soaked his pancakes in a thick pool of honey.

"I tell you I am fine, now. The leg is as good as new," he told her as he proceeded to put a large dripping bite in his mouth.

"Just the same, you should be more cautious of working," she reminded him.

"Humph," he retorted, his mouth being too full to speak. A drop of honey landed on the three week's growth of his beard. He took his napkin and wiped it clean as he listened to Alana, who was not going to wait for him to speak.

"I also think you should allow Billy to pick them up. You are not up to the long ride. Besides, the stage will probably be late and you will have to wait, and not be able to rest," Alana pointed a finger at him as she shook it in warning.

"Will you stop? I tell you I am fine," he said firmly.

Although he continually complained about it, he was

thoroughly enjoying Alana's mothering. Over the past few weeks she had cared for his every need. When he got bored one day and joined her in the kitchen, he received a scolding more severe than any Lizzie had ever given him as a boy. She promptly ushered him back to his room and made him lie back down on his bed. Brandon really enjoyed having Alana tuck him in. He also liked having her entering his bedroom as if she belonged there. It led to many a fine fantasy to help fill the times she was away with one chore or another. Many times he would refuse to stay in bed any longer unless she sat and talked to him. He finally had a chance to get her attention away from Billy and on him. He was taking advantage of the situation. If he felt she had spent too much time in the kitchen getting Billy something to eat, he would make an appearance and instantly have Alana by his side, scolding him as she marched him back to bed, leaving Billy to find his own supper.

The days seemed to fly by as the time grew near for the family's return. He knew things would soon resume a normal pace, and Lizzie would no doubt take over as his nursemaid. He was not as eager to see the family as Alana seemed to be. The only reason he chose to pick them up was because Alana said she wanted to go. He certainly did not want Billy to carry her in, giving him a chance to be alone with her—not after having kept them apart so successfully over the last few weeks.

"Alana," he said softly.

"What is it?" she answered as she reached to take his empty plate.

"I just wanted to tell you how much I appreciate what you have done for me over the past few weeks. I realize I have acted pretty contrary sometimes, but I really do appreciate it," he told her taking her hand in his as he spoke.

"I enjoyed it. Believe me, I did," she told him allowing him to raise her hand to his lips. Expecting the beard to scratch her hand as it appeared very coarse and stiff, she was pleasantly surprised at its softness.

"I certainly made a mess of your little holiday. I truly am

sorry," he added as he stood up to be able to look down into her eyes.

"As I said before, I enjoyed it," she whispered, his closeness taking her breath away.

"Well, I hope you accept this friendly kiss of gratitude," he said as he leaned forward. At first he moved toward her cheek, but instead, he pressed his lips gently to hers. The soft hair of his beard pleasantly tickled her chin. At first, she had not cared for his idea of growing this beard. The thought of hiding his handsome face behind a mass of dark hair upset her. Now that it was growing full, she found it was really very appealing. There was something extremely masculine about it and brought even more attention to his pale blue eyes and the dark long lashes surrounding them. At this moment, she was finding it felt nice, very nice, against her face, as well.

When he pulled away, he said softly, "There is nothing wrong with a little kiss between friends is there?"

"Certainly not," Alana agreed.

Again, he leaned forward, pulling her close. This time the kiss was more than one between friends, and each knew it. The sound of the kitchen door opening broke the kiss as Alana pulled away.

"The surrey is ready when you are," Billy said as he walked into the dining room. The unsettled looks on Brandon and Alana's faces made him wonder just what he had interrupted.

"Let's get going," Brandon grumbled as he marched out. When he realized he had just left Billy and Alana alone, he quickly returned and added sweetly, "Coming Alana?"

"As soon as I put these dishes in the water and get my coat," she answered.

Just before stepping outside, she checked her reflection in the window to make certain her hair was still in place. Not being ready to wear it down in town, she had put it up in a thick array of curls.

The ride into town went too quickly for either of them as they discussed anything that came to mind, avoiding only any mention of the kiss. It was exactly 10:00 when they pulled up behind the post office. Alana got out to do some quick shopping while Brandon stopped to talk to an elderly man on the courthouse lawn.

Alana went into DeLane's Dry Goods to pick out a few things to give the children for Christmas. Here it was, just weeks away, and she had not taken the time to make the gifts that she had planned to. Not wanting to cause the family any delay from getting on home, she quickly chose appropriate gifts and carried them to the counter to pay for them.

While waiting for Mr. DeLane to finish wrapping the purchases of another woman, she overheard him say, "Well, according to the letter, she has already left California and should be home sometime before the week is out. Can you believe it? She is coming home to stay."

Fear crept through her as she listened closely to the woman's reply, "I imagine you are very excited about seeing your little girl after all of these years."

"I am excited, but I do hate the circumstances. Even though I was not fond of the man, I hated hearing of her husband's death. But she is still young and has plenty of time to get over it," he told her in a hopeful tone as he handed the woman her package. "Have a good day, Mrs. Maxwell." Then he turned to Alana, "How are you, today?"

"Fine," she replied bluntly.

"You enjoying this fine sunny day? It is almost warm enough to leave off your coat," he said, trying to strike up a friendly conversation.

"It is fine," she replied as she looked out of the window trying to get over the news that she had just overheard. She did not have to ask him who they were talking about. She knew. Stephanie was coming back. Alana's stomach felt suddenly weak as the thought of Brandon's little sweetheart returning to Gilmer and probably to Brandon as well.

Silently she picked up the packages, even though Mr. DeLane offered to have his boy carry them for her and walked out. She saw Brandon talking to Archie in front of the post office. Evidently the stage was late. She carried her purchases to the carriage and put them in the back.

Feeling a strong need to sit down, she climbed into the carriage. While resting, she watched Brandon, wondering how he was going to react to the news and whether or not he had been told anything about it yet. She also noticed how handsome he was with his new well-groomed beard. That and the suit he was wearing reminded her of a good-looking young scholar or a wise professor. She was watching how he spoke so intently to his friend, using his hands freely as he spoke. When he caught sight of her looking their way, he waved for her to join them. Slowly she climbed out and walked over to stand beside him. She could not keep her thoughts from wandering back over the devastating words she had overheard in the store.

Her thoughts were concentrated on the horrendous effects it might have when she felt Brandon's hand slip around her waist and heard him remark, "And this little lady helped nurse me back to health. I owe her a lot." He proudly pulled her closer to his side as he continued to exaggerate to Archie about his fight with death. Archie listened attentively until he caught sight of the stagecoach as it rounded the corner.

"Here they come!" he shouted and stepped out on the street, wanting to be the first to greet Lilian. Momentarily, Alana forgot about Stephanie and eagerly stepped down to greet everyone with open arms. Angela was the first out of the stage after the driver opened the door. She ran to Alana who knelt down and welcomed her home with a hug and a kiss. Lilian stepped out next and received her welcome from Archie and Brandon. One by one, the others climbed out and, one by one, Alana made her way to hug and kiss them all. She was so excited she even grabbed Lizzie and gave her a big squeeze. Lizzie laughed aloud, but offered a protest, "Miss Alana, you better watch who you is huggin' in public. These people is getting their eyes full."

"So what?" Alana asked as she grabbed her and hugged her again. She had not realized just how much she had missed everyone until now. She found herself beginning to cry when Angela clutched onto her hand and told her that she had missed her terribly.

"I missed you, too. So did Smoky," she said as she sniffed back a happy sob.

"Smoky! Is he okay?" Angela asked eagerly.

"He is fine. In fact, he is a-might bit spoiled. I am afraid I let him more or less have his run of the place," Alana told her.

"Come on, Uncle Brandon, let's go home. Hurry up, I want to see Smoky," she said in a rush as she ran to prod her uncle along. Brandon heard her words, yet he took his own sweet time walking back to the carriage, mostly to tease Angela. She was so exasperated that she finally got behind him and pushed him along.

Crowded closely together on the carriage, everyone tried to talk at once. Each wanted to give his or her story of what happened during the trip. Lilian had to hush the children several times before they got home as the chatter grew too loud to bear. Unable to concentrate on any one child's enthusiasm, Alana told them they would be able to tell her all about their trip tomorrow on paper.

"Tomorrow's assignment will be to write a three-page report explaining what you did on your trip to New Orleans. And it will be graded," she warned them.

Most of the children were silent for the rest of the way home, trying to decide what to put in their paper. Lilian finally saw her chance to ask why Brandon was home so early and was astounded over the story Brandon related to her about the snake bite and how Alana had nursed him back to health. He tried unsuccessfully to convince his sister that he was as healthy as he ever had been. But Lilian and Lizzie both agreed he would be restricted to the house most of the next two weeks.

Lizzie also ordered that he go back to bed as soon as they were home, "You will do nobody no good if you go workin' yourself to death."

"Here, here!" Alana heard herself say.

As soon as Brandon was out of the carriage, Lizzie hustled him away to his room. Alana laughed aloud at the boyish pout tightening at the corners of his mouth.

Billy came out of the barn to greet everyone. He carried the trunk to the kitchen under Lilian's orders. Alana offered to help her unpack, and followed them into the kitchen. The children ran to their rooms to get out of their traveling clothes. Lilian told Billy to unload the rest of the packages, putting them in her room to be sorted out later. After he left, Lilian told Alana all about their trip.

"It was tiring but, oh, so much fun!" She ended her tale with an exhausted smile.

"Why did Anne and Douglas not come back with you? Are they planning to stay a while?"

Lilian's smile faded, "It is the baby. She caught some sort of cough that ran with a high fever, and refused to nurse for several days. She was getting better when we left, but still has a ways to go until she will be healthy again. They are waiting until she is fit for travel. I offered to bring the boys home with me, but they decided against it. I shall certainly be glad when they do get home and I can see for myself that the poor little thing is better."

"How horrible," Alana said, as a cold chill quivered down her spine. "I hate to think of that precious doll going through such a thing so soon in her short life."

"She is a beauty, isn't she?" Lilian agreed. "Going to be a real heartbreaker."

The word heartbreaker for some reason made Alana remember the news of Stephanie's nearing return. "Guess what I overheard at DeLane's Dry Goods today?"

"Alana, I never would have guessed you would be one to gossip," Lilian teased her, not catching the serious tone in Alana's voice.

"It is not exactly gossip—well, not exactly. It is just something I heard Mr. DeLane telling a woman this morning," Alana continued, not wanting to hear the words coming from her own mouth, authenticating her worst fear.

"What, that his darling Stephanie is coming back to Texas?" Lilian mused.

"You knew?" Alana questioned her, displeased with Lilian's easy tone of voice.

"I was kidding!" she told her. Her eyes grew larger as she asked for verification, "Stephanie's really coming home?"

Alana could only shake her head to affirm Lilian's question.

"To stay?" Lilian asked with a worried look twisting across her face.

Alana's lower lip began to tremble as she again nodded an affirmation.

"Oh, my dearest God!" Lilian replied almost breathlessly. "Does Brandon know?"

Still unable to speak, Alana shrugged her shoulders in an attempt to tell her that she had no idea. Lilian thought silently for a moment. When she finally spoke, she wanted to know when Stephanie was supposed to be back.

Trying desperately to regain her composure, she took a deep breath, "He said that she would be home before the week is out," she said slowly and as clearly as she could.

Lilian looked at Alana closely, "You care a great deal for my brother, don't you?" She hoped Alana would answer honestly.

"We are just friends," Alana replied, not wanting to make things worse by having Lilian feel sorry for her. There was nothing even his sister could do to make Brandon forget Stephanie.

"Is that the way you want it? To be friends?" Lilian asked cautiously, knowing it was really none of her business, but still she did want to know.

"That is the way it is," Alana said simply, wishing there could be more between them than friendship. She had allowed that second kiss this morning to build up her hopes again, only to have them shattered by such horrible news. Brandon's only love was about to return and as a widow no less. Realizing her sniveling would get her nowhere, she took another deep breath and said firmly, "Some friend I am. I should be happy for Brandon. His dreams might finally come true and I should be glad of that fact." The words 'but I am not' echoed in her mind as she tried to pretend to Lilian that she was having a change in heart.

Lilian did not respond, but continued to separate the dirty clothes from the clean ones. She saw through Alana's false front and felt deeply sorry for her friend. She realized sadly that with Stephanie home, Alana's chances were slim. She had so hoped Alana and Brandon would get together. She had even risked angering Anne by using Cynthia as a cause to unite them. "If only Stephanie had stayed in California," she thought as she slammed the empty trunk shut and locked it.

It was after the children had eaten supper that evening and had excused themselves, leaving only Brandon, Alana, and Lilian sitting at the table, that Lilian mentioned the news to Brandon. Alana watched him carefully, noticing how he actually seemed terrified when hearing of Stephanie's timely return.

"How do you know?" he asked finding Lilian's words hard to believe.

"Alana overheard her father tell one of his customers this morning," Lilian stated simply.

He turned and looked at Alana, wondering how much she knew about Stephanie.

"Why is she coming back to Texas?" he asked, trying not to seem terribly concerned.

"He did not say, only that she was to be home before the week is out," Alana said quietly, hoping she could keep control of the devastation she felt inside.

"So soon?" he asked. He sat quietly a moment trying to soak the news in. His Stephanie was coming back and he was not certain if he was angry at her, or even if he still loved her, yet the thought stirred hidden emotions dwelling deep within him. He had thought about her often, but with mixed emotions. Now the thought of Stephanie returning was planted furthermost in his mind as he asked to be excused and quickly walked out.

Lilian and Alana were watching him leave when Lizzie walked in, "What is goin' on here? You two look like you just lost your best friend."

"I think I have," Alana whispered under her breath as Lilian told Lizzie what had happened.

"Oh my!" Lizzie remarked, looking at Alana, knowing just how much the news had to be crushing her.

"Excuse me, I need to prepare for tomorrow's class," Alana told them, and quickly stood and walked out. She heard Lizzie say, "Oh my!" again just before she went through the door.

Tears were streaming down her face by the time she closed the door to her room. Hopelessly, she flung herself on her bed and cried herself to sleep.

Awaiting the inevitable news of Stephanie's arrival, Alana found she could not concentrate on her teaching. She managed to go through the motions and keep her class in order, although she felt her life was falling apart.

It was Sunday afternoon before the subject of Stephanie came up again. Lizzie had made a pot of hot cocoa and everyone was sitting around the fireplace in the parlor when Lilian mentioned she had heard the news at church of Stephanie's arrival in Gilmer early Saturday morning.

"I know," Brandon told her.

Alana listened solemnly as Brandon explained that Roth had mentioned it to him in passing the night before. "He never misses anything," he chuckled.

"Have you seen her, yet?" Lilian asked casually.

"Haven't had a reason to," he said simply, his smile fading. Then, he purposely changed the subject to the fact that Christmas was less than three weeks away.

Although everyone else was now discussing their plans for Christmas, Alana's thoughts dwelled solely on the fact that Stephanie was back. It was an actuality; she could not change it, or hope to. She decided she might as well try to learn to live with it. Stephanie was back and certain to again become part of Brandon's life. It was inevitable.

Angela noticed Alana was not paying attention and walked over to stand in front of her, "Don't you want Saint Nicholas to bring you anything special?" she wanted to know.

"Saint Nicholas?" Alana asked, trying to orient herself into the conversation. "Saint Nicholas only brings things for little girls and little boys and only if they have been very, very good."

"Uh-unh, he always brings something for everybody," Angela assured her.

"Well, I do not think he even knows where I am, so I

doubt he will leave me anything," Alana said. She allowed the nasty thought to cross her suddenly fiendish mind: She relished the idea of St. Nicholas leaving a one-way ticket back to California under Stephanie's tree.

"But Saint Nicholas knows everything!" Angela insisted. "Yet, he cannot get you what you want if you do not put it down on this list."

"What list?"

"The list we are making for Brandon to burn in the fireplace early on Christmas Eve. Saint Nicholas then reads the smoke and knows what to pack for us." she replied, a wrinkle forming a notch in her forehead. "Did you not ever make a list for Saint Nicholas?"

"Oh, I most certainly did. But, I always gave mine to my mother months in advance for her to mail to him," Alana answered realizing that all of the children were looking at her curiously. "Well, I did," she insisted.

"What if he did not get it in time?" Mickey wanted to know.

"I never had to find out. My letters must have reached him in plenty of time. I always received at least one of the items from the list."

"You must not have been very good, if you only got one thing. I always get everything I ask for," Mickey said proudly.

Alana raised an eyebrow at that statement, "Well, Saint Nicholas did not have the funds back then that he does now," she answered, wondering just how generous St. Nick was to these children.

"Do you want to put your name on our list or not?" Angela asked, growing tired of all of this talk.

"You can put my name down, but put 'not particular' down beside it. I think I shall allow Santa to decide what I need, if anything," she said simply. "Is that okay? May I do that?"

"I reckon you can," Angela said, wondering if St. Nicholas accepted such an order. "But you are taking quite a chance, if you ask me."

"No one asked you," Brandon teased. "Now I have everyone's name down except Lizzie. Go get her and let's see what she wants Saint Nicholas to leave her this Christmas."

All of the children ran off to find Lizzie. While they were gone, Brandon looked over his list and chuckled to Lilian, "Looks like your children are growing up. Both Jake and Brenda asked for fancy clothes instead of toys. I cannot imagine Brenda wanting a party dress and a red velvet choker instead of a tea set or a pretty doll. The years pass by quickly, don't they? I remember when y'all came up for Christmas and Pop got Jake a drum and Brenda a wooden flute. You swore one day you would get even as they danced around making a God-awful noise."

"He just laughed and told me I was paying for my raising," she laughed as she thought back to that Christmas so many years ago when the whole family was together. "Are you asking Douglas and Anne over for Christmas dinner again this year?"

"If they get back in time, I shall. But, there won't be a turkey or any venison this year since I did not get any hunting done. I guess a ham or a chicken or two will have to do," he was saying when the children returned with Lizzie in tow.

"Here she is," Angela announced as she helped Mickey push from behind while the other four tugged on her arms.

"Y'all makin' out Saint Nick's list are ya?" she asked. Brandon showed her the paper. "Well, let me think, what should he bring old Lizzie?" she pondered.

"I know what you want," Angela announced proudly.

"What's that, child?" Lizzie wondered.

"A pretty silver music box like the one you always stop and look at in Mr. DeLane's store," she replied.

"My, no! That thing is too costly. I'd be more near gettin' what I want if I ask for a new pair of shoes. That is what I'll ask for, a new pair of Sunday-go-to-meetin' shoes," Lizzie decided.

"But, you are always admiring that music box in town," Angela insisted, stamping her foot.

"What would I do with that music box? It is made to put fine jewelry in. I don't have no need for such a fancy,"

Lizzie told her with a chuckle.

"You could take that wedding band your man gave you out of that silly old snuff tin, and put it in the music box!" Angela explained, finding it hard to understand why Lizzie felt she had to need something in order to ask St. Nicholas to bring it.

The smile dropped from Lizzie's face, "I would rather ask for a new pair of shoes child. My old ones are beyond repairin'," she said in a awkwardly grave tone.

Brandon saw the need of a change in subject and read aloud as he wrote, "And Lizzie is asking you for a fine new pair of Sunday-go-to-meeting shoes." As he folded the paper, he remarked, "That takes care of everyone. We will be all ready when the time comes to burn the list." He tucked the letter away and asked if there was any more hot cocoa.

"There is some more in the pan on the stove," Lizzie replied, and ran out of the room as fast as her stocky legs could carry her.

The jovial talk of Christmas helped Alana forget about Stephanie for the afternoon. She listened quietly as the children reminisced over their Christmases past. As the afternoon grew late, Lilian reminded them it was time to get ready for supper. The children raced to their rooms to wash their hands and comb their hair. Lilian followed to make certain Mickey washed both of his hands properly, front and back, as he had a tendency to dip them in the water and wipe them dry on his trousers.

Alana closed the book she had planned to read, but never did, and got up to get ready for supper herself when Brandon grabbed her by the arm.

"Just a minute, I have a favor I need to ask you," he said awkwardly, his gaze avoiding her eyes.

Alana had never known him to be afraid to look her in the eye. Usually it was just the opposite as she rarely could look him in the eye. Somehow, she knew before he spoke that what ever the favor was, it had something to do with Stephanie.

Hiding the fear she felt, she replied smoothly, "Certainly, what is it?"

"I am planning to stop by and pay a short visit to my old friend Stephanie DeLane tomorrow evening. I am expected to welcome her home," he said rather sheepishly as he avoided telling her the whole truth, unaware she already knew about the part of his past when he had courted Stephanie and had sworn to marry her.

"Yes, that would be nice," Alana said evenly, as a huge knot began to tighten in her throat, causing her voice to strain as she asked, "But what can I do? You mentioned a favor?"

Taking a deep breath and talking quickly, he replied, "I want you to go with me. I would like for you to meet her. You two might become good friends." He winced at his own words, which were not the ones he had planned to use. He had promised himself that he was going to be open about this part of his past with Alana, but had failed miserably to do so.

The cold lump in Alana's throat was melting away by the hot anger rising inside of her. Her jaw flinched as she replied rather curtly, "Certainly, I shall go with you. What is a friend for if she cannot lend a little support when needed? Besides, we would not want her knowing you have been pining away for her all of these years, do we?" She was angry that he had tried to keep the truth from her.

Astonished at her accuracy, Brandon asked, "You know about me and Stephanie?"

"I know," she replied bluntly. Deciding if she was going to learn to live with it, she had better begin now. In a somewhat calmer voice she added, "And I shall gladly help you convince her that your life was not destroyed by her thoughtlessness. If you want me to act out the part of your lady friend, I shall." Actually, the thought of Stephanie possibly feeling even a small degree of the jealousy she herself was trying to get over, delighted her in a satanic way.

Brandon looked at her curiously. He did not know if he liked having such easy cooperation or not. He had hoped to find at least a twinge of jealousy in her eyes, yet he found none.

Noticing a look of uncertainty in Brandon's eyes, Alana added, "Do not worry so. I can pull it off. By the time we leave her house tomorrow night, she will totally believe I am madly in love with you." As she freed her arm from Brandon's grip, she thought sadly, "How could she believe otherwise when it is the truth?"

In a turmoil of mixed emotions, Brandon watched her go. Having sworn never to allow himself to love again, he now found he had two women he deeply cared for, and both had rejected his love in one way or another. Alana wanted nothing more than his friendship, a curtailment he detested, and Stephanie had chosen riches and fame over him many years ago. Deciding it was a good time for a drink, he skipped supper and finished the bottle of whiskey Billy had opened. He was sorry Billy had wasted so much of it on that blasted wound. He knew he could be asleep much sooner if he had the total contents of the bottle.

Failing to wake in time, Brandon also missed breakfast the next morning. Without telling Lilian, avoiding a silly argument about whether or not he was up to it, he saddled his horse and rode off to find Billy. He wanted to know what needed to be done today and help do it. Hard work would keep his mind off of everything else. He was afraid that if he had too much time to think about his plans to visit Stephanie, he might back out. But he felt there was no need in prolonging their reunion. He may as well find out tonight if he still felt anything for her or if she cared for him.

Since Billy offered to share his lunch with him, Brandon saw no need to return until it was time to get ready. He had left word with Lizzie of his plans to leave by 5:00. He wanted to arrive at Stephanie's just after dark.

It was shortly after 4:00 when he returned. He went directly to the kitchen where Lizzie was under orders to have a warm bath waiting. Quickly he dressed in black dress trousers with a matching long-waisted jacket. He wore a white silk shirt with short flounces of silk plaited at the cuffs and down the front, and a broad light-blue cravat around his neck, tucked into the open collar. He brushed his hair several times before he was satisfied with it. Shortly after 5:00, he knocked at Alana's door, hoping to find her ready, unaware she had been ready and restlessly pacing the floor for over half an hour.

When Alana answered the door, she received the reaction she had hoped for. Brandon's mouth fell open in amazement as he admired her. She had borrowed one of Lilian's gowns for the evening. It was a beautiful creation of fancy gray lace over black satin. The bodice was daringly cut, although Alana was certain such a thing was far more attractive on a figure filled as well as Lilian's was. The clinging gown was worn with only a single petticoat, taking any shape it had from the soft curve of Alana's slender hips. At her neck was the black choker with the tiny golden teardrop pendant in the center that Lilian had purchased last summer. Alana's hair had been put up in a magnificent array of curls with the help of Lizzie, who seemed to be quite an expert on styling hair. Had Brandon not have seemed completely dumbfounded by her appearance, Alana would have been crushed.

"Will I do?" she asked, batting her brown eyes at him.

"Damn!" is all Brandon managed to say, making a three syllabled word out of it, as he took in Alana's uncanny beauty.

"If you do not like it, I can change in a moment's time," she offered sweetly.

"No, don't! You are beautiful!" he exclaimed, unable to stop staring at her. A smile slowly worked its way across his face as he thought of how Stephanie was going to feel twinges of jealousy when she met Alana. She did hate to encounter anyone who was as beautiful if not more so than Stephanie knew she was.

It was well after dark when they pulled in front of a stately two-storied colonial house, painted white with black shutters. Tall white columns stood the height of both stories, supporting the high ceiling over the huge walkway. Large globular lanterns hung from thick black chains, lighting the way to the heavy oak double doors. Brandon removed his overcoat and laid it neatly across his arm before pulling the cord to the wrought-iron bell that hung just above the door. They both held their breath as they waited for the door to open.

Within a few moments, a tall slender Negro man in very stiff formal attire opened the door. His eyes grew wide as he raised an eyebrow in surprise. He recognized Brandon immediately.

"Good evening, Everett, would you be so kind as to tell Miss DeLane, uh, Mrs. Ellison that she has visitors—that is, if she is receiving."

The elderly black man peeked around the door to see who was with Brandon and raised both eyebrows at Alana, standing demurely at Brandon's side. "Come on in, Mr. Warren, I'll go tell her y'all are here."

Brandon stepped aside, allowing Alana to precede him. He followed her inside, closing the door behind them. Hooking his arm in hers, they waited nervously for Stephanie to come.

Alana was impressed with the decor of this fashionable home. A wide elaborate stairway circled down from the second floor with a highly polished wooden handrail on either side. A fabulous crystal chandelier hung above them the height of two men and nearly as wide. Shining pieces of silver highlighted the room in the shapes of decanters, fancy trays, and wall frames. She never expected a shopkeeper to live so lavishly.

Noting her amazement, Brandon offered a brief explanation, "Stephanie's mother was the daughter of a successful shipper in New Orleans. He had his own line of ships that traveled the entire globe. She inherited everything when he died," he whispered.

"Why does he even bother with his store?" she asked him, finding this show of wealth overwhelming. She had been impressed with the Montaqua house, but this place was in a class all alone. Sadly, she realized she had more than another woman working against her.

"They only inherited this fortune about eight years ago, just a little while before her mother died," he continued.

"But why does he still run that store?" she repeated, wondering why he did not hire someone else to run the business for him.

Before Brandon could answer, Everett had returned. He bowed at the waist as he said stiffly, "She has asked me to see you to the outer parlor. If you would be so kind as to follow me."

With Alana on Brandon's arm, they followed Everett into the next room. Alana was less impressed with the so-called outer parlor. The room was tasteful, but not as elaborate as the formal entry. The floors were not made of marble as in the other room. An expensive tapestry one would expect to see used as a wall hanging was centered on the heavily waxed wood floors. The French décor was done in several soft shades of violet contrasted with pieces of blue porcelain lining the mantle over the fireplace as well as spotted about on the many polished tables. A special collection of porcelain birds was displayed in tall glass cabinets on either side of a huge bay window that overlooked the well-manicured gardens outside the house.

Curious to see the view made possible by the bright moonlight, Alana pulled away and walked over to the window. Brandon allowed Everett to take his coat, then stood silently watching her with his hands clasped behind him. He was beginning to wish he had left Alana out of this. He knew Stephanie could be cruel and Alana in no way would deserve the treatment he was afraid she would receive. Stephanie truly hated any form of competition, especially if it came in the form of anyone as beautiful as Alana.

The soft sound of footsteps nearing the doorway captured Brandon's attention as well as Alana's. They turned around in time to see Stephanie make a grand entrance. To Alana's dismay and Brandon's delight, Stephanie was stunning. Her long blond hair was pulled back and soft ringlets allowed to fall down the back of her head, just barely touching her shoulders. A jeweled comb gently held the delicate curls in place. Although her soft skin was still smooth and her ivory complexion clear, Alana guessed her age to be near that of Brandon's. She had on a pale green gown with emerald green trim that Alana felt clashed with the surroundings pitifully, but knew Brandon would never notice such a thing. She smiled as she thought how Cynthia would not let such a thing go unnoticed; something clever would have to be said. As Stephanie approached Brandon, unaware of his watchful companion nearby, Alana saw that her gown especially matched her uncanny green eyes.

Alana froze as Stephanie held out her hand as if the weight of it was too much for her dainty arm to bear, "Brandon, I was hoping you would come. If you had not visited soon, I was going to send Everett out to drag you into town. I have missed you dreadfully."

Brandon took the hand in both of his as he softly replied, "It has been a long time. The years have treated you well."

"And you as well. I expected to see a change, but I never expected to see you with a beard. I remember you unsuccessfully tried to grow one when you were sixteen. I truly hated it. But, I do like this one. I must admit it is quite handsome. No, you are extremely handsome," she told him with a smile of approval.

Alana cringed inside as Stephanie lowered her lashes and looked up at him dolefully, "I was afraid you might be angry with me." A pout was forced on her lips as she added, "I was such a silly fool!"

Trying to avoid the spell she seemed to be casting on him, Brandon held his hand out to Alana, "Stephanie, there is someone I would like for you to meet," he began in a strained voice.

"Oh, yes, Everett mentioned that you had brought a friend. I told him to bring tea for all of us. Any friend of yours is welcome—" she stopped in midsentence as she turned to greet this friend of Brandon's and saw Alana coming to claim Brandon's outstretched arm. Slowly, she finished her sentence with a fading smile—"in my father's home."

"I would like for you to meet the beautiful Alana Stambridge, my dearest friend," he said as he smiled down at Alana.

Playing her role to the hilt, Alana laid her head on his shoulder and in her most charming voice replied, "Oh, Brandon, you are going to make me blush."

She hated using the same line Cynthia had relied on so many times, but it seemed effective.

"Alana, dear, I would like for you to meet an old friend of mine, Stephanie—Ellison, isn't it?"

Feeling the sharpness of his voice, Stephanie nodded politely to Alana.

"Pleased to meet you. I have heard so much about you that I feel we are already friends," Alana said with a proper nod of her own head, not letting go of Brandon even long enough to offer Stephanie her hand.

"And I am pleased to meet you, too, to be sure. But, I must admit, I have heard nothing of you. Are you from around here?" Stephanie asked rather coolly.

Trying to avoid admitting that she was in reality employed by Brandon, she simply answered, "I moved here only recently. Actually, I am from New York."

Before Stephanie could question her further, Everett appeared at the door, carrying a footed silver tray with a complete silver tea service and a plate of fancy little cakes. "Where shall I set this, madam?"

Irritated by the interruption, she answered briskly, "Oh, set it anywhere!" Then with obvious constraint, she invited Brandon and Alana to sit with her and enjoy a cup of tea.

As Everett poured the tea, Stephanie placed the cups on saucers. Before handing Brandon his tea, she offered to lace it with a bit of her father's imported brandy. At his approval, she doused it generously. Just before she handed Alana hers, Stephanie piled several cakes on the side of the saucer, mentioning how delicious they were. She then picked up her own saucer, neglecting to place even a single cake on the saucer, and motioned for them to sit. Stephanie sat on the opposite side of Brandon and effectively managed to monopolize his attention as she began to question him about many of their old friends and reminded him of the happy times they had spent together so many years ago. She opened the crystal decanter and offered Brandon more of the brandy. She kept refilling his cup with the brandy alone, at Brandon's request, as she continued her flirtations. Slowly, Brandon's coolness toward Stephanie melted and they began laughing together over some of the antics Roth and Brandon had pulled as boys. Alana noticed he began to turn his back to her, forcing her to sit silently, unable to join in on their conversation.

As the hour grew late, Brandon finally insisted they had to be going. Before calling Everett to bring Brandon his coat, she took his hand in hers and invited him to a special party her father was planning in her honor.

"You just have to come. Many of our old friends will be invited," she said sweetly.

Alana felt defeated. Stephanie had succeeded in winning Brandon's heart back. She was so certain of Stephanie's overwhelming victory, she could hardly believe her ears when she heard Brandon reply, "Of course, Stephie, we would love to come. Wouldn't we, Alana?" He reached out to her with his free hand.

Jumping at the chance to repay Stephanie for the many hours she had just spent gazing longingly at Brandon's back, Alana leaned over and snuggled against his side, "We would not miss it for the world."

"Then, it is settled, you are coming. Everett will be by with the formal invitation when the exact date has been set," she told them as they got up to leave. Just before they reached the door, Stephanie pulled Brandon back. "Brandon, may I speak to you alone? It will only take a minute. You do not mind, do you Alana?"

"Certainly not," she lied through a forced smile. "I will just wait for you in here, Brandon, darling," she told them as she stepped through the doorway into the entry hall.

She casually walked about the room looking at the various paintings, pretending not to notice as Stephanie took his hand and held it to her cheek as she spoke. Alana could tell by her overwrought expression that Stephanie was again trying to explain how sorry she was for her actions of the past. Alana could barely believe it when Stephanie managed to produce a few tears. "Purely for effect," thought Alana angrily. She felt certain this little outbreak of sincerity was not coming from the heart. There was just something false about it. When Brandon bent over and kissed Stephanie on the cheek, Alana turned a shoulder to them and acted as if she was completely unconcerned. More than the minute Stephanie had asked for passed, and Alana felt herself rapidly growing impatient. She was ready to pace the floor by the time Brandon escorted Stephanie into the room.

"Will you have Everett bring my coat, Stephie?" she heard him ask as they came near her.

"I shall get it for you," Stephanie replied in a mellow tone as she stepped inside a small door just below the stairway. "Here it is," she told him as she handed it to him and followed them to the door. Just as they were about to step outside, she reached out for Brandon's cheek and touched the soft beard covering it lightly. "Thank you, Brandon," she said simply.

Once they were safely outside and the door closed behind them, Alana asked casually, "Thank you for what?"

Brandon smiled briefly as he replied, "Oh, nothing." Then noticing Alana was shivering from the cold December night air, Brandon asked her where her coat was.

Rather than admit her vanity had kept her from bringing that ugly coat of hers, and afraid it might spoil the dress, Alana lied, "I got mud on it Sunday and Lizzie has not cleaned it yet."

"Here, take mine. I still have my undercoat," he offered as he stopped to hold it open for her.

Being colder than she was vain, Alana slipped her tiny arms into Brandon's coat and wrapped its width around her twice. Brandon found it impossible not to laugh at Alana's comical appearance. The sleeves bagged down over her hands and the hem nearly dragged the ground. Alana looked down at herself and had to laugh too. They were still laughing about it when they were in the carriage and headed home.

When Alana managed to catch her breath and calm her laughter a bit, she asked the question that was furthermost on her mind, "Why are you including me in Stephanie's party?"

"Because I do not think I am ready to face her alone; not

yet anyway. I need for her to believe you are in her way. I hope you did not become upset. You won't mind going with me, will you?" he asked, looking hopefully down at her.

"I think you could handle her alone," Alana replied evenly.

"I am just not ready. Not yet," he said simply. After a pause, he added, "Who knows, you might enjoy yourself. All of Gilmer's finest is certain to turn out for the party and that should include many available young men."

He watched carefully for her reaction, somewhat glad she did not seem interested. The fact was that it had not interested her at all. Instead, it had crushed her that Brandon had the same as suggested she go to the party to find someone else. Alana remained quiet for the remainder of the ride home. Overly tired from the whole ordeal and from the sleepless night before, Alana caught herself drifting into sleep.

Brandon noticed Alana's head nodding sleepily. Since the back of the seat was not high enough to lean back against, he put his arm around her and pulled her gently to him, allowing her head to rest against his shoulder. Too sleepy to find reason to object, Alana fell asleep in his arms. Holding her close, Brandon enjoyed these peaceful moments, feeling as if he were in possession of a precious angel. He watched the evening shadows dance across her sweet face tilted against his arm, wondering if any man would ever conquer her heart. Even Billy had failed miserably. Somehow that relationship seemed to be losing ground. He knew whoever did finally win her love, Billy would probably despise him. How he wished it could be himself that someday gained Alana's affections.

All too soon, they turned into the driveway to Montaqua. Noticing the barn doors were left open, Brandon decided to park the carriage inside. He planned to carry Alana to her room, but as the carriage stopped, Alana awoke. She was still a little groggy when Brandon climbed down and offered his hand to help her down. Still very sleepy, Alana slipped as she reached out to take that hand. Before she could fall very far, Brandon reached out and caught her by her waist. In order to get a secure grip through the bulky coat, he had to pull her very close. As he eased her to the ground, he felt her body slide against that of his own. Before she could collect her thoughts, she could smell the liquor of his breath close to her as he pressed his lips to hers. At first she tried to resist, but as an unfamiliar passion surged through her body, any fears she may have had were quickly overpowered. She gave up the struggle and chose to go with these innermost desires. She allowed him to pull her closer and gently kiss her all about her face. She found it difficult to breathe as he began kissing the length of her neck and found herself gasping for air. Her heart was beating so wildly, she felt certain that even Brandon could hear its pounding. The more his lips touched the tender flesh along her neck the more she wanted to have them there. Her thoughts blended with her feelings as she anxiously wanted to have him.

Just as Brandon's hungry mouth returned to hers, a ray of light fell across her face. Startled by it, Alana pulled quickly away. Brandon turned to determine the culprit of such an untimely intrusion. He saw Billy coming out of his room at the other side of the barn, carrying a large lantern by his side. In a sleepy voice, he asked, "Brandon, is that you?"

"Yes, Billy, it's me," he answered sourly. "We just returned from town and I was about to unhitch the horses."

"We? Alana, you still here?" he yawned.

After a short pause, she answered carefully, "Yes, but I was just about to go to my room, unless you two need me for something."

"No, I will help Brandon bed down the horse. You just go on to your room. You gotta teach class tomorrow, you know." Billy put the lantern on top of a tall barrel and began unbuckling the harness, stopping once and again to rub his tousled head. He was totally unaware that he had interrupted anything of importance.

With very little enthusiasm in her voice, Alana offered them a quick goodnight and walked out. Brandon watched longingly as she disappeared into the shadows.

He was barely able to overcome the strong desire he had to wrap his fingers firmly around Billy's throat and squeeze.

Chapter Ten

Alana was not looking forward to this evening at all. Especially not after Brandon had made such a point to apologize to her for what he termed as "taking dreadful advantage" of her. The excuse he offered for such an outrageous act was the near-drunken state he felt he must have been in. He blamed the brandy on an empty stomach and claimed he would never have put their friendship in such jeopardy had he been sober. The words felt like a spiteful slap across the face after having spent the rest of that night reliving those precious moments over and over in her dreams. Then to have him come to her that very next morning and explain in so many words that he had to have been drunk to have kissed her. She was hurt deeply. She was also infuriated with herself for once again building great hopes on another such false foundation. Although she was angry at Brandon for hurting her so, she was more angry at herself for allowing him to do so. Several times after that, she wanted to tell Brandon she could not go with him to the party, but something inside of her always prevented her from doing so. Now it was too late to back out. The party was only hours away. Besides, they had promised Archie and Lilian their company for the evening.

Hoping to make the best of a bad situation, Alana chose to wear one of the beautiful gowns from the enormous selection in Lilian's closet. Lilian had insisted since Alana felt none of her own dresses would do. At first, she worried someone might recognize the gown as Lilian's and have a snide remark or two. But, with her own accessories and having a completely different type of figure to give the fashion an entirely different shape, she decided that the chances of anyone guessing this gown was Lilian's were fairly slim.

The gown she had selected was of her favorite color, a deep royal gold. Delicate brown lace trimmed the long billowing sleeves, tiny waist, and the plunging neckline. She planned to wear the necklace that her father had given her, bearing a delicately sculptured golden cross. Not owning a proper dress coat, she chose to carry a brown shawl to wrap around her shoulders in case she should become chilled. Since Archie planned to hire an enclosed carriage for the evening, the shawl should be more than sufficient and would not clash with the gown. It was cut full at the shoulders and in the skirt, but tapered drastically at the waist. It had been so tight four days ago, when she first tried it on, that she had refused to eat anything since. She hoped that she could get by without having to wear a restraint, which was usually quite obvious to anyone who cared to observe a lady's waist.

While waiting for Lizzie to come style her hair again, Alana decided to try the dress on without her restraints. To her delight, it buttoned at the waist quite easily. She admired herself in the mirror for a moment, before taking it off again to avoid mussing it.

Impatiently she divided her attention between the clock at her bedside and the window facing the patio. Worried that it might take longer than planned to do her hair, she began nervously tapping her fingertips against the windowpane. Eventually, annoyed by her own repetitious racket, she stepped away from the window and began to pace about the room. Minutes deceived her as being hours and she decided that she had better try to do something with her hair herself. She barely had it brushed out when Lizzie's knock finally came.

"Come in, please," she said with obvious relief, putting the brush aside.

"You ready for me to make you beautiful?" Lizzie asked as she closed the door behind her.

"I won't ask for miracles, just do the best you can," Alana pleaded while looking disgustedly in the mirror at what Lizzie had to work with. Her hair had become horridly dry over the past few weeks, attempting to adhere to the bristles of her brush whenever she pulled it away. "Good luck. You are going to need it," she pouted.

"Let me do the worryin', you just sit still," Lizzie ordered as she began to unload the contents of a small cloth bag that she had brought with her.

Alana watched silently as Lizzie set the items on her vanity until she noticed Lizzie set down a jar of hand oil. "What do you need that for? My hands are not dry."

"Just watch," Lizzie said simply as she dipped a pudgy finger into the yellow liquid. She rubbed it generously all over her hands and then began to run them gently through Alana's long brown hair. As she did, the hair began to lay down and its natural sheen seemed to return. Taking a large brush in hand, Lizzie was able to smooth the hair out. After pulling the front hair up and tying it at the top of her head out of the way, Lizzie began working with the back part. She pulled a long iron rod with a wooden handle out of the bag and waved it through the flames in the fireplace. Alana looked frightened as Lizzie began wrapping long strands around the hot piece of metal.

"Won't that burn my hair?" she asked fearfully.

"What? This?" Lizzie asked innocently. "This is just my magic wand. You might better just shut your eyes and let me do my magic. I will tell you when I'm through."

Alana did close her eyes, peeking occasionally only to see a total disarray of hair. Then with orders to quit that peeking, she held them tightly closed, listening to Lizzie hum a melody familiar to her. When Lizzie finally commanded Alana to open her eyes, Alana found that Lizzie had indeed cast a magic spell on her hair. It was beautiful. The front swept down, back, and then up where Lizzie had arranged the ends in a fabulous display of tiny finger curls. Several long thick ringlets hung low in the back, held in place by a large golden comb decorated with tiny black pearls that Alana did not recognize. Before she could ask about it, Lizzie told her that it was Lilian's and that she had to use it because she needed its width. Alana was glad she did because of its beauty.

After looking at it for a long moment, she said gratefully, "Lizzie, I feel that I owe you a miracle."

"You don't owe me nothin'. You just have a good time at that party. Don't let nobody keep you from enjoyin' yourself. You hear?" Lizzie remarked as she wagged her finger just inches from Alana's nose.

"I hear," Alana assured her, trying to pull her nose in to avoid a painful confrontation with that finger.

Before leaving to check on Lilian's progress, Lizzie took time to help Alana button and hook the back of her gown and to hook up her shoes so that she would not muss her hair. Once she was alone, Alana used her last half hour to practice a smooth walk and an appealing little smile. As the time grew near to leave, Alana's pulse quickened. It was so disheartening to know that no matter how nice she looked or how pleasant she tried to be, Brandon was destined to be with Stephanie. Yet, still she had to try.

When Brandon knocked at her door, she placed the sweet little smile she had been practicing with on her face and greeted him cheerfully.

"Archie is here. Are you ready?" Brandon asked as he allowed his gaze to take in every beautiful detail of Alana's appearance.

"Certainly," she replied widening her smile and stepped outside into the cool evening air. Graciously she slipped her arm in the one he presented to her. After he closed her door, he laid his free hand on top of hers and escorted her to the carriage where Lilian and Archie were waiting.

As he opened the door to the carriage, he remarked with a devilish smile, "You have truly outdone yourself tonight."

"Then you approve?" she asked simply.

"Oh, I approve all right. I can hardly wait to see everyone's eyes turn our way when I walk in with you by my side."

"If they do, it will be you they admire," she said earnestly as she looked at the handsome gray formal coat that he wore over a vest with fancy trousers made of the same gray material as the coat. He wore a blue silk shirt with flounces of ruffles at the opened neck and at the exposed cuffs. A silver diamond-shaped pin was placed in the front of the dark blue scarf that was loosely tied at his neck and tucked neatly into his shirt front. The silver chain to his pocket watch was handsomely draped across his vest.

She climbed into the carriage, and sat across from Archie and Lilian who were deeply involved in an exchange of their own compliments. Lilian had purposely worn a gown of violet, Archie's favorite color. It was not as daringly cut as many of her evening gowns were, but it did have a low neckline, trimmed in thick black ruffles. Three layers of identical black ruffles also adorned the cuffs and the base of the full-cut skirt. She carried a black silk cape over her arm and had a black sequined bag dangling from her fingertips. Brandon and Alana both had to agree when Archie described her as heavenly.

By the time they arrived at Stephanie's house, Archie had eased everyone's obvious anticipation by executing several tall tales. He even managed to make Alana laugh at his ridiculous stories, despite the dread that weighted her heart. As the laughter they shared dwindled away, they neared the front door. Brandon stood restlessly aside as Archie rang the bell to announce their presence.

An eternal moment later, Everett opened the door with a greeting that seemed to be growing old on his tongue, "Welcome, please come in. You will find the rest of the guests just down the hall in the parlor. Some have begun to enter the ballroom although the music will not begin until nine o'clock. Please, enjoy yourself," he said in a monotone, weary from repetition as he closed the door.

"May I take your coats," he offered automatically.

As they handed him their coats and wraps, voices could be heard drifting down the dimly lit hallway. Brandon immediately offered Alana his arm as the group proceeded down the hallway to the first of the three doors brightly lit from a dazzling number of candles and lamps within the rooms. The heavy blend of voices grew louder as they stepped inside the large room that Alana guessed had to be the formal parlor.

Looking around the room for the sight of Stephanie, Alana's eyes took in the splendor of this room. There were thick carpets the color of red wine covering the floor, and heavy matching drapes hung the full length of the windows and were parted slightly, allowing a view of the lamplit gardens, which looked magnificent in spite of the absence of spring or summer flowers. On either side of the windows sat two huge tables engulfed in a wide selection of tasty treats. Huge glass bowls of a ruby-colored drink were constantly being dipped into and served in the delicate crystal cups that surrounded them. Rows of holly decorated the border of the table, making the setting festive. Christmas was now less than two weeks away. The furniture, elaborately upholstered in reds and blacks, had been pushed against the walls to allow more room for the guests to mingle. Two huge crystal chandeliers were richly highlighted by hundreds of individual candles. Many tall candelabras glowed brightly on several of the highly polished tables set stategically about the room. Alana found all of this grandeur a little disheartening, but more to her dislike was the woman she spotted heading their way.

Stephanie was wearing a gorgeous gown fashioned from an extravagant red velvet and trimmed with an intricate white lace. The skimp of her neckline revealed the ample swell of her richly endowed bosom above which an exquisite silver necklace with a large ruby, worked into an engraved background, was barely noticed. Her deep-green eyes were fastened on Brandon's face as she made her way through the crowded room to greet her special guest with a lingering kiss.

Alana felt every muscle tighten as she listened to Brandon's open appraisal of Stephanie. What hurt worse than the praise Brandon offered so easily was the fact that each word was absolutely true. Stephanie was especially becoming tonight. Every strand of her golden hair was perfectly placed. The front was pulled back into several short ringlets, which hung over the remaining tresses allowed to flow freely down her back. There was not a flaw to be found and Alana searched quite carefully for one. She watched Brandon's expression as Stephanie, in turn, complimented him lavishly. His eyes revealed the positive effect her flirtations were having on him. Alana wished dearly that she could master the womanly art as well as Stephanie had. She noted the shy way she lowered her lashes even when she intended to peer up at Brandon and how she slightly wrinkled her nose when she laughed at anything witty Brandon had to say. Alana was aware Stephanie was very adept in her ability to captivate a man, especially Brandon, by her smooth actions. Brandon's grip on Alana's arm loosened with each bat of Stephanie's emerald eyes.

Lilian and Archie did not bother to speak with their hostess and easily maneuvered themselves around her to join in the conversation of one of the many groups gathering in the room. Alana felt awkwardly alone, even as she still stood beside Brandon, trying not to seem terribly bothered by Stephanie's successful advances toward Brandon. But she was indeed so bothered by them that she had not noticed that Roth Felton stood at her side. She was startled when he spoke her name.

"Miss Stambridge, you look simply ravishing tonight."

While she was thanking him, he held out his hand to take hers in greeting. But, rather than shake it as she supposed he would, he lifted it gently to his lips and kissed it. Turning her hand over, he gently kissed the flat of her palm in a manner that made Alana feel somewhat uncomfortable.

Brandon frowned at the way his friend lingered over a simple kiss of the hand, but Roth paid little attention to his displeasure. He proceeded to hold her hand in both of his.

"I have not seen you since that evening in Brandon's bedroom," he commented, knowing the statement would raise a few eyebrows.

Both Brandon and Stephanie complied with his wishes as their eyes grew wide at such a statement. Having been unconscious at the time, Brandon wanted to know, "When was this?"

As Roth told him, Stephanie wondered what Alana

would have been doing at Montaqua while the rest of the family was away. She still had not learned that Alana was his employee and lived on the premises. Deciding to ask Brandon about it later, she acted as if she was not in the least concerned. For now she only inquired about the snake bite and listened with a growing look of horror as he told her how he had been bitten and had tended to it himself. Alana waited proudly for him to relate the part of the story where she nursed him back to health, but it did not come. Instead, he went on to recall how Stephanie's cousin had chased her around the schoolyard with a dead chicken snake.

Noticing that Alana was excluded from this conversation, Roth saw a chance to talk with her. "Are you enjoying East Texas?"

"Oh, yes, I love East Texas. I can hardly believe that the month is December and it is barely cold enough to warrant wearing a coat," she said, keeping an ear to what Brandon was saying about the mean streak in Stephanie's cousin.

"You are from the north then?" he asked, keeping the conversation alive.

"I am from New York," she answered simply, still giving most of her attention to Brandon and Stephanie.

"New York? Fine place," he remarked. "There is always something to do in New York."

"Have you been there?" Alana asked curiously.

"Once, about ten years ago I guess. I was about seventeen and determined to join the theater."

"You are an actor?" she asked, letting her attention dwell on him.

"Not really. I wanted to be, but that is not the way it turned out. As one director put it, "Kid, ya got style, but ya just can't act," he chuckled.

"Really let you down easy, didn't he?" she laughed at the thought of it.

Brandon fell silent when he heard Alana's laughter. He realized he should be glad that she and his friend were enjoying themselves. But he was not. He was just about to ask them what was so funny, when odd notes began to be heard from the next room as the orchestra prepared to play.

"They must be about to begin," Stephanie announced excitedly, grabbing Brandon by the arm. "Come on, you must dance with me. You know how dearly I love to dance."

Reluctantly, Brandon allowed her to lead him to the double doorway of the ballroom. As they left Alana standing beside Roth, Brandon gave her a look of helplessness and shouted back over his shoulder, "We will be right back."

Stephanie smiled brightly and shouted, "No, we will not," then disappeared inside with Brandon in tow.

"She always has been able to get her way," Roth said as he watched Alana's face grow heavy with despair. "There is just something about her that a man cannot resist."

That fact was already made obvious to Alana. There was something in the way Stephanie held her head, or was it the way she used added expressions in her flirtations? It might just be the way she used her eyes. Whatever it was, Alana wished she possessed those same charms. Well, she intended to have them. With a little practice, she ought to be able to master this art of flirtation as well as anyone. Turning to Roth, she smiled sweetly and with her head turned down shyly but her eyes looking up eagerly into his, she asked, "Do you dance, Mr. Felton?"

"Mr. Felton? Please, call me Roth, as I do plan to call you Alana," he said, adding, "Yes, I love to dance. Would you do me the honor?"

Taking his arm, she replied, "It would be silly to refuse such a handsome gentleman as yourself."

The music began as soon as they stepped inside the large ballroom. Alana caught but a glimpse of the golden beauty of the room before being whisked onto the dance floor. The walls were painted a pale yellow and the wooden floors were of a highly waxed golden brown hue. Several small chairs of a blending floral print were lined against the two inner walls. The orchestra was arranged in three small rows at the far wall, leaving most of the floor for dancing or spectating. A wall-length row of windows at the end of the room revealed more of the fabulous gardens with two doors opening to a pathway made of large white stones.

Before she could locate Brandon and Stephanie among the many couples crowding the dance floor, Roth pulled her close. Taking one hand in his and placing his other hand at her waist, he began to whirl her in and out of the many other couples that were dancing. The tempo was so fast and lively that she never seemed to face one place long enough to spot Brandon, or anyone else for that matter. As the music slowed down for the second dance, she was able to look around. She finally spotted him with Stephanie over by the orchestra. Brandon held her very close to him as he slowly led her across the floor. Stephanie was using her feminine charms on him even now as she stared longingly into his eyes.

Studying Stephanie's face, Alana carefully copied her expression as she looked up into Roth's silver-blue eyes. Smiling at this attention, Roth pulled her closer. "It works!" she thought as she allowed Roth to place his cheek against her temple. So far, this little experiment with Roth was entirely successful. Soon, she would be ready to try her new-found womanly wiles on Brandon.

It was not until after the first set of melodies that Alana was able to lure Roth over to join Brandon and Stephanie. The two were stepping outside for a breath of fresh air when Alana finally managed to catch them.

"Beautiful night, is it not?" Alana mentioned casually as they came up behind Brandon hoping to get his attention.

Roth was not certain if Alana was speaking to him or not, but he answered anyway, "Yes, it is very beautiful."

At the sound of Roth's voice, Brandon turned with a look of disbelief. He had not realized that Roth was still with Alana. He had not noticed them on the dance floor, but then he did not think to look. Somehow, Stephanie had caused him to forget that he had left them together in the parlor.

"I see you are taking good care of Alana," he said, staring openly at the arm Roth had placed at her waist.

With all of the charm she could manage while battling

the jealousy she felt at the sight of Stephanie holding on to Brandon's arm, she said, "Roth is taking excellent care of me. We have danced every dance. He is a marvelous dancer."

As she said that, she smiled up at Roth and gave his arm a tiny squeeze. A frown crossed Brandon's face equal to the smile that Alana now used on Roth. He knew Roth too well and did not like the idea of Alana being so friendly with him. Roth rarely spent time with any woman for the sheer sake of companionship. He was afraid Roth might have well-laid plans for Alana. He was not certain of Alana's motives either. He had never seen her act this way. The thought of Roth's lips meeting Alana's in the heat of passion irritated the hell out of him. Roth was not the proper man for Alana. But Brandon knew he had no right to feel as he did, and tried to shrug off the ill feelings as he allowed Stephanie to put his arm around her, mentioning that she was a bit chilly.

"Why don't we all go back inside and refresh ourselves with a little punch?" Brandon suggested, putting extra emphasis on the word all.

After they returned to the parlor for the punch and cookies, Brandon made certain the foursome did not separate. He had every intention of keeping an eye on Roth, especially since he found the punch was heavily spiked. Liquor seemed to have an easy effect on most women and he feared that Alana's good judgment might be altered by it. Stephanie was not happy with the foursome but found no way to break it until the music started again.

Once out on the dance floor, she was able to cast her spell over Brandon again. This time she found it necessary to run a finger up and down the back of his neck in order to beguile him. Not far away, Alana had observed Stephanie's trick with the finger and tried tickling Roth's neck gently while looking innocently into his eyes. He pressed her closer, moving his hand from her waist to the small of her back as a result. Closing her eyes, Alana pretended she was dancing with Brandon and leaned her head against Roth's shoulder. They remained on the dance floor until the orchestra struck up a jig.

"That's not for me," Roth told her. "Why don't we enjoy another cup of punch instead."

Putting his arm around her, he escorted her back into the parlor and poured her a cup full to the brim. After the jig, the music stopped completely.

"It must be time for another intermission," Alana remarked, noticing the great number of guests entering the parlor and gathering at the punch bowls. She kept her eye on the door for Brandon and Stephanie. As the crowd thinned out, she could see him just at the other side of the door talking to a man whose back was turned to her. Although she could not see Stephanie, Alana was certain that she was still at his side and found that she was correct when the three of them stepped through the door.

Realizing that Roth had turned to see what she was looking at, she asked, "Who is that man talking to Brandon?"

Roth eyed him closely as he replied, "That is Jerroed Metkiln. He is one of the richest cattlemen around. Mr. Metkiln has quite a spread just this side of Marshall. He was a good friend of Brandon's dad."

Alana looked at the man curiously. He was an odd little man dressed in a black suit with the lapels edged in black sequins. And as if that was not flashy enough, he had on the only pair of white Western boots that Alana had ever seen. She could just imagine that he had a big white hat to cover his balding gray head as well. He continually chewed on a cigar and kept his eyes on Stephanie's bosom as they talked.

"Come on," Roth said, "Let's join them. I have some business possibilities I would like to discuss with Mr. Metkiln. This might be the perfect opportunity."

He again put his arm around Alana, and guided her through the crowd to where Brandon was still talking with the man. While the five of them were standing around talking about the latest updates in the cattle business, Stephanie's father came over to the group to ask his daughter for the next dance.

"Oh, Father, I would love to but I promised Brandon I

would dance with him,"

Before she could say any more, Brandon butted in, "Stephanie, go ahead and dance with your father. After all, you have danced every dance with me. It is only right that you dance at least once with your father."

With a strong look of protest, she replied, "Okay, Daddy, when the orchestra starts to play again, come find me and I will dance with you."

"I consider that a promise," he answered with the proud smile only a father could have. "Good evening, Miss Stambridge," he said politely as he turned to leave.

With a look of surprise, she spoke to Alana for the first time since their greeting, "You know my father?" It had never occurred to her that her father would know Alana.

"I have shopped in his store," she answered simply.

A frown closed in on Stephanie as she had not thought to ask her own father about Brandon's new friend. After all of the unanswered inquiries to her own friends about this possible dark-haired rival, her own father could be the one to supply the answers. Deciding to question her father first thing in the morning, Stephanie returned her attention to Brandon for now.

As the three men talked, it became apparent that Roth wanted an invitation to look over Mr. Metkiln's stock, telling him how interested he was in crossing his Angus cattle with other breeds in order to produce a higher quality of beef.

"Maybe you should meet Edward Stomsey. He is in the process of doing just that," Mr. Metkiln said, proud of his information. "He is standing over in the far corner there. Would you like to meet him?"

"I most certainly would!" He turned to walk away with the funny little man, when he remembered Alana, "We will be right back," he said over his shoulder as he disappeared into the crowd.

Alana felt awkward at being the odd fellow to Brandon and Stephanie once again. She tried to think of a plausible excuse to leave them, feeling that Brandon would rather be alone with his precious Stephanie. But before she could conjure up such an excuse, the music in the other room began and Stephanie's father appeared at her side ready for his dance.

Knowing that she would be leaving Brandon alone with Alana after working so hard not to, Stephanie protested, "Not yet, Father. I am not rested from the last dance."

With a wink, her father replied, "You are young, you will manage. Besides, you promised me this dance."

"That is true," Brandon reminded her, taking her hand and presenting it to her father.

Reluctantly, Stephanie allowed her father to lead her into the next room for their dance. Now they were alone, Brandon moved closer to Alana.

"Having a good time?" he asked somewhat matter-of-factly.

"I am having a marvelous time," she exaggerated, wishing instead she had stayed home. Then she would have been spared the misery of seeing Brandon and Stephanie together.

After a short pause, he asked her, "Would you care to dance?"

Her first thought was "Would I ever!" But she managed to restrain herself and answered politely, "I would love to."

Brandon put his hand at her waist as they followed several other couples into the ballroom. Once out on the floor, he took one of her hands gently in his and slipped his other hand around to the lower part of her back. Holding her closely, he began to guide her gracefully through the other couples. Although he did not hold her with the same force as Roth had, Alana was twice as aware of Brandon's touch. She was also aware of the cold stare she was receiving from Stephanie, who was never very far away, but she did not particularly care. It was Brandon's choice to ask her to dance, she did not coerce him into it. Allowing Brandon to pull her closer as the dance floor grew crowded, Alana closed her eyes and enjoyed the enchanting feel of Brandon's arms around her as they glided easily to the soft flow of the melody.

All too soon the music stopped. Alana expected Brandon to release her and try to locate Stephanie. But the orchestra quickly struck a waltz and she found that Brandon was moving her across the floor to the tri-beat of the gentle music. Alana felt as if she were floating on air, allowing Brandon to control her every movement. She wished desperately that the song would never end, but it did. As the group paused to rearrange their music sheets, Alana saw Roth working his way over to them. At the same moment he reached them, Stephanie's voice came from behind her, "There you are! I was wondering what happened to you." She innocently pretended not to have noticed them on the dance floor.

Before Brandon could reply, the musicians began a swift-moving polka. Roth reached around Alana and quickly pulled her into a lively step around the floor. Stephanie held her arms out in readiness and Brandon moved her into the flow of the crowd.

Several more dances passed before the orchestra leader announced another break. Roth suggested a bit more punch might hit the spot, and he pulled Alana along behind most of the others into the parlor. While they were waiting in the quickly forming line, Lilian and Archie approached them to say hello. They already had their punch and a few cookies as well and nibbled as they talked.

"Have you seen Brandon?" Lilian wanted to know.

"Not in the past hour," Alana hated to admit, but at that moment spotted him and Stephanie at the windows talking to another young couple.

"There he is," Alana told her, nodding in the proper direction.

"Good, I want to go over and talk him into staying later than planned. I am having such a great time, I do not want to see it end." Lilian laughed as Archie snitched two of the cookies from her napkin.

Waiting until he could clear his mouth, Archie replied, "You do not have to bother going over there. Here they come now." The four of them turned to watch as Brandon, with Stephanie still clutching his arm, came their way.

"How's it going, sis?" he asked with a wink as he came

to stand beside her.

"Why, Brandon Warren, you have had too much punch," noticing his smile stretched a little too far across his face as it did whenever he was nearing intoxication. Stephanie's silly little giggle at the remark made them realize that she also had consumed far too much of the punch herself.

"Looks like you are enjoying the punch, too," Brandon teased his sister as he pointed to the half-filled cup on her plate.

Lilian just laughed and took another sip. As she continued to discuss the many pleasantries of the evening, Roth managed to get his hands on two more cups of the ruby concoction and presented one to Alana. She sipped it lightly as she listened to Lilian's account of some of the more prominent guests present.

When the conversation finally lagged, Stephanie looked up at Brandon with an eager cunningness and said softly, "My, but it is getting stuffy in here. Brandon, could we walk outside for a breath of fresh air?" Noticing the suggestive glint in her deep-green eyes, Brandon replied that a short walk might be in order.

Soon after they left, Archie suggested to Lilian that they might enjoy a walk through DeLane's garden equally as well. That left Roth alone with Alana, who was feeling uncomfortable at Brandon's being outside all alone with Stephanie. With a warm courage building inside, she looked coyly at Roth as she had seen Stephanie peer up at Brandon.

"Why don't we take a quick walk through the gardens, too?" she asked, hoping to run into Brandon and Stephanie.

Eagerly, Roth took her empty cup and laid it aside. "I think a short walk is an excellent idea," he said, slipping his arm around her and leading her outside.

As they walked into the moonlit gardens, Roth pulled her very close, explaining, "It is a might chilly out here, but I plan to keep you warm."

Actually, warmed slightly from whatever was in the punch, Alana had not noticed the cool late-night air, but thanked him sweetly anyway. Dimly lit glass lanterns directed them deeper into the gardens. At one turn in the pathway, Alana saw a huge dark shadowy figure under a small tree that was still full and green in spite of the season. When they passed closer by, she saw that it was in fact two people. It was Brandon and Stephanie locked in an ardent embrace. Devastated, Alana dropped any plans of forcing their company and allowed Roth to lead her farther down the path. Unable to concentrate on anything but Stephanie's overwhelming victory, Alana did not realize that Roth had maneuvered her behind a stand of tall bushes. Cupping her face in his hands, he held her ready for his kiss.

Considering it as nothing more than a chance to learn more about this art of kissing, Alana closed her eyes and waited for the gentle touch of his lips against hers. But, he was not as gentle as she had expected. Instead, she found the pressure of his lips was almost painful. His hand left her face and moved across to her back and pressed her body tightly against his own. Suddenly, one hand had found its way to the low neckline and discovered her breast bulging against the pressure of his body. He started working his fingers inside her gown, not seeming to care that she had stopped returning his kiss and was trying to push him away. Kissing her even harder, he pushed his hand through to grasp her breast.

Alana found that her attempt to scream was muffled by his mouth hovering over hers. When he tried to force his tongue into her mouth, she bit him. He pulled away in pain, giving her a chance to scream out for him to stop.

A rage flowed from his eyes as he whispered angrily, through gritted teeth, "You damned little tease. All night long you have taunted me with those banty brown eyes and that inviting little smile of yours. I have waited patiently for our moment alone. You have been begging me for this all night and, my dear, I plan to let you have plenty!"

He covered her mouth with his free hand when he realized that she still intended to shout out and squeezed her cheeks in painfully against her jaw. Tears came to her eyes as he forced her to the ground.

"I am warning you, do not make a sound. I would hate to do harm to that beautiful face. For your own good, keep quiet," he told her as his nostrils flared with the fury he possessed.

Paralyzed by terror, Alana lay perfectly still as Roth began to unbutton the front of her gown. Her only movement came from her eyelids as they blinked the tears that clung to her eyes. Once he had her breasts exposed, he slowly let go of her mouth reminding her to remain silent. "Easy now, just keep quiet and I won't hurt you." A sinister smile, closely resembling a sneer, spread across his face as he slipped a hand inside the gown and violently began to knead her breast, lowering his head to roughly kiss at her neck. None of the tingling sensation that came when Brandon had kissed her neck was present as Roth nipped eagerly along her throat. As his lips began to move down to capture one of her soft round breasts, Lilian's voice was heard calling Alana's name. As she was heard coming closer, Roth whispered a quick warning, "Don't move!" Lilian now stood only a few yards from the stand of bushes that shielded them. After a moment, he added, breathlessly, "Well, it looks as if you have been spared, my lovely." As he released her, he issued another warning, "I would not let this matter get back to Brandon. Knowing him as I do, he would feel the need to defend your so-called honor. I would hate to have to stop him, and it would be permanently, as I always have a rifle where I can get to it."

Alana believed he meant every word of the threat by the killer gleam that was coming from his icy blue eyes.

Getting up and brushing herself off, she snarled, "Just don't you ever come near me again. If you do, I swear, I shall kill you." Her voice trembled as she repeated, "I swear, Roth, I shall kill you!" She stepped back as she relaced her camisole and buttoned her gown back.

"Cannot promise you that, sweets. You see, I plan to finish what we started tonight. You can depend on it. You might as well look forward to it. Now, smile," he told her as he put his arm around her and stepped out of the bushes holding her gently as if nothing more had happened than an innocent kiss. He escorted her casually across the lawn to where Lilian was returning to Archie on the terrace.

"Did I hear someone calling us?" Roth asked without a trace of guilt in his voice.

"Yes, we are getting ready to go. Archie has managed to eat himself sick. Brandon has gone inside to see if you were in there," she replied, rubbing Archie's stomach lovingly.

"Maybe we should try to find him," Roth suggested.

"No, I promised that I would meet him here. He ought to be right back."

"I wish he would hurry," Archie moaned as he leaned against the iron railing encompassing the terrace.

Alana fervently held the same wish as the feel of Roth's arm around her sickened her beyond the level of any stomach ache Archie might be having. A lifetime seemed to pass as she watched through the opened doors for Brandon. When she finally caught sight of him she wanted to run to him for protection, but with Stephanie still clinging to his arm and Roth's words still piercing her memory, she remained where she was.

"There you are," he said as they stumbled over each other. "We have to cut the evening short. The glutton here had one cookie too many or was it one cup of punch too much, old friend?" He chuckled at Archie's loud moaning at the mere mention of food or drink.

"Let's go. Come on Alana," he said throwing one heavy arm around her and, after shaking Stephanie loose, he put the other around Roth, "Old buddy, you are gonna have to tell my friend here goodbye. We gotta go," he slurred. The rank odor of liquor was all around him.

"Oh, but I hate telling such a beautiful, alluring woman goodbye," Roth said softly. "So, I will just say until tomorrow."

Chapter Eleven

"Time is over. Hand in your papers," Alana announced after checking with the timepiece that dangled from a chain around her neck. As usual Phillip was the last one to hand his paper in, but as soom as he did, Alana made the announcement. "Tomorrow is Valentine's Day. So I thought, instead of your sums, that you children might prefer to create some lovely valentines for your mothers."

The children clapped gleefully as Alana brought out a stack of colored paper, paper doilies, scraps of felt, ribbons, scissors, and several jars of paste. Even Jake, who was a bit too old to get excited over making valentines for Mother, was clapping. Alana guessed he would applaud anything that got him out of doing his long division.

"Now, if you need help, just ask me, but I would rather see what you can do on your own. You will all work together on the front table since I do not have enough scissors and glue to go around." That was her own fault. She had meant to ask Lilian to pick up several extra pairs of scissors and an extra jar or two of paste last Saturday when she and Anne went into town to shop, but let it slip her mind until after they had already left.

Alana would have gotten the supplies herself except that she tried to avoid trips into town for fear of running into Roth Felton. She had not left the ranch at all unless accompanied by several friends since that dreadful night that Roth attacked and threatened her at Stephanie's party. Only once, when she had learned that Brandon and Roth were riding over to Marshall to visit Jerroed Metkiln, had she dared go with Lilian into Gilmer. She might have stayed away then also, taking no chances whatsoever that their plans might be changed, if she had not had that special purchase to make. The small derringer she purchased at the gunsmith's was a used gun with several scratches and a chip out of the handle. Looks did not matter, it would more than suit her purpose. Besides, she did not dare try to return the next week to see the new stock the man had coming in.

Afraid the gun might accidently discharge in her cloth handbag, she next purchased a strong leather purse to insure her safety. The purse and its protective contents went with her whenever she went with Lilian to visit Anne or attend church. But, even with the gun nearby, she found herself peeking around corners and checking the face of every man that even closely resembled Roth. She also avoided Brandon, afraid he might somehow guess her problem with Roth and try to "defend her honor," as Roth had put it. She was certain that Roth could easily kill Brandon if it suited his needs. The day Roth paid Brandon a surprise visit, a cold sickening chill cut through Alana as she hid in her room for hours, waiting for him to leave. The man terrified her. Her first impression of Roth had been the appropriate one. Why she had allowed herself to change her opinion of the man on that horrifying night, she would never be certain. She found that the memory of his hands all over her haunted her often, even months later, as she tried to concentrate on the children.

A short tug on her skirt caused her to jump before she realized that it was only little Robbie with a finger pointing to a thick glob of paste in his long brown curls. "Out!" he demanded, as he made it worse by smearing it with his chubby little finger. "Out!"

With a chuckle at his fierce expression, Alana remarked, "Robbie Warren, how did you manage to get paste in your hair?"

"I dunno," was his usual reply.

"Well, come with me into my room and I shall wash it out of your hair. The rest of you be careful with the paste. We will be right back," she told them.

She picked Robbie up with a slight groan. He was like a chunk of lead. Barely over the age of three, and Alana guessed his weight to be at least thirty-five pounds. He was not grossly fat, but rather a muscular child.

It only took a few minutes to wash the paste from his hair and return to class. Ordering him to sit beside the window where the sunlight filtered through, she hoped to prevent him from getting a chill. Alana let him finish his valentine on the floor and helped him with the paste brush. She considered building a small fire, but was afraid it would make the room too hot on such a springlike afternoon. Besides, the sunlight warmed the area Robbie was working in.

Before long, he sat back and claimed to be finished; he had Alana put his name on his creation. Alana hoped Anne would recognize this as a valentine. He had chosen green paper and had pasted odd-shaped pieces of red felt to both sides of it. Pride sparkled in his little blue-green eyes as he told her to put his Ma-ma's name on the top of it.

By the time 4:00 came, which was still the time class was dismissed, everyone was finished except Angela. Alana let the other children leave, but allowed Angela to stay late and finish the elaborate heart-shaped valentine she was working so diligently on. Curious to see her little artist friend in action, Alana sat down beside her. She watched adoringly at Angela's tongue, which kept curling over her upper lip as she concentrated on her work.

Out of the blue, Angela asked almost offhandedly, "Is Uncle Brandon going to marry Mrs. Ellison?" She never looked up from the paper doily she was cutting on as she waited patiently for an answer.

"I have no idea. Why do you ask?" Alana wondered. The same question had crossed her own mind several times as time seemed to be bringing the two closer.

"Mrs. Ellison sure does ask him to eat with her a lot. She asked him to go out on a picnic out at Pilgrims's Pond tomorrow and to a party at her church next Saturday. She surely keeps him busy," she said shaking her amber curls as she continued to keep her eyes on her work.

Alana had to agree. Stephanie seemed to come up with more affairs to attend than the Queen of England. Although it still hurt to see them together, Alana had resigned herself, or at least was trying to resign herself, to accepting the growing relationship as an unchangeable fact. Trying to think about it as little as possible, Alana immersed herself into her work. When she was not teaching class, she was grading papers, planning tests, or giving one of the children special help in problem areas. On Saturdays she would go riding with Angela and sometimes Mickey around the ranch. Although the children chose to ride bareback, Alana insisted on a saddle and could not imagine ever having control of one's legs again after riding directly on the horse's bare back. Alana's favorite spot on Montaqua was at the top of the mountain. The magnificent view gave her a sense of serenity and allowed her to forget the pain of knowing Brandon loved someone else, someone twice as pretty as she could ever hope to be. She also could ease her fear of another surprise attack from Roth. No one knew for sure where she was whenever she talked Angela into riding to the top. It was like a haven for her just as the shaded pond in the front pasture was to Angela.

"I just hope he doesn't ask her to marry him. I don't want her living out here. She's too snooty and I really think she hates kids. She even considers me still a kid! Can you imagine that?" Angela asked incredulously.

Alana smiled at that last remark. Angela was always in such a hurry to grow up. She already had a beautiful life completely mapped out, including having six marvelous children of her own. Her plans also included perfect meat loaves and large rose gardens. There was no room in her dreams for crop failures, sickness, or any other type of disaster.

Not waiting for a reply from Alana, Angela went on, "If she does move out here, we are just going to have to explain things to her. There, I am finished. You like it?" Angela held up a fancy red paper heart edged in lacy pieces cut from the paper doily. Three little heartshaped pieces of felt were pasted near the top and the words "I love you, be my valentine" were neatly printed across its width.

"That is very nice. Your mother will be proud," Alana

said earnestly. Angela showed quite a knack with any type of art work.

"Mother?" Angela asked curiously, "This one is for you! I finished mother's way before class was over."

Alana took the little heart from Angela and held it delicately in her hands, "For me?" she asked, unable to believe it. As the full impact of the message hit her, tears began to fill her eyes. She was deeply touched as Angela reached over and gave her a squeeze.

"I always give my best friend a valentine," Angela said simply as she began to gather up the scraps and put them in the trash. "You are my best friend, aren't you?"

Afraid that she might cry and seem silly to Angela, Alana just nodded. She was extremely fond of the child. So much so, that she found it difficult not to show favoritism in the classroom. Teacher's pets were not thought well of by fellow classmates, even if they were brothers, sisters, and cousins.

After Angela left, Alana carried the valentine into her room with her. Taking another long look at it, she placed it between two pages of the Bible she kept near her bed, next to the pressed remains of a small rose bud. It was a nice feeling to know that a six-year-old girl could find reason enough to make such a beautiful thing just for her. It alleviated some of the pain that had become part of her life recently. She felt as if Angela were her guardian angel, always managing to bring a ray of sunshine into the gloomiest of moods.

Her mood had been very gloomy lately as she found Brandon's place at the supper table was empty more times than not. And tonight was one of the evenings Brandon was out. He had gone into Gilmer to meet Stephanie for a late dinner once again. When he did eat at home with the family, he seemed to talk only of Stephanie. Alana had grown to loathe even the mention of her name.

On Saturdays, Brandon worked like a wild man in order to get his work done in time to bathe and dress for the evening. He would arrive at Stephanie's house early and devote the entire evening to her every whim. The following Saturday seemed to be no exception. Brandon ate early and left before anyone else was up. He had to fix two broken spokes in one of the back wheels of the wagon before he could carry a load of hay to the cattle in the back pastures. Until the grass began to grow, which was predicted to be soon with the weather warming so early, Brandon made certain that hay and salt blocks were provided in each section. The winter had been rather mild and a little drier than usual, but the ponds managed to hold out. Only once had Brandon had to move cattle due to lack of water.

Alana was disappointed it did not snow even once over the winter months. It seemed strange that the sun should shine and the air be barely cool enough to make long sleeves necessary in mid-February. Why, at this time of year, New York still would be plagued by severe snow storms and dreadful frosts!

By the time Alana and Angela left on their weekly trail ride, the afternoon was extremely warm, giving everyone brighter hopes of an early spring. As they were about to ride out, Brandon and Billy returned with the empty wagon.

"Where are you two off to today?" Brandon asked as he climbed down from the wagon and stepped over beside them.

"To roam the wilds of Montaqua," Alana replied with a wink to Angela.

"Sounds exciting," Brandon laughed. "Beware of the legendary Stalker."

"The legendary Stalker?" Alana asked curiously. "Is that something you just made up?"

"No, I do not have such an imagination. Haven't you heard the local folklore of the big hairy creature that stalks through the woods throughout the southlands? He seems to prefer East Texas in early spring," Brandon said, trying to look serious.

"No, this is the first I have heard of it," Alana admitted, wondering if Brandon was not making this up on the spot.

Angela piped in, "There's a fifty-dollar reward for anyone who brings it in, dead or alive. They claim it kills animals and eats them whole. Some people even claim to have seen it, but we know it is a bunch of stuff. There are no such things as that." She sounded as if she were more trying to convince herself than Alana that the story was a farce.

"I would beware of the Stalker," Brandon repeated in a ghostly voice.

"I do not know how such silly legends get started," Alana insisted as she mounted her horse.

"I don't think you have anything to worry about," Brandon replied in an easier tone, thinking that were the creature and Alana ever to meet that his pity would be with the creature. It would not have a chance against Alana's temper.

As Alana rode away with Angela close behind, Billy mentioned how well that she had learned to ride a saddle in so short a time. Brandon jumped at his words, not having realized Billy had come up behind him.

"Yes, she is quite remarkable," Brandon agreed, wishing that he was going with them on their ride. But, he knew it would do him little good. She would just ignore him as she always did.

Whenever he believed he was making progress with her, *bam!*, she would cut him short. He rarely even saw her anymore as she found other things more important than his company. He wished she was more like Stephanie had become. He never had to worry about being ignored while around Stephanie. She saw to his every need. Why he should even bother with his thoughts of Alana when Stephanie was so good to him, he was not certain. He felt as if he truly loved Stephanie most of the time, but held special unexplored feelings for Alana at the same time. Yet it was useless to want Alana; she could never feel the same way for him. She had made it clear enough to him that he was not the man for her. With that thought pestering his mind, he began unhitching the horse. He still had a great deal of work to do.

The cool air felt good against Alana's face as she gave the horse full rein. Sawdust passed her as they neared the pond, and Angela squealed with delight. "I am going to beat you!" And she did. Sawdust had already fully stopped when Alana caught up. "You are just going to have to get you a horse as fine as mine if you ever hope to win a race with me," she announced proudly.

Before Alana could reply, Angela had hopped down and was running alongside the pond. Reaching a large stump, she sat down and began to pull her shoes off. "I am going to see if the water is warm enough to wade in," she shouted to Alana, who was just now getting her horse tied to a tree branch.

"Not me. I think it is still too cold," Alana replied cautiously as she walked over to where Angela was holding her skirts up, preparing to step into the water. Without hesitation, Angela put a foot into the water. When she did, she let out a screech, "It is freezing!"

"What did you expect?" Alana chuckled as she sat down on the stump.

With a pout, Angela stood at the edge of the chilly water, reaching over to get a handful of water as she did. Then she walked up to Alana and splattered her face with the icy water.

"See how cold it is?" she grinned.

As Alana made a playful lunge at her little impish friend, Angela began running as fast as her little legs would allow. Alana grabbed up Angela's shoes and socks, pretending she planned to throw them into the water.

When Angela came running back to rescue her shoes, Alana caught her by the arm and began to tickle her. "I shall show you what I do to mean little girls who try to give me a bath before I am ready for one."

After begging for mercy did not work, Angela tried blackmail, "Let me go or I will not go to the top of the mountain with you."

"How very clever you are Miss Brams," Alana said as she let her up. "I would hate to miss out on our trip to the top. Let's go. Last one to their horse is a rotten tomato."

After she let Angela win, they mounted the horses and headed for the trail that would lead them to the peak of the mountain. Once they reached the trail through the woods, they had to ride single file. Angela, as usual, led the way as the horses slowly climbed the hill. It was much cooler here, where the sunlight had trouble finding its way through the tall pines. Alana had a spooky feeling as they neared the top. She wondered if Brandon's remarks about the stalking creature had affected her more than she realized. It was not until they had reached the knoll at the top that she again felt at ease.

They climbed down and made a huge rock their throne. They sat silently looking through the trees at the magnificent view, pretending that it was their kingdom. Alana could hardly wait until summer when the landscape would be enchanted by the brighter greens and many colors of nature. Even with its gray hue of winter, Alana found total beauty in what she saw, most of which was Montaqua. There was a strange appeal to the richness of the land. She fully understood why Brandon was so proud of it. He had every right to be: Montaqua was magnificent.

Angela showed the same pride for the land as she pointed out special landmarks to Alana. Someday she planned to have a place like this all her own as any princess would plan to have her own kingdom. She often mentioned this future dreamland to Alana.

They remained perched on the rock for over an hour before deciding to ride back. While they were following a diifferent trail down, Alana thought she heard a rustling of leaves not far away. Dismissing it as her imagination reacting to the suggestion of a scary creature, Alana did not mention the noise to Angela. The sound grew louder as they made their way down.

Angela whispered, "What is that?" Fear was in her eyes.

Afraid that Angela would believe it was indeed the creature and become afraid of the woods, Alana decided to see just what was making such a commotion. With a finger to her lips to silence Angela, Alana climbed down from her saddle and tiptoed through the brush toward the sound. As she grew closer, she found that the noise came from a small glade hidden by the tall pines. From behind a pile of brush near the edge of the clearing she was able to see about thirty or forty head of cattle being held in a makeshift corral of tree limbs and ropes. There were two men standing on the far side with their backs to Alana. A closer look revealed that the cattle all bore the Montaqua brand.

"Rustlers," she breathed silently as fear of what to do closed in on her.

She knew that she had to go tell Brandon, but also felt that she should stay to keep an eye on them. They might try to move the cattle before she could find Brandon and bring him back. Slowly she eased her way back to where Angela was waiting fearfully on Sawdust.

"What was it?" Angela demanded to know.

Putting her finger up to her mouth again to warrant silence, Alana whispered, "Rustlers have some of Brandon's cattle penned up just over there." She pointed in the direction of the clearing. "Go tell Brandon and bring him back with you. I am going to hide in the woods and make sure they do not get away. If they leave, I shall try to follow them."

Realizing the seriousness in Alana's voice, Angela did not argue. She eased Sawdust on down the trail until she felt she was a safe distance away then she forced the horse into a full gallop. Tears began to fill Angela's eyes at the thought of not being able to find Brandon: Alana was depending on her.

Meanwhile, Alana crept back to hide behind the small pile of brush. Carefully she knelt down to the ground and tried not to move as she kept her eyes on the two men who were now leaning against a thick tree trunk. She wished she could hear what they were saying, but did not dare move from her spot.

They seemed to be watching for someone. Alana guessed it was their partner, or maybe even the leader that they were keeping a lookout for. Neither one of these men looked smart enough to plan such a thing. The rifles at their sides caused her to believe they were just gunmen hired to guard the stolen cattle. She admitted that the mastermind behind this was pretty clever to have searched for and found this clearing in an area that was hardly ever visited. She wondered if they had purposely picked Saturday because Brandon stayed in bed until noon on Sunday, giving them plenty of time to get away. She decided the thief either just stumbled into the perfect time or else knew Brandon personally.

The two men continued to look around. One of them went over to his saddlebag and pulled out a large bottle of liquor and took a generous swig.

"Good. Get stinking drunk," she thought as she watched the two men sharing the bottle.

Suddenly, a deep voice from behind her laughed aloud. "Look what we have here."

Alana turned in fear to see who had sneaked up behind her. A scream slipped from her lips as her gaze fell on Roth Felton's lustful sneer once again. The two men headed for them when they heard the scream, only to be ordered back to their post.

"I do not intend to share you with those two," he leered as he stepped closer to Alana. "And I thought I would have to leave this country without ever knowing your pleasures. I guess it is just our lucky day."

As he made another move in her direction, Alana picked up a large branch and swung it at him with all of her might. Roth laughed louder as he caught the end of it and pulled it from her hands causing her to fall to her knees as he did. His nostrils flared savagely as he pushed her with his boot, making her fall over on her back into the thick carpet of pinestraw that covered the ground.

Before she could get up, he was on top of her. Desperately, she tried to push him away, but found that she could not. As she tried to hit him, he grabbed both of her hands. Then, pulling them up over her head, he managed to secure them both with only one of his own. Gasping for breath, she managed to scream for help.

"Shut up!" he ordered as he slapped her across the face with the back of his hand.

Kneeling over her, with a leg on either side of her and still clutching her hands over her head, he reached down and ripped her blouse open. When she turned her head to avoid his kiss, he slapped her again. Pressing his fingers deeply into her already reddened cheek, he gripped her jaw and brought his face down on hers for the kiss, seemingly unaffected by the taste of blood on her lips. His mouth began making its way down her neck. The flex of her bosom as she continued her struggle excited him wildly and he grabbed for one, beginning to rub it vigorously.

"I have dreamed of you so many times," he said lustfully, his stale breath burning into her neck as he spoke.

Feeling a tug on her skirt, she screamed out again, calling out Brandon's name again and again. Angrily, he bashed her face several more times with the back of his hand until she nearly lost consciousness and could not struggle against him any longer. Able now to let go of her hands, he successfully managed to get her skirts and petticoat up to her waist. She was barely aware of what was happening as he tore her underclothing free. Rising to admire his plunder, he began to unbuckle his belt. As he did, he heard Brandon's voice in the distance call out his name. He scrambled for his rifle, which was at the base of a tree where he had discovered Alana hiding. A shot rang out. The sudden heat in his shoulder let him know that he had been hit. Abandoning the move for his rifle, he turned and ran for his horse. In a single motion, he grabbed the reins from the tree limb and swung himself into the saddle. He hunched over in pain as a second shot hit his leg. Giving the horse its own lead, he rode off into the woods. This second shot had come from Billy's rifle.

Realizing her chance to escape, Alana rolled over and tried to get up. Blood trickled from her nose as she managed to get to her knees. Finding that she was not able to stand, she rolled over on her side and clutched at her torn blouse. Feeling her nakedness under her skirt, she wanted to cry, but did not have the strength left to do so.

Brandon jumped from his horse and knelt over Alana's battered form.

"Are you all right?" he asked with a look of fear deep in his blue eyes. "Alana?"

Weakly she managed an answer, "I hurt."

"We have got to get her to the house," Brandon told Billy as he picked her up in his arms. "Sit back, I am going to put her in front of you." As Billy moved back, Brandon eased Alana into the saddle. "Now get her to the house!" he ordered.

Brandon was back in his saddle before he turned to Billy with only hate glaring from his eyes. "I am going to kill that bastard!"

The words gave Alana the strength to scream out a protest, "Brandon, don't! You could be killed!"

Turning his horse in the direction Roth had taken, he repeated his order, "Get her to the house." Without another word, he raced away.

"Brandon! Come back!" Alana cried, tears streaming down her swollen cheeks. "Brandon!" she whispered now, realizing that it was useless to shout. He was too far away. "Be careful!"

They found Lilian and Lizzie pacing the patio when they rode up to the house. At the first sight of Billy's horse, Lilian ran to meet them. When she saw Alana's bruised and swollen face and torn clothes, her face grew pale, "What happened?"

"Roth Felton assaulted her," Billy answered, offering no further explanation. "Help me get her inside. She can barely sit up."

He rode up on the patio and helped ease her down into Lizzie's waiting arms. With amazingly little effort, Lizzie carried Alana into her room as Lilian held the door open. Laying her across the bed, Lizzie began a close inspection of the many cuts and bruises.

Billy stood in the doorway watching. "You need anything?" he asked ready to do whatever was needed.

"No, I think I will just wash her up a might and let her rest," Lizzie replied as she went over to the dresser and dipped a clean cloth into the water in the pitcher. "She is gonna hurt a while, but she will be fine. Did I hear you say Roth did this? I thought it was rustlers y'all was goin' after."

"We did, but found Roth about to rape Alana," he said coldly. "We got a couple of shots off before he got away, but we no more than winged him. Brandon lit out after him with blood in his eye."

Lilian gasped at his words. "Brandon will kill him," she remarked, but then added in a chilly tone, "Or be killed."

Lizzie watched Alana's motionless form a moment then looked at Billy. The words rang true to all of them. Continuing to clean Alana's tender wounds, Lizzie offered a silent prayer for her Master Brandon. After which, she wanted to know. "Was Roth one of the rustlers?"

"Looks like it. There were about forty head penned up in one of those little glades on the top of the mountain. Two other men were involved, but got clean away before we could get as much as a look at them. I am going back up there and lead the cattle back into the back pasture. Then I think I better go into town and tell the sheriff what happened. There may be other ranchers around here missing a few head. I want to catch those guys red-handed."

"It'll be dark soon, why don't you just ride for the sheriff now and wait 'til morning to get them cows. 'Sides, those other two might still be up there somewhere. You don't need to be goin' up there alone," Lizzie said firmly, her eyes showing her deep concern.

Before Billy could turn to leave, Angela pushed him aside and ran into Alana's room to see if Alana was there. She completely ignored Lilian's remark that she was supposed to be in her room.

"You okay?" she asked fearfully, tears filling her eyes. Angela was afraid that Alana was dead.

A moment passed before Alana managed to speak. "I am okay," she said grimacing from the pain of her swollen lip. "Listen to your mother. Go back to your room. I shall see you later."

Angela's mouth trembled as she asked, "You promise?"

"Have I ever let you down? Yes, of course, I promise," Alana replied slowly, trying to smile. After Angela had left, Alana looked up at Lizzie who was placing a blanket over her, "Where is Brandon?"

"Don't you be worryin' about him now. We are goin' to leave you alone so that you can rest a while. You had quite a tirin' experience as I hear. When I come back, we will talk. For now you rest. That, Miss Alana, is an order,"

Lizzie commanded on her way to the door. She pretended not to hear Alana repeat her question as she closed the door behind her.

Determined to have her question answered with a vague recollection tormenting her of Brandon's threat to kill Roth, Alana tried to get up, but fell back onto her bed wearily. She was too weak to get up. Sleep overcame her will to stay awake as she waited for Lizzie to return.

When she opened her eyes again, the room was dark. The sharp throbbing at her temple quickly reminded her of the terrifying ordeal. Able to sit up now, Alana felt around for a match to light the lamp beside her bed. Once it was glowing, she eased out of bed, finding that she still wore the torn blouse and soiled skirt. Quickly, she pulled the ragged blouse up over her head. She flinched at the pain caused by the cloth as it brushed across her swollen cheek. Cautiously she carried the lamp over to the mirror to see how badly she was bruised. Her left eye was very swollen as was the left side of her mouth. The pain from the light touch of her own finger to her lip caused every muscle in her body to tighten.

Alana cringed as Roth's face flashed before her. She tried to shut out any further recollection of the way she was so easily overpowered and damned near raped. Suddenly she remembered Brandon's cold-blooded oath: He planned to kill the man. The dreadful thought that Brandon might be the one killed ate away at her. She looked at her clock, it was after ten. Maybe Brandon was already back, safe and sound. With that hope in her heart, she ran outside to find him. The house was dark except for the torches burning near the end of the patio. Lizzie and Lilian were sitting in the chairs in front of Brandon's room, staring out into the darkness. The night had grown cold, but it bothered Alana little.

Able to read the expressions on her friends' faces, Alana remarked, "Brandon has not returned." No one needed to reply. Alana sat down beside them and joined their vigil.

Hours passed. Still Brandon had not returned. Finally, Lilian suggested they all try to get some rest. Waiting until Alana was safely in her room, Lilian followed Lizzie inside.

It was just after daybreak when Brandon finally rode up. Everyone was in bed asleep except Alana who was leaning anxiously against her window pain, allowing its coolness to soothe her swollen cheek. At the sight of him, Alana ran outside. She hurried to meet him, but Brandon passed right by her with his rifle still clutched to his side, not bothering to speak. There was a deep cut over his forehead but the blood around it had already dried. His shirt was torn as was the knee of his pants.

Alana followed him into his study determined to find out what had happened. Silently, he lit a small lamp on his desk and proceeded to a tall cabinet on the far side of the room. Its doors opened to reveal several cut-glass decanters of liquor. Seemingly unaware of Alana's presence, he poured himself a tall glass of whiskey and drank it dry.

Overwhelmed by fear, Alana cried out, "You killed him!"

He turned to her with hate in his eyes, "No, I never got the chance. His lead was too great and he knows the country too well. He got away. I completely lost his trail. But, I swear to you, if I ever see him again, I shall kill him!"

Furiously, he slammed his glass against the wall, shattering it, and stormed through the door that led to his room.

She took a step to follow him, but decided against the idea. She had never seen such rage and was afraid he might be blaming her. Instead, she slipped back into her own room and cried herself back to sleep.

Chapter Twelve

"What are you doing?" Angela asked as she walked over to stand beside Alana.

"I thought I would clear some of these weeds out of here. It will not be long until these bushes will begin to bloom. These ugly weeds would only distract everyone's attention. We do want people to admire our rose garden, don't we?" Alana asked as she piled the weeds in one corner. "This year they should really be lovely."

"May I help?" Angela asked eagerly.

"Not in those clothes. Go change into some older clothes and you most certainly can help me," Alana replied, wiping her brow with the back of her wrist as she watched Angela scurry off to her room.

Perspiration had drenched her as she worked. The humidity of this warm mid-April morning was unbearable. The cloudy sky had deceived her into believing that it would be a cool morning, just perfect for gardening.

When Angela returned, Alana asked her to start on the other side. Slowly, the two of them worked toward the middle. Twice the humidity forced them to stop for a cool drink. As lunchtime neared, they decided to quit long enough to wash away the garden soil and eat something. The temptation to rest a while after lunch overpowered them and it was nearly two o'clock before they returned to work. By three they were finally finished with the garden but covered with dirt and sticky with perspiration.

"I surely would love a dip in the pond," Angela said in her worst Southern drawl as she tugged at her damp dress.

"I imagine the water is too cool. The sun has not shown

256

itself all day," Alana pointed out realistically.

"I don't care. I would actually prefer it cool." Angela sighed at the thought, her green eyes reflecting her honest desire for the swim.

"Well, let's go. If we freeze our ears off it won't be anyone's fault but our own. Go ask your mother while I get something to get wet in."

In just a few minutes, Alana came out of her room with the undergarments that she planned to swim in and a huge towel. She found Angela waiting rather impatiently with the shirt and the cut off trousers that she usually swam in wrapped up in a towel.

"Are we going to walk or take the horses?" Alana asked.

"Better take the horses. Ma claims it might rain. If it does, or if we should hear a storm coming, she wants us back home on the double," Angela told her while they were walking to the barn. Once inside, they discovered that Billy was not around to help them put a saddle on Alana's horse. Unable to lift the heavy contraption herself, she decided that she would just have to ride bareback. Without the stirrup needed to boost herself up, Alana discovered that she was going to have to lead the horse over to stand beside a large wooden barrel. She then had to turn a bucket upside down and set it beside the barrel before she could stairstep herself high enough to get on her horse. She felt a little silly at this long awkward procedure when Angela simply ran and jumped, landing bellydown on Sawdust's back; then, she easily swung her little leg over, sat up, and was ready to ride.

Bareback riding was worse than Alana had imagined. As she bounced around on the horses's rough backbone, she found that there was nothing to hold on to for balance and felt as if she were going to bounce right off of her horse. She was never so glad to reach any destination as she was when they finally arrived at the pond. Gently, she eased a leg over and slid to the ground. While Angela was already stripping to her underwear among a group of small bushes, Alana was trying to persuade her legs to move. By the time Alana managed to get behind a bush to change, Angela was already in her swimming garb and happily playing in the water.

"It's not too cold. Not at all. Come on, hurry up!" she squealed with delight, splashing about in the water.

"Don't rush me! My legs are moving at a different pace than the rest of me," Alana shouted from behind the bush.

When she finally did manage to get ready, she peeked around to make absolutely certain that no one had come up that should not see her in her dainties. Although Brandon was supposed to be in town having lunch with Stephanie and the boys were spending the weekend with their cousins, Alana wanted to be certain that there was no one to see her so scantily dressed. After assuring herself that they were quite alone, she trotted down to the water's edge and jumped in. The icy water prickled her skin mercilessly as it engulfed her entire body.

"I thought you said that it was not cold!" Alana screamed in such a high voice that she could barely be heard.

"Oh, is it cold? I really hadn't noticed," Angela replied innocently before breaking into a belly laugh.

"Why you little sneak!" Alana seethed playfully, and splashed her young friend with the icy water. Angela began to splash back. They were having such a good time that they did not notice darker clouds were rapidly moving in. But, Lilian noticed them and was duly worried. When the wind began to pick up, she began looking for the two. She strained her eyes against the dusty wind, but found no sign of Angela or Alana. She had begun to pace the patio as a caged cat would, watching for the two when she noticed Brandon riding up. Hurriedly, she followed him to the barn where he began to unsaddle his horse.

When he heard the moaning of the aging hinges straining under the weight of the heavy barn door as it opened, he mentioned casually, "Better return to the house, I do believe we have a storm on its way."

"Yes, I do too. I think it could be a really bad one," she replied with a mother's concern shadowing her face. "And Angela and Alana are down at the pond. They should be coming back. I specifically told Angela that if a storm moved in or if she heard even the faint rumble of thunder that she had better get herself back home immediately. But they have not returned."

"Well, there hasn't been any thunder," Brandon pointed out.

"Still they should have enough good sense to come in with such a storm brewing. Would you please go tell them to come in? I am really very worried," Lilian exclaimed, her eyes showing her deep concern.

The ugly black clouds that were gathering outside frightened her terribly. An overwhelming fear pounded at her breast. One that she had never known before.

"Will you please?" She was pleading openly.

"Certainly I will. Calm down," Brandon told her as he retightened the cinch securing his saddle, "You just go back to the house. I will bring them there."

"Hurry!"

There was a desperation in her voice that sent chills twisting down his spine as he opened the huge door to the pasture. A tremendous gust of wind jerked the door from his hands and banged it against the wall. His horse reared at the sudden movement, but Brandon managed to keep a hold of the reins. Reaching for the door again, Brandon was barely able to close it against the terrible force of wind that had developed in the few short minutes that he had been inside. As he put the heavy bar in place to secure the door against the whipping motion of the furious wind, he glanced up at the threatening sky. Low black clouds churned about in angry confusion. A raging wind grew cold and then warm again as Brandon calmed his horse well enough to mount. Urging the steed into a dead run, Brandon headed in the direction of the pond.

The gale force of the wind hampered his progress and a fierce rain was beginning to slash at him in large heavy drops. Minutes seemed endless as Brandon directed his gaze to the thick cluster of trees surrounding the pond that had just begun to display their new spring leaves. Their branches were humbly bowing to the ground as the relentless winds demanded their awesome respect. Brandon watched helplessly as a dark angry funnel let itself down from the clouds to the earth, violently claiming anything that happened in its path. The malicious demon ravished the land, seizing whole trees from the earth's grasp and effortlessly heaving them into the air.

Powerless against such an incredible force, Brandon leaped from his horse and pressed himself onto the ground, leaving his horse free to chance a run for safety. He felt the vacuum of the tornado tugging at his body. Holding tightly to the grass beneath him, Brandon closed his eyes to the terror. Small pieces of debris stung his face as he desperately clung to the small handfuls of grass that held him to the earth. The grass was beginning to pull free when he felt a gradual weakening of the tornado's grasp. His body ached with an empty weakness left by such a close realization of a violent end. As he looked around at the destruction that was left behind, his heart was suddenly overpowered by a strangely cold sensation.

Desperately he shouted out, "Angela! Alana!"

He was hardly able to hear his own voice against the tremendous wail of the tornado now surging toward the house. He thought he heard a scream, but could not be certain. Scrambling to get up, he found an unsure footing in the mud.

Struggling to get his balance, he called out again, "Angela! Alana!"

The wind had begun to die down but a heavy rain continued to fall as Brandon made his way to the massive entanglement of trees and brush. As he managed to make it through the debris, his eye caught a glimpse of something that appeared almost white through the downpour. Working his way closer, he found the crumpled body of Sawdust against the base of a downed tree. "My God!" he cried out in horror, "Angela! Alana! Where are you?"

He made his way over to an enormous bulk of tangled limbs, calling out again and again. Panic racked his body with such a great force that he had to brace himself against one of the few trees still standing. His heart grew cold with a grotesque anticipation. As he pushed himself away from the tree, he was certain that he heard a faint sobbing in the distance.

At first, he wondered if the sobs might not have come from his own lips. But, no, the sounds were coming from somewhere to his left. He traced the sound to Alana. His heart seemed to stop when he saw that Alana was kneeling over the motionless form of Angela. The large heavy trunk of a tree lay across her tiny legs. Alana's hands were left raw and bloody from trying to move the massive weight from her little friend's legs. She now sat sobbing uncontrollably in a muddy heap beside Angela, pushing the wet amber hair away from the child's face with her quivering hand. As he moved closer, Brandon first noticed a large bloody gash in Alana's arm through a jagged tear in her sleeve. He then became aware of the blood trailing out of Angela's ear and soaking into her wet mass of hair. One arm was twisted down under her back.

His throat ached with each pounding of his heart as he tried to speak. He could not. Instead, he gently pulled Alana aside and tried to lift the tree from Angela's legs. With a strength he was not aware he possessed, he heaved the jagged end of the trunk and swung it over far enough to free Angela's legs. With trembling hands, he gathered Angela into his arms. He held her lifeless form close and started to make his way out of the huge pile of ruins.

The walk back to the house seemed endless to Alana as she followed closely behind Brandon. There was a weak silence as the heavy rain let up. The only sound she heard was that of Brandon's heavy boots sloshing through the deep puddles of water and that of her mud-clad skirt slapping against her legs as she tried to keep up with Brandon's broad, steady stride. She grew weak as the unattended wound on her arm was allowed to bleed freely. Her knees wanted to buckle at the sight of Angela's legs dangling limply from Brandon's arms, but she managed to keep going.

As they approached the house, they did not notice that the roof of the barn had been scattered across the yard and patio. They walked right by the rose garden without seeing that it had been demolished by a huge piece of the metal roof. The bushes Alana and Angela had nurtured and loved so dearly were shredded. Three boundaries of the fence were crushed and broken. The small section of the covering over the walkway in front of Alana's room that had caved in also missed their attention as they walked mutely into the kitchen. Brandon stepped just inside the doorway and stopped. Alana stood quietly by his side. They silently waited for whatever was to happen next.

Lilian rushed into the room first, "Did you find—"

Her words were cut short at the sight of the limp form of her youngest child in the arms of her brother. As she stepped closer, she spied the diluted trail of blood down Brandon's rain-soaked shirt front.

Brandon could not bear to look at his sister. He was too afraid of the horror he would find on her face. Instead, he looked down at the puddle of tainted water gathering on the floor under him.

"My baby is dead?" she asked numbly, already realizing the answer.

The tears that she had held back for so long through the deaths of her husband and of her father fell swiftly and silently as she reached out to caress her dear daughter's wet cheek. Finding only a damp coldness in the touch of Angela's cheek, the color drained from Lilian. Every muscle in her face contracted, forcing her eyes to close and revealing her tightly gritted teeth through taut lips. Suddenly, her throat swelled out and she began to scream. Alana grabbed her firmly and shook her. When Lilian finally stopped screaming, Alana clutched her to her bosom and they wept in each others arms at the unbearable pain that they shared.

The woeful cries brought Lizzie bounding into the room. She stopped just a few steps inside of the doorway and cried out, "Oh, my dear Lord!"

Her usually smiling face lost all expression as she stared at Angela's bruised face. Her lower lip began to quiver as she opened her mouth and flared her nostrils to take in a deep breath. She held the breath a moment, then began to sob aloud as she allowed the air to rush out. Raising her hands above her head, she clasped them tightly together. Then, looking heavenward through tearful eyes, she pleaded aloud, "Open them pearly gates, Lord. You got yourself a real angel a-comin'."

Chapter Thirteen

Her decision was final.

Alana planned to leave just as soon as her contract expired in May. There would be too much pain to bear if she were to stay. With Brandon certain to wed Stephanie soon and the insufferable grief she held from Angela's memory smothering her here, Alana decided it would be better for her, for everyone, if she were to return to New York and seek further employment.

She was standing outside of Lilian's door trying to work up the nerve to knock. Part of her did not want to burden Lilian with this decision to quit, but part of her felt that the sooner she told her, the sooner a replacement could be found. Alana had reached the decision last week, as she watched Douglas and Brandon lower Angela's casket into the ground. Although Alana dearly wanted to be the one to hold Lilian's hand and help Archie comfort her, and in doing so, helping to comfort herself, Stephanie found it her duty to do so. It was then that Alana realized she no longer belonged. She felt she would possibly even be in the way, when Stephanie became Brandon's bride and moved to Montaqua. There was also a chance that Lilian might eventually marry Archie and move into town where again Alana knew she would not be needed.

After having waited a week to give Lilian an opportunity to regain control of her emotions, Alana felt it was time to announce her decision. Taking a deep breath, she leaned forward and tapped on the door.

"Who is it?" Lilian voice sounded weak from the past week of strain.

"Lilian, it is me, Alana," she spoke softly as she opened

he door. "May I come in for a minute?"

With a voice sounding almost relieved, Lilian replied, 'Yes, do come in."

As Alana closed the door behind her, she noticed the complete disarray of Lilian's usually immaculate room. Lilian sat in a chair beside her unmade bed with a small comforter wrapped around her legs. A tray of food that appeared untouched sat on the table beside her. The curtains were drawn, keeping the afternoon sun from breaking through. Without a lamp burning, she sat in a room of darkness and melancholy. When Alana walked over and sat on the edge of the bed, she noticed Smoky's gray head poking up out of the covers enjoying the warm comfort in Lilian's lap. An urge to weep overcame her at the sight of Angela's cat. The agony of the moment made her all the more determined to leave this place behind.

Managing to control her voice, Alana asked softly, "How are you?"

"Oh, I am going to be fine, I guess. I sent Brandon over to Anne's to get the children. She has put up with them long enough. It is time they came home. We need to strive for some sort of normalcy around here. Angela would not have wanted us to disrupt our lives so," Lilian spoke with a distant smile as if her memory had led her back to some precious moment shared with Angela. "We have to move forward with the future."

"You are right. In a way, that is why I am here. I need to tell you of my own plans for the future," Alana said lamely as she focused her attention on a crumpled pillow lying on the floor.

With her usual foresight, Lilian asked calmly, "You are planning to leave?"

"Quite frankly, I am."

"May I know why?" Lilian asked evenly, as she gently stroked Smoky's head with the tips of her fingers.

Explaining how she still felt about Brandon and how she would only be in a painfully awkward position when Stephanie moved in, Alana managed to avoid any mention of the terrible effect Angela's death had on her.

"Are you certain that Brandon cares so much for

Stephanie?" Lilian wanted to know.

"Aren't you? He spends quite a bit of time in town these days. You have heard her make reference to the probable marriage yourself. And that is one wedding I do not want to be around for. I still care for him a great deal. Actually, I grow to love Brandon more each day. I just could not bear watching him take Stephanie as his wife. Neither could I bear it if she were to become my employer. Since she discovered that I am your hired tutor, she has acted as if I were quite her lesser. To be perfectly honest, I cannot tolerate the sight of the woman."

"Me either!" Lilian said simply.

"Then you do understand?"

"Yes, I understand that. But, I do not want you to go. You are my best friend, Alana. I love you as a sister. Yet, I am not so selfish that I would ask you to stay if you would only be unhappy to do so." A tear traveled down her cheek as she asked, "When will you be leaving?"

Climbing down from the bed and kneeling at Lilian's side, Alana's voice faltered as she answered, "I shall see out my contract which ends on May tenth. I plan to leave immediately afterward." Her voice broke into sobs as she took Lilian's hand in hers, "I do not enjoy leaving you, but I just cannot bear to stay. We will always be friends. I promise to write often." After a moment of looking into Lilian's tearful eyes, Alana wrapped her arms around her friend and held her close. "I shall miss you. I really shall."

She repeated her words as she stood up, then quickly walked out of the room, closing the door behind her. She ran to her room and flung herself on her bed. The misery she felt was so overwhelming she was forced to scream out in pain. Clutching a pillow to her breast, she cried herself weak, so much so that she fell asleep.

The room was dark when she was wakened by a heavy pounding on her door. Slightly disoriented from arousing from such a sound sleep, Alana sat up in bed trying to blink away the confusion blurring her thoughts. Hearing the heavy pounding again, Alana got up to answer the door. It was Brandon.

"When you failed to come to supper, I thought I had

better check on you," he said as she opened the door.

"What time is it?" Alana asked still a little groggy.

"A little after eight."

"I have been asleep that long?" Alana declared in disbelief.

"Can you come out a minute? I would like to talk with you."

Reaching up to feel of her hair, which was a tangled mess from her sleep, she replied, "I shall be right out," and closed the door.

Quickly, she brushed her hair out and picked up her shawl. Curious as to what Brandon might want to talk to her about, Alana hurried outside.

"Would you care to sit down?" Brandon asked good-manneredly, pointing to the wooden bench just under Alana's window.

"That would be fine," she replied as she walked over to sit down. "What are you doing home? Were you not supposed to have supper at Stephanie's tonight?"

"Yes, but after Lilian asked me to bring the children back home, I decided I had better stay home just in case I was needed further. I sent word with her neighbor who works at the sawmill that I would not be coming. I am sure she will understand that the family needs are great right now."

"Surely," Alana answered, a twinge of jealousy edging her voice. "What did you want to talk with me about?"

"After supper tonight, Lilian told me that you are quitting in just a few weeks. Is that true?" he asked searching her brown eyes for a reluctance to leave.

"Yes, if there is a stage heading east on May eleventh, I shall be on it," Alana answered simply, her throat aching with the desire to burst into tears. How she wanted to stay! How she wished Angela's memory did not plague her and that Brandon had fallen in love with her and not Stephanie!

"May I know why? Lilian would not give me a reason, only that your mind seemed made up."

"There are any number of reasons. I did not mention this to Lilian, but one factor that caused me to decide to go is the pain I feel whenever something triggers my memory of Angela. It is too much for me to bear. I loved her dearly. At times, I felt as if she were my own." Tears streamed down her cheeks as she continued, "I cannot bear it. I must get away for my own sanity. Besides, you yourself said that a special tutor was not needed. These children are smart. They will do fine in any school. Phillip may need extra help, but even he has progressed well."

"Maybe I was wrong. Even I have noticed a change in the children, especially Mickey. They have learned more from you than just reading and arithmetic. Brenda has become a charming young lady and Jake has learned the manners of a fine gentleman. I am proud of them. What's more, I am proud of you. Please reconsider. I am willing to pay you twice your present salary."

"It is not the money. I just do not think I could or even should stay. My reasons may seem selfish to you, but I cannot see reason enough to stay. Lilian can get another teacher if she still sees a need there. I shall truly miss each and every one here, but I feel it is best that I go." Alana turned away as she tried to avoid looking at him.

Her heart was breaking, being so close to the only man she ever dared love and knowing his heart was in the possession of another woman, which it always had been.

"We all lost someone special when Angela was killed, but life has to go on. You cannot run away from it! Eventually, the pain will lessen and you will be able to live with it. It is not like you to run away. You are a fighter! I have always admired that about you. Why are you so willing to run away, now?" Brandon's voice grew loud with anger.

He did not want her to go, but seemed helpless at finding the words to make her stay. His own heart was aching at the thought of never seeing Alana again. He was confused and angry and was ready to admit why.

"Brandon, try to understand," Alana pleaded with him, determined not to tell him how she felt about him or his growing relationship with Stephanie.

"Well, I do not understand!" he said sternly.

He was certain she was keeping something from him. She had to be. She just had not given him enough of a reason to be leaving like this; he knew there had to be more. She just was not telling him everything.

"I am sorry. I had hoped you would understand."

"All I know is that you do not have to go!"

"I do! That is all there is to it!" Alana said sharply. Brandon threw his arms in the air in an exasperated motion. Too tired to argue, she added, in a final tone, "I am going!"

Without giving him a chance to make a reply, Alana stood up, excused herself curtly, and marched into her room. Before he could think to call her back, she had slammed the door behind her.

"Go, then. And good riddance to you!" he said under his breath, and stalked off to his study for a drink.

The next two weeks slipped by quickly enough as Alana worked with the children, helping them finish their various projects and assignments. With little spare time to make the trip into town, Alana had asked Brandon to purchase her ticket for her, but he flatly refused. With May 11th scarcely a week away, Alana decided she would have to make a special trip into town to buy her own ticket.

When Lilian discovered Alana had planned to ride into town alone, she volunteered to accompany her. Most of the ride was made in silence, each dwelling on her own thoughts. When they did talk, it was usually an observance of the beautiful wildflowers along the roadside or how warm the days were getting to be. It was as if they had a silent agreement not to mention Brandon, Angela, or Alana's nearing departure.

Allowing Alana to be alone when she purchased her ticket, Lilian offered to wait for her at Archie's restaurant. Alana promised that as soon as she had her ticket, she would join her for a lemonade.

Alana nodded politely at the now-familiar faces smiling her way as she crossed the street to the post office, which doubled as the stagecoach office. Patiently, she waited until the small elderly man she had come to know as Harry finished helping the young girl at his window tie a long piece of yarn around a small brown package. After he weighed the package and set it aside, he turned to Alana. Asking him when the earliest stage east would be after May 10th, she laid her cloth bag on the counter.

"Lemme see here," he said as he rubbed his balding head with the back of his thumb. "Says here, got one leavin' the next afternoon at around one P.M., then there's one four days later leavin' out—" he broke off his words in order to spit into a small can, then finished his sentence— "at around noon." He squinched his eyes as he stared at the schedule, making sure he had read it correctly.

"I shall need a ticket for the stage leaving on the eleventh at one," Alana said firmly as she reached into her bag to get the money.

"How far you goin'?" Harry asked as he flipped through his price schedule.

"St. Louis."

"Mind me askin' what's in St. Louis?" he asked as he ran a stubby finger down a long line of prices.

"I plan to board a train bound for New York."

"New York? What's a little girl like you goin' to New York for?" he asked as he reached for a large magnifying glass to read the tiny figures on the page.

"I am going home," Alana answered, aware that she did not hear the same warmth in her voice as she heard when most people spoke of home.

"Goin' home, huh? That's nice," he said paying little attention to his own words as he squinted through the magnifying glass, trying to read the small numbers. Finally, he just pointed to the page and said simply, "It'll be that much."

Keeping back a smile that was trying to tickle its way onto her face, Alana picked out the correct amount and laid it on the counter while he wrote the date on a small ticket.

"Thank ya, missy," he said as he picked up the money and put it away in the huge metal box. Then, placing the ticket in her hand, he added, "Have a nice day."

The smile finally broke across her face as she replied, "Same to you, sir."

As she turned, ticket in hand, to leave, she wondered

how a man could be so trusting in this day and age. With a shake of her head and a cool fresh lemonade in her thoughts, Alana headed for the Blue Swan Restaurant to join Lilian.

As she passed in front of Mr. DeLane's store, she noticed the silver music box that she and Angela had stood over so many times. The two of them had begun a savings fund to purchase the music box and give it to Lizzie on her birthday in July. Angela was in charge of the money's safekeeping. Whenever Lizzie came to town with them and stopped to listen to the music box, Angela could not keep from grinning in anticipation of the day she would present it to her. When they returned home, she would rush to her room to count the coins. At her last report they had saved nearly half of the six dollars needed to buy the music box.

After staring at the shiny little box a moment, Alana reached into her bag to see how much money she had left. The ticket had cost more than she had expected, but she still had over seven dollars in her bag. Excitedly, she rushed inside to buy the music box. Angela's dream was going to come true. Lizzie was going to have her birthday gift.

She found Mr. DeLane dusting shelves just inside the door. With a twinkle in her dark brown eyes, she asked him to wrap the music box in the window.

"You mean you are finally going to buy the thing?" he chuckled as he pushed his glasses back up on his nose. "I have seen you admiring it many times, but gave up on you ever buying it."

"It is a very special gift for a friend," Alana announced proudly as she counted out the money.

At hearing that it was a gift, Mr. DeLane offered to wrap a pretty yellow ribbon around the package. Alana thanked him and, with the package held tightly in her hands, she walked out with a smile that took over her entire face. Happily, she walked along the boarded walkway to join Lilian, but her good spirits came to a sudden halt when she noticed Brandon and Stephanie coming out of one of the shops on just the other side of the restaurant.

Carrying a large blue box under one arm and guidin,
Stephanie with the other, he escorted her across th
street. Alana was relieved that they had not seen her an
had gone in the other direction. She did not want th
humiliation Stephanie seemed to push off on her ever:
time they met.

Blinking back the stubborn tears that had found thei
way into her eyes, Alana watched Stephanie's animate
face as she flirted gaily with Brandon. Stephanie could no
have looked prettier or happier as she clutched Brandon'
arm.

Taking a deep breath, Alana pulled her eyes away fron
the happy couple and continued into the restauran·
Lilian and Archie were sitting side by side in the far corne
booth with their heads together. Alana was pleased to se·
Lilian smiling again.

"What are you two looking so happy about?"

"Shall I tell her?" Lilian asked, looking as if she coul·
hardly keep from it.

"Go ahead," Archie said brightly.

"Archie has asked me to marry him and I—I said
would. That is, if the children are agreed."

Alana's mouth fell open and hung limply as the news
slowly soaked in.

"Married?" she asked curiously as if it were a complet·
surprise to her. Slowly the corners of her mouth curle·
up as she squealed with delight, "Oh, Lilian, you ar·
getting married. That is wonderful!"

Unable to reach across Archie and feeling the urge t·
hug someone, she grabbed Archie and gave him ·
squeeze. As she sat down across from them, she aske·
almost breathlessly, "When? Where? How?"

"Paul Peterson has asked to marry Katherine. They ar·
planning to be married next April. We will get married the
very next month. Lilian has not picked a specific date yet
but it will be next May, I assure you."

Alana grasped Lilian's hand, "I am so happy for you
How wonderful it must feel to know you are going t·
marry the man you love! My very best wishes and deepes·
prayers go with you both."

The afternoon was spent making different plans. Alana felt a certain sadness that she would not be here to share the special moment, but also felt excited and happy for her friend. Lilian continued to discuss her plans on the ride home. As they pulled in the drive, she asked Alana not to mention it to anyone.

"I want to wait until we are all together before I tell the family," Lilian said softly. "Brandon will not be home for supper tonight, so I shall wait until tomorrow during lunch to make the announcement."

Alana promised to keep the secret, but wondered if Lilian was going to be able to keep quiet. Alana thought Lilian might burst. Several times she caught Lilian biting her lip as if in an effort to keep her secret inside until lunchtime. During the church services, Lilian could hardly sit still. On the way home, she tapped her finger impatiently on the seat beside her. The family had barely sat down to eat when Lilian could keep her secret no longer.

While Lizzie was still setting the food on the table, she blurted out, "I have an announcement I would like to make." After a melodramatic pause, she continued, "Archie has asked me to marry him."

A silence fell over the group. Lizzie almost dropped a large bowl of peas in Brandon's lap. Luckily it managed to land on the table. The children looked at each other oddly, showing no emotion whatsoever on their faces.

"Well, what do you have to say?" Lilian asked worriedly.

Mickey was the first to break the strange silence, "Mr. Sobey's going to be our father?"

"If I marry him, yes, he most certainly will," Lilian said firmly.

Mickey rolled his eyes around to look at Brenda sitting quietly beside him, "Yippee!" he squealed. "When you getting married?"

"Yes, Mama, when?" Brenda piped in, a smile spreading across her face.

"He wants to get married next May."

"Why so long?" John asked excitedly. "Why not sooner?"

"Yes, Mama, why not sooner?" Jim chimed in.

With a look of relief, Lilian answered the barrage of questions. Everyone was talking at once, except Brandon. He still remained silent as he listened to Lilian explain that Archie wanted to wait until Katherine was married because he wanted to move out of his present house to a larger house just outside of town. The children did not seem to mind the idea of a move.

Alana noticed Brandon's facial muscles tighten as he listened to the plans.

But when Lilian asked him what he thought, Brandon forced a smile and said simply, "I think it is wonderful."

The smile did not fool Lilian for even a moment. "Brandon, tell me what is the matter. Do you not approve of Archie Sobey?"

"I like Archie. He is a good man and it is obvious he loves you a great deal." He paused as if trying to decide whether to say more.

Impatiently, Lilian asked, "Well, then, what is wrong?"

With his lower lip protruding, forming a childish pout, he answered slowly, "I shall be left all alone out here."

Lilian's smile faded. She had not thought about that. With the children needing Lizzie, he would be alone except for Billy.

"You will still have Billy. Don't be so childish, you and Stephanie will probably be married by then." Realizing what she just said, Lilian gave Alana a painful look of apology; but Alana had begun passing the vegetables to the children, pretending to be unconcerned over the conversation.

"You are right, I am being childish," Brandon replied, feeling uncomfortable at Lilian's suggestion of marriage for Stephanie and himself. He had never really given it a serious thought. But in lieu of what was happening, maybe he should. The thought of having only Billy for company at night did not set well. A wife might just be well to consider. He knew Stephanie was willing enough. She had as much as suggested it herself, but he had successfully managed to change the subject at the time. He had to admit that she was beautiful and would keep his bed warm, but there was something wrong with the whole idea. He was trying to decide what it could be when he glanced over at Alana who was handing John the basket of rolls.

When she felt Brandon staring at her, she asked politely, "Would you care for a roll, Brandon?"

Shaking his head, he continued to look at her. His eyes took in the beauty of her delicately upturned nose, her soft silken skin, and especially her large, deep brown eyes. He enjoyed looking at her and hated even the thought of not being able to do so after next week. The more he thought of it, the more he wanted her to stay. He wished he had managed to win her heart instead of Stephanie's. Sadly, he looked away as Lilian asked him to try to be happy for her.

"Oh, I am happy for you. I should not be so selfish. You will be less than an hour's ride away. I shall be allowed to visit, shan't I?"

"Certainly, I shall expect you every Sunday for lunch and most every time you come to town, which is often enough."

"How about you, Alana? What do you think of the news? Almost makes you wish you were going to be here for the wedding doesn't it?" he asked proddingly.

"Almost does," she answered simply, feeling the sharp barb of his voice.

Knowing how Alana felt, Lilian quickly changed the subject back to her plans and kept it there for the remainder of the meal.

The meal passed quickly, as did the next week. Alana spent every waking hour with the children or with Lilian, Lizzie, or Brandon, who seemed to be around more than usual during the final days.

Tonight was her last dinner with the family. Tears crept into her eyes from time to time as she took special pains in getting dressed. The dress she wore was a new one she had purchased for Easter and had worn only the one time. The long full skirt and puffed short sleeves were both bright yellow with white lace at the edges. The short bodice and a fancy, wide-scalloped band of cloth around the hemline was a checked gingham of yellow and white. She wore low on her neck the golden heart-shaped pendant that Lilian had given her for Christmas. The front of her hair was pulled back away from her face, held in place with a simple golden comb, and allowed to blend in with the rest of her long brown curls. She decided to wear her hair down since Brandon seemed to prefer it. Delicate little curls were shaped at her temples. Overall, she was pleased at the way she looked, and hoped that Brandon would be as well.

Not wanting to waste a precious minute of the few hours she had left, Alana did not wait for the dinnerbell to sound. When she entered the dining room, she found Lilian peeking into the kitchen.

At the sound of Alana's footsteps, Lilian squealed out. "You are early."

Startled by Lilian's reaction, Alana replied curiously, "I was ready early so I thought I would see if Lizzie needed any help."

"No, she does not need any help at all. In fact, dinner is ready. You may go ring the bell for her if you would," Lilian stammered.

"I would be pleased to," Alana replied, looking at Lilian questioningly as she left the room.

When she returned, Lilian had regained her usual composure and Alana dismissed the odd behavior from her mind.

Brandon came through the kitchen door about the time the children came in from the den. Lizzie followed with a huge platter of steaming roast beef surrounded by mounds of hot vegetables cooked in the beef's savory broth. Before Lizzie could return with the rolls and butter, Brandon was carving the roast and the children were passing their plates for their servings. Alana wondered why everyone seemed to be in such a hurry when she did not want the meal to ever end. Soon everyone had been served and there was little talk as the food was quickly eaten. Before Alana had put even a small dent in the pile of vegetables and beef on her plate, Brandon had summoned Lizzie for dessert. Alana felt it odd that no one had asked for seconds of such a delicious meal, but remained quiet as she continued to eat.

She was about to put a bite of carrot into her mouth when she saw Lizzie walk in, balancing a huge chocolate cake. It was four layers high, each layer smaller than the one below it, sporting a lighted candle in the center of the top layer. Fancy roses had been shaped out of red icing around the candle. Alana's eyes dampened as she read the words "Best Wishes and Love" around the edge of the top layer.

The children all shouted "Surprise!" in unison as Lizzie set the cake in front of her. Alana found herself laughing and crying at the same time as she tried to thank everyone. Mickey was the first to suggest she cut the cake and begged for the first piece. The other children quickly passed their plates for cake, too. Suddenly, her dinner did not seem so appealing and she cut herself a large piece as well.

As she finished her cake, she noticed Mickey staring at her with a concerned look on his freckled face. Before she could clear her mouth and ask what was wrong, he threw his arms into the air and asked, "When are you going to open the present?"

"What present?" Alana asked having overlooked the small package placed beside the cake.

Reaching over and picking it up, Brandon said, "This is from all of us to you for being such a good teacher and friend."

The children leaned forward in eager anticipation as Alana slowly pulled the pretty blue paper away to reveal a black velvet-clad case. Mickey climbed to his knees in his chair in order to watch her pull the case apart.

"Oh, my!" Alana gasped as she saw the beautiful gold bracelet stretched across a black-velvet board. As she inspected it more closely, she noticed the inscription "Eternal Love" on a sculptured gold disk hanging from the bracelet. Looking up to find everyone smiling lovingly at her, she hid her face and wept.

"We did not mean to hurt your feelings," Mickey said softly, almost ready to cry himself. "We just wanted you to know we love you."

Catching her breath, Alana looked up from her wet hands and assured him, "I love you, too, Mickey. That is why I am crying. I shall miss you dreadfully."

Mickey climbed down from his seat and ran to hug Alana, "Then don't go, Miss Stambridge. Stay with us forever."

"I cannot stay," Alana sobbed holding him close.

Suddenly Brandon pushed his chair back and, without a word, walked out.

Still clutching Mickey, Alana looked to Lilian who was leaning forward on her folded hands with tears streaming down her cheeks from tightly closed eyes. Each of the children was starting to cry as well.

"I think it would be best if I went on to bed. I do have to get up early and finish packing," Alana said in a wavering voice as she let go of Mickey. "I shall see you in the morning before I leave."

She kissed Mickey on his forehead as she stood up. Then, quickly, she turned and walked outside. Tears were followed by silent sobs as she ran to the refuge of her room.

Once she had the door securely fastened behind her, she released a wail of pain so violently that she could feel the veins in her neck throb from the strain. Not wanting to dwell on sad thoughts, she lit a small lamp and began putting the last of her things away in one of her trunks. The breeze blowing through her open window had grown quite chilly. Alana walked over to close the window and pull the curtains closed. She was totally unaware that Brandon stood just inside the open doorway of his study just across the patio, watching her as he belted down a second glass of whiskey.

He was desperately trying to numb the ungodly ache throbbing deep within his chest. Knowing Alana was leaving his life forever that very next day caused the pain to swell until he felt as if his chest was about to burst. After the curtains were closed, forbidding him to observe her taunting beauty any longer, he turned again to the bottle that sat still open on his desk. He gulped down a third drink, then a fourth, fifth, and sixth. Soon the bottle was quite empty and he had not yet managed to rid himself of the lonely ache that kept plaguing him as he had hoped to.

Angered that he had not yet drunk himself senseless, he hurled the empty bottle against the wall, smashing it into pieces, and growled aloud, "Damn woman!"

He searched his desk drawers and the wall cabinets frantically in hopes of finding a forgotten bottle hidden somewhere, but found none. Angrily he began to pace the floor in front of his desk. Feeling a furious need to get outside, he walked onto the patio. The only light was a torch near the kitchen door, which was beginning to burn low. Pleased with the seclusion that the cool darkness provided, he walked on out to the garden. His attention was drawn to the barren patch of ground that had once been the prided rose garden Alana and Angela had fussed over gleefully. Only three sides of the white wooden fence still stood. The fourth side had been crushed during the storm and the pieces carted away. With Alana planning to leave, no one had cared to replace it.

Walking closer, he noticed a mangled bush caught in part of the fence with a faint sign of life still in its branches. He leaned over to pull it free and pricked his finger as he did. "Damn!" He was suddenly outraged and shouted again as he saw a drop of blood form at the tip of his finger, "Damn!"

Having had way too much to drink, Brandon allowed his temper to gain control of his actions as he stormed to her door. He raised his hand to knock, but changed his mind. With a great heave of his foot, he kicked her door open, splintering the door frame as he did. Alana gasped at the sudden invasion of her room and pulled the covers close, having just climbed into bed.

Abruptly, Brandon slammed the door closed. "Woman, I want to talk to you!" He raged as he stalked over to her bedside, "And you are damn well going to listen!"

Reaching down for her covers, he yanked them from her, revealing the skimpy pink nightshirt that clung provocatively to her body. With a fury Alana had not seen before, he grabbed her by the wrist and pulled her out of bed to stand beside him. Alana's dark eyes showed the confusion she felt, but there was no sign of fear as she quietly stared up into Brandon's piercing blue eyes.

"You and your damn rose bushes!" he spoke harshly. "The blamed things have such a beautiful delicate bloom so very soft and so very inviting. But, when you try to take it for you own, it pricks you with its blasted thorns!"

Alana's eyes did not move from his as she listened silently; not knowing what, if anything, she should say. She was not even certain what Brandon was ranting about. Brandon wrapped his other hand around her chin, grasping it firmly, as he pulled her close.

"You are just like that. So beautiful, so damned alluring, yet try to get close to you and you strike out with that barbed tongue of yours. Sharp words and stubborn pride are your thorns." He spoke with a spiteful slur as the whiskey took effect on his speech. A sinister smile crossed his lips as he pulled her even closer, "Well, my beautiful blossom, I am taking you in spite of your thorns."

He let go of her wrist and slipped his hand around her waist and pulled her tightly against him in one easy motion. Bringing his lips down to hers, he kissed her with a passion he did not recognize.

Alana's first reaction was to protest. She beat his chest with her fists. He ignored her protest as he released his firm grip on her dainty chin and quickly worked his hand around behind her head, pressing her lips tightly to his. As the warming sensation spread throughout her body, she realized she wanted him. Gently, she wrapped her arms around him and displayed the passions she had held back for so long.

Slowly, Brandon lifted his head as he searched the velvety depths of her dark eyes for a sign of the truth. Did she indeed feel something for him? In the dim lamplight all he was able to see was her turmoil of mixed emotions.

She asked in a weak voice, "What about Stephanie? You know that you love Stephanie and she—"

"Let me be the judge of my own feelings," he cut into her speech angrily, letting go of her. Then in a softer tone he continued, "It is true that I had hoped to renew the old elationship. For some reason, I had always believed that Stephanie was the only woman I could ever love. When I learned she was a widow and that she was returning here, I felt as if all my dreams were to come true at last. Stephanie proved her willingness to rekindle the smoldering flame I thought was still deep in my heart. When the old passions did not flare up, I could not understand why. Even when we kissed, my desires were not what I had expected. As I spent more and more time trying to revive something I just would not admit was forever dead, mostly because of my pride I think, I began to realize the truth."

Looking down at Alana's curious eyes, he confessed, "It was you all along. It was your sweet fragrance that lingered with me, even as I held Stephanie close. Whenever I kissed her, I could not keep those beautiful brown eyes of yours out of my thoughts. Every time I was with her, I would catch myself wondering what you were doing. It was driving me completely insane. Once when she spoke of the fabulous gardens that adorned her home in California, all I could picture in my mind was your damned little rose garden. I tried to push my thoughts of you out of my head, knowing that you would never return my love. I was like a man possessed. I still am. Alana, I cannot help myself, I love you."

Again he searched her eyes for signs of her true feelings. He needed to know what was in her heart.

"Oh, Brandon!" Alana cried, as huge tears presented themselves in her shining, dark eyes with an emotion that he still was not certain of. "I have loved you for such a long time. I believed that you could never possibly care for me so I kept my feelings deep inside where I could insure their safety. When Stephanie returned, I tried to put an end to those feelings to keep from getting hurt, but found that I could not."

He bent down and tenderly kissed away a tear that had rolled out onto her cheek, then followed a path that led down to her mouth. Gingerly, he covered her soft, now inviting lips with his own. He encircled her small frame with his strong arms. As he felt the heat of his love for

Alana surging through him, he lifted her up into his arms and carried her the few steps to her bed. She gave herself and her love to him willingly.

Chapter Fourteen

Her pink-and-white nightshirt draped over a nearby chair was the first thing that caught Alana's attention as she sa up in bed. Realizing that she was still naked, Alan grabbed her sheet and pulled it protectively around her What had happened that previous evening flooded he memory as she noticed Brandon's shirt lying across th seat of that same chair. A quick scan of the room assure her that he had already left and that it was safe enough t climb out of bed.

She dressed quickly. Checking the time, she realize that it would be at least another hour until breakfas would be served. She walked over to the window to see i anyone, especially if Brandon might be outside. The pati was deserted. The delicate slanting rays of sunligh peeping through distant clouds gave the gentle mist o the morning an adorning glory. The golden strand seemed to play a silent melody across the morning dew But, nothing else moved. Everything remained perfectl still. With a sigh of disappointment, Alana decided to g ahead and straighten the room and make the bed that sh had shared with Brandon.

As she picked up her stray clothes, she wondered if sh should put them away in the cabinet or if she should fol them neatly and place them in her trunk. In spite of al that was said and done last night, it was never mentione that she should or would stay. A sudden fear gripped he as she remembered his easy apology after the stolen kiss and passionate embrace that they had shared in the barn claiming in effect that the liquor had altered his proper judgment. Her thoughts ran cold as she considered that he might have had too much to drink again. The smell of liquor had been prominent on his breath and she realized that his speech had indeed seemed slow and awkward. Her heart sank as she realized, too, that it just could have been the liquor talking. Maybe she had wanted and even needed to believe his words so desperately that she failed to notice their falseness. After all, he never once asked her to stay.

With trembling hands, Alana wadded his shirt into a small ball and hid it in the nook of her folded arms. She had to see Brandon right away. She needed to know that he did mean everything he had said and that he indeed did want her to stay. Checking around to make sure no one was watching she walked over to the door to Brandon's study, which had been left open. Stepping inside, she softly called his name. When there was no response, she walked over to the door to Brandon's bedroom and called out his name again. There still was no response.

Leaning inside, she whispered again, "Brandon, are you in here?"

The room was vacant. His bed had not been slept in. Clothes had been strewn about and several drawers were left open. Alana laid the crumpled shirt on his bed, eased back outside, and returned to her room.

After pacing the floor trying to decide what she should or could do next, Alana chose to finish packing as if she had known all along that last night was just a fleeting moment, not important enough to alter any plans. She managed to blink back her tears as her confused feeling of hope and humiliation tumbled about inside of her. With the last of her things tucked neatly into her trunks, she closed the lids securely and locked each one. As she placed the keys in her purse, the clanging of the dinner-bell announcing breakfast caused her to jump. Determined to catch Brandon alone after they ate, Alana hurried to the table.

Lilian tried to be her usual cheerful self as she greeted Alana at the door. The children were already sitting stiffly at the table looking down at their plates in sad anticipation. Alana knew that they must be under strict orders to be on their best behavior. As she glanced fondly over them, her gaze fell on the seat beside her own that Angela had once claimed. A solemn anguish fell over her as her mind placed the small amber-haired child in the empty seat swinging her feet, which could not reach the floor, eagerly awaiting breakfast. Alana looked away to try to avoid the tears that seemed ever ready to flow. When she refocused on the chair, she could see that it was indeed empty. With a hunger pitted in her stomach to see the child, Alana decided to sit down before she grew so weak that she collapsed. As she pulled her chair away from the table, she noticed that Brandon's chair was empty. His place was not set.

She found it difficult to swallow as she attempted to clear her throat to ask Lilian, "Is Brandon not eating?"

"I guess not. He left out of here early this morning. I was not yet quite dressed when I heard the kitchen door slam and noticed him walking out toward the barn. By the time I was out of my room, he was gone. He told Lizzie not to hold breakfast and possibly not lunch for him. I think he just did not want to be around for the goodbyes. He really hates to see you go. I can tell," Lilian said in a quiet voice, hoping Alana was not hurt by her brother's childish disappearance.

Before Alana could ask anymore questions, Lizzie appeared through the large wooden door carrying a platter stacked high with buttermilk flapjacks and huge slices of ham. She carefully balanced the tray so as not to spill the two canisters of honey placed on either side.

The children's grim little faces found sudden signs of delight as their eyes took in the sight and their noses took in the smell of Lizzie's specialty, which was usually reserved for Sundays and birthdays. Somber pouts were replaced by eagerly awaiting smiles as Lizzie set the platter in the center of the table in easy reach of all of them. Aware of the children's delight, Lizzie chuckled, "There's more cookin' in the kitchen when this stack is gone. Miss Alana, you best eat an extra helpin', you is gonna need all the strength you can muster for that long trip home. I made these special for you."

Alana looked up into Lizzie's large black eyes. There were tiny red lines near the edges and a great deal of puffiness. Lizzie had been crying.

"Thank you, I appreciate your dear kindness. I promise to eat my fill. Besides, you know quite certainly that I cannot resist these delicious buttermilk cakes. I am really going to miss your wonderful cooking."

"You just bein' kind," Lizzie said with a wide grin, soaking in the flattery.

"I believe you know how good your cooking is only too well," Alana said with a wink. "You just enjoy being reminded."

With a hearty laugh, Lizzie replied, "That I do. Can't get nothin' past you, Miss Alana."

Alana smiled lovingly as Lizzie walked out of the room with a faint chuckle trailing behind her. Alana enjoyed Lizzie's laugh. If anyone could get a smile from her, even when the world seemed to be crashing in around her, it was that dear sweet Lizzie.

After the door swung closed behind Lizzie, Alana returned her attention to the table and Brandon's empty place. The broad smile that Lizzie had left Alana with faded as she remembered Lilian's words: "He just did not want to be around for the goodbyes." Trying to force away some of the anguish, Alana closed her eyes tightly and took in several deep, even breaths. She hoped to ease the violent pounding in her breast. How could she have expected to find him waiting for her with open arms and declaring his everlasting love? Why did she fail to understand that it was just the liquor talking again? She had managed to completely blank out any thoughts of that stolen kiss in the barn that Brandon casually excused as having had too much drink.

Now that she reflected back over it all, she felt a complete fool for not seeing his display of passion for what it was—a ploy to bed her as he had so many other women who fell prey to those gentle blue eyes. She should have listened more closely to Lizzie who had obviously tried to warn her that he had indeed bedded several women but loved only one—Stephanie. She had been duped by her own gullibility. Brandon was probably with his sweet Stephanie at this very moment. Suddenly she felt sorry for Stephanie. Someday the poor woman would find out what a selfish, conniving man Brandon Warren was.

Able to feel pity and rage where the pain and anguish had been, Alana managed to get through breakfast without shedding another tear. With a forced smile in front of her, Alana turned her thoughts to the children. How she would miss their bright smiling faces! Maybe someday she could return for a visit, after the hurt had a chance to heal. She might find Brenda had become a beautiful woman with children of her own and that Jake might be a handsome lawyer. With his natural knack of bending words to mean what he needed them to at any given time and his quick wit, he would certainly make a fine lawyer. She had no idea what to expect from the twins or Mickey. They seemed to always be headed in many directions at once. How she wished that she could be here to help guide which direction they finally chose. At least there was one small consolation; Lilian had promised to write her often. She would be able to keep track of them all through letters. She allowed her thoughts to drift through the possible futures for each of the children while she finished eating, after which Lilian escorted her back to her room. Their only words were carefully chosen.

"Having you completed your packing?" Lilian asked, failing to look Alana in the eye as she spoke.

"For the most part, although I feel that I am leaving something behind."

"You are leaving something behind. You are leaving a part of yourself here with us. You are leaving me many beautiful memories of a dear friend. I shall miss you dreadfully."

"You are going to cause me to begin crying again. I should be out of tears by now, but it seems that I have an endless supply. You know of my reasons for leaving. They are quite sound. My life would be miserable seeing Brandon and Stephanie wedded. Even if they were not to live happily ever after, I could not bear the misery of knowing that he had become eternally hers and will never be, nor was he ever mine."

"If he were to ask me, I would tell him just how grand an error he is making. I may just tell him anyway!" Lilian exclaimed with a toss of her head.

"No, it will only cause trouble."

"I just wish that he realized how greatly that you care for him."

Alana looked away from where Lilian stood and softly replied, "He already knows that I care for him."

"How does he know?" Lilian asked.

"He knows, that is all. But it made little difference to him."

"He is a fool!" Lilian replied shortly.

"Maybe I am the fool," Alana mumbled under her breath with her back still toward Lilian.

"What did you say?"

"Nothing of importance," Alana replied quickly adding with a smile that hid her feelings from her friend, "Oh, Lilian, I have a present for Lizzie. I forgot all about it."

"You still have plenty of time. There are another two hours before you have to leave."

"That may be true, but I want to give it to her now, while I am thinking about it," Alana said, glad that she had successfully changed the subject.

Lilian followed Alana into her room. "What is it that you have to give her?"

Alana reached into her handbag and pulled out the tiny present.

"Actually, it is from Angela, too. Remember that little silver music box that Lizzie loves to stop and listen to whenever she shops in Mr. DeLane's store?"

Lilian nodded silently, anticipating the rest of what Alana had to tell her with tears of mixed emotions welling in her eyes.

"I just could not let such an unselfish goal go unful-filled." Alana spoke softly as she finished explaining and held the little package with the pretty yellow bow lovingly in her hands, "And since I will not be able to be here at the

proper time, I decided to go ahead and make the
purchase. I planned to give it to her today before I left.
Angela would understand why I did not wait until Lizzie'
proper birthday."

"Yes, Angela was such a good loving child," Lilian said as
a large round tear made a path down her cheek. "Let's give
Lizzie the present right now."

Alana followed Lilian to the kitchen. They found Lizzie
there humming the refrain of one of her favorite hymns
as she scrubbed the breakfast dishes. She paid little
attention to Alana and Lilian as she continued to work on a
particularly stubborn spot of burned grease caked on her
favorite skillet. With a childish grin, Alana slipped the little
package on top of a stack of plates near Lizzie that had not
yet been washed.

After carefully balancing it on the edge of the top plate
so as not to get the paper sticky with the honey smeared
across it, Alana stepped back and waited. Lizzie reached
for the plate without bothering to look up. When she felt
the odd presence of the package, her humming stopped.
In a low whisper, as if talking for her own benefit, she
remarked, "My Lord, what's that doin' there?"

Bursting with excited anticipation, Alana shouted, "It is
a present for you!"

The sudden nearness of Alana's voice startled Lizzie so
that she almost dropped her present into the large pan of
dirty dishwater.

"You mean that this here is for me? Whatever for?"
Lizzie asked, her eyes wide with excitement.

Alana explained how Angela dearly wanted her to have a
special birthday present this year, and that this was to be
that present. As Lizzie tore the paper away and opened
the brown paper box, she sniffed a tear back. Her hands
trembled as she pulled the delicately designed little silver
case out.

"That dear child," she cried softly. Winding the
small key on the bottom as she had done so many times in
the store, Lizzie looked up at Alana with swollen red-
rimmed eyes, "Thank you, Miss Alana." She twisted her
face tightly to keep from crying as she removed the lid,

allowing the music to play softly. Then, as if in after-thought, Lizzie turned her black eyes heavenward and added, "Thank you too, Missy."

An awkward silence followed as the music box began to wind down. Alana leaned over and kissed Lizzie on the cheek.

"Miss Alana, you mustn't do that. White folks don't kiss on no niggers," Lizzie told her as she reached up to the place Alana's lips had touched her dark skin.

"Who says?" Alana smiled. "If Angela could be here, she would have a kiss for you, too."

Having said that, Alana quickly walked outside, hoping to be alone for a while. Sadly, she walked away from the house and stood under the shade of several large pecan trees to take one last look at Montaqua. Leaning against the sturdy trunk of one of the tall stately trees, she somberly took in the view. Soon this place would just be a memory.

Although this Montaqua had easily become a part of her, she was never to become a part of it. Her gloomy mood deepened as she looked across the large grassy fields now spotted with the many colors of spring wildflowers. The trees were once again heavy with their deep-green foliage. She tried to quench a sudden thirst she had for this Montaqua by drinking in every last detail of its bountiful beauty. As her eyes scanned the country-side, her gaze fell on the pond. Only six large trees now stood where there had once been many. Brandon and Billy had cleared the rubbish of mangled trees and bushes left by the tornado. Grass had quickly filled in the bare spots left by the uprooted trees. Some of the cattle grazed peacefully nearby. The only traces of a storm having been through were the scars left in the hearts and memories of everyone who knew and loved Angela. These scars were not so easily erased. Even time might not ever heal them.

Alana's thoughts were set so deeply in the drastic changes that had occurred and in those that were still to come that she failed to hear Billy come up behind her. It was not until he leaned against the same tree trunk that she noticed him.

With a gentle smile, he spoke, "You still planning to leave us, aren't ya? I sure wish you'd stay," he paused a moment before adding, "It isn't gonna be the same around here without you." When Alana did not respond, Billy continued, "Well, I got the surrey hooked up and ready to go. Are your trunks packed? I could go on ahead and load 'em, if they are."

After Alana told him that they were packed and ready, Billy brought the surrey to her door. She watched silently as Billy heaved one trunk at a time onto the back of the surrey and tied them down securely.

As he tucked in the ends of the heavy leather straps holding the trunks in place, he mentioned, "We will be ready to leave as soon as we've had lunch. Seems strange plannin' lunch for eleven instead of noon, but you do gotta be in Gilmer by one in case that stage is on time for a change."

As he led the horses across to a hitching post near the barn, Alana went into her room to take one final look around. She wanted to make certain that she had not left anything important. It was bad enough that she had to leave part of her heart here.

The dinnerbell ended her careful search of drawers, nooks and crannies. She knew that it was the last time that she would ever hear that now-familiar sound. As she neared the dining room for the last time, she found herself hoping that Brandon had returned and was waiting impatiently at his chair to eat. These hopes were so strong that they led her into another disappointment when she found that he had not come home.

When lunch was over, the children rushed around her to tell her goodbye. Alana held each one close, kissed them lovingly on their little cheeks, and quickly released them. It was time for her to let go. There was the future to consider. There would be other children to teach and love. There would be new friends to make. Armed with these new hopes for her tomorrows, Alana walked bravely to the surrey. She climbed up into the seat beside Billy and waved to Lilian, Lizzie, and the children. She continued to wave even after they were out of her sight. She watched the house grow smaller behind her as they pulled away from it. Slowly she turned back around in her seat to face the future, and she gasped aloud at what she saw. Brandon was coming through the front gate with the wagon he was driving, bouncing at a fast pace. Alana felt certain that her heart had completely stopped as he motioned for them to stop. She held her breath as he jumped down from the wagon and ran over to stand at her side.

Angrily he shouted up at her, "Where in the hell do you think you are going?"

"Back to New York," she replied in a questioning voice.

"After last night? You told me that you loved me. We made love. Doesn't that mean anything to you?" he asked in a loud demanding voice.

Feeling uncomfortable that Brandon was revealing all of these things in front of Billy, Alana answered softly, "You never asked me to stay."

Brandon yanked his hat off and threw it down angrily, "Woman, I told you that I loved you."

"But, Brandon Warren, I remind you that you never once asked me to stay. Then this morning I find that you had gone without a word. What was I to think?" Alana replied sharply.

"I thought you understood that I wanted you to be my wife when I carried you to bed last night. What was that to you, just your nice way of saying goodbye?"

"Wife?" Alana's voice softened at the word. "Why did you leave early this morning without telling anyone where you were going?" she asked cautiously. "Why did you not tell them that I was to stay? You simply left. Why?"

"Come here and I will show you why," he said, offering her his hand to help her down. He led her over to the wagon and tossed back the lightweight canvas cover lying across the back.

"Oh, Brandon," Alana cried when she saw that there were over two dozen rose bushes piled carefully into the back.

"Last night while you were asleep, I walked outside to get some fresh air and think things through. As I went by where your garden lay in ruins, I remembered just how proud you were over your roses and how your eyes seemed to sparkle whenever someone so much as mentioned them. I decided to ride over to Jefferson and see if I could get these," he said, proudly waving his hands over the wagon's contents. "I would have been back sooner except I decided to get this for you as well."

He reached into his shirt pocket, pulled out a small box clad in deep-red velvet, and opened it to reveal a beautiful band of gold with delicate roses engraved on the outside.

Finding that Alana was speechless, Brandon simply handed the ring to her, "You are going to marry me, aren't you?" he asked as he looked into her soft brown eyes.

Billy leaned back in his seat and pushed his straw hat forward, covering his eyes. He pretended not to notice as Alana gave Brandon the answer that he had hoped for when she stepped forward and met his lips halfway.

THE BANISHED
By H. Dyke Walton

PRICE: $3.50   T51668
CATEGORY: Historical Novel

THE SWEEPING GENERATIONAL SAGA OF A
BOLD FAMILY'S STRUGGLE TO SURVIVE IN A
WORLD OF BLOOD AND PASSION!

Russia, 1708. Towering, red-haired Kurtsev Bolinsky
escaped a count's torture chamber and escaped with
his future wife, Esther. Thus, the 150-year family saga
began. Now branded traitors to Peter the Great, the
family's generational epic journey took them to distant lands, over pirated waters, and through desires of
the flesh and soul. Their passionate quest was sus-
tained by courage, love, and family strength...

COLORADO WOMAN
By Patricia Greenlaw

PRICE: $2.50   T51589
CATEGORY: Historical Romance

Lindsay Tyler was orphaned during an Indian attack and was sent to live with her kind uncle on his Colorado ranch. Unknown to Lindsay, her uncle had an enemy, a psychopathic land baron, who would stop at nothing to obtain her uncle's ranch. As Lindsay blossomed into a beautiful and hearty woman, the land baron plotted to launch a deadly scheme to bring about Lindsay's death if he couldn't get the deed. Soon, Lindsay found herself a terrorized and abused captive on the brutal Western plains. But amid the ever-present threat of death at the hands of her ruthless captors, she surprisingly found the spark of eternal love.

THE MILL GIRLS
By George Larkin

PRICE: $2.50   T51618   CATEGORY: Novel

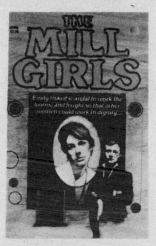

THE LIVES AND LOVES OF THE WOMEN WHO PAVED THE WAY TOWARD LIBERATION

In 1837, Emily Hatfeld left the drudgery of her New Hampshire farm and created a scandal by joining America's first female work force at a textile mill in Lowell, Massachusetts. Like the other mill girls, Emily was proud, imaginative and brimmed with dreams. She worked passionately 14 hours a day at her looms, until corruption surfaced and conditions at the mill became unbearable Through heartbreak over love, and loss of dignity at her job, Emily led the mill girls in a battle that paved the way for the new breed of working women.

A RICH NOVEL BASED ON A TRUE STORY!

SEND TO: 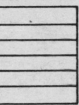 **TOWER BOOKS**
P.O. Box 511, Murry Hill Station
New York, N.Y. 10156-0511

PLEASE SEND ME THE FOLLOWING TITLES:

Quantity	Book Number	Price

**IN THE EVENT THAT WE ARE OUT OF STOCK
ON ANY OF YOUR SELECTIONS, PLEASE LIST
ALTERNATE TITLES BELOW:**

	Postage/Handling I enclose	

FOR U.S. ORDERS, add 75¢ for the first book and 25¢ for each additional book to cover cost of postage and handling. Buy five or more copies and we will pay for shipping. Sorry, no. C.O.D.'s.

FOR ORDERS SENT OUTSIDE THE U.S.A., add $1.00 for the first book and 50¢ for each additional book. PAY BY foreign draft or money order drawn on a U.S. bank, payable in U.S. ($) dollars.

☐ Please send me a free catalog.

NAME _____
(Please print)

ADDRESS _____

CITY _____ **STATE** _____ **ZIP** _____
Allow Four Weeks for Delivery